Four darkly compelling storylines converge in Florschutz's debut novel.

On a dark, rainy night in early November, John Brisdon Noxon, a middle-aged art curator, disappears. His wife, Imogen, finds his hidden journals, including one detailing Brisdon's trip to Peru as a young student—and his passionate affair with a local artist, César, which ended in tragedy. Each journal entry is addressed to Karen, Brisdon's twin sister, who disappeared when the siblings were 5 years old. Fifteen years later, Imogen and her partner, Max, gather their family around them to commemorate the closing of their lakeside resort, the Sheltering Arms. That weekend, the mysteries of Brisdon's disappearance—and of his sister's—are illuminated in a series of haunting revelations. The novel weaves together four points of view: Brisdon as a young man lived in the shadow of his sister's disappearance and haunted by the death of his parents in a plane crash. In Peru, he falls in love with César Acosta, heedless of the dangerous political climate, and is devastated by the atrocity that tears them apart. César, haunted by the same memories (and harboring a few secrets of his own), transforms into the reclusive artist CÁLA. Margaret, Brisdon's Scottish mother (once a lively young woman, now a disturbed, paranoid personality), details the events leading up to the disappearance of her daughter. Finally, Imogen, surrounded by her loved ones, is left to pick up the pieces the others have left behind. The four storylines frequently overlap, and several scenes are depicted more than once from different perspectives; as in Rashomon, instead of feeling redundant, the repetitions add depth and nuance. The settings, ranging from post-war Scotland to rural Peru to a remote Ontario lake, provide evocative, moody backdrops for the story. "As we drove on, Lima felt ominous in the dim light–a polluted, dry, decaying insomniac of a metropolis." The characters baffle and infuriate, like real people, and the unlikely series of coincidences at the end add to the uncanny, mystical feel.

Part mystery, part love story, part horror story,
this debut novel lingers like a vivid dream.

- *Kirkus Reviews*

D1496521

THE PERUVIAN BOOK OF THE DEAD

a novel

Roger J. Flaxschutz

AOS Publishing, 2023

ISBN: 978-1-990496-27-1

First edition

Cover Design: Chanelle Poupart

Visit AOS Publishing's website:
www.aospublishing.com

For Karen, in memory,
and to Dalma, with thanks

S it still and listen to my story, mis niños. Listen closely.

   There once was a great Condor, the largest bird in the world, who had grown old and blind and came to live in the hollow of a thousand year-old Hurango tree. The Inca terns and pallid doves welcomed him and decided to share their food with him because he couldn't see.

   One day, a Jaguar came along when the other birds were away. Hearing the chirping of the young chicks, she came closer to eat them. But the old Condor heard the commotion from the chicks and he called out, "Who's there?"

   On seeing the milky eyes of the Condor, the Jaguar thought, he's blind and I can trick him! So the Jaguar answered, "I'm just a poor old cat and I mean no harm. I live on the other side of the river and I only eat grass and berries."

   The Condor was soothed by the Jaguar's soft voice and her lies. He allowed her to stay with him in the hollow of the tree. The baby chicks got used to the Jaguar and were no longer afraid. Then, when the Condor fell asleep, the Jaguar devoured the little birds one by one, yum-yum-yum, and as soon as she finished all the chicks, she slipped away.

   When the terns and the doves returned, they found the bones of the chicks on the ground by the hollow tree. They cried, "The Condor has eaten our babies!"

   And then they pecked him to death.

Imogen

It's been fifteen years since Brisdon vanished into thin air.

The police were convinced my husband drove up to Shelter Lake and crashed his car through the bridge's guardrail into the reservoir below. Later, as I stood on that bridge in the rain, shivering and watching the rescue workers haul our crumpled Jetta from the water, I felt like I was in a fever dream. Images of Brisdon being swept away by the rapids began to haunt me, or Brisdon crawling to shore, disoriented and falling into a sandy pit, long over-grown with thorn bushes and thistles. At the time I prayed he would come back to me, even if I didn't truly believe he would. But prayer, when shrouded in doubt, can lead to a whole tangle of thorns.

As I look back now, this tangle must have taken root long ago, when Brisdon's twin sister Karen disappeared. She was just a little girl at the time, the poor dear. Then a few years later, Brisdon's parents died in that horrible plane crash while they were hunting for her. Max thought there was a curse on the entire Noxon family and I was the only survivor. He even wanted me to drop my married name and take his own to avoid more bad luck. But curses don't work that way. They're like fairy-tale thistles—you have to believe in them or they can't prick you.

How strange the things you remember and the things you forget. I recall the rolling sound of distant thunder as I answered the doorbell that night. I remember Detective Jablonski with his heart-shaped scar just under his widow's peak, standing there drenched from the rain. He was wearing a long raincoat and galoshes and I remember thinking I hadn't seen anyone wear galoshes in such a long time. And I remember how my heart became cotton in my mouth when he showed me his credentials and that I had pressed my nails into my palms to replace one pain with another thinking, *Brisdon, it's about Brisdon.*

What I didn't remember, until much later, was inviting the detective inside and making tea and sitting at the dining room table with him in the same spot where Brisdon and I had looked at old photographs just the night before, sepia-toned and faded images that had stirred dim memories and must have roused the devil he said haunted him all his life, a revenant who whispered into his ear and told him things he never wanted to hear.

"Do you know where your husband is, Mrs. Noxon?" Those were Detective Jablonski's first words to me. *That,* I will never forget. "When did you see him last?" he pressed. Then we were sitting in the dining room with my trembling hands wrapped around my warm mug of tea. I was afraid to bring it to my lips, afraid to even breathe. "Take your time, ma'am."

I managed to tell him I last saw Brisdon on Monday night at mother's birthday dinner at the Beechwood Club where I was the catering manager, and how he had been acting distant and distracted and how he had left so abruptly. For a moment, with this detective sitting across from me scribbling in his notebook and glancing up with his wide, quizzical face and its dour expression, it occurred to me there was more to all this. Much more.

"Would there be any reason for Mr. Noxon to go to Shelter Lake?"

I immediately thought, *yes, of course,* that was where he went.

"We recently acquired property there," I explained. "The old Shelter Lake Lodge is ours now. We're having it renovated, you see. He drove there by himself on Sunday to pay the contractors." The steam from our tea evaporated between us, like a weary ghost.

"Does your husband have any enemies, Mrs. Noxon?"

"Heavens, I hope not!"

I think that's when I started to cry, deep sobs leaving me gulping for air. The detective tried to calm me by saying it was possible Brisdon had survived the plunge and was still alive somewhere.

"Anything is possible at this point, ma'am," he said like it was all a dream play, as Max would say.

Soon everything started to unravel. I discovered Brisdon had stormed out from the museum where he was curator, the day he disappeared. He had only been back for a day, since his accident. Then, a week later, I found an old suitcase tucked under the bed containing dozens of handwritten journals, all by Brisdon and about his life before we met. It took me weeks to read them one by one. Gradually, another Brisdon came into focus. His last journal was wrapped in a book cover that read, *The Tibetan Book of the Dead*, and it was the most compelling of them all. It was the Peruvian journal he had penned while in Lima as a university student back in 1983. During that time, Brisdon had fallen for an artist named César. *Fallen in love with him*, it became clear. Brisdon never told me about his trip, or the horrors he experienced there, or his attraction to this other young man. I understand we all live three lives—a public one, a private one, and a secret one—and it turned out that Brisdon's life was all about secrets. The mystery that was Brisdon was now rising to the surface. Reading those journals dedicated to the memory of his poor lost sister made me profoundly sad.

I suppose I have Rosie to thank for starting the recent chain of extraordinary events when she came to visit and read my Tarot cards. I'd known Rosie since our days in Toronto, when we would call on the old fortune tellers above the stores in Parkdale, where Brisdon grew up. Now it was the end of August and a few guests were still hanging on at the resort: the old gentleman with his wide walrus moustache who had recently lost his wife and the middle-aged couple from Hamilton who were financial traders and just needed a peaceful, late-summer break. Soon our guests would depart. Max and I had transformed the old lodge at Shelter Lake into a modern and calming retreat. Traditionally, the last weekend of the summer meant the end of the tourist season and The Sheltering Arms, which I had named it, would close down until the spring. This time, however, we were closing down for good, selling both The Sheltering Arms *and* The Church Restaurant and leaving behind fifteen long years that had come and gone in a single breath, like a kiss goodbye from time. Max and I were in our seventies now and needed to slow down.

Rosie and I had settled ourselves at a card table in the lounge of the schoolhouse. Fifteen years ago I had decorated the lounge with bamboo furniture, rattan tables and potted palms, to help transport our guests back a hundred years to an era before all the craziness of our modern world began. Max thought it looked like the Palm Court from the *Titanic.* Now, the walrus was reading a magazine by the windows and Kai brought us loose-leaf tea in the event Rosie wanted to read my tea leaves as well.

"Just think of a question but remember that sometimes the question you are asking does not lead to the answer you are seeking."

Ambivalence was the key to the supernatural. *The dead always tell you what you want to hear.* Rosie handed me the stiff cards and I shuffled them. They had a slight odour of patchouli and bergamot and a whiff of expectation. They smelled crafty.

She laid down five cards and turned them over one at a time. The first card was The Fool. "Here we have the basis of your question, a wanderer, passing from innocence through an incredible but dangerous journey. Does this represent someone to you?"

I nodded. *Of course.* We all play the fool at times, don't we?

Satisfied, she turned over the next card. "Here we have the Ten of Swords, a violent card." A figure was lying face down on the ground, stabbed in the back with ten swords. "This can mean tragedy in the past. But here–" she turned up the Queen of Pentacles, "–this is in your immediate future. She is the Earth Mother, a charitable and truly noble soul." I thought of *my* mother, 95 years old and still spry enough to be joining us for our farewell celebration.

The next card was The Tower, a tall structure being struck by lightning with fire bursting from its roof and windows. "Beware of danger and destruction," she warned. "But this can also mean a discovery and liberation."

"It all sounds very ominous," I teased.

She shrugged. *The cards don't lie.* The final card she turned over, the card that represented the culmination of all the cards, was Death of course–isn't it always? It showed a skeleton in black armour riding a white horse. I immediately thought about my mother again and winced.

"This is not the card you think." Rosie reached out and patted my hand. "The Death card does not signify physical death but it does imply an end or a great change. You will have very little control over what is coming."

In hindsight, I can see the meaning of each of the cards in that spread. But it didn't matter how they fell, if the final card had been Justice or Judgement or even The Lovers. It would all have ended up the same.

"So what do you make of it?" I asked as Rosie gathered up the cards. "How will our last weekend celebration turn out?"

she hesitated as she wrapped the cards in a
orated with tiny signs of the zodiac, "—in all
en, you won't know what hit you."

*   *   *

It was almost noon when I heard Max's pickup truck pull
in. I knew he would be busy in his kitchen for the rest of the
day and into the evening. To celebrate the restaurant's
permanent closing, The Church was serving a ten-course
prix fixe dinner. Every table was reserved. Each course
would be paired with a fine wine, down to the sweet Spanish
Pacharán with dessert. For his swan song Max had, to my
surprise, taken the menu directly from the White Star Line.

"Don't worry, Gen, they won't mind." Max was
recreating the last first-class dinner menu from the *Titanic*
118 years later. It wasn't the first time a restaurant had done
this, but it would be the first time for Chef Max's interpretation.

"What better way for The Church to go down!" he
exclaimed.

"What's with you and the *Titanic*?" I asked. "Why not
the *Lusitania* or the *Andrea Doria*?"

His sous-chef Patrick, who was listening by the kitchen
ovens called out, "Not as sexy."

"And I think the *Andrea Doria's* last meal was steak
and kidney pie," Max added.

"What's wrong with steak and kidney pie?" I asked.

"Not sexy," Patrick called out again.

I went back to my office to fetch the menus that Isla,
my grand-niece, had printed on cream paper stock. It was
Isla's first time helping out at The Arms, which is what I
called our resort. Her cousin Atticus had returned for his
third summer with us when he could have been hanging out
with his friends at home. He was such a serious young man.

I was checking the menu for errors when I heard Kai's voice behind me. "Mrs. Noxon?"

People still called me that. I could have gone back to my maiden name of Nation or married Max to become Mrs. Wolff, as he had suggested, but staying a *Noxon* kept me connected to Brisdon.

"Yes, Kai?" This young man was the grandson of the Elder of Shelter Lake, Willie Bearheart, who had helped us long ago when Brisdon and I first took possession of the old lodge. Kai had come up behind me, ready to head out, his morning duties over. A look of guilt was written all over his face. Unlike his mother who was the housekeeper here, Kai was easy to read.

"Mom was cleaning yesterday and she found this just behind the chair." He handed me a sheet of paper. "It must have slipped off the counter. I'm so sorry but I totally forgot to give it to you." He looked anxious about it, like it was all his fault.

"That's all right. We'll see you tonight then. Last dinner, Kai. Imagine!"

As Kai hurried off I looked at the sheet which was our standard reservation form for a prospective guest. Isla printed these out each morning for me to go over before she arranged the reservations in our database.

"Isla," I called. She poked her head out of the office." I held out the sheet of paper. "Do you remember seeing this particular reservation, pet?"

She came around and took a look.

"I don't remember. Sorry."

"That's all right. It seems to have slipped through the cracks." I hurried off. Bad luck, I thought. I had to show this to Max.

A path of interlocking brick ran from the old school-house which was now the guest lounge and reception, to the old stone church, now The Church Restaurant. The dining room was quiet as I deposited all but one menu at the host stand. The square tables were covered in crisp white linen and set for dinner with chargers and crystal stemware and polished silver. This time of day the sun came streaming through the tall stained-glass windows creating prisms of light that fanned across the tabletops and got caught in the curves of the wine glasses like spirits of the old church imbibing in a singular, almost sensual type of grace.

There was a slight rattle from the kitchen at the far end. Then I heard the crash of a pan as I walked in, followed by Max growling, "*Scheisse!*" It was funny how people always swore in their mother-tongue. Max and Patrick clambered along the floor catching the apples that had rolled in every direction.

"Is the ship sinking already?"

He straightened, cleared his throat, and ordered Patrick to wash the apples. I went over and he pecked me on the cheek.

"Max, we have a new reservation."

"For dinner?" He bristled, since we were already full-up.

"No, at The Arms." I held up the sheet of paper. "Kai brought me this. It got lodged between the furniture, Max. We missed it."

He reached into the pocket of his white chef's jacket and pulled out his specs. The reservation was made in July for a booking starting on the first of September, 2030, the Sunday of the long weekend when we were closing, just two days away.

"See there," I pointed out. "The name is Lambert and there's no number of guests and no end date."

"Who is this Lambert?" Max asked.

"I have no idea," I replied, "and the credit card was accepted. We'll have to refund them now, of course, whether they stay or not because they'll be the only strangers in the middle of our family."

"Not by the end of the night."

"Oh Max!" I snatched the paper back. "That's not very helpful."

"You're refunding them anyway. Put them in our best cabin and be sure to ask your charming housekeeper to air it out first."

"Yes, I suppose—"

"There, solved. The Sheltering Arms is saved one last time."

"Will they eat with us? Won't that be awkward?"

Patrick came around from the back with his tray of cleaned Fuji apples and almost dropped them again.

"We can work something out when they get here. Now I really have to get back to playing with my food, Gen."

"Here, I almost forgot." I handed him the menu. He looked it over quickly and grunted.

"I'll post this in the kitchen to keep my staff from mixing up the courses." He took off his glasses and pecked me on the cheek.

Max, my rescuer, my Austrian knight in shining armour. Poor Brisdon fretted about me and Max when we worked together all those years ago, as if I would ever leave my husband for the Beechwood Club chef. But the workings of Lady Fate can sometimes become a self-fulfilling prophesy as she cranks her Wheel of Fortune against The Fools of The World.

Brisdon

Mad shadows are crawling across the wall like the fingers of Quasimodo's ghost. The antique clock on the mantel goes *tick...tick...tick...* as it measures out the back of time. As I sit reading *Notre-Dame de Paris*, I keep hearing a strange scraping noise. I'm at the end of my book but the last pages have been dragging on because every so often I'm forced to look up as if someone is watching me.

'...*Quand on voulut le détacher du squelette qu'il embrassait, il tomba en poussière.*'

There. Finished. I close the cover. I feel hypnotized and my eyelids grow heavy. I'm powerless as I drift off to join the undertakers from the book, with their long beards and dark surcoats. But something's wrong. I cry out, *Stop!* but it's too late. When they try to detach the lovers from their embrace, the skeletons don't crumble to dust. Instead, their bones fall into a single heap, becoming indistinguishable from one another. For a fleeting instant I am a wild bird trapped in a dark room and then the chiming of the doorbell brings me tumbling back to my body, as if I'm hearing the bells of Notre-Dame themselves.

I switch on the lamp. The hands of the old clock point to half-past six, clasped together as if in prayer. Then the doorbell rings again and I realize, *Yes, of course—the first trick-or-treaters for Halloween.* Imogen must have forgotten to turn off the porch lights before she left for work.

I push myself up from my easy chair. My leg is starting to smart. When I switch on CBC Radio 2, the room fills with a cacophony of horns and violins and the clashing of cymbals. It's the piece from Mozart's *Don Giovanni* where the hero is being dragged into the depths of hell. I've always enjoyed that part. It certainly sets the tone, and a few minutes later I'm in front of the foyer mirror wearing my costume.

Tonight I'll be the *Plague Doctor*. When I lean forward my beak taps against the glass. In the Middle Ages this same mask would have been stuffed with lavender and lemon balm and mixed with straw to cover the stench of death and decay. Now all I can smell is my own breath. And I'll be bringing my cane, not because I still need it but because, long ago, the plague doctors used to prod their unfortunate patients who were riddled with buboes and writhing with fever. They never gave a second thought to the dead rats festering in the corners or the fleas biting the ankles of their patients. As old Doctor Noxon used to say, *The art of medicine has always had its flaws.*

Sometimes misfortune happens by degrees. When Imogen drove out to the Costume Bazaar at the last minute to pick up an outfit for me, she was worried all the good costumes would be rented. As she was parking the car, she was rear-ended by a white mini-van.

"It was just a *nudge*, Brisdon," she explains, seeing my expression.

"White mini-vans are nothing but trouble," I tell her.

"The only real trouble is that the trunk won't stay shut," she admits and I roll my eyes. "I've tied it together with bungee cords."

This isn't a good start, I think. Ever since pulling out *Doctor Schnabel von Rom* from his package, I've had a sense of impending doom about this party, because sometimes misfortune happens with a big *wallop*. It's as if the shadowy, misshapen figure who has clung to me since childhood knows what's coming. He whispers into my ear, *If you want to see into the future, Brisdon, you have to move faster than time.* Somehow I know it's a *he*, but that's all I know. I shrug my shoulders to shake him off.

All dressed now with cane in hand, I turn off the radio, grab my keys from the bowl, switch off all the lights, and am out the door.

*   *   *

Next to the waning moon, Venus is twinkling above the horizon. I pull my Jetta into the *Reserved for Curator* spot at the Tamaddon Art Museum, which is better known as the *TAM*. Stepping behind the car, I see how cleverly Imogen has tied the trunk shut. To wear my mask I have to remove my glasses and the heavens become a celestial blur. As I make my way through the museum's entrance hall, the brass tip of my cane goes *clack-clack* on the marble floor. The sound rebounds throughout the foyer and into the galleries, rousing the sleeping portraits and dozing statues and the bas-reliefs of the weeping saints.

It was back in 2000 when Fiona Tamaddon, executive director of the TAM, interviewed me herself for the position of curator. I already knew that Fiona, the wealthy heiress of the Tamaddon publishing empire, had saved the old distillery from the wrecking ball swinging like a noose above its soot-stained bricks. She had hired a famous architect to reshape the building, twisting and turning its lines and topping it with a domed glass ceiling, all to house the famous Tamaddon art collection. What I didn't know was that Fiona's grandfather was Lord Tamaddon of *Brisdon*, the incredibly wealthy newspaper magnate from Scotland. You see, I am John *Brisdon* Noxon, with a broken family tree, and simply known as *Brisdon*. It was an incredible coincidence to have the same name associated with the peerage of Fiona's grandfather, and it was my foot in the door. During the interview all Fiona could talk about was Lord Tamaddon of *Brisdon* and *Brisdon House*, the ancestral home of her family located near Inverness in Loch

Ness country, and where her late father, James Tamaddon, was born.

"Have you ever seen Nessie?" I asked during the interview, trying to ease the tension in the room, even as I knew I was the perfect fit for the job.

Her back shot straight up in her chair. "Yes, of course I have! Nessie was my aunt."

I wondered if she was putting me in my place because I couldn't imagine any family naming their daughter after a sea monster. Then again, I didn't know Fiona yet and the kind of monster that ran in her veins.

Riding up in the elevator now, I adjust my mask and pull down my hat. I should be more excited, this being the first North American retrospective celebrating the reclusive artist known as CÁLA, but I can't help feeling this whole masquerade has been overdone without my recent oversight. When I step into the gallery the light that flickers over the paintings comes from tall electric candles that have been placed around the gallery to mimic real ones. Off to the side a string quartet is playing Handel's *Sarabande* in D Minor, which is quite nice, and servers in bow ties and cummerbunds are circulating with trays of wine and champagne, which is tasteful. But it's as if every move is choreographed. The shadows leap and pirouette as I try to focus without my glasses. A scarecrow walks past me and up close I recognize him as my intern, Parfait. He hands a leprechaun a glass of wine. I feel a little giddy because no one can recognize me. A couple dressed as the King of Spades and the Queen of Hearts are picking from a tower of shrimp on the food table. Marie-Antoinette swishes past me in her tall wig and wide skirts, flipping her lacy fan at me as if to shoo away death. Three Shakespearian sprites with horns and tails scamper around the chocolate fountain. King Henry has Anne Boleyn on his arm; she is wearing a green satin gown with her head tucked underneath her arm. The king laughs.

And I ask myself, *Is anyone looking at the art?*

I spy Fiona Tamaddon in the crowd, conspicuous because she isn't wearing a costume. I make my way to the adjoining galleries where CÁLA's largest work is displayed. I remove my mask to put on my glasses because I want to see the full scope of his most famous painting *The Art of Dying*. I'm too close to take it all in which is when I back right into Fiona.

"Brisdon, is that you? It *is* you!" I turn and someone dressed as Zorro is standing by her side. "I'm surprised to see you, Brisdon. I didn't recognize you."

"I should hope not."

"So you're finally back."

"Yes, but with a bit of a limp for now."

"You were injured?" Zorro asks.

"Yes, something to do with gravity and a ladder." Fiona leans in to confide in me that Zorro is our esteemed artist CÁLA, which I have already guessed. "It's an honour," I say.

Just then, one of Fiona's loyal assistants, dressed as Prince Feisal with a turban and scimitar, comes along and grabs her attention. This gives me a moment to be alone with the reclusive painter critics have tagged as *The Shadow Artist* because no one knows who CÁLA is, having hidden himself from the world for his entire illustrious career.

He moves closer—perhaps a little too close—so I inch back.

"Have we met?" I ask.

He extends his gloved hand, smiling under his black mask. *That smile...*

Fiona has detached herself from the Prince and is resuming introductions.

"This is our curator, Brisdon Noxon, who has been away for a while but has managed to make it tonight after all." I detect a touch of derision.

"Mister Brisdon." Zorro finally lets go of my hand.

His voice. The way he says *Mister Brisdon.* It's common for people to mistake my first name for my last, but this is different.

"Just Brisdon," I say.

He indicates his painting behind us. "So, *Mr. Brisdon*, what do you think of my work?"

I can't speak because the room begins to spin. *CÁLA. Why is everything so familiar?* Sweat is now trickling down my back beneath my scratchy robe. CÁLA sounds so much like *Ataccala.* I start to panic.

"Could you remove your mask?" I ask.

Fiona laughs, like a macaw. *The Shadow Artist* is gracious. "I'm sorry, I can't do that. Let me remove my sombrero."

As he does he comes up close. He has exposed the shape of his head, the copper complexion of his skin. Then he removes a glove to display the ring on his hand.

Fiona is saying something but I don't hear her. *The ring.* The milky moonstone comes alive in the candlelight, as if the whole room, the complete *vernissage*, the entire galaxy lies within that tiny stone. He rests his hand on my shoulder. Somewhere beyond the two of us, galaxies are colliding and I am being pulled into a black hole, the centre of which is the fifth floor of the Tamaddon Art Museum, right at our feet. Then the man I know as *César* lets go of my shoulder and I lose my balance, falling backwards in plain sight of all the guests and crashing into his painting. There's a screeching alarm. My mask clatters onto the floor. *The Shadow Artist* catches me and holds on until I regain my balance.

Two security guards come running. I have gone from incognito to being the centre of attention. I pick up my mask. The room flickers in time with the false candles on their stands. Everything is false. The band stops playing.

Prince Feisal clambers onto the platform and takes hold of the microphone just as the alarm is switched off.

"Now that I have your attention, ladies and gentlemen, there's no cause for alarm," Feisal says, and giggles like an imp. The speakers screech.

Then the artist who the world knows only as CÁLA—but who I unequivocally know is *César Angel Acosta*—looks straight at me and says, "*Brisdon por siempre.*" Yes, of course I remember... *Brisdon forever.* I remember *everything.* It's my curse. Then he smiles one last time... the smile that can melt Inca gold. He dons his sombrero and pulls his gauntlet back on and then Fiona escorts him away throwing me a dirty look for causing such a ruckus.

Suddenly I can't breathe. The back of my neck starts to prickle and burn. Is César looking back? I can't stay in this gallery any longer so I head to the spiral staircase for a quick descent. The heels of my shoes clang on the metal treads as I rush down the stairs. The eyes of the portraits hanging along the staircase wall are all watching me, judging me. I feel a sharp pain in my side but I keep going. Then, at last, I'm out into the cool night air. *Breathe. Breathe.* Soon I am driving home, running yellow lights and weaving across lanes. The man in the moon is looking down at me, laughing. When I walk into the house, the clock on the mantel is ticking even more loudly than usual, as if all my senses are sharpened. I set down my cane and drop my costume in a heap on a chair with the mask resting on top. Its hollow stare bores into me.

Luckily, Imogen is still at work at her club. At the sideboard I pour myself three fingers of scotch and settle back into my easy chair. My hand is trembling. I put the drink down. I remove my glasses and rub my eyes. *Fuck fuck fuck!* How did I not know that CÁLA was César? Even if no one knows who CÁLA is, I should have read the signs. I should have known that I was seeing Ataccala again, larger than life in his painting, *The Art of Dying.* I take a large gulp of scotch and feel its warmth calm me. I close my eyes and try to take myself back to that tangled journey to Ataccala, but the power of the drink and the words I had heard earlier from my little monster overtake me and instead, time starts spinning forward: I am outside myself, watching as a fragment of moonlight through the bay window travels over my face, and then the sun rises as night passes into day, and the room turns bright and then darkens to night again while the days and nights begin to move faster as time races on in a rhythm of light and shade, and soon I am moving faster than time and my skin begins to wrinkle and turn green and shrivel inside my clothes and worms begin to eat out my eyes and my skin falls off my bones as weeks and months and years flicker by and my clothes begin to disintegrate until nothing is left of me, just a skeleton from another dream, from *Notre-Dame de Paris,* and then my BlackBerry sounds on the dining room table.

I manage to reach the phone before it goes to voicemail. It's Imogen calling to see if I'm still at the party. No? Didn't I enjoy myself? *Oh Imogen of my heart, what can I say?* Her own event at the club is winding down and she is coming home.

"I can pick you up," I offer.

"I've called a taxi. I didn't expect you to be home so soon."

That will put her twenty minutes away. I make my way down to the half-door at the bottom of the cellar stairs. It's a storage space for old photo albums and travel souvenirs. I have to get down onto my hands and knees to pull out the small suitcase I shoved to the very back years ago. It's a scraped and scratched travel case that belonged to my father with art deco metal locks and corners. The leather straps have become frayed over the years. It's still locked.

I haul it all the way up to our bedroom and fling it onto the bed. Its key is hidden in my Japanese puzzle box which I keep in the bottom drawer of my bedside table. Other than the key, the box contains a few keepsakes that are important only to me: an old watch, a folded napkin, and a silver amulet and chain. I fish out the key and then hold up the medallion. I used to wear this all the time, even after I knew what it really was. I slip it into my pocket. *Not now. Focus.* I fiddle with the key in the locks until I hear them click. When I open the lid the nostalgic smell of musty paper wafts up.

The case is full of my old journals. One stands out from the rest. Yes, this is it, my book of the dead. I set it aside and lock the suitcase, shoving it under the bed and returning the key and puzzle box to its drawer. I almost trip down the stairs in my rush to find my briefcase so I can hide my journal there until tomorrow. Once that's done, I settle back into my easy chair with another scotch and wait.

When Imogen arrives home I don't tell her I met the artist CÁLA. I can't. I tell her that my costume was a hit, and she looks pleased. *Tick... tick... tick...* goes the clock on the mantel, like a metronome wagging a guilty finger at me. Imogen goes on about her event at the Beechwood Club but I'm not listening. She pours herself some red wine but only takes a few sips. She is noticeably worn out from her long day. She pecks me on the cheek.

"I'm going to bed. I have to work in the morning."

Alone now in the dim light of a single lamp, my thoughts race on. After more than thirty years, César is still wearing his moonstone ring. *How can that be?* Then again, I've kept his medallion. Has he come all this way to surprise me? Did he know that I was curator of the TAM? Has this all been a ruse, a plot? *Yes, that's it!* My mind is spinning.

Eventually I drag myself up to bed. I toss and turn, unable to sleep. The night goes on forever. Then the alarm clock surprises me at five a.m. and Imogen mumbles as I crawl out from under the covers. I peek through the bedroom blinds; it's dark and the streetlights are still on. I get ready as quietly as possible. I pad downstairs to make a pot of coffee. I'm about to write a note to Imogen when I hear her moving around above me.

"You look like you haven't slept a wink," she says ambling into the kitchen.

"I didn't."

"Why are you leaving so soon?"

"I want to beat the traffic."

"It's Sunday morning, Brisdon. There won't be any traffic."

"The contractors will be early and they'll want their cheque."

She is talking about the old Shelter Lake Lodge, located north-east of the city and where I had my fall a month ago. We would have gone up together this morning but Imogen needs to oversee a last minute brunch party at the club. At first I was disappointed when she told me; the old lodge we're renovating is really *her* pet project. But now I'm relieved. It will allow me more time alone to think. I'll re-read my Peruvian journal there to sort out the jumbled images that have been assaulting me all night. I have a type of eidetic memory, but it's flawed. Sometimes it needs a trigger and the book will bring me back to my time with César, and help me determine what I should do next. Because I have to do *something* or I'll go stark raving mad.

"I suppose they'll be boarding everything up for the winter," she says.

"I don't think they will actually board things up."

"You know what I mean." She yawns. "Is there any coffee left?"

At the foyer I grab my briefcase from the closet. "I should be home for dinner," I call out.

When I snatch the car keys from the bowl, I catch my reflection in the mirror. Imogen is right. My eyes are puffy and my pallor is like wax paper: I look like I've caught the plague.

César

I am *CÁLA*, César Ángel Luis Acosta, *The Shadow Artist.*

I like the way that sounds. A solid beginning to a mercurial story, hot like a bonfire but sad like a sea of tears, an ocean of regret. Are there really any happy endings? And just because Brisdon documented everything in that diary of his—*his* book of the dead—it doesn't mean everything was about *him*. I have to admit that years later, his book became my inspiration—so to speak. I watched him writing back then, especially late at night when he thought I was waiting for him to crawl back under the covers.

Ah, dulces recuerdos! ...to have that time back again, a time when we hardly spoke but knew each other with an intimacy I have tried all my life to regain. I've never been much for words, which is why I chose to communicate to the world with paint on canvas, with brush strokes and texture and colour. The language of art is my true mother-tongue. Even if my paintings call for interpretation, they never require translation.

To be clear, whatever Brisdon wrote down in his journal was just a half-truth. There are always two sides to every story. Those events didn't centre all around Brisdon. I was there too. As far as what comes next, I wouldn't be surprised if it's all about Brisdon all over again.

So there he stood, on the top-floor gallery at the TAM, wearing a long black robe with his plague doctor mask tucked under his arm. I could hardly believe my eyes. It really *was* Brisdon! *Dios mío*, he was as handsome and intense as ever! Age had changed him for the better, ripened him. And he was staring at my painting just as I had always imagined he would. Did he see himself there? After all, I had taken its title from the actual *Tibetan Book of the Dead*. Surely he recognized the road from Ataccala in the composition splayed out before him, larger than life.

I admit it ended badly more than thirty years ago. Ataccala broke us. I've been painting that night over and over. It accumulated into my masterpiece, *The Art of Dying*, and there it loomed right above us, testament to a hidden atrocity we had made personal.

I would have said we were opposites like Yin and Yang and that I wanted to provide the world with art and that he wanted to control the art world. But Brisdon would have disagreed—he would have said we were two Yangs moving in opposite directions. Yes, that night near Ataccala pushed us apart although Brisdon would have said *pulled*. Language and money and time were also our undoing. We lost the big picture, like looking too closely at an enormous canvas. Sometimes you can't step back far enough. Not because you will fall off the face of the earth, but because the image becomes lost beyond the horizon. Dear old Estralita used to say, *If you travel far enough you will come full circle.*

So, back then, I gave myself three goals: learn English, learn to paint, and become famous. The first two were technical, the last cabalistic. It would take years of hard work and cultivating powerful friends to achieve my objectives. I'm not stupid. It all comes down to who you know. And timing. And here we were at the TAM: fate had thrown us together to celebrate me and my body of work. Bravo CÁLA! Bravo Brisdon! The music, the imitative candle-light, the *drama*. I could even call it karma if I believed in karma and coincidence the way Brisdon did.

When I received his letter proposing a first North American retrospective of my work, I had no idea that Brisdon was the curator of the Tamaddon Art Museum. And clearly he didn't know I was CÁLA. But when my North American agent, Gilles Sevigny, showed me the confirmation letter from the TAM, I noticed that it was signed *Brisdon Noxon* below the typed signature block.

Brisdon! An art curator named *Brisdon...* That was more than serendipity! I had to think about that. I had to get it through my head what it would mean if I appeared at this event. Ever since the beginning of my career, when my first agent Jock Palmerston came up with the idea of turning me into a recluse, I never attended openings or galas or exhibits of mine or anyone else's. As *The Shadow Artist*, no one could know who I was or what I looked like.

"Don't answer them just yet," I told Gilles who, unlike Jock, easily became excited.

"Why not?"

"I need to think about it."

"What's there to think about?" But I didn't say any more. I shut myself in my studio. I painted. I gessoed over my canvas. I painted again. I delayed making a decision as long as I could.

"We need to answer them, César. I can decline for you." We were in my New York studio. Overweight and unfit, Gilles was puffing and red-faced from climbing the wide cement stairs to the loft.

"Wait," I held up my hand. I had made my decision right there and then. "I need to show up to this one."

"How will you manage that?"

"Let me take care of it."

I called the head of the gallery, and spoke with the matriarch of Canadian art herself.

"Ms. Tamaddon—"

"No, no, please call me Fiona, everyone does. What a surprise! Is it really you? The esteemed artist himself?"

I jumped right to the point. "I'll come to the opening but only in disguise."

"My, what a marvellous idea!"

"And will your curator be there?"

She didn't answer right away. She must have cupped her hand over the microphone because I could hear muffled talking in the background. Then she said clearly, "No, I'm afraid not."

"Oh!"

"He's away for an extended period, I'm sorry to say. But rest assured, you will be in good hands."

I didn't want to be in her hands, I wanted to be in Brisdon's. I laughed out loud.

"Is everything all right?"

Everything was all wrong... *Away for an extended period!* After hanging up I flopped down on a chair and then I got up and paced the way I used to when I got all fired up. Then I went to my computer and logged onto the internet. I was a recluse *and* a luddite. I searched for the name *Brisdon.* Right away I found Lord Tamaddon *of* Brisdon. I started to feel a cold sweat, that I had made a terrible mistake. Brisdon was a Tamaddon name. The Brisdon I knew wasn't related to anyone wealthy like Fiona Tamaddon. Then the old fart's picture came up, a grizzly man with mutton chops and a drinker's nose. It was clear this art museum was run by a consortium of Brisdons and not the Brisdon I expected or wanted. I would have to cancel after all.

Gilles pressed me when I told him I had changed my mind. "You can't bow out now, César. She is powerful and the TAM is prestigious. She wants to be a patron of your work."

Jock Palmerston used to say that an artist's fame comes down to a select group of people. Apparently Fiona Tamaddon was one of them.

When I arrived at my Toronto gala, the hostess wasn't in costume. The matriarch wore an average-looking gown, a Scottish tartan no less, and it wasn't flattering. She reminded me of a Buddha with a mass of red hair piled high above her wide freckled face. Gilles had done a good job of placating her because, as he maintained, you don't ever want to poke a bear with such artistic and financial clout.

I had already abandoned all hope of seeing Brisdon. He was likely the wrong Brisdon, a Tamaddon Brisdon, a false Brisdon. And here I was, anonymous in my Zorro outfit, next to Fiona Tamaddon... and then I saw the plague doctor standing before *The Art of Dying*. He removed his mask. *Y ahí estaba!* The Brisdon I remembered was standing against the backdrop of my greatest accomplishment! I knew this moment would be seared into my memory forever. I wasn't expecting to see Brisdon like that, something right out of the cloisters of San Francisco de Lima. People can change dramatically over the years, become unrecognizable from their youthful selves. But not Brisdon. Time had not changed him much at all. There was just a wisp of grey in his fair hair. His ears still stuck out and his complexion was still smooth like a northern Italian model. So handsome! He was the same Brisdon I remembered. Fiona noticed Brisdon and went over to him as he backed up right into her. I braced myself. He looked at me. He smiled without knowing what was going to happen to him. Then she mentioned Brisdon's wife. She called her *Imogen*, a character I knew from Shakespeare because Jock, cruelly, had made me read Shakespeare to learn *classic* English.

But Imogen? Brisdon's *wife!*

"You must keep this a secret, Brisdon," I could hear Fiona whisper to him, "but we have the real CÁLA here. Isn't it wonderful?"

"A pleasure to meet you," Brisdon said.

I hadn't heard that voice for years. It was richer, deeper with age. "Mr. Brisdon," I said with a smile, a joke we had once shared. "Are you enjoying my work? I have a good friend to thank for it."

I saw his reaction. He was being pulled in two directions at once. He didn't know what to think. I was being cruel, I knew. I felt a little sorry for him, being at such a disadvantage. Then he asked me to unmask myself. Just like Brisdon to ask! But of course I couldn't do that. I just laughed and Fiona laughed with me. He looked like a boy who had been punished for stealing but still had the goods in his pocket. I wouldn't be surprised if Brisdon had kept me a secret all these years, had buried our story like the dead we were both ineluctably tied to. I knew Brisdon would keep his secrets close.

I removed my glove to show him I was still wearing the moonstone ring he had given me that night in Cusco. And then he started to fall backwards so I grabbed hold of him.

I would have kissed him on the mouth there and then, like the first time in the disco, but the alarm went off and then someone was tapping on a microphone at the lectern to get everyone's attention. Fiona Tamaddon pulled me away from Brisdon before I could say anything more. I looked back. There would be no doubt he would know me now after seeing the moonstone ring.

I shouldn't have been surprised when he disappeared from the *vernissage*. Brisdon had a knack for disappearing. I first saw him at the monastery deep down in the vault when I was drawing the skulls and bones of those people who had shaped the history of Lima to only become an ignoble parade of death for tourists just like Brisdon. While I was leaning over the railing, sketching, I felt someone looking over my shoulder. When I turned, the spotlights were lighting him up from below. They cast shadows over him in a way that accentuated his features like a figure in a Fernand Léger painting, all angles and curves. Then he moved out of the light. He was shy and apologetic and I fell in love with him right there and then. But he was gone before I could close my sketchbook—vanished.

"Leave the drama for the bedroom," Carlos said to me afterwards, when I told him I had followed the tourist back through the rooms but a family with too many children was barrelling down the narrow staircase to the crypt. The last little girl fell and lay in my way, wailing, so I picked her up and handed her to her mother. By the time I came up to the stone arch entrance, my perfect stranger was gone.

He disappeared again at the disco when I introduced him to Carlos and the others. Granted, I got carried away. I was after all, a young, hot Latino and I told him so. I knew what I wanted and I wanted *him*.

His last vanishing act was at Ataccala. But that was a different type of disappearance. We had no choice but to go our separate ways. It was impossible to come back from what we had seen and done and I couldn't become involved with the police. I had to turn and walk away. It was the last time I saw him. I walked and walked as the sun got higher and stronger. When I sat down to rest in a farmer's field with sheep and goats grazing next to me I realized I was still wearing Brisdon's clothes. I looked at the ring on my hand. *Now we are married.* I was poking fun at him when I said that because he was so serious. Yet in another way I was touched. I would never be able to fully let him go.

I wish I had Brisdon's memory. My recollections of the short months Brisdon and I spent together have become hazy over time, like trying to look through a grimy, cracked window. I kept the sketchbooks from when Brisdon posed for me or when I drew him while he was sleeping. He tried to pay me for them but I never gave them to him. I never took his money. Not until the very end.

If I had my art, Brisdon had his book of the dead. He showed it to me once. I saw his neat handwriting covering page after page. I saw my name once, then again and again. On the first page I read *Dear Karen.*

"Who is Karen?" I asked.

"My sister." Then he added, "She's been gone a long time."

Brisdon had a troubled soul and I think he recognized the same in me. As Estralita used to say, *We must do the best with what we are given.* She may not have been a complicated person but she was pure. And she loved me like a mother. Perhaps, when I met Brisdon, I was looking for a mother or a father to replace the ones who abandoned me. I have always believed I am descended from the ancient line of Inca kings, but what I didn't know when I was young was all the sublime and divine hardship and suffering that comes with that regal title and which would follow me my entire life.

Margaret

When the little girl with the shimmering ribbon in her hair jumps into her mother's arms, I know I can't take these lies any longer. It's the defining moment: all the events have led up to this one and I just want to scream. The mother wears a sarong and the little girl has jet black hair just like Karen. That's all it takes, another mother holding her daughter. I look around. Everyone in the departure lounge is staring at me. I feel a sort of panic rise up to my throat, choking me. What am I doing here? If I don't get up from this horrible plastic seat and walk away before they call our flight, I'm going to lose my mind.

"Margaret?"

He's leaning into me, and I know he will start speaking in that damned quiet tone he thinks is soothing but just grates on me. And he isn't calling me *Meg,* his pet name for me, so I can tell he's getting frustrated, maybe even angry, and finding it hard to hide it.

"Margaret, what's the matter?"

We're late boarding our flight. The loudspeaker has just announced a delay due to bad weather in New York. I can't sit here any longer so I say to him, "I just can't stand it anymore, Christian." But as always, he doesn't understand what I'm really saying.

If I had only seen that little girl and her mother *before* we left for New Orleans, I wouldn't have come all this way. I would have turned around, left the departure terminal in Toronto, and taken a cab straight home. I was wrong to come with him. But I could tell he needed me here, he was so afraid that it would really be *her* this time. I knew it wouldn't be Karen—a mother always knows—but I was afraid Christian might mistake the body for hers and then we

29

would bury the wrong little girl. The New Orleans Police wanted us to come in person to identify the body because they were so sure that she was Karen Elizabeth Noxon, a decade after she vanished. They didn't send any photos. They had to bring us all this way in person, to this carnival town that's as hot as hell in June. If Christian only knew what was going through my mind right now... The fault is mine, utterly, and it's suffocating me. Once you begin a deception, it slowly rolls on, growing, until you can't stop it. It lays to waste everything in its path.

"Please don't be like that," he pleads. "We had to come. We owe it to her."

Poor Christian. But what did I really owe my daughter? Another useless journey looking into the face of another corpse. For a moment my heart had leapt to my throat when the old coroner with the crooked teeth lifted up the white sheet. *No, this can't be Karen!* Then a sweet, cheesy aroma wafted up as he pulled the sheet away. I thought, the old guy has hidden his lunch under the trolley. And for the first few moments I was actually frightened. I had never wanted this for my own daughter, no matter how I felt about her. But Christian took it harder. Something about fathers and daughters, they say. He really had adored her. I never understood why.

Granted, the dead girl did look like Karen, or at least what she might look like at fifteen years old. Christian grabbed my hand and squeezed it hard. She had been pretty, that girl lying there, before one side of her face had been smashed up. Yes, she could have been Karen, she had the right colouring and her hair was straight and black like Karen's. And there was a mole on her shoulder, just like Karen's, and that had been the impetus to call us all the way down here. Christian was crying. But I knew that this girl lying there wasn't Karen. I would know my own daughter.

The first few years after she had been abducted were the worst. I didn't know how much more I could take of the phone calls in the middle of the night or the grim faces that appeared at our front door. These disturbances didn't bring us any closer to Karen. Now it was a wrong number or a carpet cleaning salesman. No wonder salesmen look so grim. It's already 1975 and they still travel door-to-door to make their living.

After we left the stifling morgue, the detective brought us back to the police station. Christian was so pale I thought he might faint. We were shown into a stuffy room with an old stained sofa where we were invited to rest and "gather ourselves" after "our shock."

"We should try to get an earlier flight home," I suggested.

We had arrived in New Orleans the night before and we were at the police station by nine a.m. sharp. But I had no intention of staying in Louisiana for the rest of the week just because Christian had allowed for time to make arrangements to bring Karen home if the body had been hers. We had left our fifteen year-old son Brisdon alone at home and I worried he could be getting into trouble like any normal fifteen year-old. As soon as the detective left, his secretary made a few calls for us. She was a black woman with bleach-blonde hair and cherry-red lipstick. She called everyone *honey*. Then she signalled me over to her desk.

"They can't get you a direct flight tomorrow, hon, but you can fly through New York."

"What time?"

She squinted down at the paper where she had scribbled some notes. She needs glasses, I thought.

"Leave here at one p.m. and connect two hours later. That gets you home at six. That okay for you honey?"

"That will be fine. Thank you."

And here we are, in the departure terminal, much too early for our flight because I just wanted to get out of that hotel. The air conditioner was on the fritz and the room smelled. Now that I've seen that woman and her little girl, I don't think I can get on that plane. We will have to walk across the tarmac to the boarding stairs and it's already a hundred degrees out there.

"Here." Christian holds out a pack of American cigarettes. "Take one. This will calm you."

I don't smoke much as part of my effort to reinvent myself but I take one anyway and he strikes a match and lights it for me. Always the gentleman. I draw a few puffs. It tastes like power.

As I smoke he turns to fuss with his carry-on bag. I just watch him, Christian Noxon, my husband, father of my son, my rescuer and protector, my albatross, my undoing. You're supposed to stop seeing people you know well, or you see them the way you want to see them, but I always saw Christian in the same way from the moment I met him: an unfinished possibility. He will be forty-two this year but on what day no one knows. He was adopted from an orphanage back in 1933 after he was abandoned there, just a new-born *bairn* with a ticket pinned to his blanket that read *Christian*. The doctor at the orphanage had to assign him a birth date for the records. It would have been his mother that left him there, I had no doubt about that. She would carry that stigma for the rest of her life, the poor thing, no matter what her reasons. *He that hath pity upon the poor lendeth unto the Lord.*

I would have thought foundlings starting their lives with such drama would have a caul of misfortune over them for the rest of their lives. But not Christian. He was adopted almost right away by a doctor and his wife and never had to want for anything. Even as an adult he relied on them financially while I had to crawl my way out of the moors with no one's help and the world stacked against me for being a girl. But I had my looks and, apparently, my bite was worse than my bark, as Doctor John Noxon once said to me, with his subtle humour, while his sweet-faced wife Elizabeth glared at me with those piercing eyes. Her gaze unnerved me with pure witchery, as if she knew exactly what I was thinking. I certainly didn't care much for that. Who wants anyone else to know what they're on about?

Christian has the kind of face anyone can read. I always thought he looked like a Norwegian lighthouse keeper with his fair hair, long face, and scraggly beard. I can always tell what goes on behind those blue eyes of his, the same eyes he handed down to Brisdon. Christian is no good at keeping secrets, unlike Brisdon, who often withdraws into his own world as he collects secrets the way other boys collect baseball cards. Maybe he inherited that part from me, which is a shame because secrets only lead to more deceptions and create a closet full of skeletons.

Christian looks up and attempts a weak smile. What is he seeing when he looks at me? Is he seeing me pretending to relax, puffing on my cigarette? Does he notice the muscles in my neck tensing up? Could he ever understand how I want to jump up and race out of this airline terminal just to make this charade stop? I know it makes no sense to run from the inevitable; it makes more sense to head straight into it. No, he isn't seeing any of that. He never sees me. The true Maggie Campbell is invisible to him, has been obscured right from the very start.

I was born Margaret Mae Campbell but everyone knew me as Maggie before we crossed the sea to Canada. To travel over water is to be changed and that was when I lost Maggie, abandoning her to someone else, someone stronger and harder. But I get ahead of myself, as I tend to do. I was still young Maggie and living near Inverness, in a town named Crown, my ancestral home, a place I should never have left. I suspect few people alive today would remember her, a young lass coming into her own, *fair of face and full of grace*, as the saying goes. My father was hard-working and my mother, who was named Cairenn after her own mother, was tall and comely. My *wee* brother Duncan who was named after our *da* was *the child of woe* who my parents hoped had *far to go*. But he didn't. He died of diphtheria on his fourth birthday. After that my mother never smiled. Only after my brother's dying did my father start paying attention to me. This made me realize I had never been daddy's darling, that he had put all his hopes in his son, and that love for a child isn't always unconditional, and that sometimes a child has to earn it. Then the war came and so many men died fighting for our freedom. When it was finally over, I was no longer a child but a young girl, and an attractive one at that. Inverness had been spared the worst and Crown survived untouched, as had the land at *Bruidein an Ròid*, the estate we all knew as Brisdon House.

Brisdon

U p ahead the old wooden sign reads *Shelter Lake*. When I turn off the highway I'm on a gravel road that winds through an old forest. A mist hangs over the trees, their leaves tumbling down to get stuck on my windshield. The wipers smear the veins of the leaves across the pane. The sugar maples, chestnut and oak trees are on their last breath of gilded splendour. In this early light they sway blood-red and vermillion against the blue spruce and green pines. This season of ripening colour sets us apart from the rest of the world. This is Imogen's world.

A tiny white-tailed deer appears at the bend in the road. She's just a fawn and she looks directly at me. She thinks she's invisible. We watch each other for a moment, then she raises her tail and shoots off into the trees.

The stone gate leading into Shelter Lake Lodge has two pillars and a metal arch above, like an entrance into a Victorian graveyard. Latticed into the arch is a single iron word: *Shelter.* I park the car and step out into a different world, empty of the incessant hum of urban life. Sounds are trickles now, whispers. Beyond the trees, a cloud of vapour swirls across the lake.

As I gaze out over the lake, scenes from my childhood return to me. I'm no stranger to Shelter Lake. My parents and I vacationed here during the summer months when I was a boy. The screened porch of our cabin kept out the bloodthirsty mosquitos and blackflies. At night there were bonfires and music and during the day guests played croquet and horseshoes on the manicured lawn. Colourful Muskoka chairs lined the beach looking out to the water with its floating pier. The pier is still there, its boards all rotten now. Two old canoes covered in moss lie upside down near the shore. The Muskoka chairs are falling apart.

The whitewashed cabins on the hill are crumbling. All this spoilage belongs to us now. Imogen's vision will mean an entire rebuild from an outdated infrastructure of knob-and-tube wiring, lead pipes, asbestos paper and oil furnace heating. The past of Shelter Lake belongs to me and the future to her.

A few seagulls spiral down over the lake, searching for food. At first I think the noise I'm hearing is a seagull. But the high-pitched cry comes from behind me. When I hear it again, the sound is unmistakably human so I head towards it. The third time I hear the scream it is clearly someone in distress so I move faster across the long wet grass to the cabins that line the back of the property at the top of the hill.

She's a girl, just a teenager, and a menacing young man is shaking her. The girl pushes him away.

"Are you all right?" I intervene. They are as surprised to see me as I am to see them.

"None of your business, *pretty-boy*," she snaps.

"It *is* my business." I snap back.

"*Fuck off.*" He retreats into the cabin. A weak ray of sunlight shows me a tattoo on the back of his shaved head, a jaguar circling around on itself.

"Hey!" I shout back. "You can't be here. This is private property."

The boy stumbles back out. When I look into his face I can see deeper damage. These aren't just kids having a bit of fun. The girl is trembling with anger, or from something else. I take a step back. Jaguar-boy grabs hold of her and she lets out another banshee wail. The boy shouts, "Fuck you, Holly!" She reaches out and starts batting him with her fists. *Holly-go-darkly.*

"You need to get out, I won't say it again."

My heart is pounding from adrenaline when the sound of a diesel engine comes sputtering through the trees below.

The contractor's black pick-up truck appears, stopping next to my Jetta. It takes a long time before the engine cuts out as if he's just sitting there watching what will happen next.

"*Shit!*" Holly turns to me and her eyes are brooding with hate. Then she is gone into the woods like a shot, like the white-tailed deer. Jaguar-boy turns back and spits at my feet, just missing my shoes.

"We'll be back, *asshole!*"

My heart is still thudding as I head down the hill. The contractor, Francis Perry, and another man, a bit older, get out of the truck.

"You remember Willie, our resident expert?" Francis askes as Willie Bearheart extends his hand.

"Yes, good morning Willie. Very glad to see you."

"You got yourself a bit of trouble there." Francis says. He has a narrow face with close-set eyes and has a slight east coast accent that Imogen likes. *His accent makes me think we can trust him*, she says.

"Squatters," Willie points out. "It happens on these abandoned properties. Warehouses are the worst. These kids are lost. No employment up here. Just time on their hands to make trouble. I know first-hand. Lots of times their parents just kick them out and they have nowhere to go. But they're not violent."

"These two were pretty aggressive," I say. But I have to trust Willie who knows everyone in the area.

"You'll need a good alarm system," Francis suggests.

"Or get a couple of big dogs," Willie adds.

"Not climbing any more ladders, I hope?"

"I've given that up," I confess.

Francis Perry is laughing now and Willie Bearheart is shaking his head as if I'm just another urbanite to be pitied for falling off a ladder.

"Care to see what we've done with the church so far?" Francis asks.

They lead the way. The old stone Anglican church was built before the railroad snaked its way through another town further south and the population followed. The church had been converted into the dining room for the old lodge. When we enter, the morning sunlight has broken through the fog and is streaming through the four stained-glass windows. There is nothing left save the shell of the church but I can still feel its lofty symmetry and calming equilibrium. Stacks of two-by-fours now line the stone walls which are bathed in a prism of colour along the west side. The room is cluttered with small tools, a table saw, an air compressor and a drill press. The old dining tables and chairs which have replaced the original church pews are now stacked high in the centre of the room, like the work of a poltergeist. Any trace of religious artifacts, the patina of its past, has been long since removed. The kitchen at the back, built as an extension, is now completely gutted. The stained porcelain sink lies cracked on the floor with corroded plumbing pipes and rusted faucets. The original gas oven rests on its side, black with grime.

"I was thinking of running a rope down from the steeple bell to this point here." Francis indicates a place in the wall and looks up. "That way you can ring the bell when it's time for dinner."

"Imogen will like that," I say.

He has a number of questions for me about the place-ment of the new sink and range. I don't want to make these decisions alone because this will be Imogen's kitchen. Yet for a moment I can't see her in here. Instead I see Max, her new chef at the club, searing a fillet of fresh trout and sautéing vegetables over the stoves. I close my eyes and push the image away. *Damn Max!* I return to this moment feeling even more unsettled.

On the way back to his truck we pass the wishing well. My father and I used to toss dimes down into it for luck, as if this would help bring back my missing sister. There are memories scattered everywhere. Francis unrolls the construction drawings on the hood to show me some structural alterations that will have to be made. Both he and Willie hold down the corners of the blue paper.

"Certain renovations can be put off until spring. My priority is closing the place up for winter. While we're here, we'll just collect some of our equipment."

"That's fine."

"And that other cheque, Mr. Noxon—" he tries to say casually.

"Of course." Afterwards they thank me and I apologize for Imogen not being able to join me. I think they like her; she has a gift for making everyone feel irreplaceable.

As they get to work, I fetch my briefcase and the property's ring of keys from the car and head for the schoolhouse adjacent to the church. There is nothing left to indicate the building was once a school, no rows of desks, no blackboards or globes or alphabet letters on the walls. I'm standing, instead, in a worn reception area and lounge, only it's far more threadbare and smaller than I remember. It all smells stagnant and fusty, the odour of neglect. The pale particles of dust dance in the sunlight glinting through the grimy windows. The spiderwebs tremble like harp strings. There's a tall reception counter with a row of hooks behind it for the cabin keys which are all gone now. Gone too is the black dial telephone and the sign-in register where my father let me print our names. A few couches and chairs remain in what used to be a lounge warmed in the evenings by a large fireplace that is boarded up now. A few sofas have tattered blankets thrown over them to hide the wear. The upholstery is stained and torn. None of the lamps work, the lightbulbs having fizzled out long ago. Along one wall sits an old upright player piano. A stack of *National Geographic* magazines with their yellow spines are piled against its side causing another memory to flood back. With them, I had walked weightlessly on the moon with Neil Armstrong, tracked lions on safari with Bill Travers, and swam the crystal clear coral reefs with Jacques Cousteau. Now everything that is left is worn and wretched. The magazines hide in the piano's shadow, its keys like a row of rotten teeth, the ratty mohair sofa has its back to the faded paisley chairs, and the fireplace wheezes behind its nailed-up boards, like an old family tired of arguing with one another.

I dust off a nearby table with my sleeve and the dust motes twirl like tiny hurricanes in the light. I open my briefcase and set my book down on the table next to a wingback chair, its fabric shredding as if clawed by ghost-cats. *Layla.*

I hear the men shouting outside as they load equipment into the truck. Eventually the diesel engine starts up and fades away. I am finally alone.

The cover of my Peruvian journal reads *The Tibetan Book of the Dead* but long ago I stroked out the word *Tibetan* and wrote *Peruvian* above it. When I open it to the first page I read, *Dear Karen...* I have dedicated all my notebooks to my sister after she disappeared on our first Halloween night out trick-or-treating, fifty years ago. This book was my last.

I fish out the medallion and chain from my pocket and put *Saint John the Evangelist* to my lips like a sacrament. I clasp it around my neck again and settle back while my ever-present little Lucifer snarls, *Bringing all this back won't do you any good.* But how can it do any harm?

Shelter Lake fades away as I read the neat handwriting across the first few pages that will become more erratic and difficult to read, and will end with the last pages smeared with blood.

*   *   *

Lima, June 5th, 1983
   Sunday 10:00 a.m.

   Dear Karen,
   *This is the City of Kings: they called it Rimaq after the
river and then Limaq because the Inca kings couldn't
pronounce the " R". When Francisco Pizarro arrived, he
shortened the name to Lima. But I call it the City of Ashes.
The once lush and fertile oasis gradually turned into an
urban wasteland. It is now a desert of grey, the colour of
cinder and soot. It even smells grey here.*
   *I'm sitting at an outdoor café near Plaza St. Martin,
having my morning coffee. The small square tables are
covered in red-checkered tablecloths. Periodically children
come up to me dressed in rags with their hands outstretched
chanting, chiclets-chiclets-chiclets. An old man on crutches
stops to look at me and smiles. His teeth are rotten. A
commuter bus has just roared by belching out diesel fumes.*
   *This morning the roosters woke me at sunrise.
Imagine, roosters crowing in the middle of a city of five
million people! Tomorrow is my first day at the museum.
This leaves me a day to scout out my neighbourhood and
do some sightseeing. I plan to visit the famous library at the
cloisters this afternoon which is located—*

   *I can't believe it! Someone just grabbed my camera
right off the table. I jumped up and reached for the strap
but it was gone. I couldn't see who it was, just the back of
him. It was a good camera too, a Pentax K1000. I hadn't
taken one picture yet. The people at the other tables are
shaking their heads and looking at me with sympathy but I
don't want sympathy, I want my camera back. I order
another coffee and move my wallet to the front pocket of*

41

my jeans. I'm trying to see the silver lining here, like it's better to lose my camera at the beginning of my trip than later with a full roll of film inside. No one will try to snatch away my notebook, disguised as The Tibetan Book of the Dead.

*   *   *

Lima. The name sticks to my tongue like a canker sore. I should have written that down. There is so much I didn't write down during those eight weeks, so much I will need to fill in now, all my memories between these entries.

For instance, Lima wasn't at all like I had expected. My first experience of having my camera snatched away was a good lesson for me to be more careful. And yet I was still intoxicated by the exotic prospects of my summer there. I was hard-set and headstrong and nothing would bother me for very long or get under my skin that I couldn't pare away.

The opportunity to work in Peru came about during my third year at U of T, majoring in Art History with a minor in Business Admin. My plan was to become the curator of a great museum of fine arts like the National Gallery in London or the Thyssen-Bornemisza in Madrid or even the New York Met. My second year art history professor, William Cespedes, was from Lima. He offered me a job as his undergraduate teaching assistant because he liked my *entusiasmo*, he told me, and thought I could benefit from wider exposure to the art world. A colleague of his was curator at the *Museo de Arte de Lima.* If I was interested, he could write some letters and see if they would take me on *gratis* for a summer work term. It would be expensive, he warned me but I was self-sufficient thanks to the trust fund I received when I turned twenty-one, money from damages awarded to me from the airlines for the death of my parents.

I didn't like flying so when my plane's wheels touched down at the Jorge Chavez International Airport, I breathed a sigh of relief. After I left the customs hall with my suitcase, Rafael Blanco was there to greet me. Rafael was one of the assistant curators at the *Museo de Arte de Lima.* He wore large black glasses and a threadbare jacket like a typical academic. Yet there was something incredibly formal and sad about Rafael and something very kind as well. When he offered his hand it was as if I was shaking a paw.

As we exited the airport doors, dozens of men swarmed us offering their beat-up old cars as taxis, enticing us with gifts of mangoes. Rafael waved them all away. By the time we found his Volkswagen Beetle in the parking lot, the sun was beginning to set behind the barren hills of the Morro Solar. It had been a very long day. As we turned onto the highway I noticed a pervasive smell. It was an odour like nothing I had ever encountered before. It permeated everything, an arid mixture of garbage and diesel fumes, of desert winds and salt from the sea. It was my first exposure to the contrast that was Lima. We passed billboards for Inca Cola and Ducal cigarettes, adobe shacks with collapsed roofs, brown clay buildings abandoned and ruined next to pink churches and shops painted over with graffiti. The airport was not far from the city centre so I was anticipating the districts to brighten.

He saw me frowning. "Not what you expected?"

"Where are the palm trees and whitewashed colonial estates I've seen in pictures?"

"That is San Isidro and Miraflores," Rafael explained. "None of that is in Lima proper."

As we drove on, Lima felt ominous in the dim light—a polluted, dry, decaying insomniac of a metropolis.

"Why is everything so grey?"

"It is because of the sea mist which is caused when the cool winds from the ocean meets with the warmer desert climate. Lima is a desert. Do you know Herman Melville, the author?"

"Yes, *Moby-Dick.*"

"Herman Melville described Lima as '*the strangest, saddest city, and there is a higher horror in the whiteness of her woe.*' But that was more than a hundred years ago. I think it is better now."

The apartment they had found for me was located just a short walk from the museum. It was on a side street and the building's orange walls were covered in graffiti. Iron grates were secured over the windows. It had once been an elegant example of neoclassical architecture but now, in the gloaming, it appeared to be falling to pieces. Up high, on the side of the building next to the stone railing of a balcony, I could make out a frieze of an Olympian god with his herald's wand, winged sandals and traveller's cap. A tortoise was lying at his feet. Its edges had been worn away by pollution and the years.

He noticed me looking at it and said, "Our forlorn Hermes of Lima."

The apartment was on the top floor. The best part was its balcony situated off the main room next to Hermes. It overlooked the corrugated iron rooftops strewn with debris.

"I can meet you here Monday morning and walk with you to the museum. When we arrive you will need to be documented."

"I'm sure I can find my way, I could just meet you there."

He nodded. "Let me draw you a map." We found a pencil and some paper in the kitchen drawer and he drew the route. Afterwards he shook my hand again but squeezed tighter this time. When I shut the door behind him, I had to give it a shove with my shoulder before I could lock it.

* * *

Monday 5:00 a.m.

I'm too excited to sleep. After my camera was snatched away, I made my way to the convent of Saint Francis at the Plaza de Armas to see the famous library. It is supposed to contain twenty-five thousand antique texts, some of them predating the Spanish conquest of the Inca Empire.

But this wasn't to be my day! The library was closed for repairs, apparently from an earthquake over a decade ago. So I looked over a pamphlet about the ossuary, a tomb containing the remains of more than twenty-five thousand people and I thought about the coincidence of that number: there was one book in the library for each body that lay beneath it.

When I climbed down the narrow stone steps I could feel the cold and the damp rising up from the stones. I stood with the hundreds of thousands of pieces and parts of human bodies that lay sprawled in perpetual dusk around me—skulls and wrists and spines and feet and ribs entwined and layered and scattered and patterned and ordered in row upon row—centuries of death. I felt as if I was in the centre of some horrible pageant. Then something moved. Off to the side there was someone standing alone and I realized it was a young man in jeans and a T-shirt, drawing in a large sketchbook. I tried to look over his shoulder at his drawing. When my shadow fell onto the paper he turned and I stepped back, raising my hands apologetically as if caught spying, which I was. He wasn't a tourist, that much was evident. He had that rich Peruvian darkness about him. He said something to me in Spanish that I didn't quite understand so I just raised my hands again.

Lo siento, I said and he flashed me a wide smile as if forgiving me for being a tourist. I nodded and waved and

then there were footsteps and chattering from a group
coming down the narrow stone stairs.

*   *   *

That was César, of course, sketching in the catacombs of the *Basílica y Convento de San Francisco*, but I didn't know who he was then, or that he would become CÁLA, or how he would sabotage my life up until this very moment.

Once I had climbed up from the catacombs and returned to the living, I found a table on a restaurant patio for an early dinner. The gruesome bones of the dead hadn't suppressed my appetite and I realized I hadn't eaten anything since morning. I pulled the book from my camera bag looking at its false cover with its title, *The Tibetan Book of the Dead*. Next to me a waiter was writing the evening's menu on a board. When he was done I asked to borrow the marker. Then I stroked through the word *Tibetan* and wrote *Peruvian* above it. After visiting the tombs I suspected my book would be more than just a travelogue. I felt it in my bones.

*   *   *

Monday, June 6th, night

I followed Rafael's map, walking along Avenida
Abancay, passing the black hollowed-out mound of the
shrine of Our Lady of Lourdes, then down Jirón Sandia
where women in white top hats were selling cabbages and
beaded necklaces and horseshoes and wheels of cheese and
spools of coloured thread and bags and bags of spices—
lemongrass and licorice, cinnamon and mace, marjoram
and poppy seed. I reached the museum in the Parque de la

Eposición twenty minutes later. There were two armed guards at the main entrance. They wouldn't let me pass even though I explained to them I was a foreign student, starting work that morning. They just gave me blank stares and wouldn't let me through until Rafael appeared waving his credentials.

When we were inside he explained that security was very strict because of a burglary a few years back. The thieves had targeted the crowns from the Kings of Jerusalem after the First Crusade took the Holy City. The museum had feared the bandidos would melt down the gold and sell off the jewels. Fortunately, most of the artifacts had been recovered and now they were protected under shatter-proof glass.

For the rest of the day I was the centre of attention. Lucía, an assistant curator in her twenties, said in her broken English that I was beautiful and giggled into her hands like a geisha girl. I must have turned beet-red.

After Rafael gave me a cursory tour of the entire building, he brought me to the head curator's office, Francisco Barón, an older, stern looking man with a mole on the end of his nose. So this was William Cespedes' friend, I thought. They couldn't have been more different. He advised me in very good English of the planned exhibit I would be working on with Rafael, a tribute to Alberto Vargas, who had recently died. My international perspective on Vargas' work would be helpful and he hoped I would learn a lot about Peruvian art. I told him I had read a translation of his book, Pre-Columbian Art of Peru, and he seemed pleased about that. I thought Rafael was trying not to smile. I was off to a great start.

In truth, I wasn't familiar with Alberto Vargas but I didn't want to let on. As we walked to the archive rooms, Rafael told me Vargas was a world-famous Peruvian illustrator from Arequipa who had died in December at

*eighty-six years old. I suspected Vargas would have been a
1930s art-deco or cubist painter. Then Rafael asked me if I
listened to music albums, and when I told him of course, he
smiled and said, then you know him. We were in a narrow
room full of pull-out drawers filled with traditional canvasses
and drawings. Rafael picked up a record album from the
counter and turned the cover towards me. It was Candy-O
by the Cars showing a sexy woman with red hair in black
pumps lying back on a vintage car. This is Alberto Vargas,
Rafael announced wryly, the museum's macho legacy of
Peru.*

*He put the album down, took off his black-framed
glasses and stood there wiping his eyes as if he had been
laughing. Joaquin Alberto Vargas y Chavez was far from
Picasso or Klee or Kandinsky or anyone I had thought his
work might resemble. He had been an artist for the Ziegfeld
Follies in Hollywood and then the creator of the iconic
World War II era pin-ups for Esquire magazine. They were
known as Vargas Girls, beautiful and romantic women
created in watercolour and airbrush. I could feel Rafael
smiling behind me, as if anticipating my surprise. And then
we both laughed.*

June 7th - Tuesday evening

*On my second day at the museum, Lucía and I were
walking through the upper gallery together when I saw him
again, the young artist from the catacombs. When I was
surprised how busy it was so early in the day Lucía
explained that the museum was free on Tuesday mornings.
We passed an older man in a fancy cravat and felt fedora
with a feather who looked like he had stepped right out of
an Edwardian portrait. Then I spied the familiar young man
with his drawing pad sitting cross-legged on the floor. It
wasn't uncommon to see art students copying from the*

masters or groups of school children sitting in circles under a painting with paper and crayons. This stranger was taking advantage of the free admission, being young and, after noticing his worn-out runners, very likely with empty pockets.

As I passed behind him I didn't stop because Lucía was tugging at my sleeve. She invited me to dinner tomorrow night at her parents' home so I felt I owed her my attention. I glanced back just once to see if he had noticed me but he was intent on his work. Yesterday morning I thought I had dreamed him, the purple shadows deep in the crypt playing amaranthine tricks in the dust of time.

When I could get away, I went back to the gallery but he was no longer there. I kept my eye out for him throughout the day but Rafael was keeping me busy. I would have liked to have made a gesture, to have said hola to him. But I didn't see him again.

June 9th - Thursday evening

I've adopted a cat! She's a tiny black kitten that fits in the palm of my hand.

Lucía's father, Alfredo, picked us up from work yesterday in his little black Honda Civic. We drove beyond the outskirts of Lima past rows of houses that were like multi-coloured boxes. When I mentioned that it would be a long commute to work for her every day, I think her father thought I said communist and became a bit agitated until Lucía calmed him down. When we pulled up, three more adults and two children greeted us from the doorway.

The evening was filled with wine and music. They were very hospitable. Lucía, her mother and father, her sister and her husband sat around me while their two little girls climbed over their laps. The wine flowed in and out of my glass and I was sure we were dining from their best tableware. *The record player was playing ballads from a Peruvian singer Luis Abanto Morales and as Lucía showed me the album cover the smallest girl said, Gringo, and her mother scolded her. I laughed.*

When it was time to go, Alfredo was fussing under the hood of his car. Lucía was pulling on a sweater to accompany us. Seeing the hood up made me think that maybe I would be spending the night. That's when her father shut the hood and we headed off.

As we turned onto the highway I heard a mewing noise from somewhere inside the car. That's when Lucía told me there was a cat in the engine. A gato, she giggled.

I had them to stop the car on the side of the highway. We all got out and started looking, opening up the hood again, and the trunk. That's when Alfredo pulled a tiny black kitten out from the wheelhouse of the back tire and handed her to me.

On our return to Lima, sitting in the back seat next to Lucía, the cat clung onto my shirt with its tiny sharp claws, mewing and mewing. The song Layla was playing on the radio. By the time we got to my apartment the little thing had settled down and I bid Lucía and her father a heart-felt thank you and Layla and I went in for the night.

*   *   *

My involvement with César Ángel Acosta began because of a cat. In addition, I wouldn't have followed the path that led us to our night just beyond Ataccala if it hadn't been for a black cat.

Since time out of mind, cats have been catalysts. Egyptians revered them and shaved off their own eyebrows when a cat died. In central Europe they burned bags of cats in ancient rituals and spread their ashes to bring good luck. In China, at the beginning of the world, the gods appointed cats to oversee the running of their new creation. The Greeks would blame the cat. In Rome a papal bull was issued denouncing cats as evil and in league with Satan. In Persia cats were magic.

I asked everyone I knew at the museum if they wanted a kitten. On top of having to leave after my assignment, I was allergic to her. I asked the curatorial staff and the construction crew who were setting up the galleries for the new exhibitions, but apparently there were too many feral cats in Lima haunting the streets at night. I didn't want to leave Layla to that fate. Lucía tried to help. We posted an ad on the bulletin board in the small staff lounge. To get there, Lucía and I had to walk across the large inner courtyard with its black-and-white checkered marble floor. Her heels clicked on the glassy marble and when we stopped we became human chess pieces on a large board, the King in a white button-down shirt and the Queen in a short red dress. We laughed and hopped from square to square.

"White King takes black Queen," I said.

"*Jaque mate!*" She giggled into her hands.

But there were no replies to our ad. Layla would be mine for the time being, regardless of my itchy eyes and sneezing fits.

I had never been to the Pacific Ocean so Lucía wanted to take me to the beach at Miraflores. It was a warm Saturday and I wore a bathing suit under my jeans. She met me at Plaza de Armas under the statue of Pizarro, herculean atop his sturdy warhorse, sword pointing towards the presidential palace. We took a bus and we bounced about on plastic bench seats and all I could smell was the stench of diesel fumes through the open windows. Lucía held onto my arm as Lima passed by, a city of crumbling buildings and shanties, unabashed poverty outside of the downtown core, even more pronounced in the noon-day sun.

Out on the ocean pier of Miraflores near the Costa Verde beach, a new restaurant on stilts was being built over the rocky breakwater. *La Rosa Náutica* was styled from the Victorian era with rose-coloured planks and awnings, ornamental spindles and an elaborate double-roof gazebo with pointed towers. To me, it couldn't have looked more peculiar than the Taj Mahal on the moon.

The beach was spattered with people brave enough to go into the cold water. We stripped out of our clothes and hid them with our shoes in a crevice in the rocks. Then we ran in, battered by the waves, laughing and shrieking at the cold. The salt buoyed us together and the waves tumbled us apart. Beside her in the sand I leaned over and kissed her. She returned my embrace. I let my hand wander to her breast and she moaned and her kisses became more passionate. Then she abruptly pulled away.

"No, no, no," she moaned, turned over and started to cry.

I asked her what was wrong but she wouldn't answer. Eventually we made our way back to the rocks and dressed in silence. The bus ride back into Lima was awkward. She sat at the window staring out, not moving until she finally smiled when her father came to pick her up. But the smile was for him.

*   *   *

Saturday June 11th, afternoon

I made my way back to the café off Plaza St. Martin where a week ago I had lost the camera. I was asking the waiter if he wanted a cat when a voice behind me asked if it was a gato or a gata?

I turned and there he was, Hermes from the frieze but in the flesh—my elusive young artist. He asked me in

English if he could join me. Of course I said and made room. It's a she, I told him, a gata.

Maybe my aunt or uncles will take your gata, he replied. That would be great, I said, but I don't even know your name. He answered, Luis César but everyone calls me César. And yours? I said, John Brisdon but everyone calls me Brisdon. We laughed at that. We shook hands over the table. Do you remember me? I asked him. He turned shy. Yes, he said. Yes, of course.

For the next while we switched back and forth from English to Spanish. He said he wanted to learn English. I asked him if he wanted to come to a movie with me—it would be in English with Spanish subtitles. Yes, he said, he would like that.

After he left I've stayed behind to write this all down right away thinking, he's not a Caesar like the emperor of Rome, no, he pronounces his name Say-czar, with the emphasis on the czar, like the ancient kings of Peru. He says he is descended from a direct line leading right back to them.

June 13th, morning

César and I went to see The Year of Living Dangerously. It was a few years old but I hadn't seen it yet. The film was very good and I really enjoyed the music. Afterwards, we went to Café Godoy across the street, named after Armando Robles Godoy, the Peruvian film-maker who had screened all his films at this theatre.

He asked me my last name so I wrote it out on a napkin: NOXON, in capital letters. This is the perfect palindrome, I told him. He looked at me not under-standing. It is the same backwards and forwards, inverted and upside down. César liked that. He particularly liked the name Brisdon. He said it over and over, Mister Brisdon,

Mister Brisdon, and I laughed and said no, not Mister, just Brisdon, but he waved the idea away and continued to repeat, Mister Brisdon, Mister Brisdon, cementing it to memory, waving the napkin around like a flag until my name was just a blur in the night air.

Now I feel my world has become a palindrome, as if César has turned me upside down and inside out.

* * *

My responsibilities at the museum soon escalated. Señor Barón must have been pleased with my work because I had now been assigned to another assistant curator to help oversee a second planned exhibit. It was to be a display of Goya's etchings, an international travelling exhibition originating at the Prado and, incredibly, Lima would be its first venue in the Americas after it left Madrid. Our museum's other assistant curator was a small woman in her sixties with grey hair that she kept pulled back in a tight chignon. Silvery stands of hair floated in the air above her head like the cilia of an underwater creature. Rafael introduced us.

"Brisdon, I'd like to present Señora Manuela Goya."

"You are really Señora Goya?"

"Yes, of course." Her English had a slight British accent.

"Are you related to the artist? Is that why they gave you this exhibit?"

"The exhibit of the artist Francisco José de Goya y Lucientes?" Her voice had risen in astonishment. "No, of course not!"

I looked to Rafael to see if he would rescue me from my gaffe but he stayed perfectly still and expressionless even though his eyes were laughing.

"But thank you for asking," she continued. "You will find the life of a man in his name. For a woman not so much."

Later, when she was explaining a very technical procedure to me in Spanish I interrupted her. "*Lo siento,* Señora Goya, but my vocabulary is still a bit rusty."

"*No hay problema,*" she replied. "You can lick the stamps and seal the envelopes." She glanced over her glasses at me and winced. "And please call me Manuela. Señora Goya was my mother-in-law, God rest her soul. Finally."

I found myself immersed in a game of contrasts as I divided my time between the exhibits of my two mentors: Vargas, a model of dreams and Goya, the stuff of nightmares. I didn't want Raf to think I was playing favourites with Manuela's exhibit so I thought it was a good time to take him up on an offer of a night out together. I had taken to calling him Raf and he told me there was only one other person that called him by that name but I wasn't going to find out about that until we went out for drinks—to loosen our tongues.

*   *   *

June 15th, Wednesday night

> *Layla has a new home.*
> *César and I took the bus to the northern district of Independencia, where he lives with his aunt and her two little girls an hour's ride away. I carried Layla inside my coat. While on the bus, Layla got nervous and started to squirm around and I had to keep stuffing her back into my jacket and talking to her which César thought was funny.*
> *Independencia was a neighbourhood of cement houses row upon row. Some were painted pink or red or orange*

*while others had been left grey. Dented garbage bins lined
the streets. I met his tiny Aunt Estralita who seemed very
nice and who could only say hello and goodbye in English.
Two shy little girls stood in the shadow of the room behind
her with their fingers in their noses. We went around back
and I set Layla down in a little garden while a huge orange
tabby cat looked on. Estralita served us coffee in a sparsely
furnished living room. The iconic television set had rabbit-
ears. The porcelain cups she used to serve our coffee was
riddled with the fine crazed lines of wear and tear.*

    *When I took the bus back to Lima from Independ-
encia it was already dark. Here in Lima night fell like an
axe. The bus broke down a long way from the city centre
and we all had to get out. I was disoriented. I found a
restaurant called El Pulpo with a long bar and ordered a
cerveza. The bartender wasn't Peruvian. He was a strapping
ginger with a bandana around his head and his sleeves
rolled up displaying tattooed arms. Here you go, he said in
English. I asked him how he knew I spoke English. Ya look
English, mate, he said. His name was Craig Riley and he
was from Australia. When I told him my name was
Brisdon, he laughed and called me Brisbane. I spent the
night drinking one cerveza after another talking about art
and culture and Peru until the restaurant closed and then
we sat together at the bar and kept on drinking. His knee
kept grazing mine. I looked into his eyes and they were the
light blue of the Caribbean Sea and there was a strange look
to them. I noticed his wedding ring. Are you married, I
asked. Yes, my wife owns the place, he answered. But she's
away in Iquitos.*

    *Finally, when it was time to leave, he told me I was too
drunk to make it home and that their apartment was
upstairs if I wanted to pass out. He had his hand on my
shoulder. Something was telling me to stay, perhaps my little
demon was whispering yes yes yes, abandon yourself to this*

moment. *But I just shook my head no no no, and Craig Riley and I stumbled out into the street where he found me a taxi home.*

* * *

True to his word, Rafael and I went out after work that Friday night. We had kept ourselves busy in the archives later than usual because Rafael joked that he didn't like to drink in daylight. *Like a vampire,* I thought. Dusk had fallen by the time we left the museum and the air felt heavy like rain.

"Don't worry, it never rains in Lima," Rafael professed.

The bar wasn't far so we walked. It was built to resemble a British pub with Tudor-style half-timbered plaster walls and a long bar of rough wood that looked like it would provide plenty of free splinters. The place was airless and crowded and as we arrived a couple were leaving so we took their places at the bar. The seats were still warm.

Rafael bought the drinks, waving away my objections and my offer of a smoke.

"Not my vice," he said, "but please go ahead. Now about you and Lucía—" I didn't say anything. He just stared at me with that serious look of his. "Something has happened."

So, he had noticed. "I don't know what happened," I admitted.

"She is engaged to be married," Rafael said. That was all he needed to say. Those had been rueful tears, guilty, culpable sobs and I was blameless. Rafael took a sip of his beer. "Women are complicated beings," he said and I wondered where that was coming from. "The Vargas girls. You like them?"

I shrugged. "Sure."

"So you like the exhibit?" I didn't know what he was getting at. He looked me straight in the eye and slammed the palm of his hand onto the rough countertop. "*Mierda!* It's bullshit!" he exclaimed. I laughed so suddenly I spit out some of my beer. He went on. "Francisco Barón assigned it to me because he hates me."

"Why does he hate you?"

"He hates me because I am gay."

That took me by surprise. He stared into his beer as if not trying to surprise me at all. I thought I should say something but he went on.

"The exhibit is progressive but it is vulgar at the same time. Our mission statement should be to collect, preserve and exhibit Indigenous and Spanish art to advance public knowledge of these works at the highest level, not playing to the crowd."

I sat up straight on my bar stool. He had my attention. "I couldn't agree more."

"*Si*, Señor Vargas is a true Peruvian, born in Arequipa. But he moved away when he was very young and only became famous in Hollywood, not Peru. And not to speak ill of the dead—God rest his soul—but I don't see the connection to his depictions of American beauties and the history of Latin America. The true history of Latin America is a horror story and it remains so to this day."

"I suppose there could be worse ideas for exhibits," I offered.

He looked at me through his glass and smiled. "I like your attitude, Brisdon."

I raised my glass in salute. "To unusual partnerships."

"*Salud.*"

"So Raf, why does Señor Barón hate you for being gay?" I had to ask.

"*Machismo*," he answered. "It is still prevalent in Peru, even in modern times. We are a very Catholic country and the general attitude towards homosexuality is hostile." He tipped his beer glass back and finished it and held up two fingers to the bartender. "You know, it was my idea to secure the Goya exhibit for our museum. Because of Goya's Little Prisoner Series. Yes, Manuela is wonderful, I love her, but dirty politics are at play."

Two more glasses of beer arrived. Two girls with painted red lips got up and started dancing to *Blondie* in the narrow aisle between the businessmen and the tourists, spilling drinks at one of the tables. The bartender barked a warning and they sat back down.

"But the director gave you an intern. If he hates you, what does that say about me?"

Rafael laughed. "Yes, I don't think he expected you to be such a bright young man. Sometimes an intern can be a burden. But you showed yourself very quickly and that is why he has made me share you with Manuela. For the coveted Goyas."

"What was it about the Little Prisoner Series that affected you?"

"Señor Barón knows about my connection to the penal institution and my attempts to protest the conditions here in our own prisons."

"Were you in prison?"

"Not I, no." And then he took a sip of beer and said in a half-whisper, "Perfecto." I wasn't sure I heard him correctly. For a moment he appeared to be weighing whether or not to continue.

"You said Perfecto?" I leaned in.

He continued. "It is not illegal to be gay in Peru. Not for sixty years which is very enlightened for a Hispanic country. But it is illegal for anyone in the military to be gay. Perfecto was a *capitán* in the Revolutionary Armed Forces which we called *Gobierno Revolucionario de las Fuerzas Armadas*. This was military rule in the early seventies. He was very handsome, like you, but older. You are a younger version of Perfecto. I was very taken aback when I met you at the airport."

"What happened to him?"

"It is my fault that Perfecto is in prison. We were not young but we were foolish. We thought we hid it very well. We all have to hide, legal or not, wearing masks like *bandidos.* It was hard for us to meet so we arranged that I would drive home in the afternoon and I would wait for him. He would make his excuses with his squadron and drive over in the military car, still in his *capitán* uniform and we would spend an hour together, even though an hour was never enough. One day one of his comrades saw him leave and return. The military police set up a surveillance. They broke down the door of my apartment. By the looks on their faces they were not expecting what they found. Instead they were looking for weapons or drugs. We were so foolish."

"That couldn't happen where I come from."

"Don't be so certain, my friend. The police hit me repeatedly with the butts of their rifles and dragged Perfecto away. Because I was a civilian, they reported that I was complicit in Perfecto's crime to my supervisor at the *Museo,* Señor Barón. This was when my troubles started at the museum. Different treatment. Longer hours. Work I did not want. Señor Barón is still attached to the old establishment, the *machismo* of Peru. He disciplined me for taking those afternoons off, reducing my pay even though I always made up for the time."

"And Perfecto was sent to prison?"

"Yes, Perfecto was arrested and court-martialled and given a twenty year sentence. It was the maximum penalty because he was a high ranking officer and was caught while on duty. If the crime had been on his own time, his punishment would have been less severe but he still would have been punished."

"I'm very sorry, Rafael."

"Yes, I understand. When I tried to visit him they turned me away. He was married you see, so only his family could see him. I asked Manuela to go to see him, to say she was a relative and report back to me. But I know she did not tell me everything, at least she did not tell me about the worst parts. When the policies at the prison relaxed a few years ago, I tried to see him again. While I waited for him I got a look at the prison conditions. They were horrible. There were cockroaches and mice and rats. There was mold on the walls. The plumbing did not work. I waited many hours there but I never got to see Perfecto. Instead, I have been doing everything I can to petition the government for prison reform but it is...an uphill battle, I think you say. I always feel they are watching me still, ten years later. *Oh dios mío,* it is tiring." Rafael was staring into his beer glass now, his voice betrayed his frustration. "Peru is a contradiction. It is a monstrous beauty. Last year I don't think you would have been able to obtain a student visa. I am surprised they didn't close the airport again, after Lucanamarca." I just looked at him. "Lucanamarca," he repeated. Again, my blank stare. "The massacre at Lucanamarca. The communist party retaliated against the murder of their leader and killed all the villagers. I fear we are entering a very long and bloody war."

"I didn't know it was so bad." In truth, I knew nothing at all. I had been willfully ignorant about the politics of Peru and I didn't want Rafael to know.

Rafael shook his head and moved his shoulders back, stretching his neck from side to side as if exercising out a kink. "It is very complicated, my friend. Perhaps war is too strong a term. It is political unrest with gunfire. A new constitution was approved four years ago and the communist party is against it and is lashing out. Many civilians and soldiers have already died but Lucanamarca was the worst. Perhaps Perfecto would have died in one of the attacks so maybe he is safer where he is. I take comfort in that sometimes. If you go travelling you must be very aware of your surroundings. You will love the country of Peru but you will not love crossing paths with Señor Guzmán."

I wasn't sure what he meant by that but I lifted my glass again, safe in my innocence. For a moment the noise of the bar rose to a pitch like a communal hysteria and I now understood why Rafael had chosen this location to talk to me, so no one could hear us.

"You are very young and have everything before you. You may not always make the right choices but try to make smart choices." He had resumed his aloof countenance. "Now let us circle back to our dear Lucía..."

*　　*　　*

Monday June 20th

César invited me to a dance club to meet his friends Saturday night. We danced and drank and when I went to find the washroom César followed me. By then I was quite drunk. In the upper hallway César pushed me against the wall and we kissed and to be honest I felt a thrill when you know you are doing something so completely wrong! That's when I pushed him away and took off and afterwards, back at the apartment, I went out to the balcony and smoked and paced. I felt hot. Then cold. Lima stared to spin. César's face was the pale moon, his caresses were the flapping pigeons, his mouth not just on mine again but inside mine, down my throat and into the pit of my stomach. I fell to my knees and vomited up the entire evening.

Then, this morning, César was sitting on the steps of the museum when I arrived for work.

At first I thought he must know the museum was closed or he was just confused and then I felt stupid because he was obviously waiting for me. I was both afraid and relieved. He looked up as I walked over. I stopped on the steps above him and he didn't move as if he was allowing me all the power.

Hola, he said. I said hola back. I sat down on the steps next to him and fumbled for my pack of Ducals. I'm sorry about running off, I said. His face brightened. I'm sorry too, he said. I'm sure he saw a nervous quiver as I lit my cigarette.

I don't have any other way to find you, he admitted. No, I guess you don't. Why do you want to find me, I asked him. We're friends, he said. But that's all, I said. No, he answered, no.

I thought I could hear the beat of the music from the disco in my head but it was my heart racing. Smoke burned my eyes. I blinked a few times until the sting went away.

I'm a hot Latino, he said. Yes, I agreed, you made that very clear. He smiled and butted my shoulder with his. Maybe you liked it. Okay, maybe, I admitted. Maybe me too, he said. We both laughed.

I took a few more puffs and then threw the cigarette down, scrunching it under my shoe. I got up. I told him I had to get to work and thought that would be the end of it. He just looked up at me with that expression teetering on the edge of hurt and longing and I thought, fuck fuck fuck...

Friday June 24th, morning

César has been staying with me for the last week but had to go back to Independencia for a change of clothing. This time, when I came out of the museum, he wasn't there.

I sat on the steps and smoked while I waited. Soon Manuela passed by and I waved. After about forty minutes I decided he wasn't going to show up.

As I was climbing the stairs to my apartment, I had a feeling there was someone in the stairwell. When I reached the top landing there he was, sitting with his head on his knees propped against my apartment door. When he lifted his head the side of his face was crimson and his lip had been split open.

I brought him in and no matter how much I prompted, he didn't want to talk about it. He didn't want to go out either. He didn't want to be seen at all. I had an unopened bottle of scotch and a pack of playing cards. I poured us a drink. When he sipped it he winced. He didn't know any card games so I taught him how to play Crazy Eights and Go Fish. Then I turned on the radio and after he had more scotch he started to dance around the room and I laughed and joined him. We decided to redecorate the apartment, pulling out nails with an old hammer I found in the bottom kitchen drawer and moving the pictures around. Then we rearranged the furniture to match the art, which threw the rooms into chaos and we sat on the floor laughing. Then the music from Saturday Night Fever started playing on the radio and we got up and danced to oh oh oh oh stayin' alive, stayin' alive, and we cackled and howled until our sides hurt from laughing.

Later, when we were lying on the bed which was now in the living room, César said he planned to be very rich one day. Doing what, I asked him. Being a famous artist of course, he replied, so that he and his art would live on forever. I asked him what artists he admired. He didn't understand at first and then I thought he would tell me some obscure name, like Alberto Vargas, but he did something that amazed me. He started naming artists, not just one, or two, but dozens. We made a game of it:

Botticelli I said. Donatello, he said. Dürer I said. Clouet he said. I tried to stump him. I said, Filippo Lippi. He countered with Filippino Lippi. Touché, I laughed. Who's that, he asked. I laughed even harder.

And so it went on: Titian and Canaletto, Giottino and Vecchietta, Raphael and Tintoretto, until we were tongue-tied and I pulled him gently to me so as not to hurt his bruises.

Brisdon por siempre, he whispered into my ear.

Tuesday July 28th

César handed me a small medallion and chain today. It has a nice weight and looks to be made of silver: one side shows the full face of a man etched in delicate relief, with a low brow, full lips and a slim nose, a beatific and angelic face—and the other side displays writing that reminds me of the script from the dead sea scrolls.

You like it, he asks. Of course I like it, I say. It is you, he says. I just stare at him. It is John the Saint, John the lover of Jesus, the first one to follow him, he continues. I realize he is saying it's the image of John the Evangelist and it's obviously an heirloom in immaculate condition, almost a museum piece. I can't imagine its value. I know César doesn't have two soles to rub together. Yes, I really love it, César, I say, I've never seen anything like it. I fold him into my arms and hold him and there is that warm stirring again, that thrill of the taboo, but he backs away first and makes me promise to keep the medallion a secret between us and he won't tell me why.

Cross my heart and hope to die, I say.

* * *

65

Manuela Goya invited me to dinner at her home to celebrate the completion of the main phase of our project. We had been working tirelessly on a schematic for the placement of works coming from the Prado and I had resolved some of the more difficult issues. I think she was pleased with the outcome. She even smiled once or twice. We agreed to break up the monotony of the work week with a little party, as she put it. I reminded her I was allergic to cats. She promised she wouldn't serve cat. Before I arrived at her apartment which was in the nicer district of Surquillo not far from San Isidro, I bought a bunch of fragrant flowers from a cart parked in the street owned by a woman in a white top hat who smiled at me with shiny gold teeth.

Manuela's apartment was richly decorated: the furniture was a mixture of Queen Anne and Chippendale with Asian influences. Her walls were filled with oil paintings and watercolours and shadow-framed antiquities. Her floors were covered with oriental carpets. The air was scented with potpourri and I suspected that smoking was *prohibido.*

She appeared at her door in a kimono of forest green silk and her grey hair was no longer in a bun but flowed down her back. She thanked me for the flowers and arranged them in a vase which she placed on a carved walnut table. She saw me looking at the table as she primped the flowers.

"Did you study furniture design, Brisdon?"

"Yes, but it wasn't part of the core curriculum."

She brought out a bottle of Rioja from the sideboard with two tall-stemmed glasses. She had many beautiful things. I felt César's medallion against my skin, another beautiful thing she would appreciate, I was certain.

She handed me a glass and said, "Let's listen to some music, shall we?" She thumbed through the albums next to the record player. "Classical? Jazz?"

"Jazz." I answered.

She pulled out a record and put it on the turntable. The music was familiar: Keith Jarrett's *The Köln Concert.* When I heard the piano notes I felt a little lost. I always associated this music with my parents. The album had just come out the year they died. She brought a platter of cheese and fruit and it felt like we were far away from Lima.

"I'm not making *ceviche* tonight or *anticuchos* or any-thing Peruvian. I hope you enjoy spaghetti and meat-balls."

I laughed. "That's perfect. A welcome change."

"So, Brisdon, you're studying art history?"

"My focus is on the period between early medieval art and the gothic era."

"Beware. Art historians love to classify works according to different time scales. But art is not a linear historical phenomenon. Everything depends on time and place. Medieval art may be a seventh century fresco in Aachen or a sixteenth century triptych in Venice, even if the medieval period rarely stretched so far."

"You are saying the dark ages were shorter than people realized."

"Exactly, my good man."

"Where did you study, Manuela?"

She looked a little shy just then, as if afraid to sound proud. "In Europe. Mostly Spain and Italy. *Firenze* is my favourite city and the Uffizi galleries," she kissed her fingers, "*sono bellissime.*"

The piano music filled the room. For just a moment her expression softened as she went back to that time. We talked about the Goya exhibit. She had an affinity for him, she told me, because Goya went deaf and that set off his dark period. When I asked why this was important to her, she smiled and tapped her left ear.

"I'm deaf on this side, my dear."

"Oh. I didn't know—"

"All my life," she admitted. "Few people know."

Then I joined her in the kitchen where she browned the meat and stirred the sauce and boiled the water for the pasta. I leaned against the counter as she reminisced about her time working at the National Gallery in London with its rich Medieval art collection and how she came back home to Peru to take care of her father, being the only surviving daughter of a once large family. Her father had been a very high official in the Peruvian army, a three-star general, "*General de División*," she stated stoically, but I also detected a trace of cynicism. She said that it was because of her father that she had helped Rafael.

"At the prison?" I asked.

"Yes. He has told you his story?"

"He has, yes."

She considered for a moment as she stirred the pot. "Then he thinks very highly of you. What did he tell you?"

"About Perfecto. About the arrest. How you helped him when he couldn't visit him."

She kept working over the three burners of the stove, perhaps so she didn't have to look at me.

"Things were not the way they seemed," she finally said. "But first, let us finish preparing dinner. Could you flip the record please."

I hadn't noticed the hissing hiccup from the record needle. We moved to the dining room with our steaming bowls of pasta. She sat at the end and motioned for me to sit on her right. Now I understood why she tilted her head at times.

"Why were things not the way they seemed?" I asked.

"I shouldn't have said that."

"He is a mutual friend," I said twirling my fork in my bowl.

"Yes, so please remember that." She ate a few bites then put down her fork. "I went to the prison for Rafael as he had asked of me, because they wouldn't let him see his boyfriend. I told them I was Perfecto's aunt. I had never met him. Rafael didn't even have a photograph to show me. I only knew how much he cared for him. I did not know what to expect." She took a sip of wine. "When Perfecto came into the visitor's room he was just skin and bone. The guards had broken his arms and they had not healed properly. He must have been a mere echo of his former self, the one Rafael had loved so much."

"I understand why you wouldn't tell Rafael."

"Oh I told him about how Perfecto looked. And the conditions of the prison. I did not tell him that when I let Perfecto know who I was he had lunged at me, that he tried to strangle me with his chained hands and it took the guards all their strength to pry him away. He left shouting curses at Rafael. I have never before seen so much hate in anyone." We sat in silence for a moment. "I wanted to tell him but his heart was so full with the idea of their love that I couldn't see him destroyed any further."

"I understand," I said.

"It became complicated when Rafael would ask me to go on repeat visits for him. Avoiding the truth was putting a strain on our friendship. I think he knows I won't go back. He no longer asks. He hasn't asked you, has he?"

"No."

"Good. You should know the truth in case he tries to get you involved, for whatever reason. Love is irrational."

"Yes, I know."

She smiled. "What do you know of love at your age?"

"I'm not that young. I'm twenty-three, Manuela."

She laughed. "You have a far way to go. Do you have someone special at home?"

"No, not really."

She thought for a moment as she sipped her wine, reddening her lips.

"And here?" I just looked up from my pasta at her but I couldn't answer. "Is it that boy? The one who took your cat?" I still didn't speak. I was surprised yet not surprised.

"His name is César," I finally said.

"Ah!" She sipped her wine. "César the emperor. Sounds full of himself."

"He's the opposite of that."

"And you are lovers?"

My palms started to get clammy so I wiped them on my napkin.

"I have never met anyone quite like him," I deflected. "He lives with his aunt. They're poor."

"So you want to help him?"

I nodded. "He wants to be a famous artist. I've seen his sketches. He has talent."

"Well that's something. Just be careful, Brisdon. It is not easy for gays in Lima. Or anywhere in South America for that matter."

"I'm not gay!" I blurted out and knew how absurd that sounded. My mouth gaped open like a dying fish. Manuela just looked at me.

"Then you are bisexual?"

I understood she had entrusted me with her story of Perfecto and was expecting this confidence in return.

"Maybe," I replied. "I'm experimenting."

"Actually, I'm skeptical when people say they are experimenting. We are not pendulums. But let's leave it at that, shall we? I think the world has a long way to go before it truly understands the human sexual condition and I only want to be sure that Emperor César is not taking advantage of you."

"He is braver than I am."

"Brisdon, I too have learned to be brave. I've had three husbands so I know what I am." She paused for effect. "Happily single!" We laughed together. "But tonight isn't about me. It's about my protégé." She raised her glass to me. "To you, young man, and to true love wherever you can find it."

"*Salud*," I said and we clinked glasses.

"Now for dessert." She rose from the table and for a moment I saw the trace of a roguish smile, as if she had enticed me to say exactly what she had wanted to hear. "Do you prefer something sweet or savoury?"

*   *   *

July 18th, midnight

I am falling victim to the strangeness of time here. The hands of all the clocks move forward but time stands still. I carefully undo the clasp of my medallion. I want to hold it again, to rub my thumb over the likeness of the saint, as if calling him out of his two thousand year-old sleep. It's like rubbing my thumb across a tiny crown of thorns. César is asleep in my bed but I hear noises above me as if he has lifted out of his body and is hovering over me, watching me write these words in my book of the dead... turning the pages himself with his ghostly fingers.

July 19th, night

César went back to Independencia. He has taken my duffle bag full of laundry for his aunt to wash. He now spends most nights at my apartment and he wears my clothes when he needs to change his.

I found one of my shirts that he had worn at the bottom of the wardrobe. I lay on the bed and put it to my face and breathed in his scent. Now I understand why people do that: it sets off some sort of chemical reaction in the brain, releasing pheromones or hormones, or whatever

*it is that abandons you to something greater than yourself.
You lie there and just shut your eyes and draw in breath
after breath. Fuck fuck fuck!*

July 21st, morning

*César returns with my clothes all washed and folded.
He brought his sketchbook. He wants to sketch me. Only
nude, he says, like true life-drawing models. I strip off my
clothes and lie back on the bed. Like this, I ask. Yes, he
replies as he pulls up a chair. I watch him concentrating as
he works. His expression is fierce. I try to smile but it
doesn't reflect back on him. Then he flips the page over,
moves his chair to the other side of the bed and begins
another sketch. I close my eyes. I let his pencils and
charcoal etch me out and wash over me like a river of
cinders.*

July 23rd, morning

*I've started working on my travel itinerary. But César
says he won't come with me. Why not, I ask. It's dangerous,
he says. No, it's not, I shoot back. I try to calm down.
What's the real reason, I ask. Money, he says. I have
money, I tell him. It's not right, he replies. Why isn't it
right, I challenge him. Well that did it. It was the first time
we had argued like that, all flying knives and broken glass.
And this time I was the one who had to get out of the
apartment. I had to clear my head.*

*   *   *

That morning, after my argument with César, I went back to
the spot at the beach where I had spent time with Lucía and
sat under the noon-day sun, thinking about what I was doing

until I understood there would be no answers for me in the sea. *Fool! Fool!* the seagulls screeched above me. *Go back! Go Back!* the waves rasped below me. The wind tousled my hair like my mother used to do.

I knew I had to stop fighting myself. I got up and brushed myself off, scrambled across the rocks to the stairs which led back to the main road and ran for the Lima Centre bus. I bounced on the ripped plastic seat with my head against the greasy window pane as Lima slid by, got off the bus, crossed the busy intersection at Avenue Iquitos, traversed the Plaza Manco Cápac passing an old man selling roasted nuts with his monkey on a rope, laughed with a shoeshine boy in a red cap who tried to polish my running shoes while I waited at the stoplight, crossed over to my side of the street at a cart of fruits and vegetables abandoned in the hot sun and entered my apartment building where I scaled the stairs two at a time, fumbled with my keys while trying to catch my breath, dropped them, scooped them up again, shoved the door open and entered the apartment to find César in my boxer shorts, leaning over the bathroom sink as he was finishing shaving with my razor. He looked up into the mirror, startled at my sudden reflection because my arrival had been drowned out by the running faucet. My chest was still heaving from racing up the stairs. There was another mirror on the wall behind the sink and from my angle, our reflections created an infinity mirror where we were both momentarily caught in a vortex of infinite distance. I only saw this for a moment. Then César turned, a bit of shaving cream left on his chin. He moved towards me and all was forgiven, our world no longer infinite, I realized, but definite.

* * *

July 23rd, later

When I got back to the apartment after clearing my head, I said, César, if you have no money I will pay you. For what, he asked. For your drawings of me. I'll pay you twenty—no fifty dollars for every drawing. You don't have that much, he said. Yes I do, I said. Still, that's too much he stressed. If you plan to be famous one day you can pay me back, I countered.

This melted him. Later, lying in bed facing each other with a dark river of dying stars flowing between us, he just looked at me sadly. We are only postponing the inevitable, he whispered in Spanish.

Without hope there is no despair, I thought.

Thursday, July 28th

During my last week at the museum, Francisco Barón summoned me to his office.

He motioned for me to sit in the leather chair in front of his desk then opened a silver cigarette box and offered me one but I declined it politely. I watched him take his time as he lit up. A gesture of power. My impression of him had greatly altered over the last eight weeks. I had first sat in this very chair, a little damp under the collar, my stomach in knots. But not anymore.

Cómo estás Brisdon, he asks. Muy bien, gracias, I reply. He asks me about my intentions and I realize he means aspirations so I say I would like your job, Señor Barón.

He smiled but it was like a dog showing its teeth. He had my letter of recommendation ready. We are very pleased with your work with us, Brisdon, he says.

For a fleeting instant I want to tell him that I have been having carnal relations with a young man, a hot Latin man and that it is love like any other, just like Rafael and

Perfecto, and that he should try it instead of being a self-righteous hypocrite... But we just stood to shake hands: the ceremony, the code, the ritual. It is a type of defeat yet I am different now, and need to appreciate little victories...

*   *   *

On my last day the staff threw me a going away party. At three in the afternoon we assembled in the large boardroom and the table was laid with sweet confections, beer and sparkling wine. Señor Barón made an appearance and warned everybody that I could be their next boss. Manuela was aloof, as always, or perhaps her head had been turned with her deaf ear to the group. Rafael put his arm around me in front of everybody as he raised a toast with his plastic cup. Lucía kissed me on the cheek as if all was forgiven.

Rafael took me aside. "I'll pick up your suitcase tonight and keep it until you return to Lima. Are you sure you won't need it?"

I thanked him. "I'm just going to pack a duffel bag."

"And you're travelling alone?"

"No," I admitted. "But you already know that. You've been talking to Manuela."

"Yes, I have. I'm worried I've been a bad influence on you."

"No, Raf, it's just a coincidence."

"There's no such thing as coincidence."

"Now you sound like Manuela."

Before I left the party, Rafael hugged me and whispered for me to be careful as Manuela had done, as if they knew what was in store for us on the road to Ataccala. All I knew was that César was waiting for me outside on the front steps and we would be starting a new adventure together.

César

Our families can cause us the worst kind of damage. My dear mother, Mariposa, was no more than a ghost of a woman while my father was General Edmundo Francisco Acosta of the National Police in Ayacucho. He was a big man with a big ego and a booming voice that carried to the end of town. He reminded me of Zeus from my mythology books, not because of his super strength but because he enforced a type of resplendent brutality in the name of justice. His cruelty against villains and outlaws was legendary. At the same time he was privately involved with them. Even as early as 1969, the summer the Americans landed on the moon, one of Peru's greatest enemies-to-be, Señor Manuel Rubén Abimael Guzmán Reynoso, was a guest at our dinner table. Also known as *Presidente Gonzalo*, the leader of Shining Path started as a professor of philosophy at the National University of San Cristóbal del Huamanga in Ayacucho and my father treated him as an ally. Corruption in the police community was more common in outlying states where each sheriff was king. I believe now my father's true desire was to be king. All I remembered of Señor Guzmán was that he chewed with his mouth open and when he spoke, tiny bits of food came flying out, landing on mama's lace tablecloth.

We lived in the Central Sierra, one of the poorest districts of Peru, in a large house surrounded by *flor del Inca* bushes. Vines climbed up the outer walls and arched over the windows. We had four servants: Esmerelda, Reyna, Reina and Rosquete. They were from a family that had served the Acostas for generations; some say their lineage extended back to the Wari, pre-dating the Incas. Esmerelda was the matriarch. She was half a girl high and two girls wide and I never saw her smile in all the years I knew her. Reyna and Reina were her twin daughters, one a spinster, the other a widow. One wore blue every day, the other black. I called them the twin bruises. Rosquete was Reina's daughter. She was a little older than me, as round as a doughnut and exceedingly shy. She had a malformed lip and spoke with a lisp and her eyes were enormous behind her thick glasses. All the girls doted on my mother who was frail, with skin as translucent as a glasswing butterfly nervously fluttering in the shadow of the great hulking Edmundo. My father was three hundred pounds of muscle and fat and never stopped sweating. His size bode well for him in his influential role in the police force. He had been shot once when he had been a captain and because he was big even then, he didn't realize it until two days later when he developed a fever and my mother smelled pus. He claimed bullets would never bring him down because of his god-like connection to the Inca kings.

Everything changed for me the day a short-tailed swift flew into my open bedroom window and it took Esmerelda and both her daughters to chase it back out.

"A bird in the house is good luck," Esmerelda mumbled as they started to clean up the guano the bird had left on the wallpaper in its terrified flapping throughout the room. "But this time not so much."

I was almost fifteen and parts of my brain were still under construction, including where romantic love exerted its powers. I was also a boy who liked other boys and such things would not be tolerated by any family, rich or poor, especially ours which was to be a model of Family Values to the community. It was Saturday. Mama was out viewing new wallpaper samples that had come into the hardware store. My little brother Diego was playing with friends outside and Esmerelda and her girls had gone shopping. It was the perfect opportunity to sneak Pío through the back door and up to my room. Pío was two years older and we liked each other just a bit too much. We were in different grades in school but we sought each other out: in secluded rooms, under stairs, behind garbage bins, wherever we could be alone. He was a head taller than me and his shoulders had already filled out and he smelled of wood shavings from his father's carpentry shop, the way Jesus would have smelled. So when the entire family was away he snuck over and I propped a wooden chair under the door knob of my room to keep anyone out, especially my little brother who had an insatiable curiosity. That day, my father came home unexpectedly because he had spilled coffee on his uniform. Not finding anyone home, he stomped upstairs. We didn't hear my father's heavy tread on the stairs because our heads were buried in the pillows. We didn't really know what we were doing, mostly fumbling and groping and kissing because Pío loved kissing. My father could hear the bed creaking through the door. He crashed in sending the chair into splinters. General Edmundo Francisco Acosta stomped in so hard that the mirror over my dresser fell off its stand and shattered on the floor. He pulled us apart and began punching me with his fists and I had the sensation of being pummelled underwater. The blows felt warm and purifying. The searing pain only started later. Poor Pío received the worst of Edmundo's wrath because not only did my father smash his face in and bend his nose for life but he threw him onto the tiny shards of mirror which took the nurses at the hospital six hours to pull out of his skin.

Edmundo grabbed me by my wrist and dragged me down to the living room. He told me to sit in the old chair by the Chinese vase and not to move. Later, Esmerelda helped Pío down the stairs and out the back door where he had come in but this time leaving a trail of blood behind him. The servants, the neighbours, everyone would have heard my father yelling:

"Worthless *maricon.* You are no son of mine!"

I sat still, completely naked, my face bloodied and blue. I was still sitting there with my father in the next chair when my mother came home. She screamed. Edmundo was calmly smoking a cigar and blew smoke rings that quivered in the air.

"Did you know about our *poco mariquita* of a son?" he asked her.

I looked at her as she stood there and for the first time I couldn't see through her. She saw me ever-so-carefully shake my head. "No Edmundo, I did not," she lied. "But please have mercy on our boy."

He didn't. He couldn't be the General of Police without a macho mirror of himself. I was his first born son and now I was his greatest disappointment. That night I could hear my parents arguing downstairs. It was the first time I had ever heard my mother raise her voice. My fate was being decided. That night I lay awake and cried thinking about Pío, of Mama, of little Diego too afraid to come out of his bedroom, of all the things I would lose because I couldn't help who I was.

"You are no longer my son," Edmundo said quietly when we were alone. He was still wearing his full-dress uniform as if to intimidate me, as if I was a criminal. He was sweating profusely even though the evening was cool. "I want you to understand one thing, Luis César Ángel Acosta, I cannot control what you do anymore. But if you ever come up against the law for whatever reason, anywhere in Peru, *anywhere*, I will know it. And I will ensure they will lock you up and you will be the catamite for every prisoner and the punching bag for every prison guard until there is nothing left of you. *Lo entiendes?*"

I stood in the front room, not moving, barely blinking. My heart was hurting and I was clenching my fists. I was fifteen and the same height as my father. I looked down at the gun in his holster for just a second. He must have seen my angry thought of shooting him dead pass over my face like a shadow because he belted me so hard that I had a headache for a week. I never saw him alive again.

Thanks to my mother's quick thinking, I was shipped off to her older sister and husband in Miraflores. I was too young for military conscription. Luckily mandatory military service would end before I turned eighteen. I was fortunate that my mother's quick intervention saved me from the streets. My aunt and uncle were reasonably well off in their manicured suburb of Lima, a far cry from the peasant city of Ayacucho. But the person I would eventually come home to every night was not Aunt María. It would be Estralita, their housekeeper who lived in Independencia and who travelled to Miraflores every day. It would be Estralita who would love me the most. I ended up living with Estralita and her daughter Rosa in Independencia a few years later because my real aunt and uncle blamed me for burning down their house.

*   *   *

The welcome I received from my aunt and uncle was lukewarm. The atmosphere in their home was as cool as their temperaments. Uncle Javier was a small, level-headed man who worked in an architectural firm in the centre of Lima. He was a successful architect even though the first bridge his company built had collapsed in Chimbote just after it was completed. Granted, there had been an earthquake, so Javier maintained it had not been a structural issue, it had been God. At the tribunal, God won the argument but Javier never built another bridge.

When he was home he enjoyed watching his brand new Admiral colour television set which I didn't like at all because I thought the Spanish shows were mostly one-dimensional and the few American programs that were dubbed in Spanish were silly, especially because the words didn't match the movement of their mouths. Aunt María wore an air of suspicion about her like a dark cape. I felt her eyes watching me while I did my homework, while I played *Chinchón* with their only daughter Luna, even while I slept. Luna, on the other hand, was excited to have her cousin move in. She was two years younger and past playing with dolls, looking forward now to playing cards or board games for two. She had been a tomboy. She used to keep her hair cut short, fall out of trees, and impale herself on fences. Now she was growing her hair long and wearing make-up and dresses.

Estralita watched over us while Aunt María was busy as patroness of the arts. She spent her time at lunches and launches, organizing donations to artists and museums and chairing special events with the aim of creating a more beautiful Lima. Estralita had been part of their family since Luna was a little girl. The first nanny, a leathery-skinned woman from Puno, moved back to Lake Titicaca to take care of her mother, Estralita told me. The old nanny had come from Uros, a floating island made of reeds that had been created centuries ago.

"They consider themselves to be descended from the oldest people on earth," she said as I was helping her in the kitchen, slicing chirimoya and guava fruit for a pie. "Legend says they existed before the sun and they cannot drown or be struck by lightning."

"That's convenient for people on an island," I pointed out and we laughed together because she knew the fanciful tales that had so captured Luna would just bounce off me. Estralita understood who I was and accepted me right away. She asked me about the boys at school: had I met anyone nice? Then one day I came home with a bruised face.

"Nice boys with big fists," I told her.

"Ah César, they are not mad at you," she said applying a cold dishcloth to my eye. "They are just afraid of themselves."

"No, they are just dumbasses," I pouted. "There's no hope for them."

At that moment Aunt María walked in and let out a startled cry.

"Boys will be boys," Estralita told her. "I have it under control, Doña María."

Estralita had her own home in a poor district north of the city. She lived with her grown daughter, Rosa, and Rosa's two little daughters, and Estralita claimed that the story of their bastard husbands was destined to repeat itself over the generations.

"The demands of our family grew too tiresome for one husband and too hectic for the other," Rosa admitted.

"I warned her," Estralita sighed. "Our family is doomed to failed marriages."

Failed marriages were forbidden in my family. I had watched my mother suffer under the ancient patriarchal cycle of dominance and bullying. My aunt and uncle on the other hand were passionate in their work but their marriage survived on a platform of indifference. So I really owed the seed of my success to my Aunt María who was always buying beautiful works of art and taking the time to explain them to me. My interest in art helped lower her guard of mistrust that still hovered around her.

"What's that, Aunt María?" She was unwrapping a small sculpture from a crate.

"This is a Henry Moore," she said, pulling it free from the shredded newspaper. The sculpture was part elephant, part woman.

"It's beautiful," I said. "It wants to be touched."

"Yes it does," she agreed. "But if you do that I will cut off your fingers."

Another day I asked, "What about this?" It was a painting in an ornate gilded frame hung in a place of prominence. It showed a woman's face and body all disjointed as if someone had taken a machete to her and then glued her back with their eyes closed.

"That's a Picasso."

"Why does it look like that?" I made a face. I didn't like it at all.

She left me standing there with my finger still pointing at the painting and went into her husband's study. I had never been inside Uncle Javier's sanctuary. I followed and poked my nose through the door. All I could see was a drafting table under the tall shuttered windows with drawing tools and papers and books scattered over every surface. I watched Aunt María open the bevelled-glass door of a tall cabinet and pull out a stack of heavy books. I followed her into the living room and she dropped them down onto the coffee table with a thud.

"Here. These will answer all your questions."

They were art history books and some of them were the size and weight of the gravestones in the cemetery where my aunt took us to visit our relatives. The cemetery was guarded by two neoclassical angels atop the stone columns of the archway.

"You will find the exact replicas of those statues in these books," she explained as if both the angels and the books were gateways to the mysteries of the past.

I spent months reading and rereading Janson's *Historia General del Arte*. I grew enraptured by the Winged Victory of Samothrace which was on the cover. She was the greatest masterpiece of Hellenistic sculpture and the book taught me about the invisible force of the space around her. I skipped backward and forward in time and place, from Leonardo and Michelangelo in the high Italian renaissance to Blake and Canova of the neoclassical, and then back to the cathedrals of Gothic Germany. Aunt María watched me periodically, which I had become accustomed to. Then she gave me some advice.

"Start at the beginning and move forward chronologically. It will all make more sense that way."

One day, because she noticed that my attention to art did not waver like Luna's who flitted from one infatuation to another, she took me to the *Museo de Arte de Lima.* It was on that Friday at the end of September 1978 when bandits wearing ski masks and brandishing assault rifles stormed the museum. They had headed directly for the Roman galleries, smashing glass cases with the butts of their rifles and snatching up the bejewelled crowns and ornaments. I didn't want to be in the room where they all converged, I was just passing through to where my aunt was viewing the Egyptian sarcophagi. I backed up against a life-size statue of Jesus on the cross to stay out of their way. Once they had snatched up their booty they started shooting into the ceiling. There were shouts and screams as people ducked for cover. They kept shooting as they ran, dislodging the plaster and mouldings which crumbled over the floor and the sculptures and paintings in room after room, releasing a cloud of dust that followed them out to their waiting getaway car.

That was when I saw it lying on the floor covered by pieces of glass. They had missed it because it was so small. I crawled over and felt a sharp pain as I cut my hand on the shards. The label from inside the case lay on the floor. It read, *Saint John the Evangelist, circa 40 - 60 AD.* I picked the object up: it was some sort of amulet on a chain. I didn't have time to look at it properly because I could hear footsteps running in my direction accompanied by more shouting. I clamped my hand around it just as the museum guards rushed in.

Somehow I had wiped my bloody hand on my face because everyone thought I had been shot. The guards kept telling me that everything was going to be all right. A man in a suit with a mole on the end of his nose crouched down next to me.

"Don't move, son. Help is on the way."

"I'm all right," I responded. I kept my prize clenched in my hand.

When Aunt María found me and they realized I wasn't shot or even wounded, I was allowed to stand. I slipped the amulet into my pocket. I don't know why I kept it. It wasn't because of its value. I had no idea of the value of antiquities, I only knew that it was beautiful. Perhaps after all the ugliness of being beaten and threatened and cast away, I just wanted a piece of beauty for myself.

The museum was closed for a time and the reports of the theft were in all the newspapers and on radio and television broadcasts. The news made no mention of any amulet, as if it were too insignificant. That calmed me. I stopped biting my nails when the news moved on to other events: Vietnam was attacking Cambodia, the African Nation Congress tried to poison its five hundred members, and there was another horrible plane crash in the United States. Amidst all this carnage I was set free. Every night before going to sleep I would pull the medallion out from its hiding spot under the bed and look it over in the nightlight, marvelling at the intricacy of the face of the saint on one side and the writing as mysterious as hieroglyphics on the other. I wanted to try it on but the clasp was too difficult to undo and I didn't want to break it, so I just lay in bed, and after everyone had gone to sleep, I set it on my chest to feel him against my skin, as if the real saint had been miraculously transferred from the amulet into my own body and he was caressing me, covering me with his beauty and his wisdom. Having the true image of the gentle Apostle

John weighing on my chest filled me with a luxurious desire, like a stupor resplendent with sacred and profane emotions, covering me like silk and then like a scourge.

*   *   *

After the drama of the robbery had faded, my sweet, innocent cousin Luna noticed that I was still submerging myself in her mother's art books instead of paying attention to her. She had grown from a gangly tomboy to an attractive young lady. She lived in the centre of her own world. Her friends were curious about me when they visited at the house. I was almost seventeen and fair game.

"That's just my cousin," she said to her best friend Julia as they sat gossiping in her bedroom and plotting the conquest of their next boyfriends. I was standing in the hallway outside her door which was open just a crack. I pushed it a bit wider to hear better.

"Do you want to know what I heard?" Julia asked.

"What?"

"That your cousin is sweet on boys."

"No he is not!"

"That's what Alma says. Her brother told her."

"Then Alma's brother is sweet on boys!"

I was surprised by the vehemence of her support for me. But she wasn't doing that for me. She was doing it for her image and status and because I suspected she had a crush on me.

And this was where it all came apart. Luna chose a Sunday evening when her parents were out and the servants off duty, much like I had plotted with Pío. Luna was convinced she could seduce me. She must have spent all afternoon preparing. By nightfall she had lit scented candles all around her bedroom, on the dresser, on the bedside table, on the desk, on her stack of schoolbooks, on the floor. There were dozens of candles filling the room with a heady ambrosia so strong that I imagined her cat pawing at the door to get out. She had put on a very revealing red dress, although there was not much to reveal. She usually kept her long hair up in a ponytail but tonight she had let it loose to cascade down her back.

"César," she called from over the banister as I was heading to the kitchen to help myself to a pot of chicken and rice Estralita had left for us because she didn't work on the weekends. I was surprised that Luna was home since I hadn't seen her all evening.

"What?" I hollered.

"I need you," she called.

"Why?" I yelled back rubbing my eyes from the steam off the pot.

"Pleeeeeeze!"

I put the lid back down. I remember thinking *now what?* as I took the stairs two at a time. I pushed open her bedroom door.

What I didn't expect was the bordello lighting and the heady odour of perfume with Luna poised seductively on her bed in that tight red dress with her tiny bosom heaving.

"What are you doing?" I asked.

"Come sit on the bed, César," she said breathlessly and patted the space beside her.

"Why?"

"Don't you like what you see?"

I almost laughed but I suddenly understood the serious implications of what was happening. Instead, I tried to reason with her.

"But I'm your cousin!"

"Don't you find me attractive César?"

"Luna, you are a blood relative. It's against the law."

"Just a kiss."

"No."

She stood up, petulant. "So I'm not pretty enough to kiss?"

"It's not that Luna!"

"Do you think you are better than me?

"*Esto es desagradable!*"

She grabbed a candle and moved towards me seductively, like she was Lauren Bacall about to light Bogie's cigarette. "Don't you like my dress?"

"Yes." I didn't know what to say.

"Don't you like my hair?"

"Yes, but Luna—"

"If you don't kiss me I will burn my hair off," she threatened, raising the candle.

I would never quite be sure if she had done it by accident or on purpose. Before I knew it her hair and her dress were in flames. She began to shriek, "*Look what you've done, look what you've done!*" I leapt at her to snuff out the flames and all I could smell was her burning hair. She screamed and backed into the curtain of her bedroom window. The curtain caught fire and then the flames followed along the wooden frame and beams extending across the ceiling. I grabbed the comforter from the bed and covered her in it to snuff out the fire that was consuming her. By then the entire room was engulfed. I knew that both she and I would never recover from this.

She ran shrieking out of the room and down the stairs and out the door with the comforter wrapped around her. I managed to duck into my room and grab my only possession worth saving: the medallion. As I reached the front door, I heard a noise and stopped. I turned back, calling *Kitty, Kitty, Kitty* until I found the cat cowering under the dining room table and threw her out the dining room window. Black smoke was billowing down the stairs by then. I could feel the furnace heat of the flames as the roof caught fire. Then I grabbed the Henry Moore from its sacred niche and wrenched the Picasso off the wall. By the time I got outside, the neighbours were coming out of their houses and the flames were licking at the pair of upstairs windows like the eyes of a laughing devil.

As for saving Kitty, Picasso, and Mr. Moore, no one ever thanked me.

*   *   *

Luna was permanently scarred by the fire. The skin on one side of her face would grow leathery like a reptile. She didn't lose her beauty because of it, she only lost her youthful arrogance and some of her self-confidence. They were replaced by rage. She unleashed a frenzy of reproach from her scorched lips, lambasting me as a sinner and a sadist, a flighty pansy, a fairy who had been jealous of her hair. No one believed me when I said she had done it to herself. The empathy obviously belonged to the girl wrapped from head to toe in white bandages.

My uncle's house was too damaged to be habitable and even if it had been, I wouldn't have been welcomed back. Estralita showed up at the house in Miraflores on Monday morning having no idea of what had happened. She stood in the street and just stared at the charred remains. Our housekeeper had no more house to keep. She found me shuffling around nearby. I told her what had really happened and that my aunt and uncle were at their daughter's bedside at the hospital. Estralita crossed herself, put her arm around my drooping shoulders, and led me away.

"What if they come to arrest me?" I asked.

"I won't let them," she replied. "You'll live with me."

Over the next year, I spent many hours secluded in the small dusty rooms of the National Library in the city centre reading art history books. Then one day, while walking along one of the hallways with its shiny marble floors as my old shoes squeaked with each step, I came across a notice on the bulletin board for English lessons for beginners. Learning English could be my ticket out of Peru, I hoped. A ticket to a better life.

The lessons were being given by a tall Argentinian man with a bow tie in an airless room on the top floor of the National Library for two hours every Tuesday and Thursday evening. I would hang around the centre of the city on those afternoons, waiting for six o'clock, sitting on steps or benches, meeting people my age, trying to stay out of trouble because they were all a bit rougher and more desperate than I was. That was when I met Carlos. He was sitting alone in a café with his long legs crossed, his fingernails painted pink, wearing a wide-brimmed Panama hat. He motioned for me to join him. He told me his hat had been woven in Ecuador by little boys sold into slavery. I didn't believe him but I enjoyed his sense of affectation. He introduced me to Jorge and Jojo, Darius and many of his other friends. We all had the same streak of bad luck in us. But none of them came close to how I felt about Pío.

"You never forget your first love," Estralita sighed once while we were both feeling nostalgic. She was thinking back to her own past when she was young and impressionable. "My first love was Fabio Castillo who worked in the copper mines near Trujillo. He was only eighteen. The mine had collapsed in an earthquake one Monday morning and Fabio had escaped. He walked all the way into town with his face and clothes black from soot. I saw him leaning against a lamp post smoking a cigarette and when he saw me he smiled and all I saw were those brilliant white teeth."

"So you fell in love with his teeth?"

She blushed. "Yes, that was the first part of him. But I wouldn't recommend falling for a miner, César. They dig into your heart and mine all the good out of it."

I wasn't sure if Pío had been my first love. "How do you know?" I asked.

"You just do."

Carlos and his group went to a disco club on Saturday nights called Babylon. Women often danced together which was acceptable but men didn't dance with men—except at Babylon. No one there would be heckled.

On one hot day in January, Carlos and I were sitting at a café when I told him about my plan to improve my English with the help of tourists looking for conversation.

"They will want more than conversation from you," he winked. But it was really a warning.

I picked up my coffee spoon and took a bite from his dessert. He slapped my hand and my sketchbook which was perched on my lap slid to the ground. When I picked it up he said, "Do you always carry that around with you?"

"Not always. Well, most of the time."

"I know a lot about art, *pequeño* César."

"You do?"

"Yes, I make it my business." He grinned. "Draw my portrait."

I set the sketchbook on my lap, pulled some stubby charcoal pencils from my pocket and began sketching. I tried to catch the mischievous sparkle in his eyes.

"Are you finished yet?"

"You make a poor model," I said and this made Carlos laugh so hard he spilled his coffee. I had to finish quickly because he couldn't sit still, wiping the tears from his eyes and sopping up the coffee with his napkin. I turned the page around for him. Maybe he thought it was going to be a caricature. Instead I thought it captured his innocence and his insolence in a long and remote face full of contradictions. He just sat there studying it.

"Can I have it?" he asked.

"Of course." I tore the page from the book.

When I wasn't drawing I approached tourists to improve my English. "Hello nice ladies," I would say to girls in alpaca sweaters and backpacks, "Do you speak English?" Most of the time they would look afraid and scurry away.

But the men were different, especially those who recognized and were drawn to that cloud of sorrow hanging over me. One evening I accepted a dinner invitation from Sergei, a man from Belarus, who had a square jaw and scars on his face as if he had been doused in acid. I had shown him around the city but his English was no better than his Spanish. Occasionally, he lapsed into Russian and his voice was low and guttural and it wasn't long before I detected an angry streak in him. Because I couldn't understand his English very well I just nodded a lot.

"Where are you staying?" I asked him.

"Hotel Bolivar. You want come to room?"

"Oh, I wasn't inferring that. Are you a businessman?"

"*Tak.*"

The waiter appeared. "We'll have the Chicken Kiev," I ordered in Spanish. He took away our menus and left us alone.

"Kiev is nice," Sergei said. "You know where is Kiev?"

"In Poland?" I had no idea.

He slammed his fist down hard and the tableware jumped. "No! Not Poland!" he shouted. And then calmed himself. People at other tables were looking at us. "We hate Polish," he went on, his voice rising again. "They try to leave Soviet Union. If everyone leave Soviet Union then Soviet Union dies. Then family starve. Do you want family to starve?"

"No Señor," I said. I started to get up.

He slammed his hand down again. "*Sit!*"

I sat back down. I tried to calm him with my smile, the one Carlos said could melt Inca gold. It didn't melt Sergei, it heated him up. His pale neck turned red and he reached over and grabbed my arm.

"Please, Señor..."

Shadows fell across the table. I looked up. Two very tall older men were standing behind Sergei. One was wearing a cravat and the other a bow-tie and fedora. They looked as if they had stepped straight out of another era.

"Let go of our friend," the one in the fedora growled back in Spanish.

The other one repeated in English, "*Let him go!*" His voice sounded familiar.

Sergei was startled and let go of my arm. He twisted in his chair, craning his red neck to see who was standing behind him.

"Our friend is leaving with us," the one in the bow-tie said in perfect English. As he held out his hand to me I suddenly knew him. He was my English teacher.

*   *   *

The men who so dramatically intervened, leaving Sergei alone to devour two chicken Kiev dinners, were from Argentina. They were refugees. A decade earlier they had escaped from Argentina's homosexual purge, enforced by the military. In Argentina, gays were considered sexual deviants. These two men fled before being *forcibly disappeared*, as the Argentinian people called it. They left everything behind. Even though Peru had been under a dictatorship at the time, there appeared to be less active persecution here. They knew they were going from the fire into the frying pan, as they put it, but escaping had been their only hope.

Once we had left the restaurant, the three of us made our way along Jirón de la Unión. They walked one on each side of me like body guards.

"You are César, right? I have been instructing you in English."

"Yes, of course, I know you now." My ego was a bit bruised. "I had the situation under control."

They smiled. "Sure you did. You're a tough kid."

"He's not that tough, José," the one in the cravat said. "Did you see the neck on that wrestler?"

"Are you still hungry César?"

"No, I lost my appetite pretty quick."

"Where do you live?"

"Independencia."

"Oh!"

"Where are we going?" I asked them.

"Our home," my teacher announced, lifting his fedora. "I'm José Juan. This is Juan José."

"Really?"

They smiled sheepishly and nodded. They brought me to their moderate house in San Isidro painted red and yellow with a tall wrought-iron gate. José Juan removed his hat and bow tie while Juan José put ice on my arm where Sergei had grabbed me. The skin was already turning purple. They fussed about me as if they believed in my father's claim of a noble bloodline leading back to the Inca kings.

While they made tea I made myself comfortable on the sofa and told them the story of how my father had banished me from my home and how I ended up living with the housekeeper Estralita who I called *aunt* now because she was more of an aunt to me than my own Aunt María. They sat and listened with wide eyes, occasionally glancing at one another. Then they told me about their clandestine flight from Argentina and the disappearance of their friends who were abducted from their beds in the middle of the night.

"We want you to be safe," Juan José explained.

"In order to be safe you must always be on your guard," José Juan clarified.

"Latin America has a history of these problems," Juan José told me. "Did you know, dear César, that before the Spanish arrived in Argentina, there were three sexes? The third one was called *Weye,* a mix between male and female. The Spanish thought the local people were savages for engaging in unnatural sexual activity. Sodomy was one of the reasons the Spanish conquistadors declared war against them, annihilating them. Sodomy was punishable then by burning at the stake." He sat back with his tea. "Methods change over time but the intent to persecute is the same."

"History repeats itself," José Juan added.

I called them my *uncles.* They recognized the insatiable artist in me and bought me art supplies and a leather satchel with a shoulder strap to carry my sketch books. They made me aware of the admission-free entrance hours at the *Museo de Arte* on Tuesdays. I had never been back since the robbery, which I told them about, but not the part about the medallion. I just said I was afraid the *bandidos* would return.

"You need to get over it."

More importantly, José Juan let me have full access to the National Library of Peru. He worked there as an assistant librarian and gave English lessons part-time. After all, he had been a Professor of English at the University of Buenos Aires before the military purge. He knew all the best art books and where they were kept in the archives. Together with the archivist, I was shown delicate book plates of intricate prints and etchings hidden for generations and unseen by the general public. Whenever we were together, José Juan and I spoke English so that I didn't have to be a tourist guide any more. We all knew it was his attempt to keep me out of trouble, which wasn't easy to do for a nineteen year-old set free at night in Lima city.

Between the library, the museum and my uncles' home in San Isidro, I had found an alternative education and sanctuary. Soon, I returned to Estralita's house in Independencia only to sleep.

*   *   *

I first saw Brisdon playing tourist on an afternoon in June. I remember it was a Sunday because admission was free and I had told José Juan and Juan José that I wanted to sketch the bones of the dead in the catacombs of the Convent of San Francisco.

"Drawing skeletons?" José Juan clarified.

"That is very dark," Juan José remarked, stirring tomato and cucumber slices into a frying pan with chilies, lime and cilantro for the dish he was preparing.

"He's going through a dark phase," José Juan said from the kitchen table, looking up from *El Comercia,* the oldest newspaper in Peru.

"It's not a phase," I insisted. "I am going to be famous one day for rendering the dark side of the soul."

"Can you pass me the dark side of that bowl, César?"

"Are you making *ceviche?*" I asked.

"I do as the Peruvians do." Juan José said as he chopped up another tomato.

"Doesn't Argentina have *ceviche?*"

He turned to me with the large knife blade raised, the juice of the tomato dripping from its edge like blood. "Argentina has *carne de res!*"

My dark phase was the beginning of a lifetime of painting shadows. I could see the dusky and indistinct auras that followed each one of us like the devil. I had been schooled on the devil, been preached on him in church, and raised by him at home. I learned to reach down into my nightmares like William Blake or Salvador Dali. At its highest level, art was euphoric and intellectual; at its lowest, corporeal, even carnal. Somehow I would bring the two together.

I tried to explain this to Carlos one afternoon while we were sitting on a bench in the park next to Neptune's fountain which had dried up and was now a basin for pigeons. Carlos was getting ready to head off to work. I had no idea what Carlos did. We were sipping from our bottles of Inca Cola through paper straws and imagining the water falling in the fountain in front of us.

"Ha, ha, that is very funny, my *pequeño* César." He slouched down, his long legs crossed.

"What is funny?"

"That you want art lessons."

"Why is that funny?"

He sat up and looked at me. "You really don't know?"

"Know what?"

"About my life drawing classes."

I sat up straighter too. "You are taking life drawing classes?"

"No." He laughed so loudly the two militia guards patrolling the park looked our way. "I am one of the models at the life drawing classes. *Nel nudo* as the Italians would say."

"You are? Where?"

He laughed again and swept his hand towards the building at the far end of the park. It was the *Museo de Arte Italiano*.

I thought for a moment. "How much do these classes cost?"

"Nothing you can afford, I'm afraid."

"Oh." I pouted.

He thought for a moment. "Let me ask Señor Gonzales for a favour. He owes me. Once the other models didn't show up and I had to pose alone for two hours and I had a kink in my neck for a week, which raised eyebrows."

That afternoon, Carlos spoke to the instructor about me. He showed him the portrait I had drawn on that hot day at the outdoor café. Mario Gonzales was a little balding man with thick eyeglasses who wore a white lab coat. On the afternoons when he was teaching a session, all I needed to do was to show up with a large pad of paper and my charcoal pencils. If there was an easel available I was allowed to discretely set up behind everyone else. Señor Gonzales explained the exercises, then would circulate among the dozen or so student artists, stopping to comment or suggest an improvement while they drew. Even if I wasn't paying, he gave me his time. "Try to balance your positive and negative space," he would say, or "Keep your eye on the subject and let your hand do the work." The woman pulled her robe back around her skinny torso after half an hour and then Carlos climbed to the platform. He dropped his robe and stretched backwards on his chair. I could see his ribs under his skin, the way his diaphragm moved as he breathed to hold his pose. Both his finger and toe nails were painted bright yellow. I couldn't help but notice how large his member was. Near the end of the session, when Mario Gonzales made his way to my easel, I was drawing an elaborate detail of Carlos' genitals.

"Young man, that is not part of the exercise," he admonished.

"I'm sorry," I said, and drew back the overturned paper to the drawing of Carlos I had completed.

The art director stood back. He smiled. "*Bellissimo!*" The other artists at their easels craned their heads in our direction. "You show promise, young man, even if you lack focus."

Sketching the bones from the crypt was just another kind of anatomy study until my next life drawing class. The shy tourist who would become *Mister Brisdon* caught me off-guard on my first trip into the darker parts of the soul. I thought I was alone in the catacombs until I felt someone staring over my shoulder. When I turned I saw unequivocal beauty standing there in the low light. He was the exact opposite of what I was trying to capture. I chased after him. When he disappeared among the columns and rose bushes of the convent, I cursed him. He had made me lose the sweetness of my dark moments in the crypt below.

I saw Brisdon again a few days later, on a Tuesday morning at the *Museo de Arte de Lima*. I had overcome my fear of returning there. I chose a painting to sketch and sat cross-legged on the floor below it. From the corner of my eye I saw a handsome *gringo* pass by. I caught him glancing at me. Even in the bright light of day I recognized him. Both he and the girl he was with were wearing museum badges. How was that possible? A *gringo* tourist working in this museum? Maybe I had it wrong. Maybe he was a dignitary or patron of the arts like Aunt María and this young lady from the museum was giving him a tour. No! No! He was too young. Or maybe he was the son of a foreign diplomat. Or, or...

Juan José moved on to another gallery and I stayed hoping the young man from the catacombs would come back the same way. But he didn't. When Juan José had finished with the upper galleries and was ready to leave, I packed up my satchel and went with him to meet José Juan for lunch. Over my *trucha de agua dulce* I became lost in my thoughts about this stranger from the crypt.

Then, like magic, we met again at an outdoor café near the Plaza de Armas. He needed a home for his cat so I promised to ask my uncles and Aunt Estralita. My uncles fell over laughing when I told them the story of Brisdon's cat.

"A tourist with a cat!" Juan José exclaimed.

"Harry and Tonto!" José Juan added.

"Would you like to take his cat?" I asked. "It's very small."

"For the love of God, no!" Juan José cried out. "They grow!"

"They're vindictive," José Juan added as he cleaned his tan-coloured brogues with a stiff brush. "If you don't pay enough attention to them they piss all over your shoes."

"I'm going to ask Estralita and Rosa to take it," I said, so they wouldn't think I was trying to force them into anything. "For the little girls."

"Don't they already have a cat?" José Juan asked.

"Yes, an old tabby."

"Then they can take care of another one," José Juan piped up. "Cat people often have more than one."

"Like tattoos," José Juan exclaimed, starting on his other shoe.

"Some people even have tattoos *of* cats," Juan José said, which I thought was strange so I wondered if they had their own tattoos hidden under their long sleeves and ruffled shirts.

*   *   *

Aunt Estralita adopted Brisdon's little cat and to celebrate, the following Saturday night I took Brisdon to Babylon and introduced him to my friends.

"Is that your new boyfriend?" Carlos teased me.

"He's your knight in shining armour," Darius teased. He was sprouting a new military brush cut. "Is he smart too?"

"Probably not if he's with César." That was Jorge who weighed two hundred and fifty pounds of pure muscle.

"He can understand you," I warned them.

100

"Only if he can hear us," Jojo said leaning into my ear over the booming music. Jojo reminded me of a toucan the way his hair stuck up.

"If you don't want him, I'll take him," Darius teased.

We all moved to the dance floor. Brisdon said he didn't dance but I liked the way his body moved. Then Brisdon excused himself. I followed him. We were in an empty hallway as the walls and ceiling vibrated from the boom-boom of the music, like a crazy heartbeat. I pressed him against the wall. When I put my lips to his he enjoyed it because you know when someone enjoys it. Then he got his straight-boy act up and gave me a hard push back so that I stumbled.

Ah, I thought. The chink in his armour.

The hallway suddenly got crowded with people thinking we were having a brawl. Brisdon walked away. He just disappeared. This time I didn't follow him.

"What happened?" Carlos asked when I came back down alone.

"Nothing," I answered. "He left."

"Was it something we said? We were only kidding."

I decided not to say anything to my uncles so they wouldn't try to talk any sense into me. Early on Monday morning I arrived at the museum and sat on the front steps until Brisdon arrived. From that moment everything between us changed. Not only did we renew our friendship but by the end of the week we were inseparable. He wanted to spend all his free time with me. At first he was afraid that our intimacy would be dirty, that it would hurt, that it would emasculate him, and that he would be ashamed. Every night we broke through an imaginary barrier. Every morning he woke less anxious and reserved. Every day he was happier.

One night as we lay quietly in bed, Brisdon propped himself up against a pillow, lit a cigarette and asked, "What are you thinking?"

I was imagining a pack of jaguars leaping through the open balcony door to find us lying here, just flesh for them to devour, to rip open our throats with their jaws and tear out our hearts with their claws.

"I am thinking of jaguars," I answered.

The next time I saw Brisdon I would look like I had been attacked by one, with gashes on my cheek, my eyes blackened and my face bruised. I was with Carlos and our clan, leaving Babylon at two in the morning. Jorge and Jojo had stopped to smooch in the alley. That was when a group of roughnecks looking for trouble jumped us. They were all over us, five of them so we were outnumbered. At first we thought they were there to rob us but it was more personal than that. They aimed for our crotches and kept kicking poor Jojo while he was on the ground. Jorge and I fought them off while Carlos pulled Jojo out of the way. When I came back to Independencia in the morning, Estralita cried as Rosa put cold towels on my wounds. Brisdon's little black cat watched us from the windowsill.

I was supposed to meet up with Brisdon after work that Friday. By then the swelling had gone down but my bruises had grown into purple and brown welts around my cheek and eye and along one side of my ribs. I decided to wait outside the building where he lived so no one would see me in this condition. After a while I followed someone in. I climbed the stairs to Brisdon's apartment and waited against his door.

Every scenario raced through my mind. He wasn't coming back. He was getting drunk in a bar. He had met someone else. I hung my bruised head. Then I heard footsteps on the stairs. I looked up and there he was with an expression of surprise and then alarm.

"I don't want to talk about it," I told him. I dulled my aches and stings and wounded ego with his scotch. We played card games and danced to American songs on the radio. Only Brisdon knew the words so I took them from his mouth and hid them in a secret compartment of my mind to listen to them when he was gone.

"*Brisdon por siempre,*" I said to him as we lay together letting the night air from the open window cool our bodies. But what I was really thinking was, *You for me and me for you in Peru.*

During the night I awoke hearing Estralita's voice telling me, *To have nothing is to have everything.* I realized I needed to take my most valuable possession and give it away because this act would purify me. The next day I dug out the box hidden at the bottom of my dresser and slipped the medallion with its chain into my pocket. When I gave it to Brisdon, his joy reverberated around the room, shaking the glasses and plates in the cupboards and jarring the paintings which we had rehung on his walls the night before. I attached the chain around his neck. I was still afraid I would damage the clasp, after all it was incredibly old. It didn't have any springs, it was all in the way it twisted together, and I managed to close it.

For the rest of our time together he never took it off.

*   *   *

My wounds healed slowly—my ribs and the side of my face changed colours almost by the day, sometimes by the hour. When I looked at my ribs in the mirror, the evolution of the bruises fascinated me with their muted golds and reds and browns and purples all mixing together slowly like the sky of a sunset on a vast sea of storms.

During our last days together in Lima, I would stay over at Brisdon's apartment and he would lend me his clothes. Then I would take a bundle of his laundry home and Estralita would wash and dry and iron them, *for the young man who brought the cat.*

When I think back, those hours were like a dream, surreal and intangible. Early one morning, as we lay together fighting against the dawn, the colours in his apartment turned from indigo to periwinkle and the light from both the moon and the sun shone together through the terrace window so that we felt immortal under a spell that wouldn't let us detach no matter how much the pull of our different worlds tried to separate us.

Then at the end of July, Brisdon had finished with his job at the museum and was ready to leave for our trip across Peru. I still had my misgivings—I would have rather we stayed in Lima. The next morning I had to be at the train station by six a.m. I had slept on the sofa in my uncles' sunroom that night but I couldn't get comfortable. I kept turning over the argument about money we had had when Brisdon had stormed out of his apartment only to return all apologetic and offering to buy my drawings so I would have pocket money. My Inca pride got in the way of everything. So when I arrived at the train station all bleary-eyed and soporific, I settled onto a bench and watched the travellers slowly arrive for the first trains. As I waited for Brisdon I was growing so tired that I may have fallen asleep sitting up because in the early morning light that splintered through the tall station windows, each person passing by turned into supernatural beings, slender monsters with scales and tails and sapphires for eyes, archangels with the tips of their feathery wings dipped in frankincense and dainty seraphim clinging to each other and crying, *Holy! Holy! Holy!*, translucent but deadly as sea-snakes.

Much of what I remember about our trip before we reached Ataccala is a blur. What I do recall was our climb up to Huayna Picchu where we stood above the ruins of Machu Picchu looking down into the Inca valley. It was glamorous through Brisdon's eyes but I only saw a lost city, a desolate empire high above the others, a graveyard testament to a transitory life. It had ended, like Brisdon and I were going to end. Machu Picchu was the greatest ending of them all. For Brisdon it was magic. For me it was the point you reach where everything starts to recede, to drop away and you realize you can never get any of it back. Everything becomes achromatic. The flames smoulder. The magic turns to ashes.

"Look where we are!" Brisdon exclaimed as we stood on the top of the mountain next to a hornet's nest. "Can you feel it, César?"

Brisdon put his arm around me. He believed we were here because of another type of destiny from where, below us, the Inca kings had walked. What he didn't understand was that their ghosts were still walking through me and stabbing at my heart.

I remember swatting at hornets. When we descended from that mountain everything started to unravel.

Margaret

I was the postmaster's daughter—which was how I got to know everyone in our village of Crown as well as the surrounding farms and estates. During the war years I would accompany my *da* on his rounds when he delivered the post and the people would come out of their houses to see us. I was Duncan Campbell's showpiece, his *bonnie lassie*, and I got used to the attention. When my father wasn't sorting and delivering the mail, he butchered pigs in his shed for a network of neighbours and local clients. *Never underestimate the value of your neighbours,* he declared once while his hogs snorted and squealed. *Now look away, lass!* he called out as the axe fell, but I never did.

Fortunately for us, my father's postal job kept him in Crown and out of the war. Scotland was an industrial stronghold, rich in factories and coal mines. And even more fortunate, the Germans thought that RAF Inverness was but a seaplane base, and what danger were sea planes to anyone? So the Luftwaffe passed us over in search of meatier targets.

The year the war ended I was fifteen and that's when my father broke his leg. It would be the beginning of the end for Maggie. My *da* had been chasing a hog that had escaped its pen one brisk Sunday afternoon when the late May winds off the North Sea reached all the way across the plain. Pigs are smart and this one knew the sound of the axe. My father misstepped over the stones and gullies while chasing the hog and it took them six hours to find my *da*. Afterwards, he was still able to sort the post from his chair, so I took over the delivery during the summer months, just until he recovered. I knew the route and I knew the people and we all expected my father to return to the job in full force by September.

That was how I got to know the Tamaddon family who owned Brisdon House because they received a great deal of letters and parcels. They had a daughter named Vanessa who we all knew as Nessie, and a younger son named James who was two years my senior, and who I knew from the church choir before he went off to boarding school. He was scrawny then but had a beautiful voice, I remembered, and a kindly disposition. Years passed, and when I saw him again he was a *braw* young man and I, now a young woman, couldn't help but notice the change in his height, his strong hands, and the new depth to his voice.

I didn't think much of Nessie Tamaddon. She had always been cold and haughty around me and was overly protective of her little brother. When you looked at her you saw Elizabeth Angela Marguerite Bowes-Lyon herself, the last Empress consort of India. I was intrigued by the new James Tamaddon, but I knew his summer at Brisdon House would be short. During these long warm days he would hunt red deer and grouse and join the annual pheasant shoot that took place on the estate. It was a bit cruel, I thought, raising the pheasants in captivity all year in order to release them to be shot. It wasn't the shooting I found cruel but the birds that escaped the buck shot and the retrievers had no idea how to survive in the wild and would be dead within a year. After this, James would be off to school again. He had his sights set on Cambridge. As the only Tamaddon son, James usually got his way.

The Tamaddon clan had always been well-off landed gentry in Bruidein County. James' father, Hiram Tamaddon, was the patriarch of Brisdon House which had been passed on down through the ages, and even if he came from old money, he was good at making new *lowie*, because he was buying up all the insolvent newspapers in the land. The war, or much more accurately, the pains of reconstruction, became an opportunity for him. He started in Scotland in

1938 with the *Highlander Press* which everyone knew as *The Lander,* and then during and after the war obtained other newspapers that teetered on fragile financial legs across the United Kingdom.

"Money begets money," my father used to say as we ate our evening meal of salted beef with wild nettles and turnips.

My mother was setting her barley cakes on the table when she added, "And no money begets bread crusts."

I entered Brisdon House for the first time on an unusually hot July afternoon. It was Friday and my last run of the week. I was delivering a book wrapped in brown paper that had travelled all the way from *Hatchards* in London, booksellers to the King and Queen. Bruidein Hall had been conceived in the classic E-shape of a Tudor mansion with its gables and mullioned windows, stone dressings and a stone balustrade. To reach the house I had to ride up the long gravelled drive, past the orchard house and gardener's cottage that was abandoned now, all the way to the side entrance where one of the servants would hear me ringing my bicycle bell and appear to collect the letters. This time, however, the short woman with wiry grey hair known simply as Cook was outside ready to wash out a large copper pot with a hose. She looked up and saw my laboured ride up to the house and the perspiration on my brow as I stopped next to her.

"My poor lass," she said putting down the pot. "Ye must come in for something cool to drink. Lemonade, perhaps?"

"Thank you, that sounds lovely." The idea of iced lemonade put me in seventh heaven, not so much because I was hot and thirsty but because, like so many simple things that were rationed during those long war years, like biscuits and tea and butter and eggs, the thought of fresh lemons sang from the heavens.

Cook took the package and led me through some long and dreary corridors to the manor's spacious kitchen. The first thing that struck me was how the kitchen was still all original with its huge fireplace and smooth stone walls and floor. A tall wooden cabinet with glass panes displayed pewter jugs and silver dishes, polished stemware and copper pots and pans, one after the other in neatly organized rows. There were only a few modern appliances like the oven range and ice box. In the centre of the room stood an enormous oak table that was as old as the house and served a multitude of purposes, from chopping and carving and arranging meals to holding festive staff dinners decked out in linen and wildflowers. Then there was the rare and solemn occasion of a death in the household where the body would be prepared and laid out upon it.

Perhaps it was a trick of the light filtering through the single high window but at first I thought Cook and I were alone there. Then something moved and I realized James Tamaddon was sitting at the end of the long table with a tall glass to his lips.

"Master James," Cook announced, "I've brought you some company."

"Oh hello Maggie," James greeted me, raising his glass like a toast. "Did you bring us the post?" I saw he was grinning at me like a Cheshire cat under those curly locks of his.

"Why don't ye pour our hard working lass here a glass of lemonade?" Cook suggested, which he proceeded to do from the ceramic pitcher resting next to him. I thought that was so utterly strange, the servant instructing the master to serve the guest. It must have shown on my face because when he came around the table to hand me my glass he started to laugh.

"We're in Cook's domain. She's in charge here."

I heard a gruff *harumph* as Cook handed the small parcel to James. "This is for madam. She's been waiting on this so please be sure she receives it."

I savoured my first sip of the cool drink that was both sour and sweet. Cook busied herself with some small pots and then mumbled something about her big pot still sitting dirty outside. She left us alone.

James put the package down on the table and leaned in a little closer to me. I was very aware of my blue uniform that had lost all its starch under its brown leather straps and belt. I was still hot and there were perspiration stains under my arms. I couldn't have been a very pretty sight.

"Is it good, your lemonade?"

"Delicious."

"Do you really deliver the post for your father?"

"Until the bone in his leg heals. He fell, you see, and is on the mend."

"Yes, I see. Bad luck that."

We sipped our drinks. I noticed his formal schooling had diminished his brogue. He spoke like an Englishman.

"Until school begins at least," I added not really knowing what else to say. We weren't looking at each other. Then I said, "I'm surprised to see you down here."

"This is my home, you know."

"That's not what I mean. Isn't this—"

He laughed again. "This isn't the eighteen hundreds, Maggie, although I do come here to get away when it gets as stuffy and boring upstairs as if it were the eighteen hundreds again. Especially when my father entertains. He doesn't want me hanging around while he conducts his business as if I might find out he's doing something unethical. So I come here where things are happening, where people keep busy with simple things. Honest things."

"They don't mind? The staff?"

"I grew up with them. There's only a few of them left, Cook and Charlotte and Mrs. Mackenzie. Did you know that Mrs. Mackenzie's first name happens to be Mackenzie too?"

We both laughed. "Bad luck," I said. My hand was resting on the table and he reached over and put his hand on top of mine.

"Then there's Sarah and Maidie which is funny too because Maidie is actually the maid."

"No footman then?"

"No Mister Footman or *Monsieur* Valet or Master Page. That all went down with the *Titanic*. And no *Herr* Butler either. That was over when Germany surrendered."

"Then they're all women, who's left," I noted. "That's why you like it here so much."

"Why Maggie, what a forward thing for you to say! Except for our driver Simple Simon, that would be true. Actually Simon's not simple at all, that's cruel. Regardless, you're right. I shall always prefer the company of women."

"I see." I hadn't pulled my hand away. It was like he had full control of me by that simple touch.

"This is where the real people are, people who aren't afraid to get their hands dirty. Or pedal a bicycle up a dusty laneway on a hot day to deliver a parcel."

When we kissed all I could think about was being in my pretty floral-patterned summer dress instead of my ugly uniform, with my impossible hair smoothed back instead of stuffed under this cap, and in peep-toed pumps instead of these clumsy shoes. How could I be attractive to him now? Then I heard Cook whistling to herself as she came along the corridor as if she knew exactly what was happening because she had orchestrated it and was announcing herself in time for us to compose ourselves. When Cook walked in with her big scrubbed pot, James snatched up the parcel from the table.

"Stay for dinner," he announced out of the blue.

Cook set the pot down and glared at him.

"I mustn't. I have to be home, my parents are expecting me."

"Then tomorrow night. It's Saturday. I'll ask Cook to make something for us. We'll eat down here."

There he was, finally being the stalwart Tamaddon heir. Cook couldn't say no. Instead, she shot him another look that said, *What trouble are you getting yourself into now?*

Later on my bicycle, I peddled home as if a demon possessed me, my already unruly hair spilling out from my cap and dancing from the windspeed. My world was going to change: I knew that suddenly and inexplicably, but I was still young and full of hope then and I thought changes were for the better, that vistas of opportunities were ahead instead of the darker road I would eventually swerve to take.

*　　*　　*

As I prepared myself the next evening for the dinner at Brisdon House, my mother came into my bedroom to help me with my hair. I had a huge mop of red curls that I could never control. As she drew the hairbrush through them it got stuck and she had to pull. I cried out.

"Wicked hair, wicked girl," she sighed.

The easiest way to look presentable was to clip it all back out of my face. My mother wanted me to use the diamond studded clips but I thought they looked like cheap paste, which they were, and I preferred to be under-whelming tonight eating in Cook's kitchen. But my mother didn't know that.

"I still find it odd that the Tamaddons would invite you to dinner." I could see her reflection through the looking glass in front of my vanity table. Her face seemed funny reversed like that.

"As I said, Mrs. Tamaddon was very appreciative that I rode all the way out to deliver her book. She wanted to thank me."

I could tell by her expression she still had doubts. She finished my hair with plain black clips and stepped back to admire her work.

"I didn't think Irma Tamaddon had a grateful bone in her body," she said.

I shouldn't have been surprised my mother knew Mrs. Tamaddon. Bruidein County was a tightly knit community. I would have to watch my step.

"I quite get along with her daughter Nessie," I added, stretching the truth. "She must have had some influence. We could become friends."

"What would that young woman want with a wee lass like you?" My mother just shook her head and surrendered to an invisible enemy.

I heard my father shouting from downstairs, "The car is here, Maggie."

I gave my father a kiss on the cheek as I had to pass him to get to the front door. He wasn't going to press me with any questions because he needed me to run his postal route. Instead he said, "Now mind Maggie you are home early enough even if tomorrow isn't a work day."

"Don't worry about me," I told him.

My mother came running after me before I was out the door.

"I almost forgot." She handed me a basket of coloured dried strawflowers to take with me. She said no one should ever arrive as a guest without presenting a gift to the host no matter how modest, especially if the host was Irma Tamaddon because the help would talk and it would circle back around to my mother. "Everything circles around, my wee Maggie."

When the driver dropped me off I went to the side door with the strawflowers like a servant but it was all fun and subterfuge and even a little thrilling. Cook brought me in. They had set a spot at the end of the huge kitchen table where modest Maidie and silly Sarah, as James called them, were sure to keep an eye on us.

James was waiting for me there. He wore a yellow summer jumper over a white dress shirt with modern collars. He took the basket of dried flowers from me and situated it on the table between our two place settings.

"You look very nice tonight, Maggie."

"Thank you." I had learned you should always accept a compliment gracefully but to never return it so the focus wouldn't leave you.

Cook retired to another room because she had done her full day and was ready to go home. The help didn't live in Brisdon House any longer. That was another era entirely, James pointed out. Rising wages forced the Tamaddons to lose a number of employees because it was all about the bottom line. This was how the world really turned, he told me, as if he was trying to emulate his father.

Sarah, a very pale girl I knew from the village, served us summer soup with cucumber, spring onions and black pepper. That was followed by roast pheasant in buttermilk and Parisienne potatoes in fragrant oil. I had never experienced food quite like this, not because we were poor but because of the long years of rations and lack of imports. Scottish food could be very basic. There was no wine, of course, but Cook had made us lemonade again and there was plenty of apple cider at hand.

While we were starting our main course, Cook came in without an apron and her purse in hand.

"I'll be on my way," she told us. "Everyone else is out this evening, so you could have eaten in the dining room upstairs after all." She smirked.

"What fun would that be?" James said.

I think Cook enjoyed an argument. "There's no need to hide such a lovely young lady."

"I'm not hiding Maggie, I'm just avoiding all the pomp and circumstance up there. It can be unbearably stuffy if you ask me."

"No one's asking ye." She laughed triumphantly and left.

When we were alone, James reached over and took my hand.

I said, "I think you're really hiding me from your sister."

"I think that's possible. Are you enjoying everything?"

"Yes, thank you, it's all delicious. The pheasant is as tender as cheese."

"I wanted a saddle of venison but Cook is waiting for father to return from Edinburgh before preparing one." Now he sounded like he was showing off. "She said it's too masculine a meal for a young lady."

We both laughed at that. Sarah came in and busied herself with the silver and a buffing cloth. "Don't mind me," she said.

"Cook only plays at being confrontational," I pointed out to him. I could see she cared about James.

"We are family down here although Nessie wouldn't be caught dead doing this. And Cook was right. I shouldn't be hiding you. Next time we'll eat in the dining room."

"Next time?"

He grew a bit shy for just a moment. "If—if you'd like to."

I laughed. "Yes, I'd like to." Brisdon House held a fascination for me because of its history and all the wealth it represented. Then I teased him with, "If the dining room is at all worth seeing. I wouldn't know."

He smiled. "Is that your way of asking to see the house?" I nodded. We threw down our napkins and ran off leaving Sarah wondering if we were coming back for dessert. James clasped my hand and led me through a narrow hallway and up the stone back stairs. When we reached the landing he kept pulling me as if he was trying to evade something or someone. But James assured me that Nessie was in Inverness dining with friends, Lord Tamaddon in Edinburgh on business, and Lady Tamaddon was overseeing choir practice at Kirkhill. We passed through some tall, panelled doors and into the main hall. There was a wide central staircase, magnificently cantilevered without supporting pillars, its treads and risers covered in deep burgundy carpeting. He sat on one of the lower steps and pulled me down next to him.

"The tour begins here," he announced just like the guides who showed tourists the ruins of Urquhart Caste on the headlands that overlooked Loch Ness. "Said staircase where you are now perched was part of the original house which was built by Peter Cullen, an English architect who completed it in 1703." He pointed upwards. "And this bannister, just above your head, has been used as a slide on countless occasions by yours-truly who was only intercepted once."

"Was yours-truly punished?"

"With a belt." He did a kind of thinker's pose. "But it was probably for something else entirely. I can't remember. Luckily, children have short memories."

"Not me, I remember everything," I boasted.

"Is that right? What did you have for lunch on Tuesday last?"

I faltered, of course, having no recollection. "Watercress sandwiches," I lied and he knew it and I punched him in the arm.

He went on, "My great ancestor Adam Tamaddon won Brisdon House in a game of cards around 1750 and the Tamaddon clan have been the owners now for nearly two hundred years."

"Won't Nessie inherit? She's the eldest."

"As the male heir I shall be the legal successor," he boasted. "And Nessie doesn't want it. She'd rather live in a fancy London townhouse with a rich banker husband so she'll never have to work a day in her life."

I thought there was an entirely different kind work involved in achieving that life but I didn't want to side with Nessie so I asked instead, "What about the ghost?"

"So you've heard about our ghost."

"Everybody's heard about your ghost."

"I suppose." He sighed and leaned back against the steps. "Every country estate has its ghost and she's pretty old now."

I leaned into him as he crossed his long legs. "She?"

"Yes. Fionola Gosling. She was the wife of Sir Hamish Gosling, the original owner. Lord and Lady Gosling built Bruidein Hall as it was called back then. They say she locked herself in the Blue Room and starved her infant daughter to death."

"Whatever for?"

"Because she couldn't give Lord Gosling a male heir. As the story goes, Lord Gosling succumbed to drink, and became penniless and homeless after that card game with my great-great-great-grandfather." He thought for a second. "I don't think I've put in enough *greats*."

"I'm sure you did."

"When my ancestors renovated the house in the late 1800s, the bones of the child were discovered under the

117

hearthstone of the fireplace in the Blue Room. To this day Lady Gosling wanders the halls looking for her lost little girl. Or repenting or having just gone mad. At least that's what my sister says. She won't go in there."

"Afraid of being cursed, is she?"

"I don't know. Girls seem far more susceptible to superstition, like believing seagulls are the souls of dead sailors and all that rot."

"I don't believe it either!" I insisted. I didn't want him to think I put any credence into old wives' tales.

"Then you won't be afraid to see the Blue Room?"

"Of course not!"

He jumped to his feet, took me by the hand again, and as we climbed the steps I could almost feel the shadows moving in a menacing sort of step with us. Brisdon House was dimmer and more brooding than I imagined, even with electricity installed. But I didn't mind. I followed him along the upper landing and down another panelled hallway with the framed oil portraits of fussy old men in whiskers and tired-looking women in their finest gowns with embroidered pearls and dainty lace. Even if these were not my relations, I felt close to them. I was falling in love with Brisdon House, as if it were my destiny to be here.

We took another narrower stairway up to yet another floor. We seemed to walk and walk, past closed door after closed door. There were narrow tables along the walls with dried flower arrangements set upon them much like the gift my mother had pushed into my hands. This is where it will end up, I thought, somewhere only the ghost of Lady Gosling will see.

"No one comes up here," James said, as if reading my thoughts. The air was warm as if all the heat of the house had collected to this spot. There was a distinct odour, like old pumpkins gathered from a field. It was neither pleasant nor disagreeable, an odour I could live with if I had to, an aroma I would identify with Brisdon House for the rest of my life.

We came to a stop at a door that was a bit larger than the others. I could see there had once been a large bolt or lock there, long since removed. I felt a chill as he opened the door and we went in, as if we had climbed up to a sudden change of altitude.

"Here we have the Blue Room," he announced.

It was a sombre bedroom facing west, with the draperies drawn against the setting sun. A ray of orange light trickled through a slivered gap and the dust motes seemed to glitter as if on fire. James found the light switch. The room lit up. It was indeed blue, the wallpaper, the coverlet, the carpet on the wooden plank floor, all full of blue, patterned and latticed and suffused with blue. Then I noticed the stone of the fireplace had blue in it too. James went over to it.

"The blue hue of the stone is why this is called the Blue Room. The decorating decisions are additions over the years by the over-zealous mistresses of Brisdon House. They're just artifice." I didn't think he was using that word correctly, nor would I become one of those mistresses, but I didn't interrupt him. "It happened in here. She strangled the child and let it lie on the hearth for days." He grinned slyly and I knew that part was true artifice.

"I don't feel anything strange."

He sighed. "Then Lady Gosling is probably not interested in haunting you."

He moved closer to me. I was suddenly aware of the blue stone, the blue iris and periwinkle patterns on the draperies and the blue silken coverlet. "Why is that?"

"Because you don't scare easily."

Bluebells on the wallpaper. Blue threads in the carpet. Eyes of deep blue staring into mine with a look I had never seen before. Was I giving him the same look? I closed my eyes as we kissed again and the blue faded into gold like flames in the hearth. In our innocence we forgot to close the door. There was a sudden noise from the hall that grew louder, like a cry, and then I realized it wasn't a cry at all but a series of shrieks. As we pulled away from each other a scruffy-looking Corgi came scampering in, yapping away and jumping at us both.

"Sweet Mother of God!" James exclaimed, probably in relief. "Get down Crackers!"

I sat on the bed, all flushed from so many surprises. The bed bounced softly under me.

"Crackers?" I asked. "Like Queen Elizabeth's Corgi?"

"It's Nessie's dog."

"Of course."

With that he fell onto the bed beside me laughing as the dog danced and snapped, much like Nessie would have done if she had caught us.

* * *

The midges were driving me crazy. Something about a fair girl with red hair was most appetizing to them. The second Sunday of August was the annual summer social at Brisdon House and James talked his mother into inviting our family. Traditionally, the event was to celebrate the beginning of harvest, when the hedgerows were full of berries and the nights grew cooler, but James called it the "*bite back the midges party*" to make me feel better because I was becoming riddled with tiny red spots on my upper arms and lower legs.

All the notable families were invited: you didn't have to have an estate to be included in this cabal, or even be wealthy, but you needed a title or a standing like commissioner or doctor. Sadly, we were the wrong side of the Campbells and the humble county postmaster didn't pass muster. So when we received the invitation, my *da* was at first perplexed, then angry, and then looked at it as an opportunity. Duncan Campbell, even as a lame duck, was always looking for an opportunity.

"We cannae go," my mother warned him. "More than that, you cannae go with that leg of yours."

"Fetch me a cane then. We'll call for a taxicab to drive us."

"Why-ever do you want to go there?"

"Because the Postmaster General usually attends and I can have a wee chat with him about my future." He tapped his leg. We were at the dinner table. I didn't know what he meant, exactly. I expected him to fully recover and return to work about the same time I returned to school.

The day of the party, my mother rubbed calamine lotion into my skin where the midges had left their little red pock-marks. We all dressed in our finest, father in his dinner jacket with its velvet lapel and mother in a black gown appliquéd with a shimmering peacock and feathers that extended up and over her shoulder. That dress harked back to the art-deco style of the thirties, as if she had never looked at a clothing catalogue since the war. I was in a simple flowered frock with a lacy shawl that had real mother-of-pearl beads embroidered into it, like in the portraits I had seen in Brisdon House. Even though these were our best Campbell outfits, I was still afraid we would look like the poor relations. But when the taxicab pulled into the crowded drive, I breathed a sigh of relief because it was far more casual than I expected, it was a *Ceilidh* after all, where everyone wore breathable clothing and women were in flat, lightweight shoes. Perhaps we were even a bit overdressed, which in my mother's eyes was impossible.

The sun was lazing over the hilltops. There was a fire pit burning outside and the bagpipes were skirling and men were crossing paths in their kilts and plaids with their buckles and sporrans and the young handsome ones wore *ghillie* shirts with their sleeves rolled up to their elbows showing off their brawny arms. There were close to a hundred people there so we wouldn't stand out no matter what we looked like. Still holding onto my mother's arm, I glanced around searching out James. My father found a chair at the first opportunity to relieve the weight on his poor leg. Eventually I detached myself from them and when I still didn't spot James I found my way down to the kitchen hoping that I would find him there.

"How pretty you look, young lass," Cook said to me as she rushed past holding a tray of deviled eggs. It was obvious she and Charlotte and Mrs. Mackenzie were too busy to chat and James was not among the others bustling about. I felt foolish suddenly, looking for the young master in his own kitchen. The heaviness of the steam and the heady aroma of seafood and tarragon overtook me. I breathed it all in like an enchantment, like I was Mrs. James Tamaddon of Brisdon House checking on the kitchen staff during my annual event, ensuring that everything for the buffet was as I had planned it.

I met James coming up through the back way, where he had led me down weeks ago. He was in a kilt as well, with his fly plaid brooch, and he wore a Victorian collared shirt and formal jacket as befitting the son and heir of the house.

"There you are," he said. "I've been looking for you."

"And I you."

"I thought you may have come down here. I've met your parents. Or rather, they met me. They knew who I was straight away but I have to confess I didn't recognize your father without his uniform and cap."

"He wants to meet the Postmaster General," I said.

"I'll arrange that for him then."

"Do you have to do it straight away?" I hoped he understood there was no need to return to the party just yet.

We were alone here, sheltered by the wooden panelling, the noise of the party muffled and distant. Even the skirl of the pipes seemed lulling from where we stood.

He picked up on my nuance and bent in and kissed me. We stayed like that for a while, probably for less than a minute, and definitely not long enough for me. He tasted like jasmine and smelled of wool.

"That's much better, James Tamaddon of Brisdon House."

"So is that what you came for then?"

"I came to dance and to have some champagne..."

"Well then?" He took hold of my hand pulling me along the corridor and just in time because Mrs. Mackenzie came around the corner with a silver platter of chilled brown trout and shaking her head so we took flight around the corner and climbed the last set of stairs until we were lifted up and into the dazzling light of the grand hall.

The doors to the veranda were thrown wide open and a group of older men in full regalia were dancing the Sword Dance while their wives and daughters looked on, heads tilted to the side with their sleepy smiles as they clapped in time to the music. I felt tradition run deep here; we were descended from the *Picti* after all, and we had survived Vikings and Romans and Norwegians and now the Germans. I was situating myself to fit snugly into all this, a poor Campbell lass with dreams of being mistress of Brisdon House.

We were standing outside against a wall of vines when Simon the chauffeur appeared. He was carrying a camera. Apparently, when he wasn't driving the Tamaddons he was taking pictures as an amateur photographer.

"You make a lovely couple," he said, just to encourage us and he snapped away, the flash blinding us.

"May I have a copy?" I asked him.

"Of course you may, *m'lady*," he said and bowed and we all laughed.

James brought me a glass of champagne to sip behind a drapery that separated two rooms, so no one would see. Then we danced amongst the wealthy and the beautiful, under the watchful eyes of his parents at one end of the room and mine at the other, and, of course, Miss Nessie Tamaddon, who seemed more amused than resentful. She didn't speak to me. She kept herself busy with her own league, the kind of refined young people from Edinburgh or London who would break in half if you put them to work on the moors. There and then I nick-named them *The Lavender Lot* and James laughed so hard that the nearest guests turned to stare. To avoid any further embarrassment, we fled. He snatched an unopened bottle of Bollinger chilling in a silver bucket on the veranda and led me down to the grassy lawn that was like a carpet under a blanket of stars.

"Where are you taking me?"

"To the gardener's cottage."

"My *da* will be looking for me," I warned him.

"Not for a while. I introduced him to old Terry Vass-Walsh who you call the Postmaster General and I call *The Indelible Stamp of Boredom*."

We went to the cottage which was unlocked and he popped the cork of the champagne bottle a little too quickly so that the drink spilled in gushes of white foam that he tried to capture with his mouth and we laughed together. Then he put the bottle down onto the floor and we kissed. It was the most natural thing, all sea spray and sunlight in this dark *bothan* on the edge of the grounds. I didn't know what to expect. I understood there would be fumbling and awkwardness. I knew there would be pain. I thought it would be over in a few moments. I never believed there could be such a wild and profound release from the days that bound me, and the nights that pressed down on my throat as I tried to sleep, and that the pain would fade away, along with the last of my ignorance, and be replaced by something that would rattle within me for the rest of my days.

*　　*　　*

By late August the rains came and a cooling mist hung over the magenta bell heather and golden furze that had spread over the Highland hills. The summer nights were getting shorter and I knew it wouldn't be long until my father took over his postal route and I would be returning to school just as James would be sent away to his, and I wouldn't see him for ages and ages.

After the party I visited Brisdon House as often as modesty allowed. I wasn't able to avoid Nessie for very long. The stables at Brisdon House were at the back and Nessie liked to ride in the late afternoons which I thought was strange for a girl who craved city life. James said he had something to show me and to come by the following Sunday afternoon. I rode my bicycle so I didn't have tell my father where I was going and when I peddled up the long lane to Brisdon House, I could see Nessie perched on her chestnut mare and her little yelping Corgi was with her, jumping and barking around the mare's legs. As I stood on the bike pedal gliding to a stop, Nessie walked her horse over to me. I leaned my bicycle against the wall. The mare snorted as if announcing herself. Nessie was up high against the sun so I had to shield my eyes in order to see her.

"Hello Maggie Campbell," she called from her perch. She had a pointy nose, much like her Corgi, and I wondered if pets grew to look like their owners or if it was the other way around.

"Oh, hello Nessie."

"Are you visiting my brother or are you delivering the post today?"

"It's Sunday," I said.

"Do you ride?" she challenged. The mare pranced and snorted. Crackers had run up to me now and was yapping at my feet.

"I can ride," I replied. I wasn't very experienced but what country girl didn't learn to ride a horse before she learned to ride a bicycle? Just then James emerged from the doorway.

Nessie saw him. "Splendid. We should go riding together sometime. I will let you know."

When hell freezes over, I thought. She turned and trotted off. Crackers ran after her but eventually stopped and lay down in the grass, panting.

"Oh good, you've come," James exclaimed with a wave. "Stay where you are. I'll be right back."

He headed off in the other direction. A few minutes later I heard the sound of an automobile engine. When I stood up, a shiny maroon convertible came barrelling around the house with James in the driver's seat. He was beaming.

"Like it?" he called out as he pulled up next to me. The motor was loud.

"What is it?" I asked over the noise. "It looks like a plucked turkey."

"It's a brand new Triumph 1800 Roadster," he replied happily. He reached over and opened the door almost banging my knees.

"I didn't know you could drive."

"There's a lot you don't know about me." I got in. "It arrived a few days ago. It's my pre-graduation present from my father. It's more or less a bribe so I'll obtain good grades."

"That's clever, actually."

He was gripping the steering wheel like he was already speeding along the roadway. I liked the interior, with its tan leather bench seat and its shiny wooden dashboard and glove box. The movable roof was pinned down in a leather arc behind us.

"Engine is a four-cylinder valve with a downdraught Solex carburetor." He was boasting.

"What does that mean?"

"It can go fast."

"How fast?"

"She can reach a speed of seventy-five miles per hour."

"It's a she now?"

He blushed. "Where do you want to go?"

"To the sea."

"It's gonnae take an hour to get there," he warned, "and another hour to get back."

I could detect his brogue beneath his clipped words when he forgot to be someone else, most likely that person his father wanted him to be.

"I've nowhere else to be."

With that he threw the car into gear and the gravel shot up behind us.

James took me all the way to the Chanonry Point Lighthouse at Gob na Cananaich on the North Sea. From there we watched the bottlenose dolphins as they fished and played in the wild currents. I don't think I was ever happier in my life as we sat in his roadster in that secluded spot, the wind off the water crisp and full of buoyant promise. He pulled me closer into the crux of his arm, my head on his shoulder. We stayed to watch the sky turning red like a blood orange. Before leaving, James pulled out a tartan wool blanket from the dickey seat. He draped it around my shoulders.

"It could get cold. Should I put up the top?"

"No, I'll be fine."

As we drove, the sky moved through deeper shades of pink and red until it was almost crimson. I've heard people say they find Scotland grey and damp and yes, it does rain a great deal. But the sun always comes out and fills our world with colour, the mauve thistle, the green bog myrtle, the purple peat and the rusty red stag amongst the golden heather. I never felt freer as I clutched his warm arm. He geared down to miss a herd of goats and then geared up again. He noticed me watching as he turned into the last roadway before Brisdon House.

"You want to learn?"

He pulled over to the side of the road. I straightened. "Here? Now?"

"Why not? See that light up ahead? That's the house. That's as far as you have to go."

"What if I crash the thing?"

"I have faith in you. And between here and there, what can you hit?"

So we switched places and he taught me to drive. He demonstrated how to regulate the clutch with the gas, to switch gears, to steer and, most importantly, he couldn't stress enough, how to brake. In no time I was driving down the final stretch of road, first shrieking and then laughing, but driving, truly driving.

I steered into the curved lane that led up to the front of Brisdon House, at almost exactly the same spot where we had started out earlier that afternoon. It could have been because of the long shadows, or the unfamiliarity of driving, or trying to think about too many rules at the same time, or just plain bad luck, but I didn't hear the familiar yapping of Crackers over the engine nor see the Corgi dart out in front of me. By the time I pushed down hard on the brake, I could feel the thud-thud of the tyres over the dog. I cried out.

"Clutch!" James yelled. As I stomped down on the pedal with my left foot he pushed the gear stick into park and turned off the ignition. When the engine cut out there was an ugly silence. We looked at each other in the dusky light. Then we heard a weak whimper from under the car. James jumped out and I just leaned my head on the steering wheel and shut my eyes. James pulled the wee dog out from the undercarriage on the driver's side. I turned to look. Even in the waning light I could see Cracker's confused expression, his tongue hanging limply out of the side of his mouth and his eyes all glassy as he wriggled and struggled for life, like the pigs my father slaughtered. I had broken the poor little thing's back.

"How horrible," I said.

"Give me that blanket," James demanded in a very take-control way. I got out of the car and handed him the blanket. I wanted to show him I was good in a crisis. He spread it on the ground and lay the dog gently upon it. I thought, *life hangs on for as long as possible.*

I knelt beside him and we watched the wee thing die. Oddly there was no blood.

"I'm so sorry," was all I could think to say.

"I know." He wrapped the Corgi in the blanket and then looked at me with a pained expression. "Nessie will be livid. She'll make father take the car away from me."

"Tell her I was driving."

"Even worse."

I thought for a moment as we stayed on our knees as if in prayer for the lifeless bundle before us. I reached out and clasped his arm.

"Then don't tell her."

He looked at me and the world around us grew darker and darker. "What do you mean?"

"No one needs to know."

He glanced up to Brisdon House. All the windows were in shadow.

"Maybe no one saw a thing," I said. I could almost hear him considering.

"I donnae know."

I stood up and he had to raise his head to look at me. It gave me the advantage.

"We could bury it in the woods. It's Nessie's fault. She shouldn't have let Crackers out in the first place. This is all because of her carelessness. Crackers could very well have run off chasing a hare or a deer for that matter." He just stared at me as if weighing the consequences so I said, "There are no consequences. You're leaving for school soon. She'll just get another Corgi and name it... well, *Biscuits.*"

With that he couldn't stifle a snigger. "I suppose..."

"Can you get hold of a shovel without anyone noticing?"

He considered for a moment. "Yes."

So I stayed with little Crackers in his tartan death-shroud while James headed towards the gardener's cottage. When he came back he handed me the shovel. He didn't want to get back into the car and make more noise driving off again. So he carried Crackers as we walked across the lawn and into the woods. Luckily there was a moon so we could see our way down a hill and across a small creek until we were far enough away from the house and found some soft ground without any tree roots.

As he dug, I couldn't get it out of my head that it was like burying a child. The spirits of the forest were whispering to each other and looking down upon us with their shining amber eyes, shaking their heads like they would have done with poor Fionola Gosling. Maybe she hadn't murdered her wee daughter at all. It may have been an accident, or the *bairn* had just died and there was no one to blame. I heard that happened sometimes. Whatever the cause, I suddenly knew that Fionola would walk the halls of Brisdon House until the end of time, wringing her hands in shame.

*   *   *

My own world soon fell apart, as if burying Crackers in the woods and hiding the truth had cursed us both.

On a Tuesday morning, very early, James telephoned from Brisdon House. He sounded like he hadn't slept, his voice raspy and far away, whereas I had slept soundly with his yellow jumper against my pillow. I remember dreaming of yellow. If Brisdon House was blue, the rest of the world was yellow. I saw shades of yellow everywhere, bright sunlit yellow, canary, daffodil and butter yellow, pale yellow just like when the moon hangs over the hills of heather on a hot summer night, caught in the jaws of the clouds.

"I need to see you, Maggie," he fretted.

"I have my rounds to do," I whisper-shouted into the receiver, worried my *da* would be angry at having been awakened by the pealing of the telephone bells.

"Then come after. I'll be here."

I wondered if he wanted to bring me back to the gardener's cottage. I would go with him again but he would have to insist, he would have to pull me there because I wasn't that kind of girl. Then I thought, no, that wouldn't be it. What if he wanted to discuss the guilt that weighed upon both of us? I imagined his sister's reaction to the disappearance of her dog, of Nessie out on the expanse of their private grounds perched on her mare calling out over and over for her precious Corgi. Instead of our little secret drawing us closer as I had hoped, I now worried it would pull us apart.

He had been watching for me because when I pulled up on my bicycle he came out straight away. We didn't head to the gardener's cottage. Instead he led me into the woods, the same path we had taken with poor dead Crackers just a few nights ago. We crossed the stream again and when we reached the spot, the make-shift grave had been dug up and the blanket lay in shreds on the ground nearby.

"Wild animals," he said.

"You didn't bury him deep enough," I scolded. There were large purple flies buzzing annoyingly around the blanket. "What do we do?"

"There's nothing to be done. But that's not the only reason I brought you here, Maggie."

"Why then?"

We moved away from the flies and he sat me down on a bed of pine needles and told me his father had returned from a business trip and had called him into the study to say that it was inappropriate for him to be seeing a simple girl like me, like Maggie Campbell, the postmaster's daughter, and that he was to stop this foolishness immediately, once and for all.

"I expected that."

"He was wicked. He threatened my education. I'm going to Cambridge you know."

"I'm happy for you."

"I'm sorry Maggie. I'll try to see you when I get back for holidays but it has to be in secret."

I picked up a stick from the ground and began peeling off its dead bark with my fingernail. I was considering my options. "I'll go with you to Cambridge then. I'll find a job there."

"Oh Maggie—"

The look on his face said it all. I was a girl in love but I was also Margaret Campbell, a woman now, no longer a naïve lass.

"I see."

"I don't mean to break your heart, Maggie." His voice rasped with misery but I wasn't sure if it was a wretchedness from love or from pity.

I scrambled up from the ground so that I was above him when I said, "My heart is not broken, James. It's cankered. Now it's all cankered hearts and spoiled blood."

He just looked up at me, a boy breaking out of his own innocence. "As is mine, Maggie. Ever since I first met you, it's tied itself into knots and now—" He was faltering. He believed he loved me. "But we both knew I had to leave for school—"

As he tried to get up I took the stick and poked him hard with it and he fell back down into the dirt. And that's how I left him, alone on the ground with the supernatural beings of the forest, the dryads and the nymphs and the torn-up body of the little dog we had tried to bury forever.

Imogen

The night Max had his heart attack, Brisdon was convinced I was having an affair. We were all at the Beechwood Club staff Christmas party and I was dancing with Chef Max who, being a big, burly man with a beard, was dressed as Santa Claus. Brisdon didn't want to join me on the dance floor even though I tried to coax him. Brisdon preferred drinking his fine scotch and watching from the sidelines, chatting to the bartender, so I grabbed Santa by the belt and we danced. Then Max started to feel unwell. He went all red in the face and his mouth was moving like a fish out of water. He reached out for me and I grabbed hold of him and that's when I heard Brisdon's voice shouting over the music:

"Let go of my wife!"

As Brisdon charged towards us everything happened at once. The other guests realized we were in a crisis and quickly stepped in to help. We managed to get Max to a booth and loosen his costume so he could breathe easier.

"I can't feel my hands," Max whispered.

"He's having a heart attack," someone said from the crowd. Guests were reaching for their phones. The music stopped.

Later, when the paramedics were strapping Max onto the gurney, he was still awake but confused.

"I'm going with him," I told Brisdon, realizing people may have thought his shout had stopped Max's heart.

"Is there anyone I can call for him?" he asked.

"Haven't you done enough?"

I held Max's hand in the ambulance. For a chef's hand with its burns and calluses, it was softer than I imagined. Max wasn't married, I knew that, and any family he had was back home in Austria. There was a distant cousin in

Innsbruck and a wealthy widowed aunt in Salzburg who had recently died, his *Tante Fini* as he called her.

When Max talked about his past and about working as a chef in some of the best restaurants in Vienna, I could relate to him because my own mother was from Germany and I had chosen a West Berlin culinary school to study cooking. That was where I met Brisdon, who was in West Germany working at the *Neue Nationalgalerie* that summer of '89, just before the Berlin Wall fell. I fell in love with Brisdon on that crisp November night we ran out to join the crowd gathering at the crumbing wall, cheering and singing and drinking champagne until dawn.

What Max didn't tell me, at first, was that his *Tante Fini* had willed him and his only cousin her considerable fortune. He didn't want anyone to know he didn't need to work any longer. But being a chef is in your blood; there's no escaping it.

"I was just a boy when I wandered into a restaurant kitchen," he told me, "when I was struck with a momentary dizziness as I realized that being there *just felt right*. I never looked back. Now, with money behind me, I only look ahead. Everything is a dream play where anything is possible. The fear of failure has evaporated like a reduction for a sauce, a braise for angels."

Having a healthy bank account allowed Max to take a chance on me and my epicurean vision for The Sheltering Arms. My inspiration had been the wine-themed bed and breakfast Brisdon and I had discovered during our trip along the eastern seaboard one summer. I no longer recalled the name of the Japanese lady who ran *The Little Grape*, but my dream of running The Arms was planted in my imagination because of that vacation. But the reality was that we were buying a dilapidated summer resort, cob-webbed and smelling of musty mid-century decay, to turn it into that dream. Incredibly, it was also a place Brisdon remembered from his summers as a boy. We were going to create something extraordinary with his memories and my vision. I pictured Brisdon managing the resort and I would take care of the restaurant and kitchen. I would finally be chef. Then Max came along and everything changed.

I knew straight away I would have to ask Max to become the chef at our resort when the time came because he could do all the things I couldn't—he had such clever and innovative ideas. Then I made the mistake of mentioning this to Brisdon which started the rusty chain of jealous events that would shackle us until the end.

*   *   *

The first time Max set foot on the property was during the police investigation into Brisdon's disappearance. A few days after Detective Jablonski gave me the unsettling news of Brisdon's crash into the river, the detective called to ask me to come meet him at Shelter Lake. They were still dragging the lake for Brisdon's body. I no longer had a car; it still lay in the rapids as far as I knew. It was Max who suggested that he could drive me to Shelter Lake to meet the police. My sister-in-law Mercy was staying with me but Max thought I needed someone less emotional by my side. Dear Max was trying to offer me a sense of *normal* in the midst of all this madness.

A cold November rain was washing away the colours of autumn, like the rapids that seemed to have washed Brisdon away. When Max drove under the old sign that simply read *Shelter* above the stone pillars, there were police cars and other vehicles already parked on the other side. The police had been searching the property for clues or evidence that could lead us to Brisdon; maybe Brisdon was lying unconscious somewhere.

"Mrs. Noxon." Detective Jablonski greeted us in the parking lot. I was a bit disconcerted by all the activity buzzing about my tranquil dream resort.

"Good morning Detective. This is my colleague Maximilian Wolff who was good enough to bring me here."

"Detective Anton Jablonski." They shook hands. They studied one another for a moment. I realized we were all suspects until Brisdon was found.

"Max is my colleague from work," I elaborated. "The chef at our club."

The detective kept staring at him.

"Yes, she takes her chef wherever she goes," Max said.

Detective Jablonski ran his hand through his wet hair and turned his attention to me. "I didn't realize you're related to Superintendent Morgan Nation."

"Yes, he's my brother." Morgan, my eldest brother, was married to Mercy who was now my closest friend.

We were joined by a young police officer. She was carrying a clear plastic bag. Detective Jablonski took it from her.

"Have you found something?" I asked quickly. Max stayed quiet now and just watched everything unfold, like in his dream play.

"Yes." He showed me the bag. It contained a pair of eyeglasses. "Do you recognize these?"

"Oh dear, they look like Brisdon's." I turned to Max. He shrugged. I looked closer: tortoise shell plastic frames. "Yes, yes they are, but that doesn't make sense."

"What doesn't make sense, Mrs. Noxon?"

"Brisdon wouldn't have driven without them. He's terribly near-sighted."

"Noted, thank you. Would you mind coming this way please?"

As they led us to the schoolhouse Max trailed behind. There was a hum from an emergency generator.

"The door was found unlocked," Detective Jablonski continued. "Is that unusual?"

"The contractors keep it locked up."

"Do you have keys?"

"Yes, but we keep them in the car."

We stepped inside, into an ugly white light one would find in a basement morgue.

"If you could just take a good look around the room, Mrs. Noxon. Does anything seem out of place?" Max was standing behind me. I wanted to move forward but the detective stopped me. "Except I can't let you in any further right now."

The floodlights brought out every shoddy detail of the neglected lounge but I saw it right away: the piano was lying on its back in the middle of the room. The magazines that had been stacked against it were now scattered all over the floor.

"That!" I said. "The piano on the floor. Did the contractors try to move it?"

"We've already spoken to them. They were still working yesterday but they say they didn't come in here."

"Then I don't know," I said. It was all a bit much. Detective Jablonski motioned to where a pair of wingback chairs sat facing each other. I didn't remember them like that but Brisdon had been here on Sunday and most likely on Monday night as well.

"We found blood splatter on these chairs," the detective indicated. "Would you know anything about that?"

Both the detective and police officer were watching us as if measuring our reactions. I supposed that's really why they brought me down here.

"I haven't been here for weeks," I said.

"Your husband was here on Sunday, you say?"

"Yes, he met with the contractors. He paid them and gave instructions to close up for the winter. Did they not verify that with you?"

"Yes, ma'am."

"Brisdon didn't come home Sunday night with any blood on him. We even stayed up late drinking wine and looking at old photographs."

I thought, *But Monday night.* I didn't know anything about Monday night.

The officer spoke up. "Were you aware there were squatters in your cabins at the back of the property?"

"Squatters?" Max asked from behind me, as if it was a new word.

"Vagrants. Kids, we think."

"No, I didn't know that."

"Apparently they had a slight altercation with your husband. Your contractor, Francis Perry, advised us."

"Brisdon didn't mention anything about that to me. Do you think it means anything?"

"We're not sure, ma'am."

Max said dryly, "Everything means something."

Detective Jablonski put on his plastic gloves and moved into the "crime scene" while the officer stayed with us and continued to smile. She was becoming a bit irksome. There was really nothing to smile about. Then the detective returned with another bag.

"We found this empty bottle of scotch lying on the floor."

"Bowmore?" I asked.

"Yes, is that significant?"

"No—just that Brisdon brought it with us the day he fell from the ladder."

"When was that?"

"Just over a month ago."

"I see." He seemed to think for a moment. "Did your husband drink a lot, Mrs. Noxon?"

I knew where this was heading: Brisdon, drinking alone up here then getting behind the wheel of his car without his glasses and crashing through the guardrail of the bridge over the rapids, to be swept away. It was crazy. I was trembling.

"I think that's enough, detective." Max spoke up from behind me.

"Yes, all right. But please don't leave the property just yet."

As Max led me back to the truck I remembered the lost look in Brisdon's eyes when he excused himself from Klara's dinner, those blue eyes pleading for my forgiveness. Or my permission. Or even my blessing. Half-way to the truck the officer caught up with us. She smiled sympathetically as the rain trickled off her police cap.

"I understand how difficult this is for you. Detective Jablonski needs to know if you could come to the site of the accident. Are you up to that?"

I looked briefly at Max. "Yes, I think so."

"My condolences in this difficult time," she said as if there was no expectation of finding Brisdon alive.

When we reached his truck I said to Max, "It doesn't feel like he's dead. I can't explain it, but it just doesn't feel right to me. What if he's still here somewhere?"

"Then call out for him."

I looked around. I heard the shrill mewing of a seagull then nothing but the rain. I looked up to the endless grey sky and shouted out Brisdon's name as loud as I could. Once. Twice. The sound of my voice echoed through the trees and then faded into the mist over the lake. That made me feel empty, but also better somehow.

Later, we stood at the bridge where Brisdon had crashed through the guardrail, watching the workers in thick yellow raincoats tow the bashed-in carcass of our Jetta from the rapids. There was police tape around the broken railing and the sidewalk was closed off. I just wanted everything to be over. A chill was entering my bones as we stood there in the rain.

"Why do I have to see this?" I asked the detective.

"Can you think of any reason why your husband would be on this bridge?" It wasn't close to the route Brisdon and I would take to get to the lodge.

"No," I answered.

The detective stared out across the bridge with me. "Take a good look, Mrs. Noxon."

I heard the grinding sound of metal from either the crane or the car itself. Max noticed me shivering again. "I think that's enough, detective," he said.

"Of course. If you can think of anything else, please don't hesitate to contact me."

"Yes, yes. I will."

"I'm sorry to have taken up your time but you have been very helpful."

"I have?"

"Yes, ma'am."

Not long after that Max and I were driving back on the highway. A few miles out he pulled his truck into a rest-stop with small restaurant.

"Hungry?" he asked. I shook my head. "How about a hot cup of coffee then?"

"Yes, that sounds good."

Inside the diner I stirred the sugar into my coffee absentmindedly, the spoon going around and around in the cup until Max reached over and put his hand on mine.

"The sugar has dissolved, Gennie."

It was the first time he used that pet name. I smiled. "Thank you for saving my life."

He sat back whistling between his teeth. "Be careful—"

"Why is that?"

"When you save someone's life you become responsible for them."

"Oh Max, you have such a funny sense of humour!"

When I realized what I had said, we laughed. I felt lighter. Max could be a wolf in the kitchen but he was always a lamb with me. I sipped my coffee and the chill of the morning began to dissipate.

Only later did Max admit he wanted to bring me to Shelter Lake to see the place himself because he liked the idea of a secluded resort with a kitchen where he could have full license to create his own style. He had no idea I had already thought of him there, under other circumstances, of course. We didn't speak about Shelter Lake for the rest of the drive back. We hardly spoke at all. Mesmerized by the rhythmic swaying of the wind-shield wipers, I closed my eyes and drifted off.

*   *   *

"Imogen, I'm so sorry for your loss."

"Thank you, Fiona."

Fiona Tamaddon extended her hand to me at her office door. She had invited me to meet her at the museum a few days after my drive to Shelter Lake with Max. I wanted to say that no one knew for certain that Brisdon was dead but I felt it wise not to say too much. She indicated a chair while she sat shielded behind her large mahogany desk.

"I should start by mentioning that the police were here yesterday. They were asking about Brisdon and all this mess."

I took offence to her calling my predicament a *mess.* I never cared much for Fiona Tamaddon. I always felt that she had a hidden agenda. Those glazed-over eyes in her wide face never let you know what she was thinking. She often came across as scattered, but I thought that was just an act. On top of being heir to a communications empire and a patron of the arts, she also owned the Beechwood Club. Technically, both Brisdon and I worked for her.

"We'll have your husband's things sent to you," she said and before I could ask her if she wasn't being a bit premature in her certainty that Brisdon wasn't coming back she said, "But the reason I called you here is about the club."

Here it comes, I thought.

"I'm letting you know that the Beechwood Club management team is making an announcement to all staff today but you won't be there, of course. I'm afraid the club is to be closed, effective immediately."

For a few moments I couldn't react. Then I asked, "What about the club members and functions they have booked?"

She waved her hand as if shooing away a fly. "Yes, well, it's all between my lawyers and the members' lawyers now. I have it all in hand, Imogen. It's all about the bottom line, you know."

I thought about losing my job, my dining room staff, Max—all after losing Brisdon too.

"How horrible! Why are you doing this, Fiona?"

At first she didn't look like she would answer. A haughty, triumphant expression crossed her face. "The odds on maintaining a successful fitness and dining club financed through members' debentures were stacked against me from the start, Imogen. Never stay with a losing venture, it will drag you down and waste your time."

I stood up abruptly. "I guess that means I'm wasting yours."

She didn't have the grace to respond to that. "Parfait will see you out." Then she actually snapped her fingers to summon the young man who had shown me in. She didn't stand or extend her hand. I couldn't leave fast enough.

I was a bit shell-shocked as he led me out. Then I gathered myself. "Your name is Parfait?"

"Yes, madame."

"You were Brisdon's intern. I remember him mentioning you." He grinned, showing a row of glistening white teeth as Brisdon had once described them.

When we entered the towering glass lobby he stopped.

"Mr. Noxon confided in me before he left. I don't think I would be betraying him if I told you what he said. May I show you?"

We took the elevator to the top floor. The sign read, *The Art of Dying: A Retrospective.* There were a few other people milling about, looking at the exhibit. Most of the art was huge and disturbing. Parfait led me to one particular painting, the size of the entire wall.

"This is *The Art of Dying,*" he indicated.

I took it in, a type of *Guernica* but darker. Parfait stood next to me, his hands clasped behind his back, shifting his weight from foot to foot as if waiting for me to see something.

"What about this painting, Parfait?"

"You don't notice it right away," he confessed. "The work was painted in a way that draws your eye up and never down far enough. At the bottom here..." He moved forward, indicating. "I think you'll see it."

I did. What was painted there in life-size was unequivocally the young Brisdon I had known in Berlin, naked and sprawled on a bed of bones. His pallor was a deathly green and his hands held a bouquet of prickly hawthorn to his chest. Every part of him was painted in meticulous detail. Even, I thought, *with love.*

Parfait read my expression. "Mr. Noxon admitted to me that he had known the painter. Do you think that's important? I mean, to help find him?"

I didn't know what to think. I knew nothing about this exhibit or artist other than he was secretive and famous. Everything was moving too fast.

"I'm sorry, Parfait," I said. "I'm not sure what it means."

He took me back to the lobby and walked me out to the rental car I had parked in the empty curator's spot. I thanked him for showing me the painting and as I drove off, I wondered what other surprises were in store for me.

*   *   *

I lay the small leather suitcase on the bedspread. I had discovered it tucked away under the bed and sent Mercy to the kitchen to get a paring knife to unlock it. Once we pried it open, I pulled out dozens of notebooks and I was glad Mercy was there with me because no one would have believed it.

"His diaries," she said as we read the first pages from a yellow spiral notebook. "Did you know anything about this?"

"No, not a thing."

"Who's Karen?" she asked, noticing each notebook started with *Dear Karen.*

"Maybe his sister?" I guessed. "He never mentioned anyone else named Karen." We picked up the notebooks one by one and flipped through them. "They go back years and years," I said. I began to have second thoughts. I closed the one in my hands. "I don't know, Mercy. Maybe we shouldn't—"

"You're worried that he might come back and find out?"

"Yes, or just because they're private."

Mercy sat back holding a book that looked different from the others.

"If Morgan disappeared, I'd want to know everything about him, no matter how long ago it happened."

Mercy placed the book back in the suitcase. She must have understood that Brisdon's disappearance was still too fresh. "You're right, it's too much too soon. Let me help you put these away."

A few days later after Mercy went home, I brought the old suitcase to the dining room table. I left it closed. A day went by. Two. I didn't open it again until the morning of the third day. It took me a while to sort through the notebooks because I wanted to read them in chronological order. Every morning I'd make a pot of coffee, carry my mug to the living room and sit in Brisdon's easy chair next to the bay window to read.

Mon. Nov. 25/74

Last night I left my body again. I was waking into that half-sleep state with my body shaking as though an electric current was running through it. The vibrations pulsated from my head to my toes and back again. I wanted to float up as I had done before. As I concentrated, I realized there was someone else in my bed. I rotated my astral body from my physical one and found not a person but some sort of horrible creature lying there beside me, the one who I always felt was watching me. I cried out and then everything was gone, everything had fallen quiet except for the mad thumping of my heart.

I put the journal down on my lap. This was not what I expected from a fifteen year-old boy. Friends of ours had two sons around that age as well but they were busy with soccer and hockey and girls and, as they kept grumbling, getting into all sorts of mischief. I was discovering that Brisdon may not have had only one secret life, but many. Astral bodies. Horrible creatures watching him. What vein of darkness ran through his line that ended with Brisdon and his twin sister Karen each disappearing fifty years apart?

I went to the kitchen to pour myself another coffee. As I stirred in the milk, I looked back through the doorway to the easy chair still rocking from when I had gotten up. How strange, I thought. Was Brisdon sitting there now, watching me, angry because I had betrayed his trust?

I picked up another book from the pile.

Sept. 24/75

Yesterday was my sixteenth birthday.

Grandfather came into my room last night and gave me dad's wallet. He said it was found among the debris of the plane wreckage. Inside were some American dollars and credit cards and the laundry ticket from his real mother. I didn't want it. I didn't want any of it. The wallet burned in my hands. I hated my grandfather for doing this to me. When I looked at it I wouldn't remember my father as he was, but how he and mum ended up, that they had pulled this wallet from his charred or broken body, or there had been just a leg left and the wallet had stuck in the pocket.

Every entry was vivid in its own way. Then something he had written would grab me by the throat, the most disturbing of all being his *Peruvian* book of the dead. I noticed the cover was a facsimile of *The Tibetan Book of the Dead*, the book that Brisdon had talked about so enthusiastically when we were dating in West Berlin. I knew it had captivated his imagination and was the crux of the spiritual Brisdon I knew, a man who professed to follow no specific doctrine but never removed his holy medallion from around his neck. That icon had been a gift from his time in Peru, he told me, but that was all he told me, and I recognized that his trip to Peru had been an indelible force that had shaped him into the man he became. So, of course, I was curious when I opened it up to the first page.

Lima, June 5th, 1983
Sunday 10:00 a.m.

Dear Karen,
This is the City of Kings: they called it Rimaq after the river and then Limaq because the Inca kings couldn't pronounce the "R". When Francisco Pizarro arrived, he shortened the name to Lima. But I call it the City of Ashes. The once lush and fertile oasis gradually turned into an urban wasteland. It is now a desert of grey, the colour of cinder and soot. It even smells grey here.

I read some of his entries over and over. My coffee grew cold. It was as if the whole room turned cold as Brisdon revealed his true self.

...I realize he is saying it's the image of John the Evangelist and is obviously an heirloom in immaculate condition, almost a museum piece. I can't imagine its value. I know César doesn't have two soles to rub together. Yes, I really love it, César, I say, I've never seen anything like it. I fold him into my arms and hold him and there is that warm stirring again, that thrill of the taboo, but he backs away first and makes me promise to keep the medallion a secret between us and he won't tell me why...

I had to push through my own wonder and credulity to keep reading. Page after page I felt his fears and his frustrations and his awakening through César.

How could Brisdon have kept this from us? Was there anyone in his life, other than César, who knew about what they had been through? I put the book down and stood up from the table. My back was stiff. My eyesight was getting blurred. I was forgetting to blink. I rubbed my eyes. I stretched and sat back down. I had to keep going.

I found one of my shirts that he had worn at the bottom of the wardrobe. I lay on the bed and put it to my face and breathed in his scent...

I got up again. I washed my coffee mug out in the kitchen sink. I straightened the cushions on the sofa. I put away a coat that lay draped over the chair in the entrance hall. All the time I was thinking, *how could you not have said anything to me, Brisdon?*

I went back to the table and read his journal to the end, to the final pages that were stained a reddish brown, like dried blood. Then I started over again from the beginning, to re-live his lament of innocence lost in the face of inexorable cruelty, something no one should be forced to endure while searching for meaning in their own heart.

*   *   *

After Brisdon's disappearance, I didn't have the energy to look for a new job. Max stayed in the background at first. But when spring arrived, I recognized a deeper attachment to him simmering under the surface. Discovering that my husband may have been leading a double life, even if just emotionally, made me braver, so when Max held out his arms to me one evening, I went into them and never left.

One day, Max suggested we could speed things up, that we could sell our homes for added equity and hire additional contractors to finish the property on Shelter Lake within a year.

"Where would we live?" I asked.

"We could buy a trailer," he suggested. "A big one. Park it on the property. Sell it when we're done with it."

That Easter I brought Max to the family dinner. It was being held at my brother Curan's home. Over dinner, Curan's wife Nancy glared at us from across the table and said, "I can't believe you are considering moving into a trailer. At Brisdon's childhood resort!"

Our mother, at the head of the table, merely said, "Here we go again."

"I think it's perfectly acceptable for our sister to start living again," My youngest brother Oliver sided with me. But there was no need to take sides. There were no sides to this.

"I'm just saying," Nancy went on, her back straight as a board against her chair, "I really loved Brisdon."

I bristled. As if I hadn't loved him. Max, bearing the evening with impunity, just sat back in his chair and dabbed the ends of his moustache with his napkin. I bit my tongue. Their oldest daughter Harper, who was studying to become an Anglican minister, sat squirming in her seat.

"Perhaps we should pray for Uncle Brisdon's soul," she suggested meekly.

"I think we should pray for your Aunt Imogen's soul," Nancy retorted.

Curan shot her a look that said, *Don't be such a bitch.* I hadn't realized how much their marriage strings had come unravelled. By the end of the year they would be divorced.

Max cleared his throat and raised his glass. "Let's have a toast instead. To Brisdon. May he be happy wherever he is, or at rest, whichever is best."

That was fifteen years ago. Any minute now they would all be arriving for our last summer-end gathering at The Arms. Over the past few years it had become too difficult to corral the nieces and nephews, all grown up with children of their own, with camp and summer vacations ending and back-to-school shopping keeping them busy. So it would be immediate family only. I understood. But I still had Atticus here, Morgan and Mercy's nineteen year-old grandson, and Isla, Curan's sixteen year-old granddaughter, and Harper was joining her dad who had a stroke a few years back, in order to help him with the drive up. That would make ten of us and more than enough family to bid farewell to The Arms.

When I heard the cars arriving, I called out for Max but he was busy getting lunch ready for the group. Our two labs, Jasper and Sandro, skirted excitedly around my legs. The first to arrive were mother and Oliver in his old diesel jeep that was built like a tank and carried the matriarch like a queen. I stretched out my arms to them while the dogs came after me, barking and prancing. The other cars followed like in a procession, the doors flying open, every-one rushing around, embracing each other, the blue jays and cardinals hopping on the grassy slope up to the cabins and the rippling lake catching the sun behind us and setting the world ablaze in light.

I went around the jeep and gave my mother a gentle hug.

"I won't break," she said, "but I think I'll have a little lie-down before dinner. Your father sends his love."

"What's that mum?" I asked.

"Your father, dear. He's so happy for you."

"He is?" I shot a worried glance at Oliver. Father had been dead for thirty years.

"It's inevitable," Oliver shrugged. Mother heard him and scowled. Then he took her by the arm. "First let's head over to those nice chairs where you can sit and watch all your kids paying their respects like a rehearsal for your funeral."

"Oliver!" I admonished, but Klara just laughed with him. *Mothers and their sons*, I thought.

Mercy, still so elegant and beautiful in her late sixties, the smooth Ghanaian skin on her arms glistening darkly in the bright sunlight, brought over a gift basket tied together with a bright yellow ribbon and bow. Under the cellophane were clusters of soaps and lotions.

"It's all perishable," Mercy said. "And it's not food or beer. I wouldn't presume."

"Were we supposed to bring beer?" Morgan asked from the car.

"Which cottage did you assign to us, my dear?" Mercy asked. "And where's my darling grandson?"

"Atticus!" I called, "Isla!" The two of them were huddled conspiratorially in the schoolhouse doorway across the lawn. "Would you please show our guests to their cottages?"

Curan called out to his granddaughter, "Come on Isla, you're no longer the boss. Come help us with our bags."

Atticus came over and Morgan ruffled his curly black hair.

"Hi grandad." Atticus fell into him like Jasper would do with me sometimes. He never did that with his own father.

"Hey buddy, don't forget to give your grandma a kiss." Mercy came around the car. Her bloodline ran strong through Atticus. He had her poise and liked to keep to himself, unlike his cousin Isla who seemed to be everywhere at the same time.

"Handsome as ever," Mercy said and handed him a duffle bag. "Thank you, Atticus."

I found myself alone with my niece Harper.

"I don't remember if I told you, but I've moved to another church down in London."

"I know London. Brisdon's grandparents lived there."

"Yes that's right. And I remember Uncle Brisdon."

"You do?"

"I remember him from Christmas. Some people just stay clear in your memory." The sun was in her eyes so she shielded them with her hand as she looked at the church. "I have always loved this church, Auntie. Are you sure you want to leave all this behind?"

"No, I'm not sure. But we're not getting any younger. Sometimes I don't see it anymore, I just see the work." I shielded my eyes as well against the glinting water beyond us.

"So you've really sold it! Whatever will Uncle Max do without his restaurant?"

There were still a few more details to iron out but she was right. Such a change at this stage of our lives was causing us both excitement and anxiety.

"Shelter Lake has kept us both feeling young." I turned to the group that had gathered around the Muskoka chairs. "Let's go see mother Klara."

"Nana is God's gift to us all," Harper sighed.

When we reached Klara I pulled Oliver over to one side. "About Mum—"

"Yes, she has her moments." He lit a cigarette. "Where have you put her tonight?"

"You'll both stay with us. But it's a non-smoking resort, Oliver."

"Surely you'll make an exception for mother's keeper."

Oliver had always proffered himself as a pariah but he also had a big heart, taking over as mother's custodian. "I suppose..."

"Don't worry, Mo, I'm just doing it for the inheritance."

With that, the church bell began to peal. Max was pulling its knotted rope from the kitchen. The sounding of the dinner bell carried all the way from the beach to the cabins on the hill.

"Lunch is served!"

*　　*　　*

The next morning a mist hung over the lake. I stood watching it from our terrace doors as the coffee machine gurgled. It was the first of September. The chill of dawn was lifting, dissolving. I dressed and took my mug of steaming coffee down to the water's edge as I enjoyed doing on beautiful summer mornings such as this. Purely by habit, I made my way to the flat rocks at the edge of the lake. I liked sitting there, breathing in the cool air of a new day. It was peaceful. This morning none of my family appeared to be up yet, except for Max who was already working in the restaurant kitchen cracking eggs for our breakfast. When I finished my coffee I decided to see who was awake. I heard the mournful wail of loons hidden by the brume. Coffee cup in hand, I strode up the green expanse behind the schoolhouse, past the residence we had already closed for the season, and up to the row of cabins. The lawn had recently been cut and clipped blades of grass lying in the morning dew stuck to my shoes. The aroma was heady and I knew, by moving back to the city, I would miss this.

"I'm your wake-up call," I shouted out to the arc of white cabins.

I wasn't surprised that no one was stirring. We had all stayed up late, congregating in the schoolhouse lounge. I was surprised that Klara had stayed to the end, lucid and cheerful, sipping cognac. Curan and Harper took turns on the old player piano. When the night air grew chilled, Morgan brought in kindling and Max poked at the fireplace until the flames reared up. I had placed the antique clock from home on the mantel, the one Brisdon had liked so much; it still worked as it loudly ticked off the seconds into the wee hours. Max brought over imported beer and some very nice wines and liqueurs from the restaurant bar.

"We have to drink it all up," he told everyone.

"No we don't," I contradicted loudly.

"Benedictine, anyone?" It was his favourite.

"*Deo, Optimo, Maximo,*" Harper intoned, accepting a snifter. *To God, Most Good, Most Great.*

Atticus started to yawn and stretch and was the first to bid the family good-night. I followed him to the reception desk to rummage through the drawer for another corkscrew because the antique brass one had gone missing. Max avoided most screw-cap wines. Soon Oliver came in after having a smoke, holding the neck of his bottle of beer between two fingers.

"Always at work," he said to me. He was teetering a bit. We were all in our cups. "You should have seen Atticus racing up the hill like he had left the baby in the bathwater."

"That's throwing out the baby with the bathwater."

"What are you going to do without all your bathrooms, Mo?"

"Harper was asking the same question."

"You're sure you're not making a mistake?"

"To be honest, I really don't know. But if we don't make our move now, nothing will change."

"That's not true. Everything changes without any help. Just look at me." He grinned like a Cheshire cat.

"What's that quote? The more things change, the more they stay the same..."

Now, coffee mug in hand, I called out again, "Come on you lazy Nations, wake up!" A face appeared at one of the windows and Isla waved at me. At least someone was awake. I moved to the last cabin. Atticus was sometimes impossible to wake up when he and Isla were staying with us. I had moved them to the coveted cabins to make room for Klara and Oliver. I remember sometimes having to go in his bedroom and actually shake Atticus awake.

I went up to the side window which was open. I could hear Atticus speaking. I came closer wondering who he was talking to so early in the morning. I was going to knock on his window to surprise him when I heard him say:

"You know I won't be coming back next year."

I was suddenly embarrassed to be eavesdropping, a foolish old woman lurking outside her grand-nephew's cabin. I started to move away when I heard another voice speak.

"You have to make up your mind *now*. Later will be too late, Atticus."

"Shit, Kai—I don't want to be without you anymore. "

Kai. That was Kai Bearheart with him. I'd heard too much. For three years now Atticus had come back to The Arms to work over the summer holidays while Kai had been working here. Everything started to make sense now. They had managed to keep it quiet. I was in a déjà-vu and felt light-headed. For a moment I was back with Brisdon.

"Can't you tell your family?"

"My dad would freak."

"Then let's just get out of here tomorrow," Kai said. "My mom wouldn't understand either. I've got friends who can put us up. We don't need anybody else."

That did it. I couldn't stand there and let this go on one more second.

"Atticus!" I barked at the window. I heard a loud *Shit!* and a sound like the flapping wings of giant birds trapped in a cage. "I'm coming in!" Every cottage had a back exit and I wasn't naïve. I scooted around and just as I thought, the door flew open and Kai stood there holding his shirt and his shoes.

"*Shit Mrs. Noxon!*"

"Not so fast." I put my coffee mug on the step and moved ahead, backing him into the room. Atticus was in his briefs, scrambling under the bed for the rest of his clothes. An empty wine bottle sat on a table next to two tumblers with the missing corkscrew. He looked mortified.

"Auntie, what are you doing?"

I forced Kai further inside so that he backed up against the bed and fell onto it. Condom wrappers slid to the floor. "Jesus! Busted!" Kai exclaimed.

I wasn't born yesterday. "At least you're using them," I said.

"Please don't say anything about this."

He climbed onto the bed next to Kai but their guard was up and they kept their distance.

"I'm sorry—" Atticus started to say but I cut him off.

"What are you afraid of? That your families won't accept you?"

"Mom won't," said Kai straight out. "Ever since she found God she harps on that *thou shall not lie with another man* shit."

"Maybe she'll surprise you." I looked to Atticus. "And your excuse?"

"Dad," was all he said.

"And granddad?" I knew Morgan, who had just been tousling his hair, would be open-minded.

"No, granddad's probably cool. He married grandma." Yes, I thought, a white policeman marrying a black woman in the seventies was brave.

"Well then, you have no enemies here. So why all the secrecy?"

"The world isn't as advanced as you'd think," he said. "Kids still commit suicide. I've heard stories. It can be ugly."

I was surprised at that—with the last twenty years of zero-tolerance against hatred taught in schools. "I would have thought that things have changed—"

The moment I uttered those words, I heard it coming, like one of Brisdon's inexplicable moments of coincidence.

"The more things change the more they stay the same, Auntie." I just shook my head, more at myself than for them, which they wouldn't understand.

"Listen, your Uncle Brisdon—" I hesitated. Or would they understand?

"Yes, Auntie?"

"Your Uncle Brisdon, well I suspect he was gay. Deep down I think he was unhappy in his skin. There. I've said it. No one knows. I guess I'm a bit of a hypocrite telling you to be brave when I've kept that quiet all this time."

They just stared, not speaking. Then Kai broke the silence. "Really? That's cool."

"Well I wouldn't quite say that. It was a different time."

"Like the bathhouse raids at Stonewall?"

"I think that was all over by then, Kai. But still, it was complicated for Brisdon. People are complicated."

"And the people who follow *Leviticus*?" Kai asked, trying to be clever, I thought. A contrarian. And a good match for Atticus. Harper once talked about that verse. She had denounced the general interpretation, and pointed out that during the time of *Leviticus* men lived herding cattle and worshiping a vengeful and terrible God. Women were stoned to death if they didn't remain pure until marriage. Disobeying a priest could get you killed. *Leviticus* spoke of adultery, sex with animals, prostitutes, daughters-in-law, cousins, sisters and aunts, but it said nothing about loving someone of the same sex.

"Leviticus was probably just a repressed old man," I said to Kai who couldn't hide his smile. "Some things don't change easily. The world has always been plagued with prejudice and self-righteous hypocrisies, but you can never give up fighting against it."

Atticus slumped as if defeated. "Why does it always have to be war?"

"Everything is a battle, Atticus."

"What happened to Mr. Noxon?" Kai asked.

"No one knows. His car went over the bridge at the rapids here at Shelter Lake and he was never found."

"He could be alive then?"

"I lost that hope a long time ago."

"How is that about us?" Atticus asked.

"Secrets of the heart are the worst. I will regret for the rest of my life the night my husband drove off that bridge. I still feel it's my fault. Don't make anyone feel that way. Don't keep secrets. Don't deny yourself an authentic life the way Uncle Brisdon denied himself."

"Shit, Aunt Imogen, you're not going to *out* us in front of everyone, are you?"

Here they sat before me, side by side after being together all night, fearful for their happiness yet still happy. How normal that was. How utterly normal and wonderful.

"No, I won't do that. It's not my place." I moved to the front door leaving them together to figure things out because they had no choice. In the end we never do.

Brisdon

Sunday July 31st, on the train to Cusco

César has dozed off on the seat beside me as the tourist train jostles its way high up into the Andes. It's a twelve hour train ride from Lima. We met at the main train station at dawn and for a moment I was afraid he wouldn't show up, that he had been beaten up again or he had cold feet. But there he was with his own duffle bag in the middle of the terminal and I felt lightheaded. I had hardly slept. I had lain awake during the night solving all the world's problems except my own.

I have left Lima behind. Beyond us the mountains have turned into desert rocks, an endless mass of dead hills. Above them a condor circles over the thousand spiny plants thrusting upwards out of the rock. Peru—where the desert won't leave the sea alone—where the sky won't let the mountains sleep.

Now the train is passing by fields and fields of orange flowers. What sort of dream am I in?

Later—

In the afternoon the train came to a sudden stop next to a small farming village. There were cows on the tracks. We were able to get off the train for a while. The day was cool and there was a gentle drizzle but it was a relief to stretch our legs. We mingled and talked to tourists from other cars.

The villagers must have known right away that the train had stopped because they came with baskets of Inca Cola and carpets and flowers and cigarettes and silver bangles to sell to us at the side of the tracks. Above us in the light drizzle, the clouds covered the tops of the cyan-coloured mountains. There was a hollow, endless echo in my head. César explained that it was the altitude and I needed coca tea. I gave César a handful of coins to buy something to drink. He returned with bottles of warm beer and a bag of mangoes.

When the train moved on, people had changed seats and we found ourselves facing a young German couple. We shared our mangos with them. She was all legs, blonde and pretty. He was fair-haired and scruffy and reminded me of my own father. They were wearing identical moonstone rings. I recognized the moonstone gems right away. My mother wore a moonstone ring so whenever I see a moonstone, I think of her.

Do you know about the fable of the moonstone, I asked them. My father had read it aloud to me from a book of fables. There was a living spirit within the stone, created when it was washed up on the shore from the sea, etched smooth in the sand. When the sun and the moon reached harmony in the heavens, once every twenty-one years, the moonstone received its luminescence that would last for eternity. Or so went the legend.

The Germans kissed. I wanted to kiss César right there, just to show them they didn't have a monopoly on love, or heaven, or moonstone rings. But the moment passed.

Later—6:00 p.m.

We must be nearing Cusco. It's getting dark. Everyone else is sleeping. The Germans are entwined in shadow in the seats across from us. César is warm against my side. My one arm cradles him, while I am able to write with my free hand. His head rests on my shoulder as we jostle to the rhythmic click-clack of the train on its tracks. I can smell César's hair. It reminds me of lilacs. I feel his rib cage

*expanding and contracting against my side. I am drowsy but
unable to sleep. I will never sleep again. There is too much
going on inside me, click-clack, click-clack. Beyond the
smudged window the rolling twilight landscape breathes
endlessly, tirelessly, stretching and pulling into the distance.
My own breathing is difficult. I can only take in short gulps
of air, maybe it's the altitude after all, as the train winds its
way up into the Andes. It's as if a weight lies on my chest
like heavy thunder, like the weight of my feelings for César.*

*   *   *

The mountains were hidden in the dark when the tourist
train pulled into Cusco. I had made a reservation at a small
guest house called *Hotel Inca* which was off the main
square. As soon as we had settled into our room, I opened
the windows. There is a pull of air as if the room suddenly
breathed in and our vista looked out onto the *Plaza de
Armas* which I thought was more quaint and beautiful than
its counterpart in Lima. There was a hush to the city as if
the altitude thinned out sound.

The next morning my neck was stiff from the cramped
bed and my head was throbbing from the altitude. Looking
out from the window I could see the mist rising from the
valleys, opening up a clear crisp day. The square and
cathedral were bathed in a different kind of light, one which
I had never seen before, all gossamer and gauze, as if the
thin air fractured not only sound but shapes and colours.

I took a lukewarm shower while César went out to buy
some coca tea for my headache. At first the tea had an
acerbic taste but soon it mellowed on my palate, another
elixir like César's kisses. We spent the morning exploring
the Inca market. Inside was a flower stall where an old
woman with a long pigtail was stuffing tin buckets with red
and white carnations, wild orchids and yellow beauty of the

night. A little girl no older than ten was carrying her baby brother on her back in a striped manta the colour of earth. Another woman in a red sweater was breast-feeding her baby surrounded by tin pots piled high like pyramids under a shiny red and green *Feliz Navidad* banner. Three old women were sitting in the shade by the market gate wearing their tall white hats and aprons surrounded by sacks of potatoes, potatoes in baskets and buckets, potatoes piled in neat rows and in shapes of animals, loose potatoes rolling on the ground and flying through the air as barefooted children played catch with them in the bright sunlight.

As César and I weaved in and out of the market booths, I came across an old man sitting at his workbench making jewellery. César went on ahead while I lingered by the jeweller. He was soldering a little Jesus statue under a blue plume of smoke that curled upward into the crisp morning air. Next to him lay a jeweller's toolbox of beading pliers like my father had in his jewellery store. My eye fell upon an array of rings with various semi-precious stones. One was a moonstone.

With César away I asked him how much he wanted for his moonstone ring.

"*Cuál?*" he asked. *Which one?*

"*Está ahí,*" I said pointing.

He handed me the ring so I could feel its weight in my hand. I held it up, admiring its intricate silver pattern etched like ocean waves. The off-white gemstone had a little hurricane raging inside it. It was magical. All my connections to the ring became clear: my father in his workshop, my mother's moonstone flashing in my eyes in the lamplight as she tucked us in at bedtime, and now César, who I would have to leave with this memory of me on his hand until I could come back to Peru for him.

I paid for the ring and quickly pocketed it before catching up with him.

* * *

Cusco, August 2nd

I carried my surprise for César in my pocket all day. While we were walking back to the hotel after dinner, I stopped and said, César, I have something for you. It can't wait. I pulled out the moonstone ring I had bought in the Cusco market and told him it was the one in the legend, the real one this time and that it was enchanted and powerful. He held out his hand and said, put it on me Mr. Brisdon and I slipped it onto his ring finger. It fit snugly. He let out a laugh that was blithe and brimming with innocence. I laughed with him. Now we are married, he exclaimed.

When pigs can fly, I replied, knowing he wouldn't understand.

August 3rd?—Wednesday? Thursday?

What day is it? I've lost all track of time. I've been so sick...

I've been lying in this rickety hotel bed for two days now, retching into a porcelain bowl César took from the kitchen downstairs. César grew worried so he brought in an old doctor with a scrappy grey beard and a worn-out bag of medicines. The doctor just grunted, like holding in a laugh. *Intoxicación alimentaria*, he said, and removed his stethoscope. A simple case of food poisoning. I needed to rest and eat dry crackers.

César made me coca tea. Because of my fever, when I took a sip it was like I had sweet anise and bergamot in my mouth. But my stomach couldn't keep it down.

When the fever broke I realized the sheets were saturated with sweat. I had taken another lukewarm shower,

got dressed, and told César I was going downstairs to get
some coffee. While I was sick he had the owner bring up a
cot, placing it next to the bed. He made sure the hotel
changed the sheets, and ran back and forth for two days,
buying bottles of mineral water, hot tea, rice-soup and
medicine.

Back in the room now I'm sweating again so my fever
has come back for a final curtain call. Is the room stifling
hot or is it me? I must lie down again...

Later—

I'm feeling much better but I'm restless. The single
lamp on the desk is throwing strange shadows around the
room. And I can't sleep anymore. I have been sleeping so
much over the past days that I have run out of things to
dream.

I watch César sleeping on the cot and I'm careful not to
disturb him. When I am stronger we will catch the tourist
train to Machu Picchu. From the window I can see the first
brush-strokes of dawn. A voice in the distance is calling out
to someone. Incredibly, impossibly, it sounds like the fakir,
the shimmering call of the muezzin...

Machu Picchu, August 6th

Machu Picchu is the apogee of all that has brought me
to this hallucination of a world.

We arrived after a two-hour train ride. The afternoon
sun was strong at that altitude and the air was cool. The
German couple told us the best views of Machu Picchu
were supposed to be from the neighbouring mountain,
Huayna Picchu, reached by a narrow trail that wound its
way up to the top. Before we climbed, César and I rested in
the shade of a single wall that had survived the destruction

*of time, and we ate the bread and cheese I had packed in
my bag and shared a bottle of spring water. Then we scaled
the trail up the mountainside, occasionally clutching a rope
attached to metal rods hammered into the rock. I was being
brave and trying to overcome my fear of heights, but at
times I had to ask César to hold on to me.*

*There was a hornet's nest at the very top of Huayna
Picchu, as if they were guarding the peak. We had to
scramble back down to a grassy plateau where there were
old steps that led nowhere. We were all alone, the
mountains shimmering green and blue around us, their tips
spearing little tufts of cloud. I looked down to the lush
agricultural terraces on the slopes and the ruins of Machu
Picchu spread out below us. I held my breath and stood
perfectly still, the rush of the Urubamba River filling my
head and the fresh air my lungs, a sorcerer's spell drawing
me upwards so that this became the absolute pinnacle of
anything I could ever dream of.*

*Something amazing is happening, César, I said and he
put his arm across my shoulder. The moment was
sacrosanct, rapturous. Can you feel it, I asked him. The
ruins. The mountains. The hornets. Us. It's all part of a
greater plan we can't even fathom. Something incredible is
happening right here and now...*

*For the first time in my life I felt free of that sinister
creature that lingered in my shadows. There were no
shadows here, there was only the sky above and the ruins
below and César next to me and it was flawless and
complete.*

*César didn't speak, as if there were no other words for
this moment. I heard the cry of a lyre-tailed nightjar. I
looked up, shading my eyes from the sun. High up the bird
dragged his long tail behind him like a kite. We, too, had
risen like the river's echo, as if we were gods awaiting our
golden chariots.*

Absolute moments are absolutely fallible. The nightjar wailed one last time and disappeared. The hornets found us. Our journey back down was wrought with caution and missteps because I could see everything we could fall into.

* * *

When we checked into the brand new tourist hotel they had built at the base of Machu Picchu, the clerk with his black hair slicked back and his ramrod posture didn't want to give up our room key because I was with César, either because César was a "local" or because we were "two men" together. It didn't matter: I was like a dog with a bone until the manager came out to apologize.

César just looked at me sadly. They had trampled all over our perfect moment.

Later, César and I made our way to the new empty dining room. The lights were dimmed. Over dinner I wanted to tell him what I had felt on Huayna Picchu, about how time and events were connected and that somehow this was all meant to be. That was when a young man came in and nodded to us and sat at a table by himself in the corner. He had a shock of black hair hanging over his forehead, round wire-rimmed glasses and a small pointed beard. I recognized him from the group of tourists who had arrived with us on the morning train.

"He seems to be alone," I said to César, so we beckoned him over.

His name was Gabriel Larco and he was a photo journalist. He ordered a bottle of red wine from the waiter and was happy to practice his English with us. I asked him how he came to be a photographer.

"I took over the business from my father who is sick. I don't even care for photography much. But because of the lack of healthcare in this country, I had no choice."

167

"Why do you say that?"

He kept his voice low as if he was bringing us into his confidence.

"Our new government is as corrupt as the last one. It is built on greed, on materialism. In order for things to change there has to be sacrifice. There is going to be a revolution, you will see."

I noticed César keeping a close watch on him, his lips pursed tight.

Larco sneered and sat back. "So where are you two going?"

"Pisco and Huancayo," I said.

"I know a man in Pisco who can drive you anywhere you want to go."

I thought this was a good idea. We wouldn't have to take the round-about way of the bus routes.

"He can even take you as far as Ayacucho along the old trails if that's what you want."

"Will he take us to Huancayo?" I asked.

"Of course," Larco replied, "just keep him in brandy. That's his name, by the way, *Brandy.*" He wrote down the name and an address on a paper napkin. "You would also like Ayacucho," he suggested.

"Not Ayacucho," César said bringing his hand down on the table.

Larco was looking straight at César as if they knew each other. "I still recommend it. I went to university there. I know many people."

César stood up abruptly. "I am going to the room," he announced and was gone without saying goodnight.

I didn't know what was happening. The wine arrived and I couldn't abandon this young man even though he had clearly provoked César. And I was curious.

"Why recommend Ayacucho?" I asked.

"It's an important town," Larco explained. "It lies south of the Sierra. Did you know the name means *Corner of Death*? That's because the battle of Ayacucho was the final and bloodiest of all the battles in the Peruvian War of Independence. Now *Corner of Death* will take on a whole new meaning."

"How so?"

"It is now the home of Peru's transformation. You've heard of Lucanamarca?"

Now I was feeling uncomfortable. I remembered Rafael telling me about Lucanamarca, that just outside the flower markets and ancient ruins lay a country at war with communist rebels wielding machetes and setting off dynamite.

"Yes," I said.

"Peru needs a popular war. The people have to rise and take back what is owed to them. The government tried to stop the presidential elections by burning the ballots but that was not enough. If you think the people that support the current government are just and good, you only need to look at what they did at Sacsamarca."

I hadn't heard of Sacsamarca. I didn't want to hear about it. I tried to say something else, to change the subject, but he wouldn't let me.

"In Sacsamarca the *secuaces* killed one of our leaders. They dragged him into the town square where they stoned him, stabbed him, set him on fire, and finally shot him. We were peaceful until this. You understand? The government brought this on themselves."

Without saying it, Gabriel Larco just laid claim as part of *Sendero Luminoso* or Shining Path, who followed the Marxist doctrine for a communist Peru. I made the connection now and understood why César had left in a huff. Rafael had told me about Lucanamarca, which was the result of Sacsamarca, I now understood, where Shining Path had retaliated for the brutal murder of their leader by even greater brutality, raiding the villages of Lucanamarca and killing all the men, women and children they could find. Seventy of them, all rounded up and shot. I was certain this Señor Larco believed the massacre of Lucanamarca had been justified.

"Rebellion is coming my friend," he warned, as if I would ever be his friend. "But I see I am scaring you." He laughed as he poured out the bottle into our glasses. The wine left a metallic taste of blood in my mouth.

*   *   *

A windstorm hit the city the day we left Cusco. There was so much wind that old windows in derelict buildings blew out onto the street shattering to pieces. A cart of roasted corn tumbled over and the owner had to run after the cobs rolling along the cobblestones. Market stalls held together by rope came apart, their makeshift metal roofs sliding down like guillotines. Everything that wasn't tied tightly was caught up in the whirlwind: buttons and beads, scarves and shoes and forks and spoons; anything light or plastic went *whoosh*, up and away. The tall white bowler hats of the market women flew off their heads and somersaulted down the alleyways.

When the wind finally died down, César and I climbed onboard the bus to Pisco. We would make the journey westward from Cusco along the coast to Pisco, where José de San Martin liberated Peru, and north again to Huancayo in the northern valley where it was rumoured that drinking from the golden cup on the altar of the cathedral would make you immortal.

"There are many very old people walking around the streets of Huancayo," César teased.

Beyond the window of the bus the reeds were ten feet tall and as red as cayenne pepper. We passed a Shell gas station, yellow and rusted-out, no longer in use, like the tamed had been pitted against the wild. A sandpiper skirted across the mountain sands.

When the bus came to a rest stop we had lunch at an outside restaurant where cold mountain water flowed down over the stones between the tables. César and I ate grilled mackerel as a glassy fisheye stared up at me without mercy. César took my pen and wrote on the napkin: *BRISDON IS LOVE,* and then used it to wipe away the crumbs from the bread we had eaten. Later I pressed the napkin between the pages of my journal as the bus carried us further into the hills.

When we got back onto the bus, someone had placed pamphlets on the seats, a haloed Jesus, his hands clasped in prayer looking up at us. While I stared out the window, dreams from another world flew past. A little boy in a yellow sweater was trying to push a boulder twice his size; a thousand swallows were gliding over a marsh; a woman wearing her top hat, her skin like charcoal, hobbled along the road followed by two baby pigs; two men who sat on a mound of red dirt, side by side, were so identical in their brown-striped ponchos and grey hats they could have been co-joined twins. Neither of them moved: they were part of the land.

The bus driver turned on the heat. It got cold at night in the desert. I began sweating into César's shirt, turning the blue fabric green. Here in Peru, even sweat turned to colour.

*   *   *

Pisco, Saturday August 13th

   I think our driver's name is really Xavier but he says his name is Brandy and I am sure it's because that's all he drinks, and he drinks all the time. I don't know if I should trust someone recommended by Gabriel Larco. But Brandy doesn't seem to have a revolutionary bone in his stout body. He is a small burnt-copper man and his eyes are always swimming in liquid. He is missing his two front teeth and he sticks his tongue through the space when he grins.

   When I saw his old van I just shook my head. It was scratched and chipped and dented around the bumpers. I used my fingernail to peel away a section of the white paint and found red underneath. Stolen, perhaps? I didn't ask.

   Now I'm having a café con leche at a restaurant patio and spending a few precious moments catching up in my journal. There is music playing from a speaker in the open window, a distinctive woman's voice singing to an African rhythm. César returns from the store with water and sandwiches. Who is singing I ask him. That is Chabuca Granda, he tells me proudly, the Mother of Peru. We listen together. The sun is hanging over the central plaza behind the beautiful San Clemente Cathedral, bathing it in gold— Inca gold—as if the Sun Gods were kissing it.

*   *   *

Years later, in an article on the history of Spanish music, I would learn that the famous Peruvian singer Chabuca Granda was really named María Isabel Granda Larco, and that she had been a singer since the age of twelve, dying that March of 1983 in Miami Florida at the age of sixty-two. Perhaps she had married a photographer and had a son named Gabriel who had gone to university in Ayacucho. Anything was possible in the dream I was living in Peru.

A few years after that, I would read in the newspapers that an earthquake had levelled the city of Pisco and that their golden cathedral had collapsed within minutes while mass was taking place inside. If I could have seen into the future, I would have lingered at Pisco longer and would have sat inside that church with the clergy and the parishioners and enjoyed the splendid statues and icons in the nave and apse, long before it was all doomed to crumble to dust. If I could have seen into the future, I would never have taken that road to Ataccala. *Ataccala...* This is what happened.

*   *   *

Ataccala, August 14th

Fuck fuck fuck!

I am prisoner of the Guardia Civil. They have put me up at the old city hotel, the Hotel Presidente. Someone sent up a tray of food but I won't even look at it. It was delivered by two men in khaki uniforms checking on me, making sure I wasn't going anywhere. Where do they think I would go? They have my passport. And I have no money. I pressed everything I had into César's hands before he went off for good.

Outside the window a car alarm goes off and I hear a girl shriek. Maybe she's just laughing but it sends chills down my spine. I need to write down what happened. I need to tell everything that—

Later

They're gone. The same two police officers came to collect my untouched dinner.

*It was just yesterday evening when César and I left
Pisco with Brandy in his old van. The country became more
barren as it grew dark and there were fewer villages the
further inland we travelled. I had bought Brandy a bottle
and told him not to drink it while driving. He grinned at me
with that idiotic expression and it didn't take long before I
smelled the cognac as he tipped his flask to his lips.*

*The cicadas were buzzing. It reminded me of home.
Soon we were passing through the town of Ataccala, just
before the road turned north to Huancayo. I wanted to stop
there for the night because I worried that Brandy would
pass out at the wheel. We had another four hours to go but
César didn't want to stop until we got to Huancayo. This is
not good country, he warned. We stayed huddled together
in the back as I kept my eye on our driver.*

*Past the town of Ataccala it was pitch black, there was
no moon, no stars, nothing but an invisible weight all
around the headlight beams and Brandy was sipping from
his flask and the music on the radio was too loud. Then the
headlights caught an animal crossing the highway in front of
us, a big black cat, its eyes lit up like fire. Brandy veered to
miss it and the van lurched off the road and into a gully. We
skidded and just about teetered over but the van righted
itself at the last moment. The engine died. I turned to
César. He was all right. Brandy had hit his head on the
steering wheel but claimed he didn't feel it. What now, I
asked. César spoke to Brandy. Mala surete, he said. Bad
luck was an understatement.*

*We got out of the van and tried to see if there was any
damage. I struck a match and the tiny flame burned my
fingers while Brandy crawled under the van.*

*It became clear we would have to go back to Ataccala
for a tractor to tow us out of the ditch but everything would
be closed down now and tomorrow was Sunday. Brandy
switched off the weak headlights to conserve battery power.*

We felt our way to a grassy patch near the van and sat together where Brandy and I smoked my last two Ducals. We watched the red tips of our cigarettes move like fireflies in the dark. The cicadas stopped screaming. I heard César take a drink from a water bottle. I don't suppose anyone else is going to come along this road at this time of night, I said. No, probablemente no. It was impossible to do anything until morning.

Brandy felt his way back to the van, leaving us alone. It was getting cold. César huddled next to me. I thought I heard something rustling nearby. The wounded animal? Do you think it's still lurking out there, hurt, bleeding and dangerous? We crawled our way back to the van. Brandy was already snoring in the front seat. César and I huddled under a scratchy alpaca blanket on the slanted floor in the back.

We didn't sleep. We were lying there trying to keep warm when I heard the sound of approaching vehicles, faint at first, then growing louder. I climbed to the front and shook Brandy awake. Thank god, I was thinking. We can get a ride to wherever they're going. Somehow both Brandy and César knew better. They pulled me back and when I resisted, Brandy covered my mouth.

The headlights bouncing through the empty fields lit up the horizon like lightning strikes. It sounded like three, maybe four trucks. We huddled in silence in the back of the van. Through the windshield we could see the lights coming closer. Then they stopped not more than two hundred feet away and their engines shut off one by one. There were shouts, like orders being given. We heard people talking and crying and then more shouting. There were women and children's voices mixed in with the men. For a moment there was an ugly silence, before the crying became shrieks. And then gunshots. Not just single shots but the rat-tat-tat of machine-gun fire. And more horrible,

horrible screaming. It took forever for the gunfire to stop and the screaming and the howls to fade away. Then the killers began yelling back and forth. There were more gunshots, single pistol-shots, as if they were finishing off stragglers. And then there was another noise, a stranger one, a rhythmic clicking and scraping and we realized the sounds were shovels hitting dirt. We kept absolutely still, huddled on the slanted floor of the van. I smelled urine. Brandy had pissed himself.

The shovelling went on and on and then there were more orders and more shouting. Another lone, distant, end-of-time gunshot. I head one of the men call out, *Enterralos aquí!* They were burying the dead.

How long had we been there? One hour? Two? It would be dawn soon. And then I was afraid more than ever before in my life—afraid of the dawn because when the sky lightened they would see the van in the ditch. They would come to investigate. There would be nowhere to hide. We would just be shot and buried with the rest.

Then everything seemed to stop. There were shouts from the senderistas and the trucks started up again. They moved off and their headlights panned the black landscape and we held our collective breath in case their headlights fell over us as they left but they didn't, they moved off until the noise of their engines died in the distance. Still, we didn't move for a very long time. We kept listening in case someone was left behind to guard the site, someone with a gun. And then it didn't matter because it was finally dawn, all scarlet and purple and blue lifting us and the world up into the next day. But not the disappeared. Not the dead.

Later—

What good is writing this all down? It's not helping those people or César or even me. A part of me was buried *with them. I am still a prisoner in this fusty hotel room. If I could only get out of here and find a way back there—*

*   *   *

But what was the use? César was gone. The incident had wrenched us apart and broke all that we had into pieces, scattering them across the desert plain.

Brandy kept drinking and passed out when it was all over. César sat down hard on the ground beside the van. His eyes were glazed over. Then we argued. I wanted to head back to Ataccala and alert the police. This was another Lucanamarca, I told him. César said the police were not to be trusted.

"*Ellos son cómplices,*" he argued.

"How do you know they're complicit?" I challenged.

"I have seen the face of the devil," César said.

"We have to tell someone!"

"*Este es el verdadero Perú,*" he said and spat on the ground.

"Real Peru or not, you can still do the right thing. For the sake of their relatives. For the living," I pleaded.

"No!" he said flatly again, watching me stand with difficulty as if the Earth was suddenly too heavy for its burden. "I won't go to the police." That was final.

"I will go to the police myself then."

"Yes, go," he said. He started to get up as well and when I tried to help him he pulled away from me. "I have to leave now."

"That's it? That's all?"

"*Sí.*"

"After everything—"

"*Sí.* It is the end of the way of things." His face was stone, his eyes shards of glass. He went to the van and grabbed his knapsack.

I pulled out every *soles* I had. "Take this." I closed his hand around the money.

"I don't need—" He stopped. He was weakening.

"Take it or come with me," I said again.

He stuffed the money into his pocket and walked away. He didn't look back. Even in the jarring morning light the image of him moving away along the side of the road was a mirage, a trick of mirrors. I felt I had left my body and was hovering half-asleep in a bed far away, trying to tell myself to wake up, that the massacre and César disappearing beyond my reach was all a dream while the dead kept crying out from the gully behind me.

I woke from my trance when I saw the first scavenger birds circling overhead. It was time to leave. I went over to Brandy who was awake and sitting against the van watching me.

"They may come back," I said. He just looked at me and I realized I was speaking English. "*Tenemos que irnos,*" I repeated.

He pushed himself up and I grabbed my bag out of the back of the van, the one César and I had used as a pillow just hours ago. I started walking back in the direction of Ataccala. Brandy followed behind me with his flask. We didn't speak. The sun was warming the plains and the birds and reptiles and insects were coming alive again. My heart began to race when I heard a car come up behind us. I pulled Brandy off the road to hide in a ditch. As the truck approached I could see it wasn't the police, it was a run-down farm truck, so we ran out to the roadway and flagged it down. There were three farmers sitting in the flatbed. They were wearing plaid and striped coats and earflap hats and were as swarthy as pirates. Brandy spoke with the driver and then nodded to me. We climbed into the back with them and they shuffled to make room for us. They appeared amused with me and broke out laughing, showing their crooked or missing teeth. Even when they smiled their eyes were hard. Brandy talked to them as we were jostled over the ruts in the road and he shared his flask around with them but, wisely, he said nothing about what happened to us.

They let us off at a garage which appeared to be closed. When the dust settled Brandy shook my hand.

"*La comisaría está en esa dirección,*" he said pointing down an empty street where I would eventually find the police station. I was on my own.

I walked towards the centre of town. There were only a few people on the streets. They looked at me strangely as they passed. *Gringo*, they were thinking. Ataccala was larger than I expected, with the *Plaza de Armas de Ataccala* and a cathedral surrounded by shops and restaurants still closed up. A woman was sweeping in front of a fruit store. No one seemed to have any idea about what had happened just outside their town. I found the police station, a long cream-coloured building with writing painted on its side: *Policia Nacional del Peru, Comisaria Sectorial, Ataccala.*

I approached the officer at the front desk. A ceiling fan was circling overhead.

"*Perdón!*" I said. The officer in his full uniform stared at me as if I was a trick of the light. "*Ha habido una masacre.*"

As if he didn't understand, he asked me where I was from. When I told him, he demanded my passport. I pulled it out of my duffle bag and he took it back to his colleagues. A minute later he came back out.

"*Billetera y papeles,*" he said.

I was worried I would be misunderstood so I decided to keep my Spanish to a minimum.

"*No hablo español, sólo inglés,*" I replied.

"*Billetera, billetera,*" he repeated and showed me his own wallet. I went back into my bag and pulled out my wallet and my airline ticket which I had stuffed inside my travellers cheques.

"*Si!*"

They led me to what must have been a small interrogation room. There was a wooden table and two straight chairs facing one another. The paint was peeling off the walls. The room smelled of stale coffee, cigarettes, and rotten fruit. I was hoping someone would speak English but no one at the station spoke any other language. I could make out a few phrases in their dialect through the open door: *We don't know. He's Canadian. Find Alejandro...*

I rummaged through my duffel bag for my cigarettes then remembered that Brandy and I had smoked them all by the side of the road. There was an ashtray sitting there full of cigarette butts stinking up the room. I felt sick again. I would never take up another cigarette if I made it through this...

Eventually two officers in khaki uniforms came in. They stood against one wall and spoke quietly to each other. Finally, another police officer in full regalia stepped in and closed the door. His straight black hair was tucked under his military cap. He was holding my passport.

"I am Major Alejandro Francisco de Paula y Cortez. So what is this about a massacre?" he asked in English.

I told him. He listened carefully as he made notes in his officer's notebook. I had to tell him about César in the event they came across Brandy and questioned him but instead of calling him César, I said his name was William Cespedes, like my professor. I don't know why I did that. I don't know what I was afraid of. Brandy wouldn't have known any different. What seemed to puzzle Major Alejandro was why I had come to the station alone. Where was the driver of the van? Where was this other passenger, Señor Cespedes? Why send the only person who does not speak Spanish to make a confession?

"It's not a confession," I corrected. "It's an account."

He raised his hands in apology. "*Si. Lo siento.*"

"I think the driver was avoiding the police," I continued. "Maybe the van was stolen?"

"So you were travelling with criminals?"

This was absurd. He was twisting my words.

"They didn't strike me as criminals, no."

"Strike you?"

Now I made a mental note to be careful with idioms. "They didn't *seem* like criminals. The driver was from Pisco and my friend was from Lima. Shouldn't we talk about the massacre?"

The Major, who was writing something down, paused to look up. "Tell me more about your friend from Lima."

"Don't you want to go check out the area where we saw the massacre?"

"You *saw* the massacre?"

"Where the massacre *happened*," I corrected. I could feel sweat dripping down my sides under my shirt. "Shouldn't we try to find it as soon as possible?"

"What is the rush? Tell me about Señor Cespedes."

I told him what he wanted to hear. I told him about my internship at the museum—he could check my student visa in my passport—and that César, now William, had agreed to be my guide but after the massacre he just took off, afraid, and I couldn't blame him. I had the impression the Major was trying to ascertain any connection with *Sendero Luminoso* just as I was being cautious about the police themselves being involved with Shining Path as César had warned. It felt like a game of chess where all the pawns had been captured then shot and buried.

The Major ran his hand through his thick black hair. A few strands fell over his forehead. "Please don't misunderstand. What you are telling us is serious."

"I've told you everything I know. I'll go now—"

181

"We prefer not yet," the Major said, stopping me as I rose from my chair.

Then one of the other men pointed down at my feet. Major Alejandro pulled my duffle bag out from underneath the table.

"This is your bag?"

I nodded. When they made to leave with it, I tried to protest but they just shut the door behind them.

With my elbows on the table, I put my head in my hands. They had my journal. They had the key to all my secrets, to me and César. They would see the napkin I had kept that said *BRISDON IS LOVE.* Gabriel Larco was mentioned in there too. All they needed to read was his name, that we had travelled together, and if he was known to them as a *senderista,* how would that look for me? Even worse, they would find out I had been lying about César's name. I could imagine where that would lead. I felt sick. My mind kept racing. César was right. I shouldn't have come. I looked at my watch but it had stopped. Was that from the impact of the crash or had time stopped...

When the door finally opened, Major Alejandro stepped in alone. I felt a rush of cool air. I hadn't realized how stifling the room had become. The Major brought back my duffel bag and set it on the table. An edge caught the heaping ash tray, spilling it onto to the floor with a clatter.

Ashes to ashes, I thought.

"Sorry for the waiting," he said.

"Did you find what you wanted?"

"No," he replied. "We could not find it."

Only then did I understood he was talking about the site of the massacre and that they had driven out to look after all.

"The van was in a ditch maybe fifteen minutes from here. Maybe twenty."

"I understand."

"But you will keep looking?" I implored.

"Yes," he said. "We know something has happened. Not here in Ataccala but in Cavelica, the next town. Thank you for your patience."

"I can leave then?"

"Sorry, no. We will make arrangements for you." I just looked at him, not understanding that I was to be their prisoner. "I will take you to the hotel now."

*   *   *

Ataccala, August 15th - Hotel Presidente

Major Alejandro, my jailer, says they are sending me back to Canada on the next Air Canada flight out of Lima. Can they do that? What sort of risk am I to them? If the entire police force in Columbia is under Pablo Escobar's payroll, does Abimael Guzmán wield the same power here? Should I be afraid?

Major Alejandro will take me to Lima himself. His uniform is impeccable and he is obviously educated but I don't trust him. I can't trust anyone. They kept me in that interrogation room for hours. They had my bag and access to my journal. When Major Alejandro brought me to my hotel room, I pulled out my book from the duffle bag and asked him straight out if he had looked through it.

Si, he said and left.

It is the end of the way of things.

*   *   *

The Major's police cruiser had a flat tire so our departure was delayed. We finally left for Lima at two in the afternoon. Major Alejandro warned me it would be a seven hour drive. We would stop in Chincha for food and gas. I saw the Major place my duffle bag in the trunk on top of an axe and shovel and a new spare tire. *What do you need that axe for?* I wanted to ask him, but kept quiet.

I sat in the back seat behind the iron grate like a criminal. There were no handles to roll down the window. I gazed through the pane at the endless expanse of desert and thought how easy it would be for the Major to pull off to the side of the road, drag me out of the cruiser and shoot me dead, then bury me in a gully somewhere. The more I thought about it, the more I realized it would be the simplest solution for them if they were complicit as César had warned. As we drove on, I grew more uneasy. Is this why I was given a police escort? When did the police ever put someone up in a hotel or put them on a plane? What was really happening? I began to panic.

"Do you have my new plane ticket?" I asked him through the grate as calmly as I could.

"No. We will get that at the airport."

"You have nothing?"

"We have confirmation," he replied, staring straight ahead.

"Can I see it?"

"I will give it to you in Lima."

My stomach churned. There would be no plane ticket. He had kept my wallet and passport. I looked out the window. There was just barren land extending miles in all directions. I couldn't remember the last time we saw another vehicle on the roadway. I glanced at the rear-view mirror and saw Major Alejandro's brown eyes staring back at me. He must have seen the expression on my face, that I knew what he was going to do, because in the middle of nowhere he pulled the cruiser to the side of the road and stopped in a cloud of dust. He started fiddling with his holster to release his revolver. Then he opened the door and slowly walked around the front of the car. It was so deliberate. So calculating. He pulled open my door. As I stepped out I prayed to see a car coming but there was nothing but a soft breeze cutting through the dust and the sound of the police cruiser's engine. I was shaking. I couldn't utter a word. I couldn't even breathe. My knees buckled and I started to fall and the Major reached out and grabbed me. Then I saw the *Air Canada* logo on the envelope in his hand. I pushed away, turning towards the car to retch onto the ground, heaving all the poisons out of me, all of Ataccala and César and Peru out into the dirt. When there was nothing left and my eyes were swimming, Major Alejandro Francisco de Paula y Cortez of the Ataccala Police put his arm around my shoulders at the side of the road because he understood. He helped me back into the cruiser and in those moments, not only did the spirit of youth leave me, but some arcane and audacious part of me died on that desert road.

*   *   *

Lima, August 16th- Gran Hotel Bolivar

I am back in the City of Ashes at the Gran Hotel Bolivar. It seems the Ataccala police department has spared no expense to keep me quiet. There is a chandelier of Murano glass over the bed and a Juliet balcony with French doors overlooking the Plaza San Martin. The wallpaper isn't peeling and the sheets and towels smell fresh. The furniture is Empire classic and there are little soaps and shampoo bottles in the bathroom.

The Major is keeping my passport until my flight tomorrow but returned my wallet with my travellers cheques so I can get money out of the bank if I need to. He advised me to stay in the hotel until he comes back for me but I'm

not staying put, no fucking way. I'll be back when Raf brings
my suitcase this evening but until then, nothing will stop me
from locating César. It's Tuesday morning and I know
where to find him...

*   *   *

I arrived at the *Museo de Arte de Lima* just before ten
o'clock when one of the security guards would open the
doors to visitors. There were just a few tourists with
backpacks waiting at the steps. I didn't see César there and I
was worried if he saw me he might turn away before I
caught sight of him. So I walked over to the park and found
a bench that was partially hidden by bushes but still
provided me with a view of the entrance.

I waited until almost noon but César didn't appear. I
hadn't made a plan so I had no idea where to go from
there. I walked around the Plaza de Armas, searching him
out. Everyone looked like him; no one looked like him. I
circled by the palace alongside the goose-stepping guards
but no César. Next I headed down Jirón de la Unión and
caught my refection in the shop windows and didn't
recognize myself. I had grown a scruffy beard. I was thinner.
At six o'clock I headed back to the hotel to meet Rafael.
When I walked in he was waiting in the lobby with my
suitcase.

"Were you waiting long?" I asked. "My watch broke—"

He just grinned and we found a couple of leather
armchairs by the ferns at the window.

"Can I buy you a beer?" he asked. "You look like you
need one."

I rubbed my rough beard. "That sounds good." I
wanted to tell Raf everything, unburden myself to him, but I
knew I wouldn't.

Rafael was watching me like he knew something was wrong. "I didn't think you were leaving so soon."

"My plans changed," was all I could say. I tried to change the subject. "How is everyone?"

"Oh yes. Manuela sends her love. Lucía and I have installed the Vargas exhibition. It was interesting to have a woman's point of view."

The drinks arrived. When I poured my beer into my glass it foamed over. Just don't ask me about César, I thought. I don't want to have to lie to you.

"I have something for you," he said, fishing through his jacket pocket. He pulled out a wrist watch and held it out to me.

I took it from him. It looked new and expensive.

"I want you to have it, Brisdon. And it's appropriate since you say yours is broken—"

I held it up. "It's very nice, Raf but—"

He cut me off. "I bought it for Perfecto, you see. For his birthday which would have been a week after they caught us and threw him in jail. I never had the chance to give it to him. I have kept it all this time but I would like you to have it now."

Bad things happen to good people, I thought. "I don't know what to say."

I took Perfecto's watch and closed the clasp around my wrist. The weight of it there felt hopeful. Then I grew sad. I wanted to tell him about Ataccala, I wanted to tell him that Perfecto hated him now and to abandon all hope with him. But most of all I wanted to tell him I understood that the history of Peru was a horror story as he had warned, but I said nothing.

"I'll think of this moment when I look at it." I displayed my wrist to him. He had set the watch to the correct time— more or less.

When we were done he held out his hand but I moved around the table and hugged him tightly.

"Until we meet again," he said, not knowing how soon it would be.

*   *   *

The next day at noon by Perfecto's watch, Major Alejandro met me in the hotel lobby. He was in full uniform and everyone must have thought he was arresting me by the way he picked up my suitcase and took my arm to lead me ahead of him and out the door. On the way to the airport I wanted to ask him if he had heard any more about the missing villagers from Cavelica but thought better of it. I would grab a newspaper at the airport.

The Major brought me to the front of the line at the check-in counter. He escorted me through security and right up to the departure gate and stood there as I disappeared on the other side. I found a seat where I could watch the Air Canada plane with its big red maple leaf parked on the tarmac. There were a number of service vehicles moving back and forth. About fifteen minutes later there was an announcement over the loudspeaker that my flight would be delayed due to technical problems. Everyone in the departure lounge started talking at once. Travellers began lining up at the desk where two young women in red and white airline uniforms were fielding questions. I waited. I found a newspaper abandoned on a seat but there was nothing about Ataccala or Cavelica. When the line thinned out, I went up to the counter to ask about the delay.

"Actually, sir, we've just been told your flight to Toronto has been cancelled. There will be an announcement shortly. We are putting everyone on another flight this evening to Vancouver and then you will be able to connect to Toronto."

"Vancouver? That's as far away from Toronto as we are."

She shrugged. "There is nothing I can do, sir."

"When is the next direct flight to Toronto after this one?"

The other agent checked. "Next Sunday. In four days."

I thought for a moment. "Can you book me on that one instead?"

They exchanged glances.

"Yes, I suppose that is possible."

When she left to start the transfer process I paced back and forth beyond the plastic seats of the waiting area. My heart was racing. Two hours later an airline representative escorted me back through security along with my suitcase and a new plane ticket. When I reached the arrivals area, I had to sit down. I had just bought myself four more days to find César.

*　　*　　*

August 18th, morning—Hotel Castella

I have been given a second chance. I never got on that flight home! It was cancelled and I got myself booked on another flight four days from now. I immediately called Raf who picked me up at the airport and I could tell he was pleased I was wearing Perfecto's gold watch. He wanted me to stay with him but I explained I had to attend to some-thing personal. That hurt him, I think, but I knew he would try to talk some sense into me and I didn't need common sense, I needed luck. I needed César.

He took me to the Hotel Castella, a cozy guest house on a narrow street in the city centre. I have a room on the roof, like a little cabana with a wide view of the rooftops of Lima. When I look down, a lone policeman in a white helmet and belt walks along the narrow street and he reminds me of Major Alejandro who thinks I am well on my way home.

Thiago and his sister Trinidad work for their parents at the hotel. Thiago is just a teenager and he tends to the reception desk. His older sister works in the tiny hotel café and does the laundry. She is beautiful. She has green eyes like a cat, like Layla. There is sibling rivalry as they vie for my attention. Trinidad, I found out, is the only surviving girl of triplets. Her other two sisters died very young but God spared her, she says. I told her I had a twin sister who I lost very young as well. I didn't expect I would tell her this, but I did, and now we have connected on another level. I'm so sorry, she said and kissed me on the cheek and I returned to my room feeling even more lost than before.

*   *   *

Because I had told Thiago I was urgently looking for a friend, their parents and proprietors, Eduardo and Rosario Castella, were sympathetic to my cause. They were up at dawn long before their son and daughter, scrubbing floors, washing walls, changing linens and preparing breakfast for the guests. They kept a colourful and ostentatious parrot in a bamboo cage behind the front desk that talked and talked until I came into the room on the first morning and then it shut right up and just stared at me. Rosario crossed herself and clasped her hands together saying it was a miracle because she had been trying to shut the bird up for years.

If I had no luck in finding César today, Eduardo promised to drive me to Independencia tomorrow, to look for César's Aunt Estralita. I only had a vague idea where the house was located because I hadn't paid attention on the bus ride, preoccupied with Layla under my jacket.

I looked for César in all the places I thought he could be. I passed by my old apartment building and then returned to the convent of San Francisco and waited in the catacombs with the bones of the dead. I took a city bus to the Café Godoy where César had repeated *Mister Brisdon* over and over. I sat drinking coffee after coffee looking for César in the crowds that passed me by. I took out my medallion from under my shirt and held it and said a prayer and tried to feel hope again. I was running out of ideas.

When I returned to the hotel the Castellas sensed my frustration.

"You will find him," Trinidad assured me. "Stranger things have happened." She was sitting close to me on a bench on the rooftop. She rested her hand on my shoulder.

Early in the morning on my last full day, Trinidad and I piled into the back of Eduardo's little blue Fiat and we headed north. Independencia looked the same with its narrow streets littered with dented garbage bins, its grey concrete homes and the occasional cantuta bush, the Peruvian magic tree. We stopped to ask a group of young men standing against an iron gate eating ice cream if they knew anyone named César or even Luis, or if they knew an older woman named Estralita. No one knew them. It was futile. My world had gone dark. The mystical mists rising from the ancient valleys of Peru had turned to slime in the gutters of Independencia.

To cheer me up, Eduardo and Trinidad drove on to Miraflores. The sun came out, piercing through the grey haze and the colours became brighter and there were palm trees and flowers along the road. And, of course, the calming sea.

I asked if they could stop and let me out at the boardwalk.

"How will you get back?" Trinidad asked.

"I'll take a bus. I've done it before."

Trinidad had her hand on my shoulder again. She was rubbing it gently. I closed my eyes and when I opened them the car had stopped.

"Come see me," Trinidad urged, "after you get back."

When they drove off I made my way down to the water's edge. The boardwalk was busier than I expected. The gothic pink restaurant on the pier was open now and people in small clusters were heading there, chattering away. I just wanted to be alone. I clambered over the rocks. The waves were crashing like small explosions. I found a place to sit by myself. I had wanted to bring César to this place, to swim and lounge by the rocks like I had done with Lucía, but César said he couldn't swim.

Today, like me, the ocean had gone mad. The water was churning and turning and convulsing with gurgling, spewing laughter. The colours of the water against the interminable horizon changed minute by minute, almost green, almost blue, then grey again.

Then I heard a familiar laugh from the boardwalk above. It was César's laugh. I couldn't mistake it, even if it was all out of context. Maybe it had only been a trick of the wind and the cawing of the seagulls. I had to know. I scrambled back over the rocks so fast I scraped my ankle on the ear of a stone with a laughing face and almost fell. I found my footing again and scaled the last rocks until I was level with the boardwalk.

I hadn't imagined it! César was there, just ahead, walking away with that same stride when he had walked away on the road from Ataccala. I called but he couldn't hear with the waves crashing and the wind whipping back in my direction. There were two men with him, one on each side. I watched as the taller one put his arm around his shoulder. They were good looking men, tourists who César had picked up after his return from Ataccala, two new adventure-seekers, restless, ready to take chances, to descend into catacombs and climb cliffs, men full of longing to be intimate with César, like I had been. They were laughing like the seagulls circling above us. I couldn't imagine what was so funny while I stood there abandoned and humiliated by the moxie of this coincidence. The shorter tourist reached out and caressed César's arm like Trinidad had done with me in the car. How they loved him already!

I climbed up onto to the boardwalk then. The three of them had disappeared somewhere beyond the walkway, gone among the Miraflores Saturday afternoon crowds. Gone for good.

When I got back to the hotel, I didn't look for Trinidad. I stayed in my cabana until it grew late and I would be alone on the roof. When I stepped out, the almost full moon above me was covering the rooftops of Lima with a silvery gauze. I pulled my medallion out from under my shirt. My hands were shaking. I tried to undo the clasp on the chain but it stuck. I clawed at it but it wouldn't release so I tore it off in anger. I felt a sting and my neck started to bleed. I held the broken chain and medallion in my hand. The saint was burning into my palm now. Then, with all my might, I hurled the medallion at the moon. It went sailing through the air, the chain its comet's tail.

Gone. Gone for good.

*   *   *

August 21st, morning - Hotel Castella

Dear Karen,
These are the last pages of my book, my last entry even if my story isn't finished.

*I rub my sore neck and the wound reopens and starts
to bleed again. Now I have smeared blood over these last
pages.*

*César has played a trick on me. Everything between us
has been a lie. Last night I stood alone on the rooftop of
this hotel and said a final prayer for the dead at Ataccala.
Then I pulled César's medallion from my neck and threw it
to the moon. It was after midnight. Trinidad found me
sitting there, alone and shivering. She sat next to me and
noticed my bleeding neck and kissed the wound. Then she
took my face in her hands and kissed me on the mouth.
We went back to my room. We undressed. Her skin
glistened in the shallow light. Her caresses were soft. The
scent of jasmine filled the air and I wondered if I was
imagining everything. Saint John was no longer watching
over me. Instead, my little demon hovered in the shadows.
The moonlight fell over us, opaque like a moonstone,
washing us with its cloudy sheen and enveloping us in its
mystery of light and dark. Then, all my loose ends melded
together.*

*Later, I climbed out of bed and found a blanket to pull
about my shoulders. I stepped out to the rooftop again. I
watched the stars try to break through the permanent grey
that hung over Lima, even at night. Somewhere a rooster
crowed. Suddenly I didn't want Trinidad in my bed. I
wanted to crawl under the warm covers and find César
there, waiting for me.*

*I know it's wrong. I know it's reckless to want César.
My longing is already getting mixed up with outrage and
revenge stirring at the pit of my stomach.*

*There, there, my demon says to me, there's nothing to
be done about a broken heart.*

*But the heart wants what the heart wants—and it wants
blood.*

César

They call it *apophenia*. I didn't know it had a name at the time, but there was something unusual about the way Brisdon saw the world, *su mundo*. He had a tendency to see meaningful connections where I couldn't, where I was certain none existed. *Dios mío!* He even told me he didn't believe in God and that he wasn't sure there was a *supreme being*. He tip-toed around me as he spoke because he knew I was a devout Catholic and always wore the crucifix my mother had given me.

"If I'm anything I'm a Buddhist," he admitted. "In Buddhism everything is connected." He really wanted me to understand. "It's like the prancing of atoms in a molecule and the music that binds the planets together as they dance around the sun."

"That is gravity," I replied. I kept looking at the moonstone ring he had bought for me at the Cusco market that day. It fit snugly on my finger but it made me sad. Then he put his hand in mine—such a brave move—as we entered the dining room of the new hotel just below Machu Picchu. That was when we met Gabriel Larco, a *senderista* and unequivocally the *enemy*. I saw it in his eyes right away, behind those tiny wire-framed spectacles like a student of Lenin.

It was a portent of things to come.

A few days later we were on our way in a dilapidated *camioneta* driven by one of Gabriel Larco's comrades who I didn't trust either. We passed through Ataccala just after nightfall heading to Huancayo. Then one of the jaguars of my dreams crossed the highway in front of us. We swerved to miss it and crashed into a ditch. We were stranded there. We were trying to make the best of it in the pitch black night when we heard the sound of trucks approaching. They

195

were driven by Shining Path militants as they pulled to a stop in the fields just beyond us, in the middle of nowhere. We heard them unload a few dozen villagers who had clearly been snatched from their beds the way they were shouting and wailing. These *senderistas* had rounded up whole families: the mothers and the fathers, the brothers and the sisters, the wives and the children of their enemies in Cavelica, and shot them all dead. *Long Live Peru!*

We were in shock. We had survived without being seen, but the worst was to come and the result would be wounds that continued to fester for months and then years, leaving scars that refused to heal. We were the survivors who had dug their way out of the clay of Ataccala.

I had no alternative but to make my way back to Lima alone. I walked a long time in the opposite direction from where Brisdon was headed to alert the police in Ataccala. I stayed away from the road so it would be easier to hide if the police drove by. A truck filled with farm workers passed me going in the opposite direction. I lay down flat on the ground whenever I heard an engine approaching. The day was as quiet as night. I felt that jaguar stalking me, ready to lunge and tear me apart at any moment. I would deserve that. When I reached Cavelica I could tell right away that something was wrong. There were too many vehicles, too many people rushing around for a Sunday. I heard shouting, crying, the same fearful sounds from the night before but without machine-gun fire. This was by far the worst place I could end up. I stayed on the outskirts of the town and weighed my options. My instincts told me to keep walking. Logic told me the night would be too cold without shelter. I found an abandoned adobe hut further along the road. The straw roof was filled with holes. Inside was an old blanket, caked with dirt and torn apart by fleas. I slept as soon as I closed my eyes. I woke up in the middle of the night, thinking I heard the grinding gears of militia trucks and prepared myself for more screaming. But my mind was haunted and playing tricks.

I caught the bus to Lima the next day and paid the driver with Brisdon's money. I watched the shoreline of the ocean as the bus travelled north on the coastal highway. The water stretched out towards an impossible horizon. *The ocean is tears*, I thought. I leaned my forehead against the window: but water has no guilt or shame, no conscience or remorse. Water is elusive the way it slips through your fingers. Water will always be true to itself. The whole ocean of tears would not be able to fill the void of despair I felt inside me.

When the bus let me out in Lima centre it was late afternoon. I hadn't bathed or eaten in two days. I walked to the National Library. It was a Monday in the middle of August and José Juan would be at work. In the main lobby the familiar guards at the desk just stared at me. I asked one of the guards who I knew as Mateo if he could find José Juan for me. His chair screeched backwards against the marble floor, the sound echoing up to the high ceiling. He hurried off.

José Juan took one look at me, grabbed his coat and brought me back home. I stayed with them for the week. My uncles must have known I was in shock the way I moved around their house like the lost spirit of Atahualpa. I couldn't go back to my aunt's house. Estralita and Rosa weren't expecting me back yet and I didn't want to face their prying eyes, their questions, their surprised and empathetic expressions. They wouldn't be like my uncles who let me suffer in silence.

I slept a great deal the first days and fought off nightmares. José Juan brought home a new sketchbook and an array of coloured pencils. I used up all the browns and blacks and greys, all the moodiest colours, grinding them down with a pen-knife as I worked. We all had our therapy and drawing the death of me and of Brisdon at Ataccala was mine.

My uncles continued to be concerned about me, especially because I wasn't eating. Juan José suggested they take me for lunch at *La Rosa Náutica*, the new seafood restaurant on the pier in Miraflores. It had just opened.

"It will be refreshing for all of us to go to the ocean front," Juan José encouraged.

"What do they have there?" José Juan asked as if they were performing a little skit for me.

"Why, there are mussels and oysters and crab and lobster and even Argentinian beef. The best beef in the world!"

They treated me to lunch that Saturday when the sun came out and lit up the elegant Victorian dining room, all in pink with bamboo and ferns and oriental vases the size of the waiters. My uncles made me laugh for the first time since I had found my way back to Lima. I still didn't have much of an appetite. I picked at my lobster salad while they sat looking at me with their wide and inquisitive chocolate-brown eyes.

"Is your heart broken?" Juan José asked.

"Not in the way you would think."

"So you think about him all the time?"

"I can't imagine *not* thinking about him."

"It's good to talk about it," José Juan assured me.

"It makes no difference," I said. "He's left Peru. He's as far away as the Milky Way."

"That's very far," Juan José agreed.

"And even sounds pretty," José Juan joined in. "You should draw that."

"I don't want to draw any more."

They both stared at me, not blinking.

"You don't?"

I managed a grin. "No. I'm done with sketching. I want to paint."

"What do you want to paint?" Juan José asked.

"Death," I replied. "In oils."

"Acrylics would be easier," José Juan suggested.

"I've had drawing lessons," I said, lifting a forkful of lobster from my plate. "Now I need painting lessons. Are they expensive?"

They looked at each other and then back to me with my raised fork, extortion through appetite.

"No more expensive than eating lobster every day," Juan José calculated.

"Let's see what we can do," José Juan gave in, and I finished everything on my plate for them.

The following week, José Juan found me a part-time job at the National Library. When I arrived on my first day, scrubbed clean and dressed in a pressed shirt, Mateo beamed and shook my hand. The few *soles* I earned went directly for painting supplies. My uncles cleared out a corner of a room in their house for me to set up my easel. Their home had more light and space than in Independencia. I laid newspapers down to protect their parquet floor. As my canvases grew in number and size, the house became inundated with my paintings, stored against the walls, tucked in between the sofa and chairs and behind the dressers and cabinets. They even hung some of my more cheerful canvases on their walls. At the beginning I had to admit most of my work was not very good.

I went back to the *Museo de Arte Italiano*. I sought out the art director, Mario Gonzales, who had given me life-drawing lessons and was busy working at his museum supervising restorations. He remembered me and smiled when I told him I no longer lacked focus. We went to the museum cafeteria. We sat on cold chairs sipping hot *mate de cocoa*. I told him painting had become my medium of choice but I needed more structure. I needed to build my technique.

"I need a maestro, Señor Gonzales. I can pay."

He thought for a moment, his cup lifted half-way to his mouth.

"To be honest, you need a Muse."

He found me both. She was a spry octogenarian named Señora María Rosa Alonso. I visited her often in her small apartment on Calle La Joya. She set my own easel next to hers and told me about her past. She had been married to the Minister of Culture. During their long and bureaucratic life, she was an art director for many museums and galleries in Lima. When the military junta took over, her husband was assassinated.

"Nineteen sixty-eight. The most politically-charged year since the two great wars. Not just for Peru but for the entire world."

"What happened?" I asked.

"The world contracted a fever that still hasn't broken."

After the death of her husband, and over the next twelve years of repression and dictatorship, she retreated into a private life of painting. As I drew my brush along the canvas she would correct my pattern and contrast. When I mixed my palette to paint a sunset she corrected my strokes. At one of our first sessions she said, "Painting is like music, César, it operates under its own rules by breaking the rules." At another session she decreed, "It's all about the light. Pay particular attention to this even if you paint a dark canvas. Light is there. It is even in the darkest parts of our being."

She taught me impasto and implied lines, variety, balance and rhythm. When I was half-way through a painting and hating it, she lamented, "There is often as much sincerity in a bad painting as in a good one."

"But I don't want to make bad paintings," I replied. "I want to create something new and innovative."

"There is nothing new under the stars, only a fresh viewpoint."

During another session she caught me putting my finger to my tongue to turn a page in my painting sketchbook. "Be careful," she warned. "Paints can be poison. They used to make yellow pigment out of arsenic and sulfide and artists have died in agony after licking their fingers." Another time she said she didn't understand what I was trying to express in my painting, so to cover my embarrassment, I glorified its lack of clarity. "Ah, maestro César," she cautioned again, "ambiguity is anathema for an artist."

"What's next?" I asked her when we came to our last session.

"Education, César. It is very important. But you don't always need a formal education if you already possess self-discipline." She handed me a book. "You need to understand the world if you want to paint it."

"What's this?"

"*Don Quixote*. Start there and never stop."

Only later, long after she had died, did I realize her effect on me: she had been my true guide through the inner world of my art because she knew there was arsenic in my heart.

*   *   *

My lifelong relationship with Jock Palmerston began at the stroke of midnight ushering in 1986. Like Brisdon, Jock was a visitor to Peru. He lived in London, but he was born in Newcastle and his hardy Geordie dialect was difficult to understand. He wasn't as handsome as Brisdon and was much older. He had the pale complexion of people who rarely saw the sun. He was in Lima to gather Peruvian artifacts for his exclusive London art gallery. We met at the

New Year's Eve celebration at the National Library, where he had been invited by one of the directors, and he caught my eye in the crowd amid multi-coloured balloons, confetti and accordion streamers. I made my way towards him.

"I knew I could bring you over with just the power of my gaze," he said.

"How is that?"

"I have a gift. I can tell everything about people just by looking at their faces."

Physiognomy would be discredited many years later but I wouldn't have argued anyway. "What can you tell about me?" I asked.

"I can tell you're an artist. I can tell you have great pride."

"You have been talking to someone about me," I laughed. "What else?"

"You are intelligent and wise beyond your age and you want to get to know me."

I was impressed with his precision and presumption. Then we all counted down the seconds to midnight. As the balloons were released, he kissed me, not like Brisdon, not shy or with a heart racing from fear, but with every intention of having more.

The month of January was bright and hot. The winds off the Pacific had blown away the grey that Brisdon hated so much and the sky turned a hard blue. Jock was uncomfortable in the heat. When we were out walking, he jumped from shade to shadow. His neck and shirt became wet and I tried not to think of my father and his incessant sweating. During the day I was busy in my make-shift studio so Jock and I usually met in the evenings at a café or in his air-conditioned suite at the Sheraton. He was here until the end of January so we made the best of our time together. With Brisdon it had been all sparks and fire; with Jock it wasn't lightning bolts but a steady stream of electricity. It felt comfortable. Maybe I was growing up.

Juan José insisted I invite Jock home for afternoon coffee. They had never met Brisdon so I couldn't disappoint them again. I was living with them by then. Rosa's children were growing and needing more space and Estralita was now the head cleaner at a golf club, closer to Independencia but working longer hours. My uncles had converted their sunroom into a bedroom and studio for me.

When Jock arrived that Sunday afternoon, Juan José set down a tray of Argentinian sweets made with vanilla dough, covered with dark chocolate and filled with *dulce de leche*. We could smell the rich aroma of coffee percolating in the kitchen. José Juan sat in his chair and smoked a cigarillo. Jock wanted to see my paintings so I pulled them all out from their hideaways to show him. He brought his camera to take pictures.

"What will you do with the photos?" I asked.

"Show them to some colleagues of mine," he answered as José Juan blew smoke rings into the air. "The international art world is run by a small and independently wealthy clique. I want to affiliate you with them and integrate you into it."

"And then what will happen?"

"If my instincts are correct, you may have to come to London."

José Juan's last smoke ring rose into the air like a phantom noose before it curled away. José Juan who understood everything we were saying, just stared at me with wide eyes because, as he told me later, I had become transparent, bathed in yellow sunlight coming through the glass doors of my studio.

"But I don't even have a passport."

"Then you should get one."

Jock Palmerston became my mentor. Over the next two years I continued to paint while Jock returned to Lima time after time, mostly for my sake.

"I want to be your agent," he told me on a visit to my uncles' house. José Juan was in the kitchen. I heard him say to Juan José in Spanish, "So that's what they're calling it these days."

"I would take a large commission," he warned me. "But you will make money with me, César."

"Enough to give back to my uncles and my Aunt Estralita?"

"As much as you want. But you are getting ahead of yourself, César."

He purchased my best canvasses. To make the transaction official, I had to present him with invoices in triplicate for a customs clearance so he could ship them to his London gallery.

José Juan continued to tutor me in English, relentlessly correcting my mistakes and making me repeat my verb tenses over and over. In the meantime, Juan José helped me secure my work visa for my trip to the United Kingdom. After all the effort and protocols and letters and paperwork and meetings in government offices with sour-faced officials under Peruvian flags and crests, the visa was just a small piece of paper attached to a blank page in my brand new passport. It allowed me six months in England. I wouldn't come back for seven years.

*   *   *

When I returned to Peru at the age of thirty-three, it was for my father's funeral. I was a British Citizen by then, able to abandon my Peruvian status and shed the ugly memories along with it. When I arrived back at our old house in Ayacucho, all the windows and all the mirrors and all the clocks had been covered in black cloth. I found my mother smaller than I remembered and stooped over. Dressed all in black she looked forlorn and more translucent than ever. She sat in a rocking chair the way she used to when she had read stories to us from an old book of fables, especially the tale of the Condor and the Jaguar which had scared Diego and made him cry. I had only wanted more.

Mama held on to me weeping during those first hours. My little brother Diego had become a handsome young man during my nineteen years away. He was broad-shouldered and big-boned like our father. He was starting to show a paunch.

"Be careful of that," I said patting him on the stomach.

Diego grinned ear to ear under his long moustache. He was doing up his police uniform jacket with its epaulettes and brass buttons in preparation for the full military funeral. He had followed in the General's footsteps. He had married a thin and mean-looking woman named Alicia who wore heavy makeup that made her resemble the drag-queens at the shows Jock took me to on Saturday nights near Leicester Square. She did not like me at all as I had tarnished the family values she was so painstakingly trying to uphold with one toddler in tow and another baby on the way. I had sullied her new family name, Acosta, just by returning here.

"So you are a famous artist," Diego said patting me on my back. "But no longer a Peruvian."

"Not famous yet," I replied, "but not struggling either. And I will always be Peruvian. After all, we are descended from Inca royalty."

"So our father believed."

"I need to ask, Diego, how did he die?"

"His heart gave out," my brother answered gravely, which was impossible because Edmundo didn't have a heart.

"So he didn't sweat to death," I said, and for a moment Diego's expression lightened. In the trace of his smile I witnessed him being released from his years of suffering under my father's iron fist. That encouraged me. "Now we're all at peace," I said to him.

As I stood with my family during the funeral, surrounded by rows of soldiers and police officers in full regalia, I knew my father's menacing warning to me was being buried along with him. Diego gave the eulogy but I couldn't focus on his words. I thought of Brisdon and how everything had ended because of my father's curse. Then there was a drum-roll and a band started to play a march that began off-tune until the sounds of their instruments blended together. Diego was at full attention, strapping and formidable. Looking at him now I saw how fate had switched our lives: I was supposed to be *Lieutenant* César Acosta. Instead, little Diego had to abandon his crayon drawings and watercolour paints, forever losing that brilliant world I knew lived hidden inside him.

"You can't choose your fate," María Rosa told me once. "But you can mould its shape."

My entire journey back to Peru was suffused in a kind of twilight sorrow. After saying farewell to Mama and Diego, and unable to avoid Alicia so I could kiss my little nephew good-bye, I travelled back to Lima to see Estralita and my uncles. Estralita was still cleaning at the golf club even though she had pains in her back and arthritis in her hands. She didn't want to stop working.

"I'll send you more money," I promised, "so you can retire."

"The devil makes work for idle hands," she replied.

Rosa had found another husband and had broken the spell that Estralita thought jinxed her family. Her two daughters had grown into gangly teenagers with rosy complexions and teasing eyes that reminded me of Luna before the fire.

My uncles had aged visibly since I left for London and didn't return as I had promised. But they didn't hold a grudge. They were not the type. I could tell their health was tenuous and they were thinner and more frail. José Juan had retired from the National Library. They spent their days dreaming of their youth in Argentina and I understood I had been that dream brought alive for them. They accompanied me to the airport to see me off and waved handkerchiefs as I disappeared through the security gate.

I knew it would be the last time I would see them.

*   *   *

As soon as I returned to London, Jock suggested that if I wanted to become more successful, I needed a hook, a moniker, a brand. We were having a night-cap in his drawing room with its elaborate crown mouldings, floor-to-ceiling floral draperies and rich Isfahan carpet. I was exhausted. I had been underway for twenty hours hop-scotching on various flights from Lima to London. I had no energy to unpack.

"Don't my paintings speak for themselves?"

"Yes, of course, but as an artist you need something to distinguish yourself from all the rest."

I sipped my cognac and relaxed. "What do you have in mind?"

"Take on a new persona for example."

"Like who?"

"Become a recluse."

"Like an outcast?" I sniffed. *Like returning to my youth in Peru...*

"Not exactly. You would stay away from the media, that's all. You wouldn't attend your shows. No one will know who you really are." He watched me with my nose in my snifter, thinking. "It's about the power of mystique, César. Why don't you sleep on it."

I did sleep on it. It stayed with me the entire night. Something was off and I couldn't put my finger on it. I enjoyed the idea of anonymity but what would I be losing in the process? I slept until noon the next day. "Just like a recluse," Jock joked while he poached some eggs for me.

"You remember that my first name isn't César?"

"All right," he said with hesitation.

I had his attention. "It's Luis. But no one's ever used it. Not even my family."

"Luis César Ángel Acosta," Jock spoke out. "That wouldn't make much of an acronym."

"If we rearrange it to César Ángel *Luis* Acosta, it comes out CÁLA," I suggested. "It means brook or stream in Spanish—"

The egg timer went off like a chime of approval. And that's when I became CÁLA. What I didn't tell Jock was that the real inspiration came from a darker place, from Atac*cala*. It was something only Brisdon would understand.

When CÁLA was born so was my self-induced seclusion as *The Shadow Artist*. The parties stopped. I was wiped off social media, something that was starting to become popular. Not being able to meet new people was difficult. As my fame expanded, my bubble shrank. My life became more restrictive. Over the next few years, my carefully orchestrated profile caught the public's attention as Jock had planned. "The hook has taken hold," he said, pleased with himself. Once again I felt shackled.

Originally, I set up my first studio on the top floor of Jock's Mayfair townhouse. He was happy to give me the entire floor because he found the air up there too stifling in summer and the heating too weak in winter. For me, it had the perfect light because of the atrium glass windows on the north side. But as my popularity grew, so did the size of my canvases. When they couldn't fit through the door we had to rent a large studio space in a warehouse in Fitzrovia. This allowed me to complete my first true signature works that would eventually lead me to celebrity status. They were my *Triumphs of Eternity*. I based them on a book I found in Jock's library, a nineteenth century English translation of Petrarch's *Triumphs*. They had been painted before but I gave them a more modern and disturbing interpretation in the spirit of Goya or Dali. They were the triumphs of eternity over time, over chastity and love, fame and death, and were, as one critic put it, *a terrible and tender splendour.*

*   *   *

For the next two years I spent most of my time working in the studio. As my art sold, Jock took his hefty commission. But I was also starting to feel the weight of his power over my work and my life like *The Triumphs of Jock over César.* Sometimes I felt I was nothing more than Jock Palmerston's creation. My seclusion brought on bouts of loneliness. I had a futon brought into the studio because there were nights when I couldn't be bothered going back to Mayfair. I didn't know how long I could keep this up this solitude.

My *Triumphs of Eternity* series was a critical and financial success but I knew from my Muse María Rosa that fortune and fame were fleeting. I couldn't allow myself a comfort zone: I needed to work on something more complex, more colossal than my *Eternities*. Then Jock received a letter from an American oil tycoon who wanted to commission a mural for the lobby of his new Manhattan office tower. He liked my work. Would I come out of seclusion to paint his mural?

"I think I should do it," I told Jock.

He furrowed his brow. "Absolutely not."

"Think of the exposure," I countered.

"And the press finding out all about you," he replied. "You will lose all we have gained, César."

We, I thought. By accepting a commission to work so far from London it was clear he was afraid of losing *us*.

The Texas magnate was Russell Matter Sr., but we were directed to send our response to Russell Matter Jr., the New York Project Manager. The Manhattan phone number was on the letterhead so when I was back in my studio I called without Jock knowing. Russell Jr. spoke with a lazy sort of drawl I found appealing, like there was a timbre of honesty in it.

The Matter offer to paint a mural in Manhattan seemed to be the right opportunity at the right time. I told Russell Matter Jr. I could be interested if certain conditions were met.

"Well then it's my right lucky day," he declared.

I spoke to Russell from my studio the next afternoon. And the next. There was always an excuse to call, to ask questions, to clarify expectations. We talked about baseball. We talked about soccer and the good-looking players from Argentina. We talked about horses and cattle. We talked about art. What we didn't talk about was our obvious attraction to the idea of each other. It wasn't long before Russell Matter Jr. flew the Concorde from New York to London with directions to my studio. On the day of his flight, I paced the studio floor waiting for him. I tried sketching ideas for the mural to impress him but nothing was working out. Again, I was trying too hard. Pages of failed attempts lay scattered on the cement floor. I watched the blending colours from the setting sun from my window. A murder of crows flew up from a tree and fluttered against a sky of brilliant pink. When the knock on the door finally

came I felt a queasy sensation, a strange anticipation I had
not felt for a very long time.

"Hello *Caesar.*" He said my name like the Roman
emperor. He was easily over six-foot-two with auburn hair
and a scruffy beard. He wore cowboy boots and a fringed
leather jacket and was completely opposite to what I had
pictured for a Manhattan property manager. I thought of
the John Wayne westerns I had seen at the one cinema in
Ayacucho when I was young. He held his cream-coloured
Stetson in one hand and a gift-wrapped box in the other.
The back of his hand was tattooed.

"Chocolates from the airport. I'm not good at gifts." He
laughed at himself which made him look boyish. When he
came in I offered him tea. He laughed again. Maybe he was
nervous. "You Brits and your tea. We don't drink tea in
Texas. Texas tea is a whole other story."

"How about some gin, then?"

"Wrong again."

"Let me guess. Bourbon."

"That's right. We should go out. For whiskey and some
dinner."

"I don't know if I should."

"You're on a pretty tight leash there, Caesar."

We took a taxi to *Simpson's in the Strand,* a place
where Russell could get a big slice of roast beef. Russell
loved the black London cabs, the way he could just walk in
and out of the back, with room to stretch his long legs.

Over dinner we talked about my recluse strategy and its
obvious flaws.

"A lone wolf is not an anchorite," he said, carving his
meat.

"That's a pretty big word."

"I have an MBA, Caesar."

"Why did you choose business?"

"Because they don't hand out degrees in rodeo, *pardner.*"

Afterwards, we ended up at Heaven. Russell spent the night dancing off his buzz and then downing more whiskey. He drew me onto the dance floor like I had done with Brisdon long ago at the Babylon nightclub. After that, when we were walking through Trafalgar Square, I asked him where he was staying.

"I dunno yet," he slurred.

"I only have a futon," I warned him.

"Hell, I'm used to sleeping in a barn." Then he whooped and his joyful, boozy voice carried across the empty square from lion to lion and we thought we could see the sky begin to lighten behind St Martin-in-the-Fields.

Later in the studio we were awakened by the shrill ringing of the telephone. By the clock on the wall it was already four in the afternoon. I scrambled to answer.

"How are you?" Jock asked.

My voice rasped out, "I'm fine."

"I called last night but you didn't pick up."

"Must have been out."

"You don't sound fine, César."

We left it at that. I crawled back under the covers. The October light spilling in through the wall of windows was already growing weaker. We had missed the day. Russell and I lay still for a long time staring at the high concrete ceiling.

"You're in trouble now," he teased.

When he extended his arm to pull me closer I saw it was tattooed with flames and roses with bleeding thorns all tightly entwined in blues and reds so that no pink skin showed through.

"I guess I'll find out," I replied. But it wasn't trouble at all because Russell had become my new-found freedom.

*   *   *

"I think you're making a mistake," Jock cautioned as we signed the contract for the Matter commission a few months later.

At first he didn't appear angry or upset but there was something simmering beneath his calm veneer.

"It's a lot of money," I pointed out. "I thought you'd be happy."

"Think of your future, César."

"I am."

When spring arrived, I flew to New York alone. I needed to see Matter Towers and explore the space for the mural. We had timed it so I could meet Russell's father, who would be in New York that week. Russell met me at the airport wearing his Stetson and cowboy boots and kissed me like a lost love returned, right in front of the crowds. No one seemed to care.

His apartment was on the Upper West Side near the Dakota, famous because of where John Lennon was shot. Once inside his hallway, Russell removed his Stetson and kicked off his boots.

"Do you prefer New York to Texas?" I asked.

"Yeah, they don't go for my kinda cowboy back home."

"What do you miss the most about home?"

"My horses. I have a couple of Andalusians, a black and a chestnut, the most beautiful creatures on the planet. Trained them myself."

I was anxious to see Matter Towers. It was early April and the air was crisp as we walked down Columbus Avenue. I was used to the bustle of London, the crowded tube, the jostling and dashing across the narrow streets but people moved differently in Manhattan, less frenetically and with longer strides. The motion seemed choreographed. When we arrived at Russell Towers, the entire block was scaffolded. I looked up. I couldn't see the top. The building demanded respect by the sheer power of the structure rising above us. I could almost feel the pressure of its weight as we walked inside. We had to wear hard hats. The lobby soared four stories high. I had a whiff of marble dust, the same smells Bernini would have breathed in as he sculpted.

"There." He pointed to a huge blank wall. "Your canvas awaits, *Señor*."

I looked up, my head back, the optic nerves of my eyes filling with serotonin, sharpening my mind, pushing my ideas into a cosmos of possibilities.

"It's like my feet aren't touching the ground," I admitted.

"If you think your head is in the clouds now..."

Before I could ask him what he meant, Russell had rounded up the foreman. Soon the three of us were shooting upwards to the top of the building in an elevator lined with plywood. Another staircase took us to a door leading outside. The roof was flat here to accommodate a helicopter landing pad. "Watch your step," the foreman warned. "And stay away from the edge. A strong gust could lift you right up—"

The wind carried the scent of the ocean. I hadn't smelled the sea since my uncles took me to *La Rosa Náutica* in Miraflores. Then, with the sun behind us, the vista of the city expanded out on all sides to the rivers and the harbours where the waves glinted in the sunlight. The twin towers of the World Trade Center were at the farthest end, the anchor at the tip of Manhattan or, as Russell put it, like the two big front teeth of a yokel. We were higher than many of the buildings around us. I had a moment of vertigo so strong I had to take hold of Russell's arm.

"Whoa there buddy, you all right?" I nodded. We were above the birds. We were above almost every other person in Manhattan, moving like ants busy in the lifecycle of this incredible colony—and I suddenly knew exactly what I would paint in the mural.

*   *   *

I met with Russell Matter Sr. for the first time a few days later. I was able to finish a few preliminary sketches of my new idea. The unfinished boardroom on the first floor smelled of sawdust and wet cement. "Daddy" wasn't who I imagined. He wasn't old or cattle-fed. He didn't talk with a cigar between his teeth. He wore a perfectly tailored business suit—*bespoke* as Jock would say—and his hair was long and silver-grey. He was striking, like his son. He shook my hand, genuinely pleased to meet me. "Junior" had spoken enthusiastically about my work, he said. I reminded him there could be no press release with my face or image. He understood. He kept checking his Rolex as if he had somewhere else to be. The rich have no time to enjoy time, I thought.

If New York revitalized my self-esteem, Russell removed the last of the shackles from my self-induced prison. I still had tall barriers installed in front of the mural to keep prying eyes from observing me as I worked. When I wasn't painting, I was wandering through the MET or the MoMA. If Russell couldn't come along because he was busy at work, then he would join me afterwards, dressed in a fine pin-striped suit and cowboy boots. We would meet for drinks at the Oyster Bar under Grand Central Station or at the White Horse in the West Village. At one Texas-themed gay bar that Russell knew, he introduced me to his friends: Lola, the flamboyant manager of the Queen of Hearts drag show in the Village; a writer couple who were at totally opposite ends of the political spectrum and threw elaborate and decadent parties; a shy accountant with his gentle manner at odds with his booming baritone when he sang in off-off

Broadway shows; friends from Jamaica and Puerto Rico and a florid Irishman fresh off the plane from Londonderry with hands and feet two sizes too big for his body. Then there was Charmian, who had the same name as Cleopatra's trusted servant but who had served Leona Helmsley, the Cleopatra of Manhattan, before *The Queen of Mean* was sent to prison. They were a multifarious crew of singers and artists, designers and stock-brokers. A late arrival was a jeweller named Jenny Chang who had a tiny shop on Seventh Avenue that was so dilapidated and covered by graffiti that it smacked of something illicit.

"Interesting ring," Jenny complimented while my hand rested on the tall bar. "Very nice moonstone. Sri Lankan?"

"No, Peruvian." I wanted to change the subject. I never talked about Brisdon or what happened to us at Ataccala.

"He rubs it every time he gets anxious," Russell added. "Like it grounds him."

On another evening, at the Queen of Hearts, Lola sidled up to us while the musicians were tuning up and the showgirls were fixing their peacock feather headdresses to their glittering hair.

"So I hear you like to give your money away," she challenged. She reminded me of Carlos under all that face paint.

"Not all of it. But there are people I know who need it more."

"Caesar's a misanthropic philanthropist." Russell clapped me on the back. "That's why I love him." It was the first time he said anything like that.

I only returned to London when my visa expired. But my stay there was short-lived. In New York the mural had created a sensation at the grand opening of Matter Towers. Russell Matter Sr. kept his word and my secret identity remained intact.

At dinner at the townhouse one night I told Jock I was moving to New York.

"I know," he just said and poured more red wine into my glass.

"You know?"

"I'm no fool."

"I would never accuse you of being that."

He was chewing his salmon very slowly as if his tongue was searching out the bones that could choke him to death.

"You know, César, you remind me of Che Guevara just before he was executed."

"That's quite the non-sequitur."

He went on. "Che was thirty-nine when he was gunned down, not much older than you are now. You know he spent time in Peru? He was going to become a doctor. He was going to make the world a better place." Jock dabbed his napkin against his pink lips. "Then he got into the wrong crowd with the Castro brothers. He became just like Shining Path. A guerrilla fighter. Che started killing people instead of healing them. And the strangest thing is that he will always be hailed as a hero."

"I don't know what you're talking about." My knife and fork clanged loudly against my plate.

He picked up the bottle and topped up my glass even though I had only taken a few sips. He raised his glass for a toast so I did the same, reluctantly. But his eyes were ugly and his tone threatening.

"You never know what the future will bring or who will bring you through it. Remember that."

*   *   *

If London is a painting, New York is a photograph. When I arrived back in Manhattan, everything seemed sharper and more edgy. The city's rhythm was hypnotic, a macrocosm of extremes, peaceful in Central Park yet exhilarating at Times Square, and above it all the taxi horns a cacophony of musical notes. Summers brought a heat unknown in London, reminding me of the costal deserts of Peru. The subway grates blew hot air upwards, smelling of sandalwood and rust. New York was a desert of steel and cement and glass with a beating heart. I knew I belonged here.

I walked everywhere. During the day the pavement shimmered. At night, the sound of my footsteps was absorbed into the slabs. The poor and the destitute lay covered in cardboard in the shadows. In Peru the children were the face of the poor. You could give them bread and cheese or a few coins, touch their small arms, rub their heads and watch them smile shyly before they moved on. There was something still hopeful left in that.

One day as I was passing a music store the thumping percussion of Donna Summer filled the air. Then a car pulled up to a stoplight next to me and the radio was blasting music from Saturday Night Fever. This all triggered a memory of Brisdon so strong that I couldn't shake it for days on end. I started seeing Brisdon everywhere, on the streets, in the bars and restaurants, disappearing down the subway stairs or entering an elevator just as the doors were closing. The back of someone going through the revolving doors of Matter Towers was Brisdon's back. The hand that slid the show tickets through the glass slot was Brisdon's hand. Once at the MET, I was convinced I saw him crossing the front lobby. I lost sight of him. I always lost sight of him. I was trying not to look up, trying not to see Brisdon dressed as a mannequin in the shop windows when I stepped from the curb and into the path of a speeding taxi.

The accident stopped traffic. The police and ambulance arrived. A crowd was gathering around me as I lay sprawled in the gutter. In between the spasms that stabbed at my leg, I pulled myself up to the curb. A pair of hands helped me, a soft pair of hands, Brisdon's hands. I looked up.

"You walked right out in front of me!" It was the taxi driver, a short man with a shaved head.

At the hospital the doctor told me the accident had crushed my right knee so that they would have to operate. While I was being pushed in a wheelchair back into my room, Russell was there, pale as a ghost, pacing back and forth like a caged tiger. The orderly helped me into the narrow bed and raised one of the side rails so I wouldn't fall out. Russell watched from the far wall.

"Are you all right?" he called from the other side of the hospital room.

"What's the matter?" I asked after the orderly left.

"I hate hospitals," he answered.

"No one likes hospitals," I commiserated.

He appeared stricken. "I'm sorry Caesar, I can't be here!"

But he didn't leave. Reluctantly, he sat beside me and took my hand. It took some prodding. Russell's aversion to hospitals stemmed from the time his father discovered his predilection for other boys when he was sixteen. But instead of Edmundo's tactic of walloping his son senseless and winding threats around his neck like a garrote, Russell Sr. instilled a different kind of cruelty. He admitted his son into a conversion therapy clinic at a Dallas hospital. Russell underwent a series of therapies, *aversive treatments* they called them, severe methods of applying electric shocks to his hands and genitals, and being given nausea-inducing drugs while they presented him with homoerotic stimuli. Like training rats in a maze.

"I wasn't stupid. I knew that I wasn't a deviant or mentally ill and that this treatment would alter nothing. I endured as much as I could and then I ran away. I lived in the streets. I did some things I wasn't proud of. My father found me in an alley with a needle in my arm. I was shaking all over. He took me back with him and we made a pact that I would keep my personal life to myself. I don't talk about it, Caesar, just like you don't talk about your life in Peru. I'd rather jump in front of a speeding subway train or off the roof of Matter Towers than be incarcerated in a room like this. I'm sorry." I understood all too well. We never mentioned it again.

There was a scar after my knee healed. "It adds character," Russell said. "Scars are natural tattoos."

I needed to get back to work. Gilles Sevigny, my new North American agent, found me studio space in a converted warehouse in Soho. I took possession on a sweltering July morning as children played at the gushing fire hydrant beneath my wall of windows, squealing and shrieking as they jumped through the jets of water. Even though the loft was noisy, it had the light I wanted and the height I needed. It was large enough to live in and had a full modern kitchen which was an improvement on my single hotplate in Fitzrovia. At night I could hear the boom-boom percussion from a neighbouring night club and, oddly, it didn't remind me of the nightclubs of New York but transported me back to Babylon and to Brisdon, as if recent memories were never as powerful as distant ones.

Soon I began working on *The Art of Dying*, the canvas that would define my life's work. It was early September 2001 and no one in Manhattan knew what was on the horizon. I was working on some sketches in my studio that sunny Tuesday morning. Then the earth shuddered. By the end of the day the ashes from the twin towers had settled over all the parked cars and the street lamps and the roofs and balconies and the windowsills in my neighbourhood. The dust of the dead hung in the air above us, enveloping us as it travelled from Battery Park, around and around the mountains of rubble and steel beams sticking out like fractured bones, up West Broadway and across Canal Street to land on the end of my paint brush.

I wouldn't let Russell or Gilles or anyone into my studio while I was working. I was driven by collective grief and personal outrage. Ataccala was the base, the twin towers the motivation. There was something both divine and wicked that lived inside each one of us, an angel and a monster, and I knew from experience that we were power-less against their resolve. I was resolved to expose the dark-ness in us all.

When I came home at night, I couldn't shake this melancholy mood, just like the pallor of incredulity and anxiety that hung over Manhattan like a fog that wouldn't lift, even after weeks and months.

*   *   *

"Let's get out of the city," Russell suggested. It was mid-October and we were in the kitchen. The cane I was still using to help me walk was leaning against the counter. The morning light was streaming through the tall east windows, bathing everything in a suffused, honeyed glow.

"Where were you thinking?"

"How about driving up to Providence. We can visit my friend Sammy. And driving along the east coast is beautiful this time of year."

We left early the next morning. I put down the window and felt the rush of cool air over my face. We stopped near Providence for lunch. Then we headed south-east, across Mount Hope Bay to the southern shore of Rhode Island on the Atlantic Ocean. We pulled into a laneway that led us to a Victorian mansion with a wrap-around veranda and a grassy knoll with a private beach of rolling sand dunes. Russell parked next to a peeling sign that read The Little Grape. It was a wine-themed bed and breakfast situated right on the Cape Cod National Seashore, secluded and exclusive and a best kept secret, Russell assured me.

I tried to let go of the city. When I stepped from the car, I was overwhelmed by the wind from the ocean. Here, the Atlantic had a different scent from the Pacific that had pressed over Lima. This ocean didn't press, it pulled. The smell of the Pacific had been sour. This fragrance was sweet and silvery and its sea foam carried a whiff of secrecy.

The front door opened and a young woman hurried down the steps calling "*Russell!*" as if he was a long lost love returning home. She was wearing a flowing silk robe and her skin was milky white and her closely-cropped hair was black as coal.

"Sammy!" She ran right into his arms and hugged him with her eyes squeezed tight.

"You don't come back enough!" she chastised.

"You look wonderful Sammy. This is Caesar."

She reminded me of a China doll that used to sit on a shelf in Luna's room before the fire had melted away the synthetic locks and eyelashes.

"It's pronounced *César* by the way. And you are the infamous Samantha?"

"Only my grandmother calls me that. I'm Sammy and definitely not infamous. Are you hungry? I left the buffet out for you. We've partnered with a new vineyard. Their Pinot Grigio is incredible. Come in, come in."

It was early afternoon and there were still a few guests in the dining room. Two men together at a table by the fireplace glanced up at us.

"We stopped on the way for lunch," Russell confessed. "But I'm parched for that Pinot."

Sammy showed us to a table by the window that looked out to the dunes and the ocean beyond. She went to fetch the wine and an ice bucket. Then she joined us.

"How do you two know each other?" I asked.

"From UT Austin," she replied. She didn't have Russell's southern drawl.

"You're not from Texas then?"

"No. But I chose Texas because I like them cowgirls, eh Russ?"

"No one calls me Russ anymore."

"I've heard you called worse." She filled our glasses.

"We were in marketing class together," he explained.

"I went on to be an entrepreneur. Russ was training to take over from his daddy. How did that turn out?"

"It's not all silver spoons, Sammy."

"Still, I'm surprised you went to work for Russell Sr. of all people. After what he did to you."

She suddenly looked stricken like she had let the cat out of the bag.

"He knows," Russell told her.

Then Sammy waved it all away and laughed, resting her hand on my arm.

"Dear César. It's like I've known you all my life." Her nails were short; her hands were used to scrubbing and laundering and cooking. "You have a rich aura."

I smiled. Russell lifted his wine glass. "Here's to rich auras, then."

I planned on reading by the water and Russell wanted to drop into some well-known antique shops. Sammy boasted having a large library on the main floor. *Take a book and leave a book*, was her motto.

After we unpacked I went down to see the library. One of the men from the dining room was sitting in a wingback chair in front of book-lined shelves extending to the ceiling. It was too late to hobble out.

He looked up. "Hello."

"Sorry, I didn't mean to disturb you."

"That's okay, I was just killing time."

He set a book down on the table in front of him. That's when I saw the cover. It had the same brown paper dust wrapper that I remembered from Brisdon's journal.

"That book—"

"Yes, *The Tibetan Book of the Dead*. Do you know it?"

"In a way."

He handed it to me. It was heavy. "It's a rare copy," he continued. "I did my thesis on Tibet and Vajrayana literature so I'm familiar with these esoteric doctrines. I was surprised to find it here."

"What is it exactly?"

"Books of the dead are about spells and prayers for someone entering the afterlife. Whether it's Egyptian or Tibetan or Theban, it all represents the same thing."

When I opened it I expected to see *Dear Karen* in Brisdon's handwriting. But inside were printed pages of text with footnotes and diagrams. On one page a buddha sat on a ring of leaves surrounded by a mirror, a conch, a lyre, a vase with flowers, and a holy cake. It was the effigy of a dead person. I flipped through the pages and stopped to read that a body, hacked to pieces, would revive again even if repeated hacking caused intense pain and suffering.

He must have noticed my expression. "It's an anthropological masterpiece. It's about the art of dying."

"*The art of dying*," I repeated out loud. I wanted to know more. "May I?"

"Yes, certainly."

I took *The Tibetan Book of the Dead* back to our suite. Russell was lounging on the bed reading a tourist magazine. I had to forget about the book for now. We stayed in for the evening, ordering dinner and wine and breathing in the clear air through the partly open terrace doors that looked out to the ocean. But for most of the evening I was somewhere else—I was back in Peru, back on that starless, moonless night and inside the painting that I knew would become *The Art of Dying*. Later, when sleep finally came, it folded over me like the earth from the graves at Ataccala.

* * *

The next morning Russell headed out to Providence with Sammy. I wanted to feel the sun on my face so I took the book and dragged an Adirondack chair down to the edge of the lawn facing the beach. I wrapped myself in a wool blanket against the cool ocean breeze.

The Tibetan Book of the Dead brought me insight and inspiration so I could build my nightmare painting of that night near Ataccala. Some of the book's passages grabbed me by the throat. I was afraid it might have been an affront to my belief in Jesus but it wasn't. Instead it was fascinating, the similarities uncanny, the sentiments universal. *The Tibetan Book of the Dead* was a prayer; the *bardo* was purgatory; the light was God; and the Wrathful and Peaceful Demons were Fallen and Risen Archangels who emanated from our own hearts and minds. I read about the ropes of death, the cutting off of heads, the pulling out of hearts, and the dining on intestines and brains. There was eating the flesh and gnawing the bones of the dying who were incapable of dying—a testament to everlasting life set down in Sanskrit a thousand years ago.

I closed my eyes. That was when I heard someone calling me, a voice you know isn't there, words that aren't words, a muffled and indiscernible language from another world. I put the book down and looked around. At first I thought it was Sammy but she and Russell wouldn't be back yet. Then I thought it was one of the guests but everyone, including the professor of anthropology, had checked out. Then I heard it again, and for a moment I thought it was my mother's voice, somehow caught on the ocean winds, and I thought: *she has died.*

I stood up from the chair. I felt cold. I draped the blanket around my shoulders. I picked up my cane and trudged through the sand to the water's edge. The dunes were high enough that I couldn't see past them. They were a ridge of miniature desert mountains. Grass grew on their tops like wisps of hair.

"*Mama—*" I called and the wind spit my words back at me. There was nothing but the wind and the waves and the seagulls now. I was filled with an incredible sadness.

I kept walking along the dunes to shake away this feeling I had, this reattachment to my past that was suddenly heavy. I used my cane to manage the uneven sand. My knee was smarting. I kept walking until I came to an inlay of rocks and clambered over them and continued along the beach as the waves lashed and crashed, trying to draw me into the sea. Seagulls gathered above, circling like buzzards.

I thought I heard the voice again, or it could have been the seagull cries as they swooped down over the dunes. I followed them inland until there was nothing else around me, just a vast emptiness like the desert sands of Peru. That was when I saw her buried in the sand, a girl with fair hair, just her head and small shoulder sticking out and a tiny hand with nails painted pale rose. Over time the wind and the rain and the ocean spray had worn away her sandy grave. It brought me back to all my sorrows: another victim in a hidden grave. A gust of wind threw sand in my face, into my mouth. I moved back and then sat down hard on the sand and wept.

I waved away the seagulls who spotted her. I sat there for a long time, thinking of different prayers, thinking about all the books of the dead, all the Ataccalas. Nothing would ever change. I kept my eyes shut. I was back on the road from Ataccala with Brisdon and he was screaming at me

and I was pulling him away from the pits where the massacred lay buried. The ghost of Brisdon returned to me, as
if he, too, were dead. I could hear more voices calling out
from beyond the lighthouses that dotted the shoreline, and
whose lonesome beams trolled the sea, raising the ghosts
from all the foundered ships lying on the ocean floor.

"*César!*"

"*Caesar!*"

Brisdon was grabbing hold of the blanket still wrapped
around my shoulders and pulling me away from the dead...

"*Oh Jesus!*"

"*He's in shock,*" a woman's voice spoke, out of place,
out of time. It was Sammy.

I opened my eyes. I was back on the shore of the
Atlantic and I was shivering. Brisdon was gone and Russell
was standing over me, just a dark shape as he blocked out
the pale sun, sinking to the horizon. Sammy was standing by
the body of the girl, being careful not to disturb anything.

"I'll go back to call the police," she said. "Will you be
all right here?"

"Yes, yes."

Russell's face was still in shadow like a dark angel. We
huddled together under the blanket as the air turned brisk
and the sun set beyond the dunes. He leaned in and
whispered, "We were afraid you had drowned."

"I'm sorry."

When the police arrived, they set up stakes and tents
and yellow tape and asked us dozens of questions. I knew I
shouldn't have been worried, but I was nervous and afraid,
even with Russell there, even if I was four thousand miles
from Peru. It would never leave me, this dread that General
Edmundo Francisco Acosta had instilled in me. Inevitably, I
found myself in the same situation I had tried so hard to
avoid when I left Brisdon that morning all those years ago,
an innocent witness to another atrocity.

"Explain to me why you came out this far?" The constable was speaking to me, a large man with a permanently furrowed brow. He was trying to catch me in a lie, to incriminate me. "What brought you to *this* point?"

What was I to tell them? That my mother had called out to me from three thousand miles away to this spot?

"The seagulls," I answered. "They kept circling and I wanted to find out why."

A half-truth was better than a full lie.

"Who is she?" Russell asked the constable. A forensic team had already assembled and they were bringing the girl out of her coffin of sand. I had to turn away.

"You don't live around here then?" the constable asked.

"We live in Manhattan," Russell repeated, "Central Park West."

They're always suspicious, I thought, it's in their DNA. Because the guilty always return to the scene of the crime.

"We've been looking for her for a long time," he finally answered. He didn't disclose any more.

"How long do we need to stay here?" Russell asked.

The sun had set. The police escorted us back to the guest house with flashlights. I was certain Russell knew there was more to my story but he didn't question me. When we were back he joined Sammy in the kitchen while I ran a hot bath in our suite. Afterwards, having retrieved the book that had so captured me, I lay on the bed in a bath robe reading about striking and slaying and licking human brains and tearing out the hearts from corpses. My eyes felt wet, as if they were brimming in a sea of primordial blood.

"Are you all right, Caesar?" Russell had come into the room with some warm cookies Sammy had baked for us.

All the chants, I thought, *all the prayers I should have said...*

I just said, "Russell, I need to call home. To Peru."

"Do you want to make the call now or can it wait until we get back?"

I looked up from the book. What if this was all for nothing? "It can wait."

When we returned to the New York apartment, the answering machine light was blinking. There were five messages from my mother who had not died. It was about my little brother Diego. He had been caught in the cross-fire of army patrols while fighting a Shining Path column that had resurfaced in Ayacucho—the resurgence of *Sendero Luminoso* our enemy now that my father was gone. Diego was the only fatality.

*   *   *

I never found out what happened to the little girl or why she was buried in the dunes. Nor could I return to Ayacucho for my little brother's funeral because by now it was too late. I spoke with my mother on the phone. She talked in whispers and I realized she was a mere trace of herself now. My widowed sister-in-law Alicia came on the line to tell me to stay in New York but to send money. There were four children by then and apparently my little Diego had been battling a gambling addiction that had left them broke. I gave in to her, of course, for everyone else's sake, and because I understood his misery and the vices he must have sought out to help mask his solitude.

When my birthday arrived that year, I pined away the day, restless and unprepared for what was ahead. That night, Russell presented me with a surprise gift. He un-buttoned his shirt to expose a bandage across his chest. When he pulled it off the words *César Por Siempre* was arced across his heart in a beautiful cursive font.

"*Vaquero loco!*" I called out. He just stood there beaming at me. "At least you spelled my name right."

Afterwards we drank tequila and Russell danced shirt-less to *Livin' La Vida Loca*, and we laughed and he fell back onto the sofa with me. Up close I could see the skin around the lettering of his tribute to me had turned red.

"You should put the bandage back on," I suggested.

"Too late now."

"Doesn't it sting?"

"Like it's on fire," he replied.

That was the beginning of Russell being on fire.

*   *   *

Russell started having night sweats and we thought it was an infection from his new tattoo. The doctor prescribed peni-cillin. The symptoms went away, the tattoo healed and he paraded around shirtless as much as possible when at home, when he was at the gym, and when he jogged through Central Park as spring weather warmed the city. A few weeks later he was on fire again. I noticed the sweat on his brow during the night. The sheets were soaking wet the next morning. When he felt better we went dancing at The Monster. But the next day he didn't bounce back. Tired and hungover, he slept the whole day and through the next night.

"I'm getting too old for this," he said but seemed to recover again.

All the same, he was gradually losing weight. There was a noticeable gap at the neck of his dress shirts. I ignored it the way we can push a disturbing thought to the back of our minds. I kept busy in my studio. Months would go by and Russell would appear much better. Meanwhile, these were exciting times for me. The Chicago MCA wanted to secure *The Art of Dying* for its permanent collection.

I went with my agent Gilles to Chicago. I kept out of the spotlight but I wanted to tour the gallery to see where my painting would be displayed and then sign the necessary paperwork in my hotel suite. Russell didn't join us. I spoke to him on the phone while I was away. The calls were brief. He was a man of few words now. When I got back from Chicago he poured me a whiskey, sat me down, and told me he had finally gone to a private clinic for tests.

"What kind of tests?"

"It's not good, Caesar."

"Is it AIDS?" I had to ask.

"No, God no. I wouldn't do that to you, Caesar. It's cancer."

Those next days and weeks lay like heavy stones on our backs. I began to hate the letter *L*. It could stand for *Light*, *Liberty* and *Luck* but it also stood for *Lymphocytic Leukaemia*.

At Christmas Russell returned home to Texas to visit his family. He wanted to break the news of his illness in person. I offered to come along but he said, *No, please, let me do this alone.*

While he was at home in Austin, I decided to visit Jock in London. Other than Russell, Jock was the only family I had left. He had forgiven me for leaving him. My mother had died not long after my brother Diego. The weight on her heart had grown too heavy and it had simply stopped while she was reaching to clasp a crucifix to pray for her dead son. Soon after, Rosa wrote to tell me that Estralita had passed away peacefully. My uncles were also gone. The money I sent them came back from the bank, *Account Closed.* It was as if they had finally vanished like they had feared would happen during Argentina's purge. I felt abandoned.

I didn't mention anything about Russell's illness to Jock. I had promised to stay until the first week in January. New Year's Eve had always been special for us. There was a dusting of snow over Mayfair when I arrived at the townhouse. He greeted me with a hug because after so long, hurt and malice fade and happier memories survive.

"You don't change a bit, César."

I thought he looked old. His hair was thinning and there were puffy pouches under his eyes and crow's feet when he smiled.

Everything else was the same, the chipped corner of the dining room wainscoting where I once had pushed my chair back too hard, the artwork along the dun and ochre coloured walls. Even the smell, the slightly musty odour of a townhouse built in the 1800's with its sash windows and Georgian floor tiles. Only we were not the same, Jock and I.

He offered me a whiskey from the bar next to the freshly cut Christmas tree festooned with twinkling lights and glistening ornaments and topped with a golden angel.

He poured out two drinks and asked, "How's Russell?"

I deflected by asking, "Where's your friend?" Jock had started seeing someone and they were planning to travel to Greece together.

"In Mykonos," he replied, twisting the cap back on the bottle.

"With someone else?"

"I'm afraid so."

"I'm sorry."

"It was mutual. He was too old for me anyway."

"How old is he?"

"Forty." We laughed. "You know me—cradle robber."

We sipped our drinks. An awkward silence followed and the path forward seemed uncertain. I missed my chance to steer the conversation from its inevitable conclusion because he said more emphatically, "And *Russell?*"

"He has cancer." We stared at each other.

"What kind of cancer, César?"

Not the good kind, I thought. "A type of leukaemia. It's bad, Jock."

He put his hand on my knee. It was reddish and speckled with liver spots. I covered it with mine.

"I'm sorry César," he said. "He's brave."

"You don't even know him."

"Whoever heard of a cowardly cowboy?" I smiled at that. "Where is he now? In hospital?"

"God no. He won't go near a hospital. He's gone back to Texas to be with his family."

"You never know what the fickle fates will deal out, César."

"He's not brave, Jock, he's bull-headed. We both ignored the symptoms." I took a sip from my drink. It burned my throat. "I should have known."

"It's not your fault, César."

"The doctor told me that if we had caught it early he may have stood a chance. He won't take chemo. He won't go into any hospital or clinic."

I didn't tell him why. We sat for a while not speaking. I finished my whiskey. Jock got up to pour me another. The Christmas lights were blinking on and off.

"I was throwing a Christmas party tomorrow with you as the special guest. A surprise, actually. I'll cancel it now."

"No, please don't. It's fine, really. I would enjoy it. Who's coming?"

"If I tell you then nothing will be a surprise. Allow me that."

"That's fair."

The party did cheer me up. Jock must have said something because our small circle of friends were subdued as they arrived, bearing red and ivory poinsettias, festively wrapped boxes and Christmas bags with wine and spirits. As the evening progressed, the food and wine and the music unravelled the tense chord that wrapped invisibly around us. Jock was the ultimate host, making sure everyone's glass was full and no one was left out of a conversation. I never fell in love with him but I remembered why I loved him. Then he caught me under the mistletoe and the guests applauded and cheered as if the long years behind us had finally disappeared.

*   *   *

When I came back from London in January, Russell hadn't returned from Texas so I spent all my time in the studio. Then early one January morning in the weak and icy light of dawn, I created a new colour. It was a combination of cold copper, verdigris, ruby and rust, so rich and strange that it was impossible to describe. I used it to paint my next canvas, an abstract work I titled *The Spirit of Russell.* I mixed more and more of that shade of sadness because I knew I would never be able to mix it again, like the colour of the dust from the hooves of the Spanish horses galloping on a Texas ranch in twilight. María Rosa once told me there were no new colours in the spectrum, and I wished she were here now to see the combination I had created, to stand with her and be surrounded by and immersed in *Russell,* and to rejoice as if I had discovered a new planet or a star. *Good job, César,* I could hear her say, *you have imagined the unimaginable.*

A week later Russell returned visibly diminished. His skin was turning to a grey pallor before my eyes. I was afraid he would become translucent like my mother and would float up and get caught in the fabric of the canopy bed above us. I watched him sleep. His breathing was raspy. His cheeks were hollow. His hair was thinning. The skin on his back was barely warm against my hand. He was becoming the effigy in my book of the dead.

One evening in July he handed me his bloodstone ring, a gift from his father on his twenty-first birthday, after they had begrudgingly accepted each other's differences.

"Take this," he said as if it were a parting gift. "It keeps falling off my hand."

That night I awoke and Russell wasn't next to me. I called out. I went into every room. I noticed Russell's office keys were missing from the tray by the door. Why would he go there now? I had a terrible feeling. I threw on some clothes and found one lonesome cab trolling along Amsterdam. I told the driver to take short cuts even though there was no traffic. When I got to the building, I rapped on the entrance door *clack-clack-clack* against the glass with the bloodstone ring on my hand. The old security guard shuffled up, recognized me, and unlocked the door.

"Mr. Matter has gone up to his old office," he said locking the door behind us. "He's not looking so good, sir."

The mural loomed over us as if the Inca gods had foreshadowed all of this: that the history of the world, of Russell and everyone we knew, would end with a whimper.

"Can you take me to the roof, please?" I could hardly get the words out. The guard just looked at me, not understanding. I was already moving towards the elevators. "I think Mr. Matter went to the roof."

The elevator ride took eons as if time was endless and cruel. We kept glancing at each other but we said nothing. We traversed a long hallway and climbed a set of stairs to find the roof of the door unlocked. I pushed it open and was back out into the hot July night, a hundred storeys above the ground. The expanse of the roof in the dark made it hard to visualize its edges beyond the spotlights. When I called out for Russell the wind carried away my voice and then killed it. I ran out to the empty helipad, all instincts of vertigo forgotten, and saw his shadow moving on the other side. I ran forward. He was climbing the balustrade. I don't think he heard me calling. His back was to me and he was looking down. I had to think fast. If a gust of wind took him he could be gone in an instant.

"*Russell, wait!*" I shouted. That's when he turned as if he had heard me. One of the enormous spotlights caught his expression and he looked as if there was a stampede of Andalusians galloping towards him and he was back in Texas in the open fields of his childhood under the maddening sun, and he was free.

We were both suspended in that moment as he fell backwards over the edge and out of sight.

*   *   *

It was a scorching July in Manhattan, hot enough to fry an egg on the sidewalk. Russell Matter flew his son's remains back home to Texas for the burial, where it was even hotter. He acted as if I was to blame.

"You may as well have put a shotgun to his head and pulled the trigger," he had snarled. "You did nothing to save him." I had no energy to argue.

When I arrived in Austin for the funeral, a car was waiting for me but I didn't see Russell Sr. until much later. It was an evening service. I was not asked to speak. I was standing alone behind the mourners, a cluster of the wealthiest families in Texas, some of them looking at me with a disdain I hadn't encountered for years. The dark world of bigotry and injustice had circled back upon me like I was doomed to this type of intolerance forever. *César Por Siempre.*

Russell's father cancelled the lease on the apartment. Gilles said he knew a good family lawyer but I refused to fight. I just asked Gilles to help me move some of our personal possessions to the studio before the movers arrived to cart everything away.

"What are your plans?" he asked me amongst the boxes piled on the cement floor.

"Maybe I'll disappear. Would anyone notice?"

But I didn't head off to a mountain in Tibet or an island in the Pacific as I had sometimes threatened. In the years following Russell's suicide, I became more of a recluse than ever. I kept working. A prestigious gallery in Toronto was developing a retrospective exhibition of my work. I received a vanilla envelope with the embossed TAM logo. Inside was a letter from J. B. Noxon, Curator, on crisp white letterhead confirming the opening date of the exhibition: October 31st, 2015. And it was signed *Brisdon.*

I didn't want to return to the limelight but I couldn't refuse this opportunity to see Brisdon again, no matter how painful it could be. After all, in my new-found solitude I was finally returning to my old self from Peru, the outcast and loner I was worried I would become again. But, somehow, I was happy with my sketch pad and charcoal pencils, needing little and missing nothing. As Estralita used to say, *You often become what you fear the most.*

Gilles encouraged me to go to the opening. "Don't throw in the towel just yet. Russell would kick your ass." He was right. A few days later I spoke with Fiona Tamaddon who said that the curator wouldn't be there. I thought I had made a big mistake, but it was decided: I would show up for an exhibition opening for the first time in my career, but in disguise. There would be works I hadn't seen for a long time including a scaled-down replica of my mural at Matter Towers. They had even obtained *The Spirit of Russell* from a private collector who had been so awed by the colour, he had bought it on sight. I met Fiona Tamaddon and when we arrived at the exhibition floor the gallery was already filling up with guests. The kitschy candlelight flickered and a plague doctor nodded to us as he walked by. I was thinking about using images of the plague in a painting when Doctor Death removed his mask in front of *The Art of Dying* and it *was* Brisdon after all, it was so unbelievably perfect. The next thing I knew, Fiona Tamaddon was taking me to him.

The rest is history. Fiona took my arm to pull me away from Brisdon before we had a chance to really speak. The man dressed as a sheik tapped his microphone and announced to the guests that the renowned artist CÁLA was among them. *Gasps! Applause!* Chatter rippled through the crowd. Later, I was whisked away to the safety of the museum offices to remove my disguise. I passed an office door with a nameplate that read: *John Brisdon Noxon, Curator.* I saw Brisdon's desk and chair, where he had been sitting while I had worked at my easel in Soho, separated by curved time and invisible space.

But the past is doomed to repeat itself. Brisdon disappeared again, as he did when I first embraced him in the thundering hallway of Babylon. *The truth always catches up with you,* Estralita also told me one night in Independencia when she saw me remove the medallion from its hiding place to give it to Brisdon. She must have always known about my darker side. And still, she had loved me.

I undressed and wrapped the hotel bathrobe around me and settled onto the bed. I considered my options. Then I reached over to the phone and pushed the button for the front desk.

"I need to extend my stay," I told the voice at the other end.

I could hear the clicking of a computer keyboard. "Of course, sir. I will leave your reservation open-ended. Have a good night."

After a few hours of tossing and turning, I switched on the lights and got up. I pulled the robe back around me. I paced the room the way I used to do in my studio, the way Brisdon used to do in his Lima apartment when he thought I was sleeping. I used to watch him from the bed as he scribbled in his book of the dead. He would often stand on the terrace wrapped in a blanket before climbing into bed, shivering and restless until I would calm him.

Is Brisdon sound asleep now? Or is he awake and thinking about me? Is he trying to rid himself of these ruthless spirits as I am? Before tonight I didn't realize how much I needed to see him. There will be fire and there will be ice. We will be rousing the dead, even if their hearts have turned to stone and their hopes to dust.

"*Caesar...*" Russell's ghost whispers as I start to drift off to sleep, "*...when you're going through hell, pardner, just keep on going.*"

Margaret

The New Orleans airport is now humming with a sound that reminds me of a swarm of bees ready to attack. Over it all the airport Muzak is playing an instrumental *Close to You*. Christian is still clutching his carry-on bag, not comprehending why I am so anxious. He really doesn't know me at all and never did. I get up and pace the tiled floor in front of the rows of people in their seats.

"What has gotten into you, Meg?"

"The devil," I answer. He continues to stare. Everything is getting too close for me. "I'm going to take a walk," I tell him.

"Don't go too far," he warns. I know there is time before they call our flight. I need fresh air. But there is no fresh air in the terminal. We are locked up inside at this point, until we are led out to the tarmac in single file like heading to our execution. And then it will be all hot, humid air mixed with jet fuel fumes. I need the cooling breezes off the North Sea at Gob na Cananaich, at the lighthouse watching dolphins like I had done with James, and not trapped in this airport, waiting to return home to our son. Brisdon wanted to come with us but that would have been just too much for me. Brisdon would have sided with his father and I would have been fighting them both all this time.

I have to walk somewhere else, breathe different air, something that smells pleasant. I spy a perfume counter at the back of the duty-free shop, something to bring me out of myself, even for a few moments. There is a row of perfume testers on display. I pick up a smokey-coloured bottle and I spray the back of my hand and stand there with my eyes shut, breathing it in. Scent can stir up all types of memories.

I smell dry wood and leather, cedar and a touch of tobacco. The aroma brings me back, but not to my cankered love for James, but to a more brutal kind—my love for Michael Murley. How much will Christian hate and despise me when he discovers everything between us began with a lie, a deception behind smoked mirrors? Because when I first met Christian and swept him off his feet, I was already pregnant with Michael Murley's child.

*   *   *

My father's leg never completely healed from his fall. During the *Ceilidh*, he had asked the Postmaster General for a letter of recommendation so he could immigrate to Canada. His elder brother Fergus was living in Toronto then and could get him a job in a mail plant. I refused to go, even if my dreams of being mistress of Brisdon House were shattered. I couldn't give up my circle of friends, my culture, my identity. But it was a losing battle. At fifteen years old, I had no recourse against the iron will of a father who had already lost one child. So I had to leave Maggie Campbell behind. It is said that to cross a large body of water is to become a changed person and so I shed Maggie, the girl full of optimism and laughter and trust, and became Margaret.

The first time I saw big red-faced Michael Murley, I thought he was exciting. He was a bit of a bad boy, a hard-drinking, blue-collar Irishman not yet thirty who loved to take me dancing at the Irish Club. We met at a diner on Queen Street. We were sitting facing one another in separate booths. He looked up from his bacon and eggs and winked at me and we got to talking. He asked me if he could join me in my booth and I let him.

"You ever notice how people don't talk to each other in this town?" he asked me.

"You don't seem to have any trouble in that department," I remarked.

"You're from Scotland, then," he noted from my accent.

"And you're Irish." That should have set off alarm bells right there and then.

The waitress in her orange uniform and starched white apron brought him a fresh cup of coffee and I watched her slowly clear away his plates from the table behind him as if she was trying to listen in.

"Only immigrants talk to immigrants," he said. It was a game of wills straight away.

I was aware of my attractiveness. I took pride in it, even if I didn't have the means to dress it up properly. "We're all immigrants here," I volleyed back and smiled.

"Jesus, Mary and Joseph!" he exclaimed, and I didn't know if he was frustrated or impressed. His expression said, *I've got to have you* and my look returned, *You've got to work for it.*

He was part owner of a construction company that was building the new courthouse across from the gates of Osgoode Hall. I was told that those tall iron gates had been built to stop the young governesses with their prams from getting through to the handsome young lawyers on the other side. Michael Murley's opinion was that it had been built to keep out the cows. We talked about home. Toronto was very different from Inverness. It had its charm but it lacked magic. It had no monsters. There was very little history compared with Scotland, even though we had Mackenzie House and the Toronto Scottish Regiment here. Casa Loma, built in 1914, was a far cry from Inverness Castle built on the site of castles going back to the eleventh century, since the time of Macbeth, King of Scotland. Instead of Chanonry Point at the mouth of the sea, with the dolphins and the whales riding the sea spray, Lake Ontario had thousands of dead alewife fish washing up onto the shores.

"Are ye homesick then, Margaret?" he asked me the first night we stayed together. He took a swig from the whiskey bottle that he had put on the floor next to my bed the way James had put down the bottle of champagne we never drank.

"I fear that being with an Irishman will be the closest I'll get to home."

Michael Murley represented the sensation of my old world meeting my new one, and in him I found a thrill that had been missing in my new life. He was tall and strong as an ox and sometimes it hurt, like he had an anger in him, even though I was certain he loved me in his own way.

My parents never met him, which was just as well. They died within the first few years of moving here, my father of heart failure, as if he had left parts of his heart in the post boxes of Crown, and my mother from an aneurism, as if life was just a cruel trick, the effort to forge a better existence across the ocean a joke on us all. I didn't laugh much after that. I was all alone. My Uncle Fergus and his family had moved to Winnipeg where it was rumoured to be so cold in the winter you could freeze to death just crossing the street.

By the time I was twenty-five I had a good administrative job at the University of Toronto Faculty of Arts and Sciences. I lived in a small apartment above a jewellery store on Queen Street West. I had a new circle of friends, mostly from work, and now I had Michael Murley who came over sometimes ready to love me for the entire night and other times to slam his fist into the wall or kick over the dining room chairs my parents had brought from Crown, all because I didn't have any more whiskey in the apartment.

One night we had an all-out screaming match and I threw a plate of food at him. It missed him but it stained the wall and he hit me hard. Then he cried. What do you do when a strapping Irishman cries in your lap but hold him and forgive him?

Then I found out I was pregnant. He came over that night all sugar and spice but stinking of whiskey and I told him. His hand flew up and he struck me hard across the face, harder than last time. I put a towel wrapped in ice from the icebox on my eye and sat on my sofa while he paced the floor, chain-smoking.

"Why did you do that?" I cried out.

"*O feck, O feck,*" he kept saying and pacing the floor like a caged animal.

"Jesus Christ, will you settle down!"

"I'm sorry, I'm sorry!" But he still didn't stop his pacing.

"You're going to have to marry me now," I said.

He stopped. He just stared at me. "No," he replied flatly.

"Why the hell not?" I cried.

"Because I'm already married!" he shouted back.

I was afraid of something like that. I had never been to his home. He only came to me for a warm body and a *feck* and I let him, fool that I was. I shouted until my voice was cracking like an old witch and then I cried. He came over to me and crouched by my knees and held onto my legs. I looked up and started kicking out and got him right in the ribs and we both yelled and screamed all over again.

"Does she know about me?"

"No."

"Coward! What's her name?"

"Never *feckin'* mind!"

"I'll find her and tell her!"

"I'll kill you Margaret, I swear!"

"Unless your wife kills you first!"

And so on. Until he stormed out trailing cigarette ash behind him. My eye throbbed under the ice and I hoped his ribs were smarting.

Now what was I to do?

*   *   *

The next morning I left late for work because it took a long time to conceal my bruised eye with make-up. That was when I formally met the man who was to become my husband. I lived above the jewellery store where he worked. We had briefly crossed paths a few times and I saw him sometimes through the large shop window when I got home from work. This time I was coming out as he was going in.

"Good morning." He had a pained look to him.

"Oh hello—"

"I'm Christian. I mean, that's my name, Christian Noxon. This is my store."

"Yes, I know. I'm Margaret. I live upstairs."

"Yes I know. Is everything all right?"

I was startled by that. Was my eye that obvious? "Why do you ask?"

"I was working last night. I don't usually stay so late. I heard a lot of ruckus upstairs and it went on for quite a while."

I relaxed my shoulders. "Oh that. A friend was visiting and we had a disagreement."

"Sounded more like an out-and-out scrap."

I was getting impatient. I was already late. "Well, it's been resolved," I lied.

"I have to tell you when he left he just held onto that lamppost there and puked in the street."

Good, I thought. I said, "Well, that's ugly, isn't it?"

"So, you're okay?"

I smiled sweetly and placed my hand on Christian-the-Jeweller's arm, like a *thank you for watching out for me.* "I am now. But I really have to catch that streetcar."

"Come into the store when you get home," he called after me. "I'll be here."

I did come into the store later that day. Christian was wearing a soldering mask as he fused together his precious metals. When he saw me he removed his mask and pushed back his blond hair with a black-smudged hand. He had a long face and the short patchy beard of someone who really wanted to grow one but couldn't. His charm lay in his smile and his blue eyes lit up as I came closer to see what he was doing.

"Are you busy at all this evening?" He seemed more shy now than this morning.

"No." I was certain Michael Murley wasn't going to be showing up any longer. He had made that perfectly clear.

So Christian took me to dinner at Ciccone's and Mama Ciccone herself fussed about us as if we were romancing or even newlyweds, which is where I first got the idea to get married. Christian talked about himself, his jeweller's apprenticeship and about being adopted. His birth mother had left him as a newborn at the Lakeshore Home for Little Children. It was 1933 during the depression, and the city orphanages were filling up. This sad and desperate woman, for whatever reason, had abandoned him with nothing but a blanket wrapped around him and a laundry ticket pinned to it with the name *Christian* scrawled on the back. He showed me the stub. I didn't know if I could abandon the child inside me like that. I thought of Fionola of Brisdon House and the kind of regret a mother would have felt. So I listened to him and I thought he was sweet and not one of the dangerous types that so attracted me and I felt he might make a good father. I worked very hard and very fast against the wishes of his parents to have us wed within two months of that dinner.

I miscarried at work a few weeks after we had returned from our honeymoon. I sat bleeding on the floor of the faculty washroom until someone found me. The Dean forced me to go by ambulance to hospital. Maybe he was the one who called Christian, I don't know. I pleaded with the doctor to not disclose anything to my husband about the baby. Dr. Stefan Petz was a greying Hungarian who reminded me of an owl. He held up his old hands as if shielding himself from me. I needed to trust him not to say anything because the fetus had been about twelve weeks along and I had told Christian I lost *our* baby, and that it had only been a few weeks old and I hadn't even known I was pregnant. I told him there had been a lot of bleeding, and that much was true, and that was why they were keeping me in hospital overnight. Nothing to worry about, really.

Afterwards, when I was alone, I cried for hours, but not because I had miscarried. For that I was actually grateful. Instead, I feared I was cursed with the fate of my own parents, that any attempt to make a change for the best would collapse in on itself.

*   *   *

The airport loudspeaker is announcing that the next flight to Anchorage Alaska is ready for boarding. Now *that's* a city where no one would know me or care about my past. I put down the perfume bottle and fret about the extent of the contempt that Christian will have for me when he learns I married him to be a father to Michael Murley's child.

Then I pick up a second tester bottle and sniff. It's another woody scent but with oriental notes this time, vanilla and myrrh and a hint of cloves. How extraordinary, smelling my past lovers as if I am drawn by scent along the path I can't avoid, to reveal everything to Christian. Because this scent as I spritz it into the air and breathe it in, is the fragrance of longing and despair, the essence of Jacques Kumar, who is unquestionably and impossibly the father of Karen, my missing daughter.

*   *   *

For the next few years Christian and I were happy, as much as peace-of-mind can be called happiness, and despite Christian's mother with her subtle attempts to disrupt our contentment. Fortunately, my new in-laws lived in London Ontario, two hours west of us, so our visits were limited to weekends and special occasions. I had no problem with old Doctor John Noxon. He was pleasing to the eye, lean and tall and a little stooped after years of bending to his wife's will. The day Christian introduced me I knew Elizabeth didn't like me. She may have been attractive once, at least enough to land a handsome doctor, but her face had grown pinched and she was as pale as a sheet as if she were afraid of sunlight.

Elizabeth Noxon left me with the impression she didn't believe her average son could snag such a vivacious girl. They called me Elizabeth Taylor at work even though the actress wasn't a red-head. And Christian's mother had a way of looking right into you. If I hadn't had a cowl of guilt covering me because of what Michael Murley had made me do, I would have been impervious to her stabbing stare. But remorse is an anxious ghost and I was intimidated by this predator smelling fear in her prey, prancing and crouching until finding the right moment to strike. What did she even know about getting pregnant? But she may have realized it was unusual for a woman who lost a three-week old fetus smaller than a poppyseed to be kept in hospital overnight. She was married to a physician after all. Even if Elizabeth

Noxon's witchery was all in my head, I believed it was real because there was no one I could talk to. I had no family, my friends would only judge me, and saying anything would ruin everything I strove to achieve including the betterment of myself as a person. I wanted to believe I had left my self-destructive tendencies with the blood on the floor of the faculty washroom.

But blood will tell. We were trying for a family now that Christian was no longer an apprentice at the jewellery store. The owner had sold the business to him. We moved into a larger house in a quiet neighbourhood not far for Christian to walk to work and convenient to the streetcar for me. But we were not having any luck with conceiving a child and I couldn't tell him that he might be the problem.

Or maybe I had done something to myself emotionally, after the miscarriage, and it had manifested into something physical, like a dark stain on my womb.

I met Professor Jacques Kumar when he arrived for his first day at the university. As administrative secretary, I had arranged his travel itinerary and his accommodations in one of the campus apartments. He was originally from Puducherry, India, or *Pondichéry*, as he pronounced it, having moved to France to teach Indian history. He was here to lecture on India's independence from France that had occurred only four years earlier.

"History is catching up with us," I overheard him tell another professor in the faculty lounge. "Soon history will be immediate because the world will be moving too fast for us to look behind us."

He was young to be a professor and I fell for him right away. I fell for him too hard and he knew it. He was exotic. I hadn't met many people from India and I was entranced by his beautiful colouring. There was something animal about his broad shoulders and large hands, something bold about his deep-set grey eyes, something spiritual about his calm demeanour and something sensual about the way he talked, with his mix of Tamil and Parisian accents, his words focused and direct as if he chose each word, every syllable, with precision so as not to be misunderstood.

At first I would see him when he came into the office looking for supplies. Then we would cross paths along the corridors between offices. One day in the faculty lounge we found each other standing side-by-side at the coffee station. The rest of the staff were lounging and chatting in over-stuffed chairs under a cloud of cigarette smoke.

"Will you join me?" he asked. We sat at a small table in the corner and he blew on his coffee cup. I felt people's eyes on us and it felt exciting.

"Is this where we talk about politics?" I teased him, seeing how far I could go.

"What do you know of Indian politics?" he asked me.

"Not much I'm afraid." I knew of Gandhi but I didn't want to sound foolish.

"Then come to my lecture," he said releasing a wide grin of perfect teeth as white as the snow he could never have imagined in Puducherry. "You may learn something of the history of France as well as India."

When it was time to go he pulled out my chair and bowed to me as if I were Marie Antoinette, the last Queen of France.

*   *   *

Professor Kumar was pacing the auditorium stage as he delivered his lecture. I was sitting in the back row, trying to take in the complex history of French rule in India so I could have a meaningful conversation with him. It wasn't only the topic that held me there, it was the power of this Bengal tiger pacing back and forth as if he were in a cage. I was entranced by the way his body moved and confused by my enchantment of him.

He stopped to sip from a glass of water resting on the podium.

"Now that France and India made a joint declaration to settle the future of the French colonies in India, the members of the Congress Party were hoping for a straightforward retreat of French power. But India began to drag its heels, fearing the people would rally against their decision to establish a referendum." He cleared his throat to continue. "But nothing is ever straightforward in politics."

I was still bundled in my overcoat when the lights came up. A few students shuffled timidly up to him to ask questions. Then, shielding his eyes against the spotlights directed onto the stage, he recognized me at the back and I could see his beautiful smile from all that distance. I got up from my seat and moved nonchalantly down the aisle towards him. He stood above me on the stage, and put his hands on his hips. I stopped directly beneath him and looked up as he stared down.

"Would you like to go for coffee, Professor?"

"Jacques."

"Then Jack it is."

As we sat across from each other in the university cafeteria he blew on his coffee cup again.

"Is that for good luck?" I asked.

"I don't enjoy my coffee too hot," he replied. His eyes were aimed at his cup and then he looked up. "That's just for coffee."

"I see." So we were playing a game.

"Do you attend all of the lectures, Margaret?" I liked the way he said my name, sort of clipped as if he were saying *Mar-get,* to catch my attention and to keep it there.

"Only when I have been invited."

"That's true. I invited you. Did you enjoy my lecture then?"

"Yes, I learned a great deal."

What I had actually learned was that the power of desire was far stronger than the power of prudence or wisdom or any rational thought. Somehow the old Margaret had resurfaced, and was enjoying herself again. I touched my face as if the bruising had returned. Then he reached over and caressed the same spot as if rubbing in something of himself.

We walked back between the campus buildings to the administration wing. It was mid-December. The trees had lost their leaves and the world was blanketed with a thin layer of frost. Winters were harsh in Toronto. I wondered how Jack would fare coming from temperate Paris and stifling hot Puducherry.

"You're here for the winter," I said even though I knew that full well because I had typed up his contract.

"Yes, until March." He pulled his coat more tightly around him.

"It gets much colder than this," I warned him.

"So I understand."

"Maybe we'll see each other again at the annual Christmas party?"

"Yes, certainly. It will be a pleasure to meet your husband." He was looking at my ring hand.

"Yes," I replied and thought, *You just took the power.*

Then he hurried off, his shoulders hunched forward and his head slightly down as if it was warmer closer to the ground.

*   *   *

The faculty Christmas party was being held at Croft Hall, a circular building with a domed ceiling, originally used as a chemistry laboratory and designed to contain any fires or explosions resulting from student experiments. Everything from that time was gone now, the beakers and conical flasks, the lab stands and microscopes. The intent was to convert the building into a planetarium but the seats hadn't been installed so it was a perfect space for a large gathering with just a hint of the heavens above.

What should have been a passing infatuation wouldn't have borne fruit if Christian had only come to the Christmas party. But December was his busiest time of the year. It kept him in his shop until late at night and I hadn't allowed for that.

"I can't make it," he admitted, meekly. He knew I had been looking forward to going. There were never enough parties in my life and I had even bought a new dress.

I didn't get angry. "I won't go either then. I'll come help you at your shop, if you like."

He just shook his head. "I don't know if that's a good idea—"

"So you're saying I'll be in the way?"

"No-no-no... I just think you shouldn't be denied a night out with your colleagues. It's Christmastime after all."

That was the permission I needed. I won't lie. There was satisfaction in Christian almost throwing me at the event where I hoped to see Jack again. That evening while my husband was hunched over his work table I put on my new dress, smoothing down its scarlet material woven through with golden thread, just like royalty, the shoulders narrow and soft and the middle pulled into a wasp waist. For luck, I fastened on my mother's opal earrings, the most valuable pieces she had owned. What kind of luck I was hoping for was still unclear. A few drinks, a flirtation... Really, what would be the harm?

When I arrived at Croft Hall there were already a hundred guests in their festive finest, mingling and chatting and sipping drinks. This lavish event reminded me of the *Ceilidh* at Brisdon House, a lifetime ago. A cloud of cigarette smoke hung under the dome of the hall as if a hundred failed experiments were happening at the same time. A string quartet of students from the Royal Conservatory was playing *O Holy Night* with their overly focused expressions. An enormous spruce tree, cut specifically for this event, was decked out with bells and bows and coloured tinsel and topped with a blinking star that hovered above the stratosphere of smoke.

"Hey Elizabeth Taylor!" Sophie called out when she saw me. We worked at desks abutting each other in our office. She had a wine glass in one hand and a cigarette in the other. "Didn't you bring your husband along?"

"I'm afraid not."

"No matter. The men just go off together once they find each other. Like dogs drawn by scent. I'm here with the girls." Two familiar women waved at me from across the room. "Do you have a drink yet? Go get one and join us. There's a bar set up by the Christmas tree."

I headed over and asked for a glass of white wine and stood looking around.

"*Mar-get.*" The familiar voice behind me was curt yet soft. I turned. "*Bonsoir, madame.*"

"How would you say that in Puducherry?"

"*Bonsoir, madame.* We're a French colony."

"Very clever, Professor Kumar. I mean, *Jack.*"

"I don't see your husband."

"Oh, do you know what my husband looks like?"

"I just mean I saw you come in alone."

So he was watching for me. "I'm afraid he had to work late tonight."

"What a shame."

Was it? Then he flashed his perfect teeth. Everything I was afraid of and was hoping for was in that smile, caught by the lights from the tree next to us, a prism of shame and yearning and cruelty and tenderness, all layered and exquisite and intoxicating like sipping at a *pousse café*.

"I'm dying for a fag," I said.

He pulled out a pack of Player's and a silver lighter from his jacket pocket. "Allow me." He lit my cigarette in his mouth and then held it out to me. I snatched it away.

"Jack! People are watching."

"I thought that's how they do it in the movies." I wanted to say this wasn't Hollywood and then he leaned in and whispered, "Perhaps we should go somewhere else?"

I thought that wasn't such a bad idea. Sophie and the girls would be searching me out but when I looked over Jack's shoulder they had disappeared into the crowd. This was our chance.

We bundled ourselves up to walk back to his residence. He didn't seem self-conscious, but what man did? A woman had to be on guard for whoever was watching. I kept my head down but my eyes remained alert all the way through the campus grounds.

His accommodations were sparsely furnished and there were no Christmas decorations. Books and folders covered a large table in the centre of the room. On it sat an Underwood typewriter with a ream of yellow paper stacked beside it.

"Let me take your coat." I let it slide off into his hands. "May I offer you a drink? I don't have much. Will Chivas do?"

"Chivas will do fine."

He disappeared into the kitchen. I heard him cracking ice cubes. *Clink-clink* they went into the glasses. He came back out and handed one to me.

"I admire a woman who drinks scotch."

"I'm Scottish."

"I know." Neither of us said much after that.

Later, I lay in the crux of his arm as we smoked. I didn't know how to feel. Grateful came to mind. Or ashamed. Gone were the days of feeling pure joy, the sensation of being set free. That had died with Maggie. The feelings were still fulfilling but not *full*, as if something was missing, a coda or an epilogue or some famous last words.

I wondered what he was thinking as he got out of bed and wrapped himself in a terrycloth bathrobe that was open enough for me to see the dark mat of hair on his chest. For a moment his brown body, his entire being was strange and misplaced in this room. Then I noticed the suitcase resting on the floor, the leather straps done up and a camel hair coat draped over it.

"You're going somewhere," I said.

"Yes. Paris. I'm leaving tomorrow to be home for Christmas."

I sat up. "Oh. I didn't know. Home to family then?"

"To my wife." I was almost knocked over. This had all happened before. Why was I surprised?

"Well!"

"Well?"

"You're not wearing a wedding band," I pointed out to cover my reaction, ashamed suddenly that I had reacted at all.

"No, I'm not. And you are."

"I should be going then."

He didn't say a word. He just lit another cigarette and sat at the table, his legs crossed, watching me dress.

When I reached St. George Street, I hailed a taxi. As it pulled up to our house there were no lights on. I hoped Christian would still be at his workbench in his store. My hair was all pressed down in spots, and I knew Jack's cologne and body sweat would linger on me. When I opened the door I called to Christian three times. Three times no answer. Three times lucky. It was dark and all I could hear was the oil furnace in the basement rattling through the heating vents. I didn't turn on any lights. I kicked off my shoes and threw my coat over the newel post. I pulled myself up the narrow stairs by the railing. I switched on the bathroom light and stared at my reflection in the mirror above the sink. My expression was hideous. I had not only slipped into the skin of old Margaret, I had created a new Margaret, an ugly and unforgivable Margaret.

I drew a bath. As the water ran I undressed and lit a cigarette and climbed into the steaming hot water. I submerged myself up to my neck, my knees sticking up like two tiny islands, my hand dangling over the edge with smoke rising from my fingers. I closed my eyes. I thought back to just an hour ago, and I wanted to hate myself but the memory of the rapture was too fresh, like an open wound. With Jack I had to bite my lip so hard I thought it would bleed because I was afraid to cry out. I had never experienced that with Michael Murley, who had been clumsy and rough, or James Tamaddon who was all champagne foam and stars, and certainly not with Christian who loved me too much. There is always a measure of anger buried in the best lovemaking. As the water steamed up, beads of perspiration covered my brow. I stuck out my tongue to catch the drips. Then I slipped further down, submerging my head and hair, dropping the cigarette onto the tile floor and holding my breath until I could hold it no longer.

Later, when I was in bed, I heard Christian come home. I heard him moving about, knocking against something in a failed attempt to be quiet. I was pretending to be asleep when he slid under the covers. My back was to him. I could feel him press against me as if he knew I was awake. My heart was racing. He must have felt it beating right through me, giving me away. But he lay back and fell asleep right away. I didn't sleep a wink.

*   *   *

It was Christmas Eve day. I had given up lying awake in bed so I got up and sat in the kitchen drinking coffee as the sun began to rise. I peeked out the window to see the morning star between the bare tree branches but it wasn't there. I wanted to be set free from the cage of my duplicity. Lack of sleep compounded my contrition and self-condemnation. I found my mother's holy cross, the one she had always worn, and clutching it between my hands I bowed my head and prayed.

I would start praying more and more from that moment on.

It was Christian's last day at the shop before closing for the holidays. He promised to be home by early afternoon. We would be spending Christmas Day with his parents so I planned a quiet dinner for us. Christmas had never been popular at home in Crown. Long ago the Scottish Parliament had banned it. We never had a tree and Hogmanay was far more important. But here, Christmas was a big event. I had purchased Christian a new leather wallet from Simpson's because the stitching of his old wallet was bursting. Inside the new one there was a small compartment where he could keep his ticket, the one with his name written by the mother he never knew.

I cooked a ham for our supper and served it with mashed potatoes and turnips. Afterwards I selected some Christmas music for the record player and we cuddled on the sofa next to our little tree, its coloured bulbs flashing on and off. I switched off the other lights and lit some candles to make the room feel cozier. It was the beginning of a cold snap and Jack Frost had touched the corners of the window panes. Then we passed our gifts to each other. Mine was just a little box. As I opened it he moved closer. Inside was an exquisite moonstone ring set in gold which was carved with meticulous detail.

"You made this for me?"

"This is the reason I couldn't have you come to the store yesterday. I was trying to finish it in time. Do you like it?"

"*Oh Christian!*" It was the most beautiful ring I had ever seen.

"Look." He took it in his fingers. His nails were still stained from work. "These are the stars, see?"

"Yes—"

"And this here, this is the sun."

"Yes, I see."

"And of course the stone is the moon. You are my stars and sun and moon, Meg. You are my heart."

I bit my lower lip this time to hold back tears of self-contempt and self-pity. It's over and done, I said to myself, and moved into his arms. Even though I was tired from my sleepless night, we loved each other into the wee hours and I thanked God again for His mercy and knew that Jesus on the eve of His birth was looking down upon me with forgiveness. I thought that everything, finally, was going to be all right.

* * *

That was sixteen years ago.

The duty-free shop is getting crowded. Someone bumps my shoulder but doesn't apologize. I move away from the perfume counter. I don't want to buy anything. I just need to get away from the prying eyes of the people at the departure gate, from that woman and her child, and from Christian. I will go back to Christian who is worrying perhaps that I won't come back at all, that he will have to get up to look for me and miss our flight. I'm not being heartless or unkind, I am just trying to collect myself, to organize my thoughts before I confess *everything* to him. Before him and before *God.*

When I leave the shop my heels click along the shiny floor. The PA system continues to drone on with more flight departures, to Austin and Minneapolis but not to New York. Apparently there's a rainstorm in New York. I still have time.

At a smoke shop I reach for a magazine from the rack then snatch my hand back. Time magazine has a picture of the shark from *Jaws*, all sharp teeth snapping right at me. I remember the Time magazine I picked up while waiting in the doctor's office the day I found out I was pregnant, like another shark was snapping at me, hungry for blood.

It was at the end of February 1959. The magazine was from the month before and had a young Fidel Castro on the cover, and when I paged through it I came across a photo of Che Guevara. I just was thinking how handsome Che was when the doctor called me in.

Over the past month I had been feeling ill and missed my period and none of this was new to me. We had been trying for a child for so long that I didn't want to say anything to Christian until I knew for sure. Old Dr. Petz gave me the news, watching me carefully because I was sure he remembered my odd behaviour when I miscarried. I wanted to smile, to show him how happy I should be but I couldn't manage any reaction at all.

"Is everything all right, Mrs. Noxon?"

"It's just a surprise," I lied. "How far along am I?"

"About eight weeks."

When I left his office I didn't return to work. I took the streetcar home hoping Christian would be at his store, which he was. The snow was blowing and it was bitterly cold. When I got in the door I let my coat fall to the floor, kicked off my boots and rushed up the stairs and into the bathroom and threw up in the toilet, not from my pregnancy but because of it, because of the fear of who the father could be. Afterwards, I undressed and crawled into bed and lay under the covers. I could hear the telephone downstairs ringing and ringing and ringing. When Christian came home I told him I was unwell so he brought me soup and unsalted crackers on a tray and I sipped flat ginger ale pretending to feel better until I decided what I would do.

The next morning I rose early and ran to catch the streetcar. I was the first one in the office. I found the lecture register and skimmed down until I found *Jacques Kumar, The Colonization and Liberation of French Occupied India, Lecture Hall B, 10:00 a.m.*

I never thought I would do this again. I slipped into the auditorium and sat in the back row until the lecture was over. As the students filed out I didn't move. I waited. When he was finally alone, dropping his notes into his briefcase, I called out his name.

He shielded his eyes against the spotlight like before. "Margaret?"

I didn't answer. This time I wasn't coming down to the stage. This time he would have to come up to me. He understood this when I didn't move. When he got to the back row he sat down.

"Why are you here?" His tone was clipped. I wasn't surprised. He had tried to reach me when he had returned from his holidays but I had avoided him. I thought I had sent out my signal loud and clear.

"You're almost done with us," I said. I realized that sounded ambiguous, personal. "I mean you're leaving soon."

"Yes, next week. Why?"

"I'm pregnant." He didn't speak. He searched my face. I let nothing show. "I'm pregnant, Jack," I repeated.

"I heard you. Are you saying I am the father?"

"I don't know. I don't know."

"When will you know?"

"Everyone will know when it's born, it will be obvious. I won't want it then."

"Margaret, you will love the child as soon as you see it."

"Why do men always tell women what they will think or feel?" I snapped.

"Then find a doctor who will take care of it."

"No, I cannot."

"And your husband?"

"What about him?"

"Let him think it is his."

"And if it's dark like you? How do I explain that? No, I want *you* to take the responsibility."

"But how? What did you expect by coming to me with this news? Did you want me to leave my wife for you? Are you going to leave your husband? There's nothing I can do, Margaret. I'll be back in France soon. It's over."

"Damn you!" I got up from the seat and pushed past him not caring if I stepped all over him. "Damn you all to hell!" I stomped out feeling like a fool. He was right. What had I hoped to achieve?

I was in a purgatory of my own making. I walked through the campus grounds in the freezing cold, my coat undone, like I was treading over hellfire. Before Jack left the next week I saw him once more, by chance, as we passed in the narrow hallway from the cafeteria. We were both with other people. I could actually feel the energy of his body in the thin space of air between us, yearning for me and his baby, I was sure of it. Then I took his file and locked it in my desk drawer so I would know how to find him.

Over the weekend, while Christian was in his shop, I paced through the house, wringing my hands and trying to calm myself. Perhaps God would be compassionate after all. Perhaps it was Christian's child in spite of everything, that I would be blessed after all this turmoil, and that God had let me survive His punishment for doubting Him because He was not only a *God of Justice*, but a *God of Mercy*. When Christian came home that night I told him I was pregnant. His reaction to the news was euphoric, all smiles and laughter and hugs and kisses. He popped the cork on a bottle of sparkling wine left over from New Year's. It was warm but there was no time to chill it so we made our toasts while the tepid bubbles danced on my tongue and I prayed, *Dear God, please let the child be blonde and fair-skinned like him.* That night I loved him desperately and clung to him long after he had fallen asleep. I would never go back to that other Margaret, I vowed. I would suffer my sins for my husband until death, no matter how much it squeezed my now tainted, blighted, gangrenous heart.

Easter came early that year. It was the end of March and we drove to Christian's parents' home for the holidays. At dinner, Christian broke the news to them that I was expecting in September. I was worried that my mother-in-law would be jealous or spiteful. Instead, she just clapped her hands and turned to me with a rare smile as if I had finally accomplished something that was worthy of her approval. But she didn't lower her gaze. Her grin gradually faded and her green eyes just glared into mine and I felt a chill, as if she were looking right into the darkest parts of me. *She knows, she knows,* I thought. She put her knife and fork down on her plate without taking her eyes from me.

"Is there something else you want to tell us?" she asked me directly and my fork stopped half-way to my mouth.

"What do you mean, mum?" Christian asked.

Her menacing smile was directed at me because when she looked at her son she became all sweet and sugary. "What names have you chosen, dear?"

The good doctor piped up, "If it's a boy he has to be named John. It's tradition." He leaned over and ruffled Christian's blonde locks. "This one came with a name pinned to him, unfortunately."

I started to laugh out of relief and John Noxon raised an eyebrow as if I had slighted him.

"You don't like the name John?"

"Oh heavens no...I mean *yes*, John is fine. It's a very fine name."

"And if a girl?" Elizabeth pressed. Clearly she was pushing for a girl to be named after her, like the start of a new tradition, but the child would end up being Liza or Lizzie. I had known a Lizzie from school in Crown. She had been a clown and a fool and no one had liked her.

I thought quickly. "Karen," I replied. "After my mother Cairenn, God rest her soul. Wouldn't that be a fine tribute to her?"

Elizabeth kept her serene expression. "That's lovely, Margaret." She sat back in her chair, defeated.

The pregnancy wasn't difficult. I stayed at my job until I was showing, which was sooner than I expected. My mother-in-law surprised me by sending a package of maternity dresses from the Eaton's catalog. I had regular appointments with Dr. Petz who I met in his office when he wasn't on duty at the hospital and he assured me everything was developing normally.

Throughout August I ballooned up, my breasts swollen and sore, while I suffered through the relentless summer heat. When Christian was at his shop I prayed a great deal. I went to church regularly, and that made me feel better because if I was watching out for God, then surely God was watching out for me...

...Until the night of September 22nd, when my water broke and I looked to God but I couldn't see Him, the pain was too great. God was not there when I packed my suitcase nor when Christian drove me to hospital nor in the delivery room. God was nowhere to be found. Instead, something evil languished in the antiseptic shadows, and between my screams I could hear it laughing.

*   *   *

"One more push!"

I did as ordered and my baby left my body. There was a scurrying about and cutting and sopping and then the mewing cry of a living thing.

"A boy!" Dr. Petz announced triumphantly as if he was taking credit. I caught a glimpse of my child in his wrinkled hands. The boy was covered in a white film and he was so tiny. He should have been much larger than that. I had gone full term and had been enormous.

"Show me—" My voice cracked as they were wiping him off.

"Everything is fine, Mrs. Noxon, you have a healthy baby boy. He's just a little undersized."

"What's that mean? Show me!" I demanded again. The doctor signalled and a nurse brought him over. He was very fair and pink and I knew right away it was my husband's child and I smiled because God had heard my prayers. Then my smile turned into a grimace from more pain and I screamed again which startled the doctor. There was another flurry of activity.

"What's happening?" I cried out.

Dr. Petz smiled reassuringly. "As I suspected, Mrs. Noxon, there is another one. You're having twins."

"Oh God!" I cried. The unbearable pains came again. But the second baby wasn't ready yet. This one was going to give me trouble. The nurses and doctor kept rotating in and out of the room where I lay. One nurse brought me ice chips and told me, "Twins is why your boy is small, dearie, it's perfectly normal. The second one is usually easier, don't worry."

The waiting was making it worse, not easier. I couldn't think of anyone I knew who had given birth to twins. At least there was no one on my side of the family. It was Christian. No one knew about Christian's family history. Maybe he had been a twin himself. We would never know. Then, four hours later, my second child was born. Dr. Petz looked tired but still smiled when the baby began to screech right away without a slap, just a little lump that could fit in your hands.

"A girl!" he announced.

When they brought her to me her skin was darker than the boy and she was covered in fine black hair. I wanted to cry out *no, no, no,* but I was seized with another jab of pain. This one was worse than all the rest.

"Now what's happening?" I managed to cry out even as my voice was failing me. My throat felt full of sharp gravel from hours of screaming.

Dr. Petz fussed around me, over me, beneath me and then leaned over and looked calmly at me. "Most extraordinary, Mrs. Noxon. You're about to have a third child."

I was clenching my teeth and my fists again. I was trying to push. I couldn't wait another four hours. I couldn't think about the fair boy or the dark girl but only this child, the child I was pushing out of me with more pain than the other two combined, and only minutes after the girl as if they had been somehow attached and the boy was an entity on his own. The third child didn't cry. There were startled faces all around me. *That's not right,* I thought. Then there was a flurry of activity and I caught a glimpse of Dr. Petz working to get it to breathe and I found my voice again and screamed out because of what I saw. The thing was twisted and malformed. I only saw it for a moment before they bundled it away but I saw teeth on the side of its face where its ear should have been and something else was missing like a shoulder or a hip. It looked like it had a claw for a hand. It wasn't a child, it was a monster. I screamed from another kind of pain, not from childbirth but from a powerful *stab-stab-stab* at my breast. I screamed and I screamed until I felt a needle in my arm and then a haze fell over me and my muscles finally relaxed. Dr. Petz was holding my hand and telling me I had a healthy son and daughter.

I was groggy. I don't know how much time had passed. "What happened?" I asked.

"We couldn't save your last child, Mrs. Noxon, I'm so very, very sorry."

"Was it a boy? A girl?"

All he said was, "You had a stillbirth, I'm afraid. Again I'm so sorry. Your other two children are healthy, Mrs. Noxon. We've had to put them in incubators and need to monitor them for the time being. It's policy and for their safety, you understand. You have nothing to worry about. But I am deeply sorry for your loss."

I just wanted to sleep but I fought it. The doctor let go of my hand as more nurses entered the room and began cleaning me.

"But I saw something, Doctor. What was wrong with the baby?"

"I'm afraid the child that died in your womb was not properly formed." Then he asked what he must have been obliged to ask. "Do you wish to see your third child, Mrs. Noxon?"

"No," I said, and fell asleep.

* * *

The hospital took care of the remains of my stillborn baby. I dreamed it lay swimming in a pool of greenish liquid inside a jar on the doctor's desk. When I woke, I was in the hospital bed and Christian was by my side. I beseeched him not to ask for the dead child, for my sake. I told him my heart was too broken and he sat in the chair next to me and cried.

Beyond a shadow of a doubt I knew the malformed devil-child that had developed inside me belonged to Jack. The boy was fair and was Christian's son, I was certain of that. Just as I knew the girl was Jack's even though none of it made sense, that it was irrational and impossible. But the proof was there as I stared at the babies in their incubators. Their colours were too different. I would then discover the girl had two different coloured eyes: her left eye was brown and her right one was grey, another abomination that screamed out she was part of the devil-child that had crawled out of my womb with her. Her blue-eyed brother was different. He was separate. He was innocent. He was perfect.

I wasn't allowed to nurse them. They were kept in incubators and were fed formula. My milk turned to water. My breasts hurt. I was almost glad the babies were being cared for by the hospital staff because some mornings I couldn't get out of bed to visit them. I couldn't face them, either of them. I would send Christian off to his shop and I would lie there reliving their birth over and over, the joy of the boy, the shock of the girl, and the horror of the thing that had been inside me with them. I lay there with my head on my pillow, my mother's cross pressed against my chest and prayed for forgiveness even though it was far too late for that.

We brought the babies home on Thanksgiving week-end, on an afternoon when the rain poured mercilessly from a bleak sky. They were still so small. While the boy slept, the girl cried. And cried. We met with Dr. Petz again, two weeks later. I wanted to get it all out into the open, to have the doctor proclaim why my daughter was different than my son. I knew the truth, but I wanted Dr. Petz to pronounce it like a minister, *These babies were created from sin.* The strangest thing of all was that Christian didn't speak of it even though the difference between them was obvious. Maybe he didn't want to upset me because of the trauma of the stillbirth, or maybe he just didn't care or he didn't see beyond two tiny babies that kept both of us up all night, every night, in a rotating factory shift of feed and change.

But I had to hear it. I had to have the doctor speak it out loud. We each held a child for Dr. Petz to examine. I took the boy and Christian held the girl and the doctor pronounced they were both healthy and growing well and told us we had nothing to worry about.

"Thank you," Christian beamed, relieved.

"Have you named them?"

"Yes," Christian answered. She was squirming in his arms but being quiet for a change. She just stared up at him with those strange eyes, the brown being Jack's eye, and the grey the devil's, there was no doubt about it. "This is Karen Elizabeth," he said.

I looked down at my blonde-haired, blue-eyed baby boy who was precious and never fussed. His eyes were normal. His eyes were all mine. "And this is John Brisdon," I said.

"Very nice. Brisdon is an interesting name."

"Yes, it's Scottish." I didn't say what the name meant, that it was my last link to a time of virtue and integrity, before a black streak ran through it all. Then I swallowed hard before I spoke. "But I need to know why they look so different—"

Christian just stared at me as if I was mad. The doctor moved back to sit much too casually on the edge of his desk for someone who was going to call me a harlot and a whore.

"Yes, a number of doctors have been interested in this case."

My children's birth was a case now. I was a file in their cabinet.

"Go on, please."

"To be honest, Mrs. Noxon, we believe that answer lies with your husband." Christian and I looked at each other. Karen started to whine in Christian's arms. "You have told us you are adopted, Mr. Noxon, without any knowledge of your parentage. Is that correct?"

"Yes."

The doctor cleared his throat. "We suspect there was a different race involved in your family history that has resurfaced in your child. Bloodlines can run like that, can even skip generations—"

"What are you saying?" Christian asked as I held my breath.

"I'm saying you may have African or South Asian blood in your family history, Mr. Noxon. Unfortunately, without any records—"

I couldn't stay silent any longer. "But they're so different!"

"Yes, Mrs. Noxon, such anomalies are rare indeed. This is quite interesting."

Interesting, I thought. We're chalking this up to a weak and tepid adjective. I didn't know whether to laugh or cry with relief.

"Thank you Dr. Petz," Christian said.

"It's the best we can do with what we know. As science develops we may have more answers."

In the back of the car on the way home, as I held both our babies, I knew what the doctor was suggesting wasn't true at all. I knew the girl was Jack's because every time I looked at her I saw him in her. A mother knows. As soon as we got home Karen began to fuss. Christian took her. John stayed asleep in my arms. The moment was bitter-sweet: sweet was the doctor planting in Christian's mind a tale of mixed races in his ancestry and bitter was the blood that ran through me and into the monster that had been part of Karen. This knowledge would punish me every time I laid eyes on her.

*   *   *

If only I could have loved my daughter the way this woman in the waiting room loves her little girl, adores her with all her heart.

I am ready to set Christian free as I make my way back to the departure gate. I have kept everything from him to save him but now it's time to save myself. Then that little girl comes darting out of the ladies room, her black hair flying behind her. She comes right at me, not really looking where she's going, just running like in a game. The mother is through the door behind her but is not fast enough, not before I catch the little girl in my own arms. Instinctively, I lift her up. She is very pretty—so different from Karen, sweeter, and more pliable perhaps, with an unsullied soul.

"Oh dear!" the mother exclaims and gives me an apologetic smile. "Thank you so much." She reaches for her child. "That was very bad, Madhuri."

For a moment I don't want to give her back, as if all my regret is culminating in this moment, the remorse for how I treated my little girl with such indifference, begrudging her the love she deserved. Then the child slides into her mother's arms and buries her tiny head into her mother's neck.

I should feel more than remorse for what I did that warm, drizzly night at the end of October. I should feel shame. But I truly believed it was necessary. Do I still believe that? Is it too late to change everything by confessing, so I may shed this guilt? I've always hoped that Christian had a heart big enough to forgive me for my transgressions. He was always forgiving me. But for what happened on that Halloween night just ten years ago, not even God or Allah or Shiva can absolve me from that.

*   *   *

In April 1964 I wrote:

Jack,

I know it has been over a year since my last letter. Are you enjoying diplomatic service? Are you still planning a return to Toronto this autumn?

I am asking because your daughter needs you.

I know I have written this before, but the situation here at home is getting worse. I am beginning to truly fear for the child. You have to take her away, Jack. My husband mistreats her. He shakes her and screams at her and I don't know what to do anymore. The older she gets the more she resembles you and he knows she is your child and hates her for it. He also strikes me in front of her if I try to intervene so I don't say anything from fear. Your daughter and I are miserable.

If you are still coming to Canada this autumn on your tour of 'information and enlightenment' as you put it, now that you are a diplomat as well as a professor, I plead for you to consider taking your daughter back with you even if your wife does not fully understand our predicament. You did this to us, Jack. Please do not forget that.

Enclosed is another photograph of Karen. You can see how she has grown. Soon she will be too old to forget the abuse.

I eagerly await your response.

Sincerely,
Margaret Noxon

And then, a few months later, in June, I softened my tone when I wrote again.

Dear Jack,
Thank you for writing to me about your wife. I am very sorry for your loss. To die so suddenly from an aneurism is a terrible blow, I know, because I lost my own mother from it as well.

Thank you also for letting me know your itinerary while in Canada later this year. That is a very ambitious schedule and I am glad your lectures will conclude in Toronto. I've moved to a new division at the university so I had no knowledge of this.

Please understand, I did not want to mislead you. I cannot go to the police, it will only anger my husband more and he will deny it. I feel he loves us in his own way but he would prefer to be rid of her, I am sure of it. I feel the best solution is still that you take your daughter away with you, back to France where she will be safe and will be loved. In your capacity as a diplomat, surely you can bring your own daughter back without anyone asking questions! It will not be a risk for you but only for me and it is a risk I am willing to take. For the child.

I look forward to meeting you in October, Jack, and further discussing these plans.

Yours truly,

Margaret

I addressed the letters to Jacques Kumar, in care of the Embassy of India, Paris France. After mailing each one, I would wring my hands with worry for days about what I was planning.

With Jack's wife passing away I was afforded an opportunity because there would be no more barrier to bringing his daughter back to France with him. Whether or not Jack had ever told his wife about Karen didn't matter anymore. And he only knew about Karen. I never told him about the boy.

The children were getting older and developing their own personalities. I called our son Brisdon now, not John. In a strange way he resembled James Tamaddon with his curly hair and handsome features, even at so young an age. Karen was just Karen, an angry little girl, always shouting and crying and running from me. It was as if I had never had a child with my own husband but with James and with Jack.

Christian adored Karen and I knew what I was writing to Jack, what I was hoping he would agree to, would break Christian's heart. I had to keep focused. Christian had no right to love her like that when his own son needed him more. Brisdon was the smart child, the calm one, the little sage. Just listening to Karen crying and screaming and stamping her feet and having to chase after her gave me throbbing headaches. Brisdon was an angel. Karen had been attached to the devil in my womb. At night I still dreamed about the thing as it crawled or slithered along the floor looking for its sister. At times I couldn't eat, I couldn't sleep. Year after year this silent torment kept going on until I thought I was going mad.

When October came and I was planning to meet Jack, I banged my face against the kitchen wall—once, twice, so it would appear as if my husband had struck me. When Christian arrived home that evening, the bruise had already risen.

"My God, your face! What happened, Meg?" He touched my cheek and I winced.

"Oh, I'm just so careless. I was picking up one of Karen's toys and banged myself on the coffee table."

"Did you ice it?"

"Of course," I lied. I wanted it to look as bad as possible. There would be no make-up on my cheek this time.

I met Jack at noon at the same diner where I had first met Michael Murley. I even sat in the same booth, seeking poetic justice by closing the circle. It was Saturday. I told Christian I had some errands to run so he took the children with him to the shop.

When I saw Jack again after five years, I didn't feel any attraction at all. I hated his smug wide face. How had I ever considered him handsome? He had dark circles under his eyes now and he was thinner than I remembered.

"You don't look like yourself," I said.

"This happens when you lose someone."

As his hand reached out, the dark hairy thing repulsed me and I recoiled from him. It was never far from my mind that the devil child had also come from his loins, and that Karen was part of that seed. But I had to be careful how I came across. I didn't want to frighten him away. So I smiled when I just wanted to scream. Instead of reaching out to take Jack's hand, I wanted to stab it with a knife.

"Are you certain about this?" he asked studying my face with the bruise on one side.

"Never more certain," I insisted. "You're flying back to France in early November?"

"The first of November."

"Ah," I said, thinking, *All Saints' Day.* He had an idea of my handing over Karen in a park or department store but I already had a plan. You always pretend to let the man take control and then you steer him in the right direction.

"Next Saturday is Halloween night," I said.

"We don't have that in France."

We had a form of it back in the Scottish Highlands when I was wee Maggie. My mother used to hollow-out turnips and carve grotesque faces and sprinkle pungent-smelling cumin and coffee grounds around the doorway to dispel the evil spirits.

"The kids will dress up and go door to door to collect candy," I explained. "I will take Karen out in a costume and—"

The waitress refilled Jack's empty coffee cup to the brim and I waited for her to leave.

"Yes?"

"Can you get a car?" I asked.

"Yes, we have a diplomatic service car."

"Then drive along our street. You can stop and I will hand her to you at the curb."

He stared, the gravity of it all overcoming him, as if he wanted to get up and run. I showed him the side of my face.

"You must do this," I implored. "Not just for my sake but for the child's."

He was visibly shaking. "Yes, yes, I understand." He drew a breath as if collecting his thoughts. "Seven o'clock. I will have a driver. I will be in the back. I will open the door. It will be a black sedan. I will ask the driver to circle the block twice."

There was a long, drawn out moment when his eyes appeared to tear up. As I sat back on the red plastic bench, triumphant, he leaned forward and his clumsy hand knocked his cup from his saucer. The piping hot coffee leapt forward like a muddy river, streaming towards me. As it flowed off the table onto my lap and legs, I didn't jump or even move. I just closed my eyes and succumbed to the cleansing mortification of my flesh.

*   *   *

That Saturday night was horrible in a way I never imagined. Planning to hand off my daughter was one thing but carrying it out was quite another. I have re-lived those hours over and over in my mind for ten years. You can only live with yourself for so long before the wrongs you have done begin to take their toll, a snake constricting you tighter every day until even the slightest breath is pure agony.

On the way home from work that Friday, I stopped off at Eaton's to buy the candy Christian would hand out and two jack-o'-lantern baskets for the children to carry, but more importantly to meet with Jack one last time. I had brought clothes for Karen in a large paper bag because she would be wearing her Halloween costume and would need her clothes and her coat. I sat at the fifth-floor coffee shop at a table in the corner and waited. When Jack didn't show up I started to panic. What if he had changed his mind and was at the jewellery store right now, threatening Christian for abusing our daughter only to find my meek and sweet husband with *two* children? Then Jack appeared sheepishly, apologizing for being late.

I pushed the envelope of documents for Karen across the table towards him. I had secured a passport for Karen by forging Christian's signature and just in case, I had included a signed letter stating that Karen Elizabeth Noxon was the daughter of Professor Jacques Kumar and that he had my permission to take our daughter to France. As a diplomat, Jack should have been able to walk right through French customs and immigration without any questions.

"Are you sure about this, Margaret?" he asked once more.

"Yes," I said even if I wasn't. I was already weakening as he flipped through the documents. "It's all there," I insisted, "passport, birth certificate, just as we agreed." I had Jack repeat our address back to me. "But don't pull up right in front of our house," I warned, "or my husband will come out and kill us both. He's a big man."

"I'm so sorry for all this, *Mar-get*," he said with a pained expression and all I could feel was triumph.

"It's too late for *sorry*," I said. "Just be there."

I didn't sleep that night. The next day, while Christian was at work, I couldn't concentrate. I sat at the kitchen table and watched Karen as she played with her farm set, throwing the cows and the horses and the little red-roofed barn across the coffee table where sweet little Brisdon was colouring quietly. Every time I wanted to back down from our scheme I witnessed the monster in her.

Christian suspected nothing. When he suggested he join us trick-or-treating so we could each take a child in hand, I had to think fast because he would want to take Karen.

"Then who will stay here and hand out candy?"

"Right. Got it."

I had sewed their wee costumes on the Singer. Brisdon wanted to be a ghost under a sheet. Instead of a princess, Karen wanted to be a bat. She loved the bats in the trees in the back yard coming alive at dusk so I sewed her a pair of brown wings and a matching robe and cape. The darker the better. When she threw a tantrum I pricked my finger with the sewing needle and showed her the blood.

"See what you made mummy do!"

I waited impatiently until Christian came home from work. I had dinner ready on the table; I needed time to dress the children and get them out before seven. I watched through the window as the daylight started to fade. After I cleared the dishes I stepped out to the front porch and lit a cigarette. I inhaled deeply, trying to calm myself. It was threatening to rain.

Christian came out to the veranda with the children and a pumpkin they had carved together with its diamond-shaped eyes and toothy lopsided grimace. I breathed in the odour of old pumpkin, the odour of Brisdon House. Then he lit a candle and set it inside the thing as they watched the flame ignite the slanted eyes, the wicked grin, the crooked teeth. They danced around it, squealing. Other neighbours were setting out their own decorations to pay homage to the dead. I looked at my daughter and thought, she'll be fine, she'll be safe, it was all for the best. I just wanted the night to be over.

While Christian got the bowl of candy ready by the door, I put Brisdon in his ghost sheet and Karen in her bat costume with its pointy ears. It took longer to dress them than I thought with all the squirming and complaining. Then the doorbell rang and my heart jumped but it was just the first set of kids calling out *Trick-or-Treat!* It was time. Jack would only circle twice.

I walked out with them, holding each one by the hand. I recognized a few neighbours on their verandas which was good because they would see us and vouch for us. After the white Johnson's Florist van drove by I let go of Brisdon's hand. He ran up to a cluster of trick-or-treaters and I knew I could leave him with them and that he would be safe. Karen dragged on my arm.

"Let me. I want to go too," she whined.

"No, Karen," I said firmly and stood still until she stopped pulling. "You're going on a trip."

"Where?" She looked at me with her two-coloured eyes, her face engulfed by her bat mask. She was playing cute now, like Shirley Temple, which always worked for Christian. But for me she was Faust.

There was a wind. Leaves tumbled along the sidewalk. The rain began to spit. I drew my Macintosh tighter around me. Soon Christian would be calling us to come in from the rain. It was seven o'clock. A black car came along the street and slowed almost to a stop next to me. I couldn't see in through the windows but I made a face that said, *You idiot, not here!* Then the car passed and continued along the street, stopping at the end. I walked briskly towards it almost dragging Karen along. The back passenger door opened over the sidewalk. Jack put his foot on the curb.

"Give her to me now," he said.

I looked to my right. Then to my left. No one in sight. I took the basket from Karen's hand and set it on the curb. Jack had both his feet out and his hands outstretched.

"You're going with this nice man," I told her. "Will you be good?"

"No!" she cried out.

Jack took our daughter in his arms. She struggled against him as he shut the door. The car pulled away, turning the corner and was out of sight.

*   *   *

My daughter was gone. I stood on the curb as the rain spit down and couldn't believe it was all over. I was numb. But it wasn't over at all, it was just beginning. Now all the work began. I turned and almost ran back along the sidewalk towards the houses lit with jack-o'-lanterns like beacons. Karen's empty pumpkin basket had fallen into the gutter and I left it there as it rolled around in the wind.

I started calling, "*Karen!*" but I was really looking for Brisdon in his little ghost sheet.

Brisdon came running to me with his basket in hand and I grabbed him and held him and whispered, "You're all right, my darling, everything is going to be all right now." Soon the neighbours were coming down their porch stairs and the rain was falling harder and finally Christian was there and we were both calling out for Karen.

Christian took hold of Brisdon, lifting the sheet over his head so he could see his face. He asked him if he and his sister were playing a game, playing hide and seek, but Brisdon just kept shaking his head *no-no-no*.

"You're scaring him," I said.

"I'll take him inside and telephone the police." As soon as they left I could breathe again. Then one of our old neighbours, wearing thick glasses that made her eyes into moons, came up to me to ask what happened.

"It's my daughter. I can't find my daughter!"

"I think I saw her, dear, she was collecting candy with the other children."

Never underestimate the value of your neighbours.

More neighbours approached us. "I can't find my daughter," I repeated. I would say this over and over for the next few hours. The more I spoke those words the more I started to believe them myself and the easier it became to swallow the shame.

When two police officers arrived, they wanted to question Brisdon and we argued about that.

"You'll not worry my little boy," I defended him. "We've already talked to him."

"We really need to question him," the sergeant insisted. They were both very tall and strapping like Michael Murley, one plain, the other handsome, but neither were smiling or flirting so I couldn't gain the upper hand.

I heaved my chest. "Please leave my son alone!"

The officer with the more pleasing face took off his cap and held it in his hands. "I'm very sorry ma'am but we really need—"

Christian cut him off. "I'll talk to him. You can watch."

It was all a red herring, of course. Brisdon told us about a white van he had seen and he made it sound ominous. I didn't say anything. Let them look for it, I thought. Let them chase their own tails.

Then a third officer appeared because the front door was slightly ajar so anyone could just walk in, and he was holding Karen's empty pumpkin basket. He just stood there as all eyes turned to him. I took my cue and broke down.

They were real, those tears. But not the way everyone in the room imagined.

Christian was concerned for Brisdon so he scooped him up and put him to bed. When he came back down the stairs, the tall sergeant, the plain one, asked us for Karen's certificate of birth.

"Why do you need that?" I asked trying not to show my alarm.

"Please, ma'am. I know you're upset. We also need a recent picture of your daughter."

"Don't worry, I'll get them," Christian said. He was off to the hallway and up the stairs again. I kept twisting the moonstone ring on my finger while the police shot questions at me, one after the other. Who were Karen's friends? Did they live nearby? What about other members of our family, aunts, uncles, grandparents? Did we have any enemies? Do we know anyone who would want to do us harm? It went on and on. Then Christian returned after an eternity and I knew he had been looking for the birth certificate. He was carrying a coloured photograph of Karen. The sergeant took a long look at it.

"Is your daughter adopted?" he asked.

"No, I am," Christian replied not understanding the reason for the question. How could he not understand? I just closed my eyes. I wanted to disappear.

"And the certificate of birth?"

"I can only find our son's."

"We'll keep looking," I added carefully, needing to say something, anything, because Jack had her birth certificate.

Eventually the police left because there was nothing more they could do. "Someone may just bring her back," the sergeant said and instructed us to stay by the phone.

Christian came to me and I stood up and he held me. He was wet from the rain. He was shivering. We sat back down together on the chesterfield and waited. I could hear the loud *tick-tick-tick* of the antique clock on the small mantel, a gift from Elizabeth and John. I hated that clock.

Christian continued to shiver. "You need to get out of those wet clothes," I said.

At my insistence, he went up to take a hot shower and change into dry clothes. I heard the bathroom door shut and the shower running. I went into the kitchen. I gripped the back of a kitchen chair and hung my head. What I really needed was a drink. We kept a bottle of bourbon up high in the cupboard. As I reached for it I thought I saw a face looking in from outside the kitchen window, a neighbour or the police still nosing around. I went to the back door and opened it. And screamed.

Jack covered my mouth with his hand. He stood there in his suit, drenched from the rain, the whites of his eyes ablaze from the kitchen light behind me. He let go.

"*Jesus Christ!*" I grabbed him and pulled him into the kitchen so no one would see us. My first thought was that he was bringing Karen back. "Why are you here? Where is Karen?"

He was dripping onto the linoleum floor. "She's at the embassy. She's being looked after. But she won't settle down, Margaret. She keeps saying she wants her Cathy doll. I don't know what to do. She won't stop screaming."

"Give her a thimble of bourbon and she'll quiet down."

"All right, all right. But can you get me that doll?"

I ran upstairs as quietly as possible past the closed bathroom door. I slipped into the bedroom where Brisdon was fast asleep. I looked to Karen's bed but her Chatty Cathy doll wasn't there.

Oh Jesus! I couldn't turn on the light and wake Brisdon so I pushed the bedroom door open a bit more to let in a triangle of light from the hallway. I searched all around then I got down on my hands and knees and looked under the bed. I heard the shower stop running. I was about to give up when I saw Brisdon holding something. Gently, I pulled back the coverlet and released the doll from his grip. He stirred and then settled back.

When I returned to the kitchen Jack was pacing the floor. I handed him the doll. He blinked at me.

"Did he hit you again?" he asked.

I must have been flushed. I put my hand to my cheek. "Yes," I murmured quickly. "He's angry. He called the police. Didn't you see all the police?"

"I did but I was careful."

I opened the kitchen door and he stepped back out into the rain again. Then I don't know what struck me but I quietly called after him, "You'll take good care of her?"

He turned to look at me with wild eyes and then was gone. That's when I heard the squeaky voice of the doll cry out one of her lines from the darkness:

"Please take me with you."

*　　*　　*

284

"Eastern Airlines flight 66 to New York John F Kennedy Airport will be ready for boarding momentarily. Thank you for your patience."

The loudspeaker announces its message along the crowded corridor as I am walking back to the departure lounge. I feel like I am swimming to shore, that a heavy stone is dragging me to the bottom of a vast sea of regret. The only way I can keep my head above water is to unburden myself to my husband, finally, utterly, inconsolably.

Now Christian is straining his neck looking for me as people are standing and taking up their bags. He slumps with relief when he sees me approaching.

"There you are!"

I sit down next to him. I can smell the scents of James Tamaddon and Michael Murley on me. I wonder if he can smell them as well.

"Christian, I have something to tell you." It is now or never. I fidget with my moonstone ring. I always fidget with that ring when I worry. I am as nervous now as on the night I handed my daughter to Jack Kumar. Then the loudspeaker makes me flinch, announcing the flight is ready to board. People begin to line up.

"Can't this wait until we get home?"

"No it can't. It's all over."

I get up from that horrible plastic seat. The woman in her sarong is lifting her daughter into her arms to carry her onto the plane. She sees me and smiles in recognition. She has a beautiful smile. I was denied that same happiness. My smiles have become all twisted jack-o'-lantern grimaces because of Karen and what I did.

Christian takes up our carry-on bags, slinging one over each shoulder. Such a gentleman. My knight in shining armour. He will need that armour. We join the line that's moving through to the gate.

"What do you mean by *it's all over?*" he asks me.

We shuffle ahead. People are half turning their heads as if they can smell fear or detect a tone of hysteria rising up from inside me. I take a few deep breaths. I am glad the plane will be full. It's better this way. On the plane I can tell my whole story and he won't be able to get up and leave or even change seats or really do anything at all. Yes, I will be safer telling him everything on the plane. I breathe easier.

"You're right. Not here. I'll explain when we're in our seats," I say.

"*Explain what?*" he presses.

I don't want to tell him anything more now, but his look, that same look he learned from his mother Elizabeth, gores into me.

"It's about our daughter," I say.

People have lined up behind us now. There is no turning back.

"What about her?" He is getting frustrated. I can see the tension in his brow, the way a single blood vessel is pulsing at his temple. But I don't answer because we've reached the counter where the young lady in the Eastern Airlines uniform checks our boarding passes and smiles at us.

"Enjoy your flight."

Brisdon

The bloodstains at the bottom of the final pages of my book of the dead have turned to rust. When I close the cover and look up, the dingy lounge of Shelter Lake Lodge seems strange. I take off my glasses and rub my eyes like Rafael used to do. When I open them again, the dusty furniture, the boarded-up fireplace, the stacks of yellow magazines against the upright piano all seem out of place in this sad and narrow world of mine. The shadows deepen. The air thickens. I am enveloped in the ether from another era.

There's only going forward now. It's time to confront César. It's time for a reckoning. It's time to dig up our dead.

A few hours later I'm standing in our kitchen as Imogen pulls a pan of her venison meatloaf out of the oven. I missed dinner. I called before I left Shelter Lake to tell her I was on my way but I sat a while longer along the shoreline in a Muskoka chair I had dragged over from a nearby shack. The sun was starting to set. Two upside down canoes covered in moss lay on cinderblocks next to me. I watched the occasional waves on the lake breaking up its glass surface as if we had our own Nessie lurking underneath while the seagulls let out their distinctive *ha-ha-ha* cry overhead. César was bigger than life now, a leviathan rising to upend my boat and take me into his jaws. *Call me Ishmael.*

Imogen's face is pulled tight and her eyes are watching me. "You're far away," she says. She has no idea. I'm deciding how to sneak up to the bedroom and replace my journal with the others hidden under the bed.

She portions out my dinner and I carry the steaming plate to the dining room. I pour some wine, swirling it in my glass as Imogen circles around the table and plops down next to me.

"Did everything go well with the contractor?"

I move my food around my plate. "Yes, Francis was there with his helper. You remember Willie? He flies that old de Havilland bush plane he named *Lizzie* after his wife."

"He's such a kind man."

"They're going to winterize the buildings and start back in the spring. We don't want them getting ahead of our budget. We also have to replace the original sinks in the restaurant kitchen. I hope you aren't too disappointed."

"That's a shame, such beautiful old porcelain."

"Stainless steel is far more efficient, Imogen."

"Yes, I know. New drainage and modern building codes and all that. Tell them to do what they think best."

She gets up and leaves me to my dinner and my thoughts. I have no appetite. My mind is circling like vultures over a carcass. The image of César keeps returning. He has come alive from my *Peruvian* book of the dead, only older and more refined. He's no longer a poor student in Lima sketching bones in an ossuary, he's the celebrated *Shadow Artist.* He's all about shadows now, seclusion and secrets.

Imogen comes back into the dining room. "I have something to show you," she says.

Oh Imogen of my heart, what now? My Saxon maiden with her Celtic name moves around the room, propelled by a hidden energy source that doesn't seem to fade even after a full day working at her club.

Now she is lugging a stack of heavy photo albums over to me.

She lays the albums down with a thud. "I was looking for a picture of us to give to mother for her birthday and came across some old photos I hadn't seen for years."

When I realize they are from the cellar, I jump.

"Where did you get those?"

"Where do you think? They were in the basement under the stairs."

"Why on earth would you go down there now?"

"Why on earth are you asking me that, Brisdon? Honestly, I don't know what's gotten into you."

I relax back in my chair and laugh, hoping she doesn't detect the edginess that strains my voice. "I'm just pulling your leg, my heart."

"Look." She sets a photo album in front of me.

"Are we doing this now?"

"Just humour me, Brisdon. Do you have something better to do?"

She pulls a chair over and gets comfortable. She opens the album. It's the kind with sticky boards covered with clear plastic. If you try to remove the pictures they get stuck in the hardened glue and tear apart.

"See," she says, pointing.

It's a colour photo that is fading to sepia where my mother and father are standing on a rocky beach, my father in his trunks and my mother in her modest one-piece. Behind them are Muskoka chairs in a row under the shade of poplar trees and beyond that a few white cabins on a hill. I must have taken the photograph.

"That's incredible," I say. "I was standing there on that same spot just a few hours ago."

"It's wonderful, isn't it? The old lodge in its heyday. How lucky you are to have these memories." She is looking at the photo, caressing it with her finger. "They look happy."

I don't remember my parents being happy. They seemed mismatched; my attractive mother with her shapely figure and my skinny father with his receding hairline and scraggly goatee. And I am cursed to remember how my mother tried to drown herself in that same lake during the last of our summer trips. My father dove in and pulled her out in time and she had blamed it on her sleeping pills but I think there was something gnawing at her under the surface. Imogen doesn't know about this. She doesn't realize that all my memories of Shelter Lake are not happy ones.

Then Imogen flips the pages to some black-and-white photographs of my mother. She couldn't have been more than fifteen and was still living in Scotland. There are three snapshots of her and a young man—clearly not my father—against the basalt rock walls of a country estate. He is wearing a kilt and she is in a fancy dress.

"Your mother was very beautiful." She runs her hand over the photos as if teasing the photographs to speak.

What child doesn't think their mother is beautiful? I will never know where these pictures were taken or who the young man was. She never talked about her life before she met my father.

Imogen turns the page. "Look, here. You and your sister."

We appear to be about five years old, so it must have been taken just before Karen disappeared. This album is another book of the dead.

"I wish I had known your sister," she says. "I'm sure I would have liked her very much."

"Yes, she was exactly the opposite of me."

"Oh Brisdon!" she scolds. "You're so lucky you can remember her."

She means my eidetic memory. Strangely, my ability to recall events so vividly is linked directly to my sister's disappearance. There is actually no such thing as an eidetic or photographic memory, it's just easier for the world to call it that. After Karen vanished, my grandfather, who was a doctor, suggested I keep a diary as a form of therapy. All that did was strengthen my memory. I developed a condition known as *hyperthymesia* where I honed my ability to remember intricate details of my personal life. This auto-biographical memory is a by-product of my long-term journal entries. In suggesting I write out my feelings that could be linked to my missing sister, my grandfather unknowingly opened up a rare opportunity for me to capture and keep my memories with crystal clarity. I can remember the colours and feel the textures, hear the sounds and detect, once more, the odours and flavours I experienced at the time. I am continuously at the centre of my own unforgettable universe.

For a few moments these pictures have brought me back to that Halloween night Karen disappeared. We were going door-to-door collecting candy. I remember the big orange plastic pumpkins we were carrying to collect our treats and I can still see that white van pulling alongside us, honking its horn before speeding away.

Then I heard my mother calling. Something was wrong and I shivered.

When I saw her I raced to her and she scooped me up into her arms. *My good boy,* she said. The next thing I remember, my father brought me home and the police were there with their guns in their holsters like cowboys. My parents were arguing. Then my father knelt down beside me and asked if I could tell him anything at all about what I saw and I told him about the white van honking its horn. That made everyone in the room very jumpy like Pinocchio before Geppetto cut his strings. A policeman brought in Karen's pumpkin candy basket and my mother started to scream and then I started to cry even if I understood I wasn't to blame and nothing made any sense. My father put me to bed.

Karen always slept in the bed next to mine. It was still made up with her Chatty Cathy doll in pony-tails resting with closed eyes, her arms raised, waiting to be lifted up and hugged. After my father turned off the lights and left the room, I crept out of bed and took up the doll. I was told boys didn't play with dolls so I climbed back into bed and partially hid her under the covers with just her face sticking out. I lay there, curled up with her and together we watched the unusual lights from outside moving against the walls. It made the butterfly and rocket ship mobiles above our beds dance as if fluttering away or blasting off. *Zoom zoom zoom we're going to the moon, if you want to take a trip, climb aboard my rocket ship...*

When I woke the next morning, Karen was still not there. And her Chatty Cathy doll was gone.

*   *   *

Imogen gets up from the dining room table and clears away my uneaten dinner. "Don't forget I'm going to the food and beverage conference next weekend, Brisdon."

"With Max?" It comes out more like an accusation than a question.

She ignores that. "And don't forget about tomorrow night."

"What's tomorrow?"

"Oh Brisdon! It's mother's birthday dinner. You can be so forgetful for someone with a perfect memory."

"Yes, yes, the Beechwood Club at six. See, I remember."

I sip from my glass of wine. The tannin is bitter, like my early adult years as an orphan. Bitter almonds, I think. Cherry pits and apple seeds.

When my parents died in that plane crash, Doctor John and Elizabeth Noxon, who once adopted my father, ended up adopting me. I was John to them; they refused to call me Brisdon as if they were trying to erase my identity. I had to leave school and move to London Ontario which was where I first heard the screaming of the cicadas on the hottest days of summer. I thought it was the hydro wires overhead buzzing from the heat.

I had stopped writing my journals a long time ago but now that the death of my parents supposedly caused a new trauma for me, my grandfather prompted me to start writing again. He gave me a set of thick black ledger books so I could write about my inner trials to help me face my fears. I still dedicated them to Karen. They became a witness to my world, the world according to Brisdon.

One morning at the breakfast table my grandfather said, "John, you must return that Victor Hugo book you took from my library, without permission."

"I'm reading it for French class," I replied.

"It's very old and very valuable. You need to learn the value of books." He brought me into his library and explained their intrinsic and accumulative worth. They were like works of art. As well as a number of rare editions, one entire side of his library was devoted to medical titles and leather-bound journals dating back to the seventeenth century. I held one in my hands.

"This is from the sixteen hundreds?" I asked, awestruck. "Could people even read back then?"

"Yes, thanks to Mr. Gutenberg. This one is a manual published in London about the bubonic plague. There are a number of curious misconceptions in this book. They called it *the disease of the poor,* which it was not, and thought that bleeding a person would let the poison seep out which was pure superstition and only spread the disease faster."

'Lord haue mercy on our souls,' it read, *'we are the poore of Londyn, do not let us dye.'*

It was during my search for another French copy of *Notre-Dame de Paris* that I came upon the notebook that I would eventually take with me to Peru. It was one of the

293

blank journals disguised as famous books in their original dust jackets on display in the bookstore window. They had *The Great Gatsby* with its glitter and blue flapper face and *The Catcher in the Rye* with its merry-go-round horse but the one that really caught my eye was in a plain brown jacket of *The Tibetan Book of the Dead*. I didn't think it was very famous but I went in and asked about it anyway.

The bookseller pulled it out for me. "It's empty, see."

"What about the real book?" I asked.

"The original is hard to find. It would cost a hundred dollars at least."

"I've got twenty dollars and fifty cents."

I bought it along with another beautiful old French edition of *Notre Dame de Paris* that would rival my grand-father's and which I have kept to this very day.

The following Saturday I spent the afternoon at the library where I was able to find an actual copy of *The Bardo Thodol*, better known as *The Tibetan Book of the Dead*. The grey-haired librarian in her horn-rimmed glasses eyed me with curiosity.

"That's a bit heavy for someone your age," she said.

"I'm doing a paper on it for school," I lied.

"Well it's all voodoo to me."

When she brought it out from the stacks, I huddled at a long oak table under a brass lamp with a yellow glass shade and read it cover to cover. It was an ancient chant for the dying who would pass from one *bardo*, a state of exist-ence between death and rebirth, to another until they saw "the light." Those who didn't see the light would be driven by the winds of *Karma* to separate from their earthly bodies, wandering and suffering until they were reborn.

It was an eighth-century description of a ghost.

*   *   *

Imogen closes the photo album and announces, "I'm going to bed."

"I'll be up soon," I promise. I'm not ready to go to bed yet. I need time to think. I drop myself into my easy chair and shut my eyes. *César is back...* In my chair of dreams I think only of César until I start to drift off and then I have returned to the *vernissage* where César is in disguise. *Brisdon por siempre*, he whispers and then we are lounging on a lumpy bed, naming the names of authors like Virginia Woolf and Thomas Wolfe, all the *wolves* of literature until the game turns from pleasure to heartache, from water to fire, until we are lying apart sweating and spent and lost forever. *O ghost come back again...*

I wake and the dream starts to fade, as it always does, to that locked part of our minds we are so rarely allowed passage.

On the way to bed I switch off the lights and climb the stairs in the dark. A single silver thread of the dream entwines itself around me as I clutch the bannister. When I reach the landing I can almost see it glistening as it trails behind me. I climb into bed next to Imogen and push my head into my pillow. Soon I am floating upwards, an astral body elusive and esoteric like the exosphere of the farthest planets. I finally unravel myself from my thread of dreams and then, once free, lift higher, moving through the cold glass panes of the bedroom window, dodging the gnarled branches of the old elm tree, then farther out into the night to find César who is finally so close, to lie once again with his living, breathing spirit, his life energy, or simply the manifestation of my maddening desire for him, to reach my ghost arms around him and to forgive him, to make everything right again.

This time, in the morning, I remember everything.

*　　*　　*

"Parfait, could you come in here for a moment?"

I am back in my office at the TAM first thing Monday morning. I wave in my intern who I saw dressed as a scarecrow at the masquerade *vernissage*. Parfait St. Pierre is Haitian and an art history major, just as I was at the *Museo de Arte de Lima*, but it was his name that struck me first: *Parfait* is French for Perfect, or *Perfecto* in Spanish, the name of the man whose watch I've worn most of my adult life. The watch died one day a few years back and no new battery or tinkering horologist could start it up again. I wondered if Rafael had died too, at the moment it had stopped. Stranger things have happened.

Parfait sits down in the chair in front of my desk.

"I'm sorry I've missed the last month of your internship. I just started to get to know you when—" I hesitate,"—well, you know, I had that stupid accident."

"All accidents are stupid, aren't they?"

I like his charming Creole accent. "So you attended our party for CÁLA Saturday night?"

"Yes, I brought my boyfriend. How did you know?"

Boyfriend? Yes, I should have seen that coming. Parfait speaks so casually, so self-assured. If I had said anything like that to Señor Barón—

"I was there. I recognized you. Did you get to meet the guest of honour?"

"No, but apparently he was the man dressed as Zorro."

"Yes, that was him. Listen Parfait, I need you to track him down."

"The artist, CÁLA?"

"Yes, exactly. I need you to arrange a call for me with his New York agent. Tell him I need to speak with *César*. That should get his attention."

"César? Sure. Anything else?"

"That will be all." I settle back thinking, *That will be more than enough.*

While I was away, Fiona Tamaddon chaired a shareholder meeting and the result is a thick, comb-bound impact assessment file which lies perilously before me and is stamped CONFIDENTIAL. I open it to the first page but can't concentrate. I keep seeing César in his mask and gauntlets and realize I don't know what he looks like now. I try to re-focus on the text but it's no use. I go through my hundreds of emails until I've had enough. I need to stretch my legs. I leave my office and take a walk through the galleries. It's Monday and the museum is closed. I climb the winding stairs. The fifth floor has been cleared of the remnants of the *vernissage*. The podium, the chairs for the band and the tall electric candles and their stands are gone. The floor has been swept of all the glitter and mopped clean of the event's dazzle. Once more, the room resembles a bright industrial loft, heavily laden with César's artwork.

It's all here, I am certain, the secret to César and his rising star, the young *Limeño* who I coached and coaxed to keep drawing, and who sketched me while he thought I slept. I go back to *The Art of Dying*. The secret must be in here, because it is a cry of sorrow and outrage. It is Ataccala. I move in closer. *And there it is.* At the bottom of the canvas he has painted a life-size corpse lying amongst the bones of the unburied, rendered with painstaking detail and it is *me*. I am the one who is rotting in the grave with my mouth open as if I have died screaming. That's *my* naked body with *my* face. The jaw is wrenched wide and the cheeks are stained with blood and tears. The open eyes are *my* blue eyes and they stare back glassy and dead, their light extinguished with the feverish dab of a tiny paintbrush.

I am gob-smacked. I make my way back down the staircase like in a dream. Parfait is hovering in front of my office.

"Excuse me, Mr. Noxon, I have reached Gilles Sevigny's office. He is able to speak with you now if you're available."

When I pick up the phone César's agent is walking on eggshells. Saying César's name has thrown him as I anticipated. "Do you know him?" he asks carefully.

"Yes, we know each other, *César and I,*" I emphasize.

There is another pause. He hasn't been in this situation before. "If you could please be discreet—"

"Yes of course. But I need to speak with him."

"I can't help you there. I don't think he's back from Toronto."

That takes me by surprise. "Do you know where he's staying?" He hesitates. I hear him breathing into the microphone. "It's important," I stress.

He gives in. "The Four Seasons."

There's nothing to do but find him myself. At noon when I leave my office, Parfait is in his cubicle eating a sandwich and reading *Crime and Punishment.*

"Watch out for that Raskolnikov," I say to catch his attention. "I'm stepping out for a while."

I hail a cab to the hotel. The doorman looks like a beefeater in his long grey jacket as he pushes the door open for me. The panelled lobby that soars above my head is empty; it's between check-out and check-in time. The young woman behind the marble reception desk looks up as I approach. She has closely cropped red hair and her lips are painted purple.

"I'm looking for one of your guests," I say. "Could you try Acosta?"

She types away at her computer hidden below the counter. She looks up.

"No, sorry."

"Try *CÁLA* please." I spell it. She types. Nothing. Of course not. *Stupid, stupid.* "He's Peruvian. My age. Does that help?"

"No sir, I'm afraid not."

I am stepping nervously from one foot to the other. Beads of sweat cluster on my brow. I think back to the game César and I played, rhyming off the names of painters we knew. It could be his system of alternative names. He could have used any one of them. Who was his favourite artist?

"Could you try *Goya?*"

She looks at me for a moment. She is reaching her limit, I can tell. She types.

"No, sir, I'm sorry. A Francisco but no Goya."

"I'll just take a seat in your lounge then, in case he passes by."

"Certainly, sir."

There is only one other person in the lounge, a woman by the window on her phone. As soon as I'm settled with a clear vantage point, a young man appears with a leather-bound menu. I'm suddenly famished; I only picked at my dinner the night before. I order a sandwich, a Perrier and an espresso. I sit munching and sipping, keeping a level gaze so I won't miss César entering or leaving the hotel. I try to check my messages but my old BlackBerry has died and the charging cord is at the office.

The purple-lipped clerk occasionally glances my way from behind the counter. At one point she leans over to the young blonde man who served me, discussing me, no doubt, because they both look briefly in my direction. Then she is gone, shift over, free of this lunatic in a suit sitting alone and waiting for a mysterious, nameless guest. I feel self-conscious just sitting here, staring at the panelling, at the huge vase of flowers on the centre table, at the green velvet drapery that separates this room from another. But if humility is the price to pay to get to César, I will pay it. So I continue to wait. After a while a different server approaches and I order another espresso and down it in one gulp. It's incredibly acerbic. Every so often a man will step out of the elevator or come through the front door, someone with dark hair, of medium build—and I start. But they aren't César.

I look at my watch. It's past three o'clock. I'm reaching for my coat to leave and put this insanity of an afternoon behind me when a man steps into the lobby, dark-skinned, slender, black hair. I stand up quickly, banging my knee against the coffee table and upending my espresso cup. The man approaches the clerk behind the counter, probably to ask if there are any messages from me, from Brisdon Noxon, his friend Brisdon, his old lover Brisdon...

"Hello!" I call and he turns. But it isn't César. He looks nothing like César. I just mumble my apologies and walk out of the hotel, flushed and feeling like an utter fool.

When I return to the museum, Parfait jumps up from his chair and follows me into my office.

"What is it, Parfait?"

"We couldn't reach you."

"Yes, I'm sorry. My phone died."

"While you were gone someone came to see you."

I stare at him. "Someone?"

"He didn't give his name but said you would know who he was."

You've got to be fucking kidding me! I just grit my teeth and say, "He did?"

"He waited for about an hour and then he left this."

Parfait hands me a generic Four Seasons Hotel business card. He watches me turn it over. César has written HOTEL LOBBY 8PM TONIGHT. It's the same handwriting from my paper napkin, *BRISDON IS LOVE.*

"Is that all?" I ask wondering if César left anything else for me.

Parfait eyes me strangely. "No, there's more. Fiona Tamaddon is looking for you."

*   *   *

Six degrees of separation is the catch-phrase for being separated by just six people from anyone else in the world. Similarly, I am convinced there are *seven degrees of coincidence*, where we are just seven events away from any other occurrence throughout all of history. Everything is mathematics and the number seven keeps recurring: seven colours in a rainbow; seven deadly sins; seven continents and seven seas; seven planets in our solar system that have influence over humanity; changes in our bodies occur biologically every seven years; in Egyptian mythology there are seven angels; in the Bible there are seven churches and seven seals; the lotus flower on Buddha's pedestal has seven petals, and on it goes...

Coincidence is not without its perils. For example, one sweltering summer, I flew to New York on museum business, spending the day at the MET arranging to move a priceless Caravaggio which was on loan to the TAM. It was unusually crowded that day because the MET was participating in the annual Museum Mile Festival. As I walked through the lobby I had the feeling someone was watching me. Later, as I was heading back to my hotel room, an ambulance and police car almost ran me off the sidewalk. A crowd was gathered at the end of the road so I veered down East 82nd Street and found an air-conditioned bar. As I took my first sip of cold beer, someone sat down on the next stool, trying to catch the bartender's eye. Then he looked at me with surprise.

"Hey, I know you," he said. "You were at the MET. You're the curator."

I looked at him. I was certain I knew him with that rugged open face. He had overalls on, like a painter or carpenter with his sleeves rolled up showing sunburnt, tattooed arms. "Yes, that's right," I replied, realizing it must have been him watching me in the lobby. "How do you know me?" I challenged.

He laughed. "I work with the team that's moving your artwork, mate." The server appeared. "I'm having what he's having," he said and thanked her with a devilish wink. "So, you're from the TAM then," he chuckled, "from *Toronto the Good*?"

"Yes, and you?"

"Canberra originally. But I've been all over South America, mostly Peru–"

And there it was. Confirmation he was the bartender from the restaurant I had ducked into on the outskirts of Lima. He smiled and his Caribbean Sea-blue eyes drew me in with the sharks and the scorpion fish and the vibrant sea anemones. What were the odds? He extended his hand. "Riley here."

I wanted to say to him, *Yes, Craig Riley from El Pulpo*, the night the bus from Independencia broke down and I stumbled into his bar. He was older of course, but still attractive with his devil-may-care attitude.

"Brisdon," I replied, shaking his hand.

"As in Brisbane?" he asked, just like before.

Later, back at his tiny apartment under a useless ceiling fan, sweating from the heat of our bodies next to each other, he said, "Get out of the closet, Brisbane."

"It's complicated."

"How complicated can it be?"

"Let's just say I'm comfortable the way I am."

Curious, he reached for the medallion around my neck. "What's this?"

I felt an irrational surge of fear he would recognize it. "It was a gift from Peru," I replied. Riley pulled at it to see it more closely.

"From a lover then?"

"Careful!" I warned.

"Looks like it should be in a museum." I winced. He was right, of course. He noticed my discomfort but thought it was because of something else. He said, "I got married too, mate. In Peru. She was the love of my life and gave me two little girls. All grown up now, my daughters. Won't speak to me."

"I'm sorry to hear that."

"So how did everything turn out for you in Lima?"

"It didn't turn out well at all."

"Did someone break your heart, Brisbane? Since my wife left I've had my heart stomped on, shat on and then hacked to shreds. When I started batting for the other team I kept getting kicked in the balls. You get used to it."

But I wasn't going to get used to it. I vowed after César never to live that kind of life. Suddenly I hated myself; I was just a hypocrite like the worst of them, lying here with Riley under the slow turn of the ceiling fan that was stirring up the old dust of broken sorrows.

*   *   *

For some reason I can't get Riley out of my head. The dangers of coincidence fill my thoughts as I make my way to see Fiona, as if the inner workings of fate are being revealed to me for just an instant, allowing me a glimpse into an incomprehensible pattern to the universe which no one else has ever seen.

I'm sweating with a new sense of dread as I tap on her open office door. Fiona looks up from behind her desk, intent on something with her reading glasses perched on the tip of her nose. Her red hair is piled on her head like a braided snake.

"You wanted to see me?"

She motions me in. "Close the door and come sit, Brisdon."

I think, *What fresh hell is this?* I say, "What can I do for you, Fiona?"

"Have you looked over the planning report?"

She is referring to the impact assessment. "No, sorry. I haven't gotten through it yet."

"I see!" She's not pleased about that.

"I had a few fires to put out."

"That's no matter then. During the period you were away the management board and I spent some time assessing our situation."

"What situation would that be?"

"We're going to be making some changes."

She is hedging. She looks back down at the papers on her desk.

"What sort of changes?" I press.

"To start, we're selling seven major pieces from our collections." She sees my surprise. "I've consulted the lawyers and my CFO. We've already retained an auction house. It's perfectly legal."

"I never said it wasn't." For the third time today, I'm thunderstruck. She avoids my gaze by paging through the document in front of her.

"The National Association of Museums is putting a new equity initiative in place." It sounds like she's reading directly from the paper in front of her. "We expect to funnel the money from the auction toward a broader equity plan and to establish dedicated funds for diversity, equity, accessibility, and inclusion programs."

This initiative isn't new. I've heard of museums in Europe selling valuable artworks by the old male masters: Mondrian and Chagall and Gerhard Richter in order to buy more work by women and artists of colour. This selling-off was labelled "thoughtless" and "irresponsible" by critics without addressing the histories of racism or sexism perpetrated by these same museums. They were attempts to avoid a broader, deeper self-examination by taking the easiest way out through financial transactions, and now to support and lengthen Fiona Tamaddon's *bottom line.*

She looks up again. "That includes developing new hiring initiatives for the museum, Brisdon."

"And what does that mean?"

"I'm sorry, Brisdon, but I'm afraid we're going to have to let you go. After fifteen years, it's time for a change, don't you think? Why don't you just retire? We're not getting any younger, are we?" She attempts a coy giggle but it's a snake's snigger. I bristle.

"I can't afford to retire, Fiona." I think of the future costs for Shelter Lake lodge. "I have obligations."

"Obligations?" She almost snorts. "Did I ever tell you about my father and *his* obligations?" She doesn't wait for me to answer. "He was old school, of course, but when it came down to it, James Tamaddon was not an astute business man. He couldn't fulfil his obligations handed down through generations. He almost lost the entire family fortune. We almost lost Brisdon House! He grew into a fussy and broken old man as if his inherited wealth could never fulfil him, as if there had been something missing all his life. 'It's all cankered hearts,' he would say, whatever that meant. His sister, my Aunt Nessie, was the eldest and should have inherited but it was the old boys club and she was just a *girl.* You see the problem, Brisdon? Nessie was the brightest one of the family, but she was only a woman. Luckily, she managed to take over at the end through her husband's influence and saved us all. No, my father's pining and drinking were his undoing. So don't talk to me about obligations."

"What are you saying, Fiona?"

"I'm saying there's no room for the old boys' club anymore, Brisdon. We need diversity in our leadership team."

"What if I told you I was gay?"

She laughs. "Oh Brisdon, really, don't tell me your problems. Even if you identified as LBTG... LBG—oh, for God's sake, what a garbage acronym! They don't make it easy for themselves and I wouldn't hire one of *them*. Gays are so—" she searches for the right word, "—so difficult to *manage*."

I don't know how I am able to stay calm. "Fiona, you are trampling over every human rights principle—"

She cuts me off. "Now Brisdon, it's as hard for me to tell you this as it is for you to hear it." I can't restrain from laughing out loud. This riles her. "If you have a problem, take it up with the Board. I'm sorry." And that was that.

When I get back to my desk Parfait is waiting for me. He must have seen the look on my face.

"Is something the matter, Mr. Noxon?"

"It's been one fuck of a day, Parfait."

He follows me into my office. "Do you mind if I ask you something?"

"Sure Parfait, what is it?"

He fidgets. "That huge CÁLA in the upper gallery, the one with the body at the bottom—" He hesitates as I bite my lower lip knowing what's coming, "That dead body, sir, it looks exactly like you." He waits for my reaction but I don't react. I can't. Something is happening to me. "Are you all right, sir?"

I am clutching the side of my desk. Then the coil inside me that has been winding tighter and tighter since I saw César just a few days ago finally springs free. Suddenly I can breathe again. The whole mechanism inside me that has squeezed me, perhaps my entire life, is now gone. I laugh. I can't stop laughing. Parfait steps back as the tears roll down my cheeks. Finally, when I wipe my eyes and catch my breath, I place a hand on Parfait's shoulder for just a moment, just long enough for him to understand the gesture is true *sympàtico.*

"Thank you for saving me."

"I don't understand."

I gather up my coat and briefcase, throwing my dead BlackBerry onto my desk. It's the end of the BlackBerry anyway. Then I address him as he stands between me and my freedom, the doorway out of this museum that has been my life, my duplicitous life, the life that is now ending.

"I'm just grateful to you, Parfait. Believe it or not, I could learn from you. There will always be a kind of divide. There will always be people to put you down, stamp all over you."

"What are you saying, Mr. Noxon?"

I shake my head. I'm making a mess of this moment like I have made a mess of every other important moment in my life. *Come clean, Brisdon. Just say it.*

"Yes, Parfait, that *is* me in the painting. The man who painted it, the man you met today with the business card, his name is César and he is CÁLA, and he and I were lovers once, and we were *in love.* And maybe we still have those same feelings, I don't know. I don't know how time has changed him or me for that matter. But I know this. Life is too short to waver between what you should do and what you have to do..."

Parfait's expression has gone from alarm to wonder and with this he breaks into a wide smile, as if I am making sense after all.

"Thanks, Mr. Noxon."

"Good luck to you, Parfait."

*   *   *

HOTEL LOBBY 8PM TONIGHT.

Gripping the steering wheel, I try to figure out what to do now. First there's Klara Nation's birthday dinner at Imogen's club. I'll have to slip out early. Imogen won't be happy about that! How can I tell her I've lost my job and possibly our hopes for Shelter Lake? How could I ever explain that I've got to see the lover who has come back into my life like Lucifer himself? It's as if I've pulled the Death card from the Tarot deck she keeps wrapped in a silk scarf in her dresser drawer.

I promised Imogen I would pick up flowers for Klara so I circle around until I find a parking spot near a florist. The shopkeeper has just locked the doors so I tap on the window and she lets me in. I glance at my watch. It's just after six.

When the elevator doors open onto the Beechwood Club dining room, I head for one of the private rooms where I can hear laughter. All heads look at me as if they've been talking about me.

"You made it," Imogen announces as if there has been doubt about that.

I say my hellos and kiss Klara on the cheek. I present her with the bouquet of Japanese anemone and flowering mint, and wish her health and happiness for many more years to come. Her eighty year-old eyes still sparkle bright blue and I take my seat between her and Imogen beneath the birthday banner they have hung above the fireplace. A server comes in with a tray of drinks and I order a scotch.

Imogen's older brother Morgan, a police detective, says, "Good of you to make it old man." Next to him his wife Mercy has the grace to thank me for coming.

Imogen taps a crystal beaker with a spoon.

"Now that we're all together, let's raise our glasses for a toast to mother!"

I raise a water glass, even though it's supposed to be bad luck, and we *clink, clink, clink* around the table, and Oliver pipes up, "I have no intention of getting old like the rest of you." Oliver is the youngest of Imogen's three brothers, the only one in the family unmarried and a bit rough around the edges.

Morgan toasts back, "Only the good die young, Oliver."

"He's so different from us, I always thought Oliver belonged to the milk man," the number two son, Curan, pipes up. His wife Nancy, who sits next to him, has an old schoolmarm tightness to her with her taught posture, closely cropped hair and wire-rimmed glasses.

Klara clears her throat to be heard. "They stopped delivering milk long before Oliver was born."

Morgan turns to me. "How's that leg of yours, by the way?"

Nancy interjects. "Curan says you fell off a ladder?"

"It's embarrassing," I confess.

"It wasn't at the time," Imogen says. "You could have been badly hurt."

All eyes on me, I give in. "It was during my birthday weekend. We were up at the resort to nose around and make plans. Imogen packed a picnic lunch. We met with the contractors and then we saw it."

"A bird's nest," Imogen interjects.

"It was under the eavestrough of the old residence. The nest was abandoned. I knew Imogen would love to make it into an Easter egg container for her grandnephew." I look at Mercy. "For little Atticus."

"What happened?" Mercy asks.

"I climbed up a ladder to get it."

"Brisdon doesn't like heights," Imogen says.

"I felt the ladder teeter but it was too late and that was the end of me. I fell hard."

"You certain she didn't kick it over?" Oliver asks.

"He managed to save the nest," Imogen adds.

"No good deed goes unpunished," Morgan pronounces.

I can barely sit through the meal. Curan brings out a book of Shakespeare and they play a game, *the danger of opening a book at random*, where you read a random passage that is supposed to make sense, like turning over a Tarot card. When it's my turn I read, "*I lodge in fear: though this is a heavenly angel, hell is here.*" Everyone laughs but I feel sick. You don't control coincidence, I want to say, coincidence controls you.

Their voices start to fade away. Klara is saying something but her voice sounds like it's coming from the end of a tunnel. I check my watch. I notice Oliver staring at me as if he knows what I'm thinking. *Like mother, like son*, someone says about Oliver. Everyone is talking at the same time and laughing and Imogen is asking the server to bring in more wine and refill the glasses. I push my glass away. No more. I have to remain alert now. I have to return to the present. I look at my watch again: *César, César, César,* the second hand ticks as it goes around. Imogen nudges me.

"What's up with you?"

My heart is pounding. I whisper back, "Can we speak for a moment? In private?"

She gives me a look that says, *Why do I feel you are going to disappoint me?* She follows me out of the room. Their stares feel like bee stings. Out in the hallway I put my hand on her arm. Her skin feels warm when it should feel like ice.

"There is somewhere I have to go. I really can't explain it now."

"Oh Brisdon!" She searches my face. I read concern in her expression. I didn't expect this reaction, a kind of warmth, even kindness. I could have fought against resentment or outrage but not this. It strikes me so hard I feel my eyes tear up. But I have to go. It's nearing eight o'clock and I can't miss César again. It will be my last chance.

"It's just..." I stammer. "It's something I can't put off. I'm sorry, Imogen."

"It's all right. I don't understand but I see it's important. When will you be back?"

"I don't know."

She calls after me, "Brisdon..." and then her voice falters. Maybe she's angry now. I look back expecting three small words to follow: *Go to hell!* or *Don't come back!*

Instead she says, "I love you."

* * *

As I drive to the Four Seasons Hotel, I still feel sick. I'm being propelled by something I can't control. Turning back now is out of the question.

There's no place to park on the street so I drive into the hotel's underground parking lot. It's almost deserted. Then I take the parking stairs two at a time up to the lobby. César isn't there yet. I approach the front desk. Luckily the same blonde clerk is still there, the one who watched me waiting for César earlier in the day. *My God, was that just this afternoon?* He recognizes me. I describe César and hand him my own business card, useless now, but it adds some credibility. On the back I have written: HOTEL PARKING GARAGE 8:00 PM. Then I stand out of the way, next to the velvet drapery so I have a view of the front desk. I check my watch again. Eight o'clock on the dot. I wait. Five minutes after eight. My heart is pounding. I'm sweating. Seven minutes. I think of a thousand things that could go wrong. I am beginning to realize the extent of my unravelling when I see him walking across the lobby. Before anything else I recognize his confident stride, unique as a fingerprint, even if he has a slight limp now. He seems smaller than I remember. He looks older and more distinguished, like a well-groomed Che Guevara at fifty. For a moment I forget my bitterness. I watch him survey the lobby and then approach the front desk to speak with the clerk who hands him my card. I disappear into the stairwell.

I wait in the parking garage by the elevator doors. I can hear the elevator approaching. I can almost feel his weight inside it. My heart continues to race. When the doors finally open and César steps out, we stand facing each other in a sort of over-bright shock from the florescent lights above us. They buzz like cicadas. The concrete walls are even greyer than my memory of Lima. César's rich complexion is mottled by the ugly light. He holds my card in his hand.

"*Touché*," he says." We both stand perfectly still.

"César," I just say. I want to touch him, embrace him, but I can't.

"This isn't the most romantic setting for a reunion," he says.

"I know. I want to take you somewhere."

"I was thinking of my suite, Brisdon. It's very nice. The penthouse."

"I have another place in mind," I say. "Follow me."

I don't give him a choice. I move in the direction of my car and I hear him behind me.

"I don't have my jacket, Brisdon. I thought we would just go upstairs." He has a slight British accent and a New Yorker's expressive tone. His English is perfect, as if this isn't really him speaking at all. I pull my remote key fob from my pocket and start the car.

"There's a place of mine just outside the city where we can be alone."

"Ah, what do you have in mind?" He is still behind me but I can sense his smirk.

"It will take a while to drive there." I warn him.

"Brisdon, I don't have my wallet and I left my phone in my jacket."

"I need you to come with me."

"No, Brisdon."

Just like Ataccala. *No, Brisdon.* I can't let him leave again. I am at the trunk of my car now, pulling at the bungee cords, loosening them. The trunk swings open.

"At least come back here," I say and I feel my voice rising in panic.

It all happens fast and far too easily even though I know how insane this whole plan is. The adrenaline has given me an extraordinary, otherworldly strength as I wrestle with him, forcing him into the empty trunk. Before he can understand what's happening, before he can struggle out, I slam the lid down and retie the bungee cords, stretching and turning them once, twice, three times around. He hollers and bangs his fists from inside. I have to catch my breath and wipe the sweat off my brow. There's still no one else in the garage, no other sounds but the hollow, eerie echo of my captive. I jump into the car and the squealing tires mixed with César's shrieks echo off the walls like a dragon wailing in a *Schadenfreude* nightmare.

At first César won't stop screaming. Then he goes quiet. I get onto the highway and speed up. A half hour passes. When he starts up again, banging on the inside of the trunk over and over while he yells and curses, I start screaming at the top of my lungs with him. That keeps him quiet for a while. The drive goes on and on, the headlights cutting through the night. I have a horrible thought that this is the night to end all nights like *Armageddon* or *Dooms-day*. Soon we are the only car on the road. I turn on the radio and crank up the volume. The music seems to soothe him. When I don't hear him for a while I begin to panic. I switch the radio off. Has he suffocated? Should I pull over and look? Then he starts up again, kicking and banging. I keep my focus on the road, and try not to think about what I'm doing or I'll go mad and crash us into a tree or an oncoming truck. My automatic high beams click to low just as we approach a police cruiser idling on the side of the road, right at the Shelter Lake sign where I need to turn. I hold my breath. What if the officer hears him? When we pass I see her staring into her digital terminal. Her skin is greenish in the light. She doesn't look up.

As I pull into the familiar drive, it's raining and the usually starry sky is hidden behind heavy clouds. There are no street lamps, no moon, no Venus, no shimmering comets, just a black void beyond the headlight beams. There will be no dawn, I worry, only *Judgement Day*.

The gravel crunches under the tires as I pull to a stop. I don't hear him. Maybe he has lost his voice from scream-ing. I leave the car engine running to keep the headlamps on. When I step from the car I have to hold onto the door because everything is spinning. A few crickets are chirping. I feel the rain on my face. It calms me. The air has a freshness, a humid late-summer smell that blankets the forest and presses itself over the surface of the hidden lake with a miasma of dispiriting dreams. I move around the car, afraid of what will happen next. I untie the bungee cords, one loop, two loops, three... and stand back.

For an instant there is nothing else but the hum of the car engine. Then César kicks the trunk wide open. He groans and pulls himself out. He stands there, lost and teetering, like he's adrift on a moving raft. He can't see through the dark beyond the headlights. He is searching for me.

"César," I call out.

"*Hijo de puta! Maldito perra!*" He finds his voice and hollers obscenities until he runs out of them and then starts all over again. Finally, out of breath, his voice cracking, he stops. His chest is heaving and he catches sight of me standing against the entrance that reads *Shelter* in an arc above me. "Are you totally *loco?*" he yells.

"I didn't want to have to do that."

"*Estúpido!* You could have killed me!"

I don't know what to say. "I'm sorry, César. But you said no—"

"You madman! What was wrong with going to a bar or my hotel room? Why force me into the boot of your fucking car?"

We stand far apart from each other, a chasm I have no idea how to bridge.

"I know, but we're here now. It's for the best, César."

"For the best of what? *For who?*"

"So you won't walk away again." There. I said it.

"*Holy Mary, Mother of God!*" He glares at me, one shadow against another.

"We can be honest with each other here. We can be ourselves."

"Out here in the middle of nowhere in the rain? We can be ourselves anywhere, *imbécil!*"

"I don't expect you to understand. Anyway it's done. We're here."

He looks around. "Where is *here*?"

"It's an old vacant resort on a lake. We can be alone. We can talk."

"Can we at least go somewhere dry?" It was starting to rain harder now.

"Are we okay, then?"

"*Dios mío!* Far from it."

"Temporary truce, then?"

César lets out a snort of disgust. "On two conditions."

"Name them."

"You don't attack me with an axe."

He almost isn't kidding. I have to laugh at that. "That's fair. The other?"

"You drive me right back to the hotel when you're finished with whatever you have to get off your chest."

"Agreed."

"And not in the boot of the car!"

"Yes, yes! Front seat."

We stand quietly then. Neither of us moves. The rain is pelting against the car.

"Well?" He's waiting for my next move. *Jaque mate.*

I grab the keys from the glove compartment and he gives me a wide berth. César follows behind as I head for the schoolhouse guided by the headlamps. The lock gives me trouble but once inside, I hit the switch for the single light bulb over the reception counter. I point the key fob at the car to shut off the engine. A few moments later the headlamps also go off. Only then do I realize that César hasn't followed me at all. He's gone.

*   *   *

"*César!*" I shout. I can hear nothing but the rain and the fluttering of moths circling the light above the reception counter. I step back outside and let my eyes adjust to the inky night.

"César!" I call again. "What are you doing? There's no one for miles."

I listen. Water is dripping into a puddle like the ticking of a clock but it's slower, exaggerated, as if I have bent time by bringing César here.

I hear him before I can see him. He hasn't run off. He is behind me and before I can turn, something strikes me hard against my back like he has clubbed me with a piece of plywood. My glasses fly off and I go toppling off the top step to land face down on the hard, wet ground. Only then do I feel the pain across my back and ribs as I lie there trying to catch my breath. I feel César's hands rummaging through my pockets. He hovers over me a moment and says, "I'm sorry too, Brisdon."

As he moves away I lift my face from the ground to shake off the shock of the blow. I don't think I'm really hurt. My glasses are lost somewhere in the wet grass beyond me. I watch his shadow open the door of my car. No! I didn't come this far for nothing. I heave myself up as César pushes the ignition switch. The engine revs up as the headlamps come on, illuminating the schoolhouse and trees in an almost supernatural white light. With as much strength as I can muster over the throbbing pain in my back, I scramble towards him. I have to put myself in his way so he will have to run me over if he wants to leave me here.

The tires spin as he makes his turn, throwing up gravel. I lurch between the headlights and the stone gate. The word *Shelter* hangs mockingly in the air. I fall in front of the car, landing on my hands and knees as the headlights burn into my eyes. But he slams on the brakes and the front bumper comes to a stop, nudging me over so that I collapse onto the wet gravel, panting, not so much from pain or trying to catch my breath, but because for a split second I thought I had miscalculated César's humanity, the same way I had felt on that distant afternoon when Major Alejandro Francisco de Paula y Cortez stepped out of the police cruiser on the side of the desert road to shoot me.

César just sits in the car, the engine running, the lights blinding me. Neither of us move. Then the engine cuts out. I hear his feet crunch on the gravel then stop as if looking to see if I'm still alive.

"César..." I say but it comes out as a gasp, an entreaty, a defence against my obvious blunder of bringing him here against his will. I hear him moving away, towards the lake.

I shake myself again and manage to stand using the hood of the car that is still hot under my palms. I am drawing my strength though self-directed anger now. I try to focus on the direction where I think César has run but everything is one giant shadow by the weak light filtering through the schoolhouse windows.

At first I have to feel my way through the trees and then I can gradually make out where I am going. Even when it's pitch black you somehow manage to see, as if we turn from human to wolf. I call out for César, baying just like a wolf, trying to listen for him. Behind me the forest is alive with its own music, the rain on the leaves, the crackling of creatures moving over twigs, the hoot of a great horned owl, the unnerving scream of a red fox. Even the lake moves with a voice, lurching like an ocean, ready to spew out a monster from its rings of hell.

I call out to César to come back, just like I wanted to do on that dusty road from Ataccala. Now I can't see if he is turning back to look at me through the black shadows, if he is laughing at me now, like he did then. Then I hear a man-made noise of scraping and thudding. I can't immediately place the sound or even the direction because it bounces off the trees and curls over the lake. Then it dawns on me that he is at the lake. I can hear more scraping and grunting and then splashing. I stumble on until my shoes dig into the sand of the beach close to where the old pier would be. Somehow the water generates its own light, a subaquatic glow that lets me see César dragging one of the old canoes into the water. Then he is up to his knees trying to climb into it, rocking precariously as he struggles for balance.

"What are you doing?" I call out. That stops him for a moment as he searches for me. Then he resumes his fight and wins and flops down into the canoe. There are no oars so he starts paddling with his hands.

"It's full of holes," I shout. "You'll sink!"

Still he pulls himself over the surface of the lake and for some reason stands up, probably because water is flooding in. He teeters at the edge and then I hear a splash as he hits the water and the canoe darts away from the push of his body leaving it.

I know the lake bed drops sharply only a few feet from shore. I hear César splashing and wallowing in the deep, until he begins yelling, calling out to me, his words choking with lake water, and I realize he can't swim.

He is thrashing and gurgling about thirty feet from shore as I clop into the water and dive forward and a deeper, slower darkness overtakes me.

When I reach him he's losing his battle against the weight of the water. I know you can drown trying to rescue someone like this because they pull you down with them. But I grab hold of César anyway and even as he fights me I drag him to shore. We both collapse onto the sand. He is coughing and hacking up the lake and I am struggling for my own breath and my entire body aches. I am on my back and César is on his stomach, retching into the sand. The rain keeps us wet so we don't feel the cold right away. I roll onto my side and put my arm on his back. I feel it rising and falling and shuddering as he coughs.

"You still can't swim, can you?"

"No, *estúpido!*" He pulls himself up.

"Not much has changed."

I can't see his expression. "Everything has changed."

In the blackness I imagine he is the César from that other time, from the City of Ashes and the desert sands of Pisco, drawing in his sketchbook, sitting petulant as I dab his black eye with a cold rag, or we are standing on Huayna Picchu with my arm around him as the mountains hum and the air buzzes with hornets and the ancient world below us whispers its secrets of sacrifice and the end of civilization.

"I want him back," I say.

"What do you mean?"

I sit up. I am starting to shiver. "We should get inside." But neither of us moves.

"Who do you want back?" he presses.

"Nothing. It was a stupid thing to say."

"It's a sad thing to say."

I scramble up and extend my hand to him. "Let's go." I use all my strength to pull him to his feet. I lead the way back towards the weak light of the schoolhouse, two ship-wrecked sailors washed up with the debris from a storm that hasn't finished raging.

*　　*　　*

"César, are you all right?"

He doesn't answer me. He is pacing under the light from above the reception counter, still dripping wet and shaking with indignation. He looks around, trying to make sense of this ratty lounge with its frayed sofas and chairs, boarded-up fireplace and upright piano in deep shadow, all ghost furniture.

He rubs his arms. "I'm cold," he says.

"What were you doing?" I grip one of the wingback chairs, its stale odour rising up as if I have released old time from its threads. Water drips off my matted hair and down the back of my neck. Without my glasses everything is slightly out of focus but it doesn't matter. None of that matters. "Where did you think you were going?"

"Away from you, *Dios mío!* What did you expect?" He grips the back of the wingback chair facing mine as if the chairs are shields to absorb our blows. "We're in a stupid loop now. Just don't think I will forgive you for all this."

"Somehow I think forgiveness is going to be a big theme for tonight." He keeps looking around, rubbing his arms from the cold.

"You didn't have to force me to be with you. I wanted to see you. I cancelled my flight to New York. I extended my hotel stay just for you."

That takes me by surprise. "I didn't know."

"How could I leave? You're the curator of my exhibition. Are you saying you didn't know who I was?"

"Yes—I mean *no*, I didn't know you were CÁLA."

His shoulders slump. "Well I wasn't certain it was you either. It was all very confusing." He goes around the chair, as if dropping his guard. "I wasn't trying to avoid you, Brisdon, I wanted to find you."

"Then why did you attack me with a board?"

"Because you stuffed me in your boot!"

"I like the way you say *boot*. But okay, point taken."

"So here we are."

"Yes, here we are." I move around to the side of the chair to face him. "No more barriers."

If this was a scene in a stage play, the set lighting would change: a single spotlight would light us up as the rest of the room would fade to black. There would be piano music from something famous, starting slow and then building, a bit thrilling, like the thundering chords of a Messiaen symphony to love, sex, God and the universe, because what else is there? And it would all be coming from the player piano in the corner. And the place where we are standing would slowly revolve because we are seeing one another for the first time, not in costumes with masks but face-to-face and alone. And our audience would be the schoolhouse children who have all grown up, who have lived and loved and lost and died as they sit watching us with round, mournful eyes.

César's expression reveals a great sadness without music or spotlights or revolving stages, as I spin with my own confused desire.

"Thirty-three years," he says.

"I've pushed everything so far down, I didn't realize I've been waiting for this," I admit.

"But not like this, I hope." He finally smiles, in the shy way he used to greet me at the Plaza St. Martin.

"No, this isn't exactly what I had in mind."

"Then you're not a complete *nutter.*"

He's trembling from the damp. We are leaving puddles on the floorboards that are turning to sludge in the dust.

"We should get dry." I pick up two knitted blankets lying over the sofas. When I shake them out I create a dust storm and we both cough. I drape one of the blankets over his shoulders. "This is the best I've got."

"You were always taking care of me." His look is no longer spiteful but encouraging.

"You took care of me once, in Cusco, when I got sick."

"I'd forgotten."

"I have a pretty good memory for these things."

I drape a blanket around my own shoulders. It is heavy and smells of damp earth. We both sit on the floor, side by side with our backs against the same heavy chairs that had just shielded us from each other.

"I had forgotten that too."

"I'm sure there are things you remember."

"*Si*," he says. "When I first saw you below the Basilica de San Francisco, I thought I had imagined you. I thought you were a celestial messenger sent down into the mastabah to bring me back up when all I wanted then was to stay in the dark."

"You never told me that."

"There was a language barrier. There were many barriers."

"Yes, there were."

"There was so much I couldn't say and so much I didn't understand—"

But back then how important were the things we had to say? I want to ask.

"I painted everything I knew from that time together."

"Yes, you put me inside your *Art of Dying!*" I exclaim.

He smiles. "I wanted you to see it. I took your likeness from the drawings that I kept of you."

César puts his hand on my knee. The colour of his moonstone ring is of an old tooth, worn down and yellowed by time.

"And you kept the ring."

"I haven't taken it off."

"Not even after what happened at Ataccala?"

"Did you go back to Ataccala, Brisdon? Did you go to the police?"

"Yes."

"What happened?"

"Do you really want to hear it, César?"

"That's why you brought me here, isn't it?"

I feel a chill again but it's not just from rescuing César from the lake.

"After we split up I found the police station. I tried to explain about the massacre. You were right. They didn't believe me or they didn't want to believe me. Or more likely, they were afraid of what I knew, as if the authorities were complicit and they were all afraid for themselves. They treated me like I was to blame. They interrogated me and held me there until they took me back to Lima to board the next flight home. But I managed to get away. I went to look for you, César."

"You were trying to find me? In Lima?"

"Yes. My flight didn't leave. Fate granted me a reprieve of four days. I searched for you every day, César. I didn't even know if you had come back to Lima. But I still went to all the places we had been together. I even went back to Independencia looking for your aunt's house but I couldn't find it. Then, when I had given up, I saw you."

"You did? I didn't know. I didn't see you, Brisdon."

"I know."

"You found me but you didn't say anything?"

"I couldn't." I glare at him. "That's when I realized what you were really all about."

"I don't understand."

"What you did, César. I'm talking about you going back to Lima after everything that happened, straight into the arms of someone else. Two lovers, actually."

He was getting agitated. "I still don't understand—"

"Tourists. You were arm and arm with two tourists as if nothing had happened between us, as if nothing between us had been real." He just stares at me trying to think, shaking his head. "I saw you with them and you were all so friendly and laughing and touching each other. The minute I was gone you moved on. It was all about the fun. They were right."

"Who were right? The police?"

"No, no. I'm not talking about the police." Both Manuela and Rafael had warned me. I went on, "This duplicity was part of the lifestyle I could never embrace. I was an idiot. I should have recognized what you were capable of when you walked away at Ataccala wearing my clothes and with my money in your pocket."

"That's cruel. But what you are saying didn't happen!"

"I saw it with my own eyes, César. Whether you remember it or not. So I went back to my hotel. There was a rooftop terrace. I paced and wrung my hands until after midnight. There was a bright moon that night. When I was alone up there I pulled your medallion of Saint John from my neck and thew it as far as I could."

"None of this makes sense. I never went with the other tourists, I was as upset about Ataccala as you were. I couldn't sleep. I couldn't eat. You were gone and I was broken."

"I know what I saw."

"You're mistaken, Brisdon. Your mind must have been playing tricks on you."

We just sit there on the floor without speaking. Then I reach under my wet shirt and pull out the medallion from around my neck.

"*Dios mío!*" he exclaims. "Didn't you just say—"

"You know what it is, don't you?" He doesn't respond.

"You just said you threw it away."

"I did. But I couldn't leave Peru like that even if I wanted to diminish the meaning of your gift, because you made a mockery of us. Early the next morning I begged the neighbours to let me up to their roof. Once there I started kicking over all the debris, the corrugated metal sheets, wooden boards, bricks, rope, shoes, a broken umbrella, even a rusted-out bicycle. I was certain your Saint John the Evangelist had landed there. I was running out of time and I was thinking this had all been for nothing..."

"But you found it."

"I've never told a soul. I've never talked about any of this to anyone. Probably no one would believe me. I had given up. I was out of time. I was about to leave the roof when I heard a noise behind me. When I turned, a giant bird had alighted on the handlebars of that old broken bicycle. The creature was all black except for a frill of white feathers to the base of its hooked neck."

"*El poderoso cóndor—*"

"Yes. I wasn't sure it was possible for a condor to travel so far inland, right into the city. It was the same type of vulture I had seen circling above the mound of graves beyond Ataccala. When it stretched out its wings it was wider than the bicycle. I stood dead still. It looked at me as it hopped down from the handlebars and around on the same spot, pecking at something. Then it just took off and I swear I could feel the ripple in the air from the way it beat its enormous wings. I went over to where it had been moving around and there it was, the medallion with its chain, even though I know I had already looked there."

César appears to be weighing the probability of my story. Then he asks, "So you wore it again?"

"No, I won't lie. I couldn't wear it. Not right away. And the chain was broken because I had ripped it off my neck when I couldn't undo it, I was so angry and disillusioned. I was torn apart like the chain. I only had it repaired once I was home."

"That thing is valuable. It's a museum piece."

"I know."

"I should have told you."

"Yes, you should have. How did you get hold of it?"

"I took it. I was in the wrong place at the wrong time. The museum was being robbed while I was visiting with my aunt. I was just a boy. They were smashing the cases and left the medallion on the floor with the broken glass. When I snatched it up I cut myself so people were worried I had been hurt and weren't looking for it."

I just look at him. How can I blame him? I had kept the medallion even after I had discovered what it was.

"I kept it hidden away," he continues. "I didn't know what to do with it. I couldn't sell it. I was only a kid. So I just hid it until I met you and you were John and you were as beautiful to me as all the statues of all the saints in Lima and so I thought you should have it." He looks me right in the eyes "I know it was wrong but it was right back then."

"I tried to return it," I admit. "Many times. I just couldn't."

He considers that for a moment. "I won't lie to you now, Brisdon. I gave that medallion to you with the best intentions and I never looked for anyone else after we parted ways on that road from Ataccala. I don't know what you saw. I have no explanation for you. I don't have a memory like you."

I don't know what to think. We sit huddled and shivering under our scratchy blankets. I feel a dull thudding behind my eyes. My devil is there, jabbing me with his hot claws. If César is telling the truth—and why would he lie to me now—then I've been living all this time on a false truth, false hopes, false dreams. Rafael had been in love with Perfecto and even if it was all flawed, he still held onto that power despite all that had been stacked against him. But I gave up that power. I hear Manuela saying, *We are not pendulums. Each desire holds a singular gravity.*

I feel heavy now and tired of fighting against that elusive weight, that burden of my own personal gravity.

"Are you all right?" César puts his hand on my shoulder like I had done with Parfait, but he leaves it there. It grounds me.

"I'm sorry," is all I can say to him.

With that, our only light over the reception counter flickers twice and goes out.

*   *   *

We are left in utter darkness once more. I don't move, hoping my eyes will adjust as they did at the lake, but the mysterious light of water no longer laps at our feet. This is darkness inside more darkness.

"There are two things I know," I say.

"What?"

"Somewhere there are candles and with them a bottle of scotch."

Imogen anticipated a black-out because of the knob-and-tube wiring that still snakes its way throughout the resort. She brought a box of old candles on our last visit and stowed them behind the reception desk. I brought the Bowmore.

I teeter as I stand up. The lack of light and sound makes me dizzy. I think of César trapped inside the trunk. *I shouldn't have done that.* I tighten the blanket around me and make my way across the room. I manage to get behind the counter without upsetting anything and then knock over a lamp. It crashes to the floor.

"Don't worry," I call out, "it wasn't the scotch."

I grope through the drawers until I find the box of candles. My fingers search around for matches. Surely Imogen would have thought to bring matches. And there they are, long wooden fireplace matches, easy to light. A spark flies up and the flame dances on its tip. I light two fat candles and locate the bottle of Bowmore I hid in the cubby. I tuck it under my arm and return to César with a candle in each hand. I feel like the plague doctor again with my blanket trailing along the floor. The light bounces off César's face. His eyes are darker than I remember, as if time has dulled their lustre. Or is it just a trick of the candlelight?

As I open the bottle I say, "I am *Doctor Schnabel von Rom* and this is your medicine." I hand it to César. He takes a swig.

"Zorro thanks you."

As we sit back on the floor something falls at the dark end of the room, as if the top *National Geographic* magazine next to the piano has slipped off its pile. The exposed piano keys flicker like a row of spoiled teeth, grinning at us.

"Things are moving around in here," César says, "Like we're not alone." We sit in silence for a while. Then César says, "I never told you."

"Never told me what?"

"About why I was afraid of the police."

"It doesn't matter," I say.

"But it does, Brisdon. My father was chief of police in Ayacucho and he hated me. He caught me with another boy and beat him to a pulp and disowned me. I was fifteen." He puts his arm around me like we are back in the Godoy movie theatre watching *The Year of Living Dangerously.* "I never told you why I had to leave you on the road at Ataccala. It was because my father threatened that if I ever had any run-ins with the police he would use his power to have me locked away and he would ensure I was tormented and beaten. I believed he was capable of that. So I couldn't be linked with the police in any way, especially in Ataccala so close to Ayacucho. I'm so sorry Brisdon."

"I wish you had told me. If you had said something—"

"I didn't want your pity. I have the stupid pride of the Inca kings—and look where it got them."

And this is where it got us, I think, just as Rafael once maintained that the true history of Latin America was a horror story. "I knew you were afraid of the police but I thought you had done something criminal."

"I was castigated for being gay. That's the right word, is it not? Castigate? So much like *castrate.* I had to leave you on that road or the police would have ensured that I was beaten to death in prison. Because of my father and what happened that night I had no choice but to walk away."

"Where did you go?"

"To the next village, to Cavelica, but there was nothing I could do there either."

"Cavelica," I repeat. "The police finally told me about Cavelica."

"I knew right away that something was wrong there. Men were shouting. Women were crying in the streets. But I couldn't say anything. I was afraid to tell anyone what we had witnessed in case the police got involved. I was able to board a bus. The police stopped the bus. They must have known something was wrong. Maybe it was because of you, Brisdon. I pretended to sleep. Maybe I was saved then because of how I looked, my clothes caked in dirt from sleeping on the ground. It was only years later when my father died that I was truly set free."

"Is that why you're a recluse, César? Help me understand."

"I'm not proud of it. I was a coward." He takes the bottle of Bowmore and drinks from it. He wipes his mouth along his wet sleeve. "Years ago I let someone talk me into being a shut-in. It was all pretense. It was all for publicity, or actually to starve publicity, to make them want more of me. But really, I realize now, it was to hide the true outcast that I was, the unsellable César Acosta, a young gay Latino boy playing in the high-stakes game of the art world. I was talented but I wasn't marketable. But I stood a chance as a mysterious anonymous painter called CÁLA."

I understood the art world was mostly politics and posturing. I understood all too well.

"I was complicit," he went on. "I allowed it to continue. I was used to a certain type of cruelty."

"I wish I had known."

"That was long after you, *amigo*. He didn't mean to be cruel, he just wanted us both to succeed. But I lost myself in

330

the process. I still cared for him afterwards, after I was set free."

"What set you free?"

He hesitates. "Someone very important to me."

"What happened to this someone?"

"He's gone."

"As in?"

"He killed himself. He threw himself off a building onto a ledge fifty floors below."

"That's horrible, César."

"He was dying of cancer. It ate him alive. He had enough. He wanted to spare us both."

His last words take the wind out of me. "You've forgiven him then."

"Yes." He takes another swig from the bottle. "But finding myself alone again, I became that recluse once more. This time willingly. I embody it now. I don't want the world to come in anymore."

"We've both been hiding," I say. "I've been hiding since Ataccala."

He looks at me. "I couldn't tell anyone what happened there."

"You've never told a soul?"

"I know it's was wrong Brisdon but I was afraid. Can you understand that now? Do you still blame me?"

"Yes," I say. "I understand and I still blame you."

"You haven't told anyone either?"

"No one knows. And I don't want to keep it bottled up anymore."

"We lay under blankets just like this."

"I wanted to stop at Ataccala but you wanted to keep going. You were afraid. You were right to be afraid."

"And then it all fell apart."

"It all went to hell. I could never talk about it either. I know I should have but it was a Pandora's box."

His expression is even more sorrowful in the candle-light.

"Then let's go," he says. "That's why you brought me here, after all. Use your gift of memory and take me back there now, Brisdon."

*   *   *

That night was as opaque and suffocating as this night here at Shelter Lake, another sky emptied of its moon and stars and promises of daylight. Out on the plains, below the Andean mountain ranges, there were no lights, no street lamps, no windows glowing, only the weak headlights of our van cutting through a lonesome, godforsaken world. The cicadas were buzzing and I thought of summers at home. Here they clustered over the grassy knolls and swarmed in the trees; they were fierce, vocal, and their incessant screaming filled the void around us, like a portent of what was to come.

We passed though the town of Ataccala heading east along the old road that cut a swath through the desert terrain. You didn't want us to stop for the night because it was too close to trouble, you said. I didn't understand because there were only a few tiny villages, clusters of houses fast asleep by the main road. Our driver Brandy was well into his cups by then and I kept my eye on him.

There was no rear seat. We sat on the floor in the back. I caught Brandy's toothless grin in the rear-view mirror. Could he see how you had become irresistible to me, how I would have to abandon myself to it all, to stop fighting how I felt about you? I was thinking even though I would have to leave Peru I would come back for you... and that was when you shouted. I looked up to see an animal on the road in front of us, a large black cat with glistening emerald eyes. The van swerved sharply and we slid off the road and into a ditch.

Later, to stay warm, we stayed in the van, Brandy settling in the front seat and you and me in the back, lying on the slanted floor until we heard the sound of trucks coming over the plain. I wanted to call to them but Brandy held his hand over my mouth. Then we heard shouts of military commands by the senderistas, the sounds of men, women and children babbling and yelling and crying, a baby wailing, and then the gunshots: the senderistas shooting and shooting until the time between screams grew less frequent and then stopped completely and, finally, the sound of shovelling as they dug a communal grave and then filled it over after the bodies were thrown in. Those moments were etched into our memories but it was what came next that I tried to forget, after the trucks drove away and after the sky brightened and Brandy passed out in the van.

"What if someone's still out there?" I whispered to you.

"I don't know." You were still clutching my arm, trying to root me there because you knew I wanted to get out to look.

"Do you think they will come back?"

"No sé, no sé," you kept saying.

I knew about Lucanamarca, that the senderistas had used machetes to hack up the villagers and then scalded them with boiling water in the open town square. I wouldn't have been surprised if their motivation on this dark plain was the same, because of another Sacsamarca, an ongoing war, but here their tactic was different, it was more calculating and sinister because they were hiding the people they buried so they would never be found.

You understood that we couldn't stay in the van any longer, that it made no difference now that the sky had brightened. We got out and took in great big gulps of air to clear our heads. I emptied my bladder into some spiny bushes. The dust from the truck tires had long since settled. I listened for the dreaded sound of the trucks returning but I heard something else.

"What's that?" I whispered.

"I don't hear anything," you whispered back.

"Wait!" I held up my hand. "There's something out there." Did they leave someone behind to guard the site? Was something moving in the direction of the grave? Maybe it was the jaguar, smelling blood. But we couldn't see. Not yet. We crouched behind the van while the world grew lighter moment by moment. Finally I leaned into you. "I'm going to look now. It's getting light enough. If any of them stayed behind we're caught anyway."

You tried to stop me but I walked around the van and looked out over the rocky terrain. There was nothing but layers of coloured light filling the sky.

"Brisdon—"

"It's okay," I called back. You came around and stood next to me and I heard it again. "Do you hear that? I'm going to look. Are you coming?"

I walked towards the upturned earth while you stayed behind. Every moment the light of dawn was getting brighter and it was easier to see the tawny lustre of the morning plain. When I reached the mass grave it was larger than I expected. The sparse grass was trampled flat. There were tire tracks and gashes in the ground and dark stains in the dirt. A metallic odour hung in the air from blood and bullets. Then the ground sloped sharply downward to a gully of freshly dug earth. I heard something, the sounds muffled like the whimpering of someone being smothered by a pillow, and I realized it was coming from the mound.

You were beside me then, grabbing my arm and trying to pull me back. "Tenemos que irnos," you whispered. "Let's go!"

I pulled away. "They're not all dead!" I cried out. The wind carried my voice to the hills.

"Shhhhh!" you warned me.

I raced forward and dropped to my knees and dug my hands into the dirt, clawing at it, pulling out great big hunks of freshly turned soil.

"Stop, Brisdon," you beseeched me. You were tugging at me but I shook you off. I kept digging until my hands hit something and I scraped away until a face appeared, a woman's face like she was asleep and I recoiled, throwing my arm up to shield me from the dead. You fell to your knees next to me.

"We need to go!" you pulled me but I shook you off again and moved to another spot and kept digging. "I can hear them! Some of them are still alive!" I gouged out chunks of soil, like a wild animal and I hit an arm and saw a hand but it was limp and dead. Again I dug, again death.

"Brisdon!" you called, loudly this time.

I heard it too: the sound of a vehicle in the distance. It was coming our way, grinding louder and louder beneath a brilliant sky.

"We can't be here," you shouted at me, grabbing me by the arm again but this time with an iron grip, pulling me up and away. We ran further into the dry field, further from the graves and the van and the road and then we dropped to the ground, lying flat on our stomachs.

It was a motorcycle. It came buzzing down the roadway and as it neared the van resting off-kilter in the ditch, it slowed. I could see the motorcycle driver hesitate and then he sped off in the same direction. Brandy must have still been inside the van, sound asleep.

"There will be more cars," you warned. "We can't dig up the bodies. Sendero Luminoso will come back in the daylight to check on what they have done in the night. They

can come any time, Brisdon. That could have been one of them. We can't stay."

"But we have to help them!" I cried. Tears filled my eyes. I felt sick and my head was throbbing. "They're still alive!" I wailed and then you raised your arm and struck me so hard that I reeled back and fell into the dirt.

I looked up. I put my hand to my jaw. You stood over me, against the light. "No, Brisdon."

"I'm going to get help," I said. "I'm going to the police in Ataccala."

"You can't do that."

"You can't stop me."

You just looked at me and we both knew by the time help arrived it would be too late.

You tried to help me up but I shook you off and scrambled up on my own. I looked one last time at the shallow graves and I thought I saw the dirt moving and I knew I would never forget, that I could never write or speak about this moment and that it would haunt my dreams and cling to me like the devil on my back who was now weeping along with me.

*   *   *

I take another swig from the bottle of Bowmore resting on the floor. The tiny candle flames are flickering from an unremitting draught. "I should have kept digging," I say. "I can still hear their cries like I'm underwater and they babble and they whimper—"

"You have to understand why I did that," César says. "You have to understand why I couldn't stay or come with you."

"I've never seen the world the same since."

"Nor have I, Brisdon. I painted that night a hundred times to rid myself of the guilt. Call it my punishment. My reckoning."

We move closer together. I put my arm around him. We stay like that for a very long time. Something rattles outside, a stray dog or hungry racoon. César looks in the direction of the sound.

"The ghosts that haunt us," I say.

"I hate myself for what happened. It is still a stain on my soul. I believe in the soul, Brisdon. I was brought up to believe it."

"And I'm cursed to relive it over and over with this damn memory of mine."

"It's made my artwork as cold as the dead," he says.

A chill rises up in my spine from my wet clothes and the emptiness of a conscience I have been waiting so long to unburden.

"We have to get out of these wet clothes," I say.

We undress like two boys going for a swim. He pulls me to him. "We need to share body warmth." He pulls one of the blankets over us both as he wraps himself around me. We settle back down onto the floorboards. I continue to shiver. The smell of his body so close to me after all this time triggers a hundred memories but they are flat now, one dimensional and too distant.

"I always planned—"

Before I can say any more he kisses me. It is inevitable, like the farewell kiss we were denied. We huddle together saying nothing, thinking nothing, hearing nothing. It's as if we have conch shells to our ears and all we can hear is the sea.

"What did you always plan?" César finally asks.

"I thought I would go back."

"To Peru?"

"Yes."

"Peru is different now."

"Not everywhere." I can't stop trembling because I feel hot now, like when frozen skin comes back to life. We are wrapped in each other, symmetrical, images in another infinity mirror, repeating ourselves over and over the way time and fate and coincidence can trick us.

We are not gods or kings or monsters, I think.

"Come back with me, César. Come back with me to Ataccala. I want to find them. Because of what we didn't do."

"You want to put their souls to rest?"

"Yes, and yours, because you believe you have one."

He stares, not moving, not blinking.

Then he says, "Yes." He says it again. "Yes, Brisdon."

He reaches out to the candles on the floor and pulls them closer.

We are mere mortals, gorged with our self-sacrifice.

Together, in a single breath, we blow out the flames.

Imogen

That morning, Max waited until nine o'clock before he pulled the church's bell-rope to signal breakfast. Morgan and Mercy were the first to arrive. We had set up the chafing dishes and I was lighting the burners under them. Max had laid out the cold foods, the pâté and peaches and chilled poached salmon left over from the first-class dinner menu of the ship that *not even God Himself could sink*.

"Morgan starves himself for three days before coming up here," Mercy admitted. Morgan, my retired policeman brother, was a large man and I thought that fasting, at his age, wouldn't be such a bad idea.

Soon Isla ambled into the restaurant with her grandfather, Curan. "Is mother coming?" he asked. With that, Oliver came in with Klara on his arm. She looked well, alert, animated, maybe even more so than her youngest son. As he passed me he whispered, *One day at a time.* Now only Atticus was missing. I wasn't surprised.

"Good morning," Harper called out and went to kiss her grandmother. "Bless you, Nana Klara."

At the coffee station I drew Morgan aside. "So, big brother."

"So, little sister."

"Is Atticus not getting along with his parents?"

He measured his words. "I understand there's a bit of tension but no one will talk about it. I guess that's why he comes up here for his summers."

"That's exactly why," I said.

"These things usually work themselves out."

Harper was surveying the buffet. "Uncle Max has out-done himself," she exclaimed.

With that, Max came in from the kitchen, carrying a tray of croissants. He looked out of place wearing a plaid shirt I thought I had thrown out long ago. I wasn't used to seeing him in the restaurant without his white chef's coat and neckerchief. He looked vulnerable.

"My ears are burning," he said.

"Who's missing?" Curan asked. Then they walked in together, Atticus with his hand around Kai's shoulder. Brave, I thought. Good man.

"Hey," he said, the baritone voice he had inherited from his grandfather breaking through the chatter. "You all know Kai."

I spoke up. "Of course we know Kai. You're very welcome, Kai."

"We're...um...together by the way," Atticus said sheepishly.

Then the murmuring started.

"Who is that with Atticus?" Klara asked, squinting.

"His new friend," Oliver replied.

"His boyfriend?" Klara asked. Oliver and I glanced at one another. Then Klara looked directly at Oliver and said flatly and without any malice, "It was *inevitable*."

Bravo, mother!

Max leaned into me. "Did you have something to do with this?"

That's when I noticed Kai's mother, Holly Bearheart, gesturing from the swinging door leading into the kitchen, as if she was too shy to come into the dining room. It was just after ten in the morning and she had arrived to collect linen and towels to service the cabins on her last weekend with us.

"What's Kai doing here?" she asked.

"It's just my family, Holly. I invited him."

She seemed to accept that. "I was on my way to the cottages when Emmet brought someone in his taxi," she explained. "They're at the schoolhouse now."

"Oh!" I had forgotten all about our latecomer guests. To cover my gaffe, I said, "I wasn't expecting them so early. Is their cottage ready?"

She just nodded.

I excused myself and made my way out the back door and up to the schoolhouse where I found a woman seated alone on a cushioned chair. I suspected this was Mrs. Lambert but there was no Mr. Lambert and there was only one large suitcase. I saw the back of her first. Her dark hair was down to her shoulders and was streaked with grey. To my chagrin, the empty lounge was still strewn with plates and glasses and bottles from last night's party. So much for a good first impression. Then the screen door banged shut loudly behind me, startling her. She stood and turned.

"Mrs. Lambert?" I asked.

As we faced each other, my eyes were taking a moment to adjust to the interior light. She was an attractive woman, older, very proper, her clothes well-tailored and probably expensive.

"*Oui*, yes, I am Corinne Lambert," Her Parisian accent sang out. When I gave her my hand, she held onto it.

"I should have been here to greet you. I'm so sorry."

"You are Imogen Noxon then?"

She let go of my hand. "Yes, again I apologize. We were all having breakfast in the dining room. My family is staying here this weekend you see—"

"Family..." she repeated. And then, even more strangely, she asked, "Are you the wife of John Brisdon Noxon?"

I was caught off guard by that. "Why yes, I suppose I still am. Why do you ask?"

She moved forward. Light falling from one of the windows streaked across her face and I saw that one of her eyes was brown and the other grey as if she was blind in one eye. She took hold of my hand again.

"I'm so very happy to finally meet you."

*   *   *

Dear Karen, I wish you would come back...

The words from Brisdon's journal ran through my mind when I realized that Karen *had* inconceivably and inexplicably returned. When Corinne Lambert took my hand and told me she was Brisdon's sister, that she had once been Karen Elizabeth Noxon, I sat down hard on the first chair within reach. The shock wouldn't have been less if Brisdon himself was standing before me.

She apologized and sat down with me. "I didn't know if I should have warned you first. But I wasn't even sure that you were the right person."

She should have. But it was also my fault for having missed the reservation.

"You're Karen Noxon?" I had to repeat.

"Yes, I *was*." She smiled. "But now I'm Corinne Lambert. I've been Corinne all my life."

I could recognize Brisdon in the shape of her face, her cheeks and chin, all the delicate traits from their beautiful mother, Margaret. But most of all she had Brisdon's smile, with its arresting warmth that had drawn me to him so long ago. The differences were disconcerting: her darker colouring, her black hair, a nose that wasn't straight and clever like Brisdon's, but aquiline, and of course, those eyes, those striking, complex eyes, and neither were blue.

I worried that this would be a difficult conversation. I said straight out, "Brisdon, your brother, has been missing and presumed dead for fifteen years. I'm so sorry."

"Oh you poor dear. Yes, I already know." I was certain my look of relief showed in my face. "Let me put your mind at rest. I only want to meet my brother's wife and to learn a little about him. It has taken me a very long time to get here."

"How long have you known?"

"My father, Jacques Kumar, died ten years ago and he left documents which made me doubt who I thought I had been all my life."

"That doesn't make sense."

"Ah, *oui*, I know, I know. It is very complicated. I was Corinne Kumar before I married and became a Lambert. I have spent many years digging for the answers. I was a journalist so I was good at digging. At one point I even put a research team together. I became *obsédée* as we say—obsessed. It put a strain on my marriage." She sat back to be more comfortable. "It has all been very confusing but it has finally led me to you, Mrs. Noxon."

"Imogen, please." *You're family,* I wanted to say.

"And you must call me Corinne. You see, I know no other name."

I brought her to the cabin Holly had made ready. I dragged her oversized suitcase by its small wheels behind us. She was on an extended trip, she told me, as we made our way up the walkway. She had spent time in the neighbourhood where she had lived until the age of five, to see if she could remember anything. Unfortunately, she didn't have the same gift of memory as her brother.

"There was a third birth, you know. We're not really twins, we're triplets."

I stopped in my tracks at the foot of the cabin. "No, I didn't know."

"It was all in the hospital archives. There was another child that didn't live."

"I don't even think Brisdon knew that."

"Those hospital documents had other interesting notes but I will save that for later." She looked around. Holly's cleaning trolly sat in front of another cabin and I could hear the sound of vacuuming. A blue jay hopped across the lawn and stopped to pick at something in the grass. A cloud of tiny flies hung in the air. The melodious call of the robin red-breast made me think of the bird's nest Brisdon had reached up to collect for me. He was still gripping it in his hand after he fell from the ladder, right where two grey squirrels were now chasing each other around and around.

"What a lovely place," Corinne remarked.

"Brisdon used to come here as a boy," I told her, pulling her suitcase up the three steps. "On summer vacation. There's even an old well where he dropped in dimes wishing you would come back some day."

"How extraordinary. I would like to see that."

"Would you like to rest first? Perhaps change? It's going to be another warm day."

I took her into the cabin, modern and bright and freshly aired out.

"*Très belle*," she said. I left her to unpack, letting her know I would be back at the main lodge when she was ready.

Harper was coming towards me as I crossed the lawn. Breakfast was over. I asked, "Is Max still in the kitchen?"

"I think he left to pick up steaks for the grill tonight. Can I help with something?"

I faltered. "I need to speak with him."

"You're as white as a ghost. What's wrong Auntie?"

I gripped her arm as if steadying myself because the gravity of Corinne Lambert's arrival suddenly pulled me to the ground.

"Something amazing has happened," I said, looking heavenward to the endless blue sky, a hallucinatory sky, and only when the seagulls began cawing and I heard Isla's peal of laughter and then Jasper and Sandro squealing and barking as they roughhoused at the water's edge—only then did all this become real.

* * *

Word spread quickly about Karen Noxon's surprise arrival. I wanted Max to be the first to know but everyone was already talking about it by the time his pick-up truck pulled into the parking lot.

"I thought old Klara would be the main attraction this weekend," Max stated with a detachment that surprised me, as if Karen was somehow bringing Brisdon back as well. In the first years, a hologram ghost of a Brisdon still alive somewhere haunted us, because we knew he could suddenly reappear in the flesh and stake his claim to everything we had. We were alone now in The Church kitchen. "Are you sure it's her, Gen? She just shows up? Anyone could claim to be Brisdon's sister."

"Who would make up something like that?"

"It's convenient that she's come on our last weekend before selling the place."

I stopped him. He was shuffling about with the wrapped steaks. "Max, look at me. Trust me. It's really her. I can see him in her. No one can fake that. And most of all there's something very few people knew. Her eyes are two different colours. No one would know that."

He was at a loss. The continuation of Brisdon's legacy was weighing on him. I went to him and wrapped my arms around him.

"Oh Gennie." He buried his head in my hair.

"You'll like her," I said to calm him. "I already do."

A while later, Corinne came along the grass in a sun dress and sandals. By then I had gone back to the schoolhouse. I had asked Holly to help me clean up the lounge and I made some Matcha tea. Corinne and I sat alone together next to the window that looked out to the water. I told her that my family was here at The Sheltering Arms this weekend and some of them had known Brisdon. I pointed them out to her. They were all very curious to meet her, I said, as was Max, my partner and love of fifteen years, the celebrated chef of The Church Restaurant.

"You're happy here."

"Yes. We have been."

"But no children."

"No. None of my own."

"May I ask, do you have any pictures of my brother?"

"Yes of course. I'll find them for you—"

She patted my hand. "There's no rush." But I would dig out the old photo albums with the snapshots of them together, and of her mother when she was young. Her strange eyes brightened at that. Then I mentioned the suitcase of journals but I didn't get to speak more about them because Max came in.

"*Enchanté, madame,*" he said in his impeccable French and kissed her hand.

He pulled up a rattan chair. I could see out the window where Isla was dragging a Muskoka chair to a shady spot for her grandfather and Atticus and Kai were playing with the dogs. I got lost in my family for a moment as Corinne was telling us about her life.

"My father's name was Jacques Kumar and he was from Pondichéry, a French colonial settlement in India. I know a great deal about French colonial India, through my father."

"You mean your adoptive father," I corrected.

"Or the man who abducted you? Just to be clear," Max added.

She dipped her head sideways like a raven thinking. "Yes, he was the man who abducted me. But he was also my biological father."

Max asked, "How is that possible?"

"Let me explain. Jacques Kumar was a Professor of Sociology and a French diplomatic attaché to India. He would make it his life's work to understand and give lectures on the French Raj. In the late nineteen-fifties, he came to the University of Toronto for a time as a guest lecturer. He stayed in residence there. He met my mother."

"Brisdon's mother?" I asked.

"Yes, *our* mother," she answered patiently and smiled. Did Max see the resemblance? "I only remember a brother because I was eventually told I had one. This could be a false memory, I'm not certain. All I know is my first memory was of my father's apartment in Paris and a woman who lived with us but who was not my mother. I never had a mother. My father told me my real mother had died. It was confusing. Then I grew up. I married Victor Lambert. And then my father died of *la covid* when he was very old. He was in a nursing home and I couldn't be with him. Maybe he would have told me then, at the end, but our last moments were stolen from us. When I began clearing out his files I found papers and a key to a safety deposit box I never knew existed. It took me to the Credit Lyonnais Bank where I discovered a foreign certificate of birth for a girl named Karen Elizabeth Noxon and letters from a woman named Margaret Noxon on University of Toronto letterhead. I didn't know Margaret Noxon was my mother yet, but what I read was disturbing. She claimed that her husband was abusing both her and her daughter. She entreated Monsieur Kumar to take Karen away to France to save her—"

"But Corinne," I interrupted, "I cannot believe that Brisdon's father was abusive. Brisdon always maintained he was the salt of the earth. He never lifted a finger against anyone."

"*Ma chère,* I only know what was written in those letters. I have no doubt there were mistruths. It has taken me all this time to sort through the tangle of contradictions that has brought me to you. *Alors,* I needed to ask—who was Karen Elizabeth Noxon? The name Corinne sounds very much like Karen, *n'est-ce pas?* So I looked into the origin of my French citizenship and I have no French certificate of birth. It was as if my life started when I was five years old."

There was a sincerity in her expression, and for a moment it was Brisdon's face. I couldn't imagine what she had endured to find her true beginnings.

"When I realized I could be this Karen Noxon, I had my journalism team dig deeper. Eventually they found a small news article in a Toronto paper. Since my father had kept my original record of birth, we were able to track down the hospital records and the name of the obstetrician, a Dr. Petz. Around the same time, Dr. Petz wrote an article in a medical journal about a case involving a multiple birth where one child died and the other two were of different origins. That paper is quite famous now because, you see, they didn't know about *superfecundation* then, where there can be two fathers and one mother. It is a rare phenom-enon, like the colour of my eyes. But I believe this phenomenon explains everything."

She sipped her tea that was growing cold but she didn't seem to mind.

"I still had my father's hairbrush. *Un test ADN* con-firmed Jacques Kumar was my biological father, which was a relief but eventually a burden, as I discovered more and more. It was a difficult time and the stress was the undoing of my marriage to Victor. How can you love someone else if you don't even know who you are?"

At that moment the schoolhouse door swung open and Harper stepped in with her father behind her, then Morgan and Mercy behind them and finally, Oliver. We all looked at them looking at us. Mercy stood with her hands to her face shaking her head.

Curan said, "Incredible. Just incredible."

"*Bonjour,*" Corinne greeted them and I knew this interruption was just the beginning. Corinne's story would have to wait or else be told in pieces and parts to the family members who would, no doubt, gather around her for the rest of the day.

"Haven't you been missing since you were five years old?" Oliver asked.

Before she could speak, Morgan asked, "Do the police know?"

"Sadly, no one would care about something that happened sixty-five years ago." She stood up to move into the room as if stepping into an inquisition.

"How terrible!" Harper exclaimed.

"No, how wonderful!" Mercy sang out as she came forward to take Corinne's hands. "You have come back to us—"

* * *

... I know I have written this before, but the situation here at home is getting worse. I am beginning to truly fear for the child. You have to take her away, Jack. My husband mistreats her. He shakes her and screams at her and I don't know what to do anymore. The older she gets the more she resembles you and he knows she is your child and hates her for it. He also strikes me in front of her if I try to intervene so I don't say anything from fear. Your daughter and I are miserable.

Corinne had brought Margaret's letters with her. She showed them to me when we went back to her cabin. The letters were hard to stomach because I knew from Brisdon that his father had been a kind and devoted husband and father, nothing like the way Margaret Noxon described him. I hoped I hadn't upset Corinne when I disputed this, because that was all she had to hold onto, a belief that her father had saved her from terrible abuse. I worried that I had just added to her confusion.

There was a cooling afternoon breeze now and clouds were billowing above the lake as if the weather was ready to turn. Corrine fetched her sweater from the dresser drawer. I suggested taking a walk along a path that cut through the forest and ended in a clearing where guests had picnics and flew kites. We would be away from my family for a while, just the two of us.

We strolled along the path that meandered through the tamarack trees, the red maples and the balsam firs. The sounds of the forest were muted. We listened to bird calls and the crunch of fallen leaves under our shoes.

"You told me your father was a historian, but what was he like? As a person?"

She looked at me with those two different eyes as if she were two people—an eye for Karen and an eye for Corinne.

"My father was a good man, even if he did steal me from my life here. I would still like to believe he saved me from something hurtful and that his motives were honest because he never raised a hand to me. All my life he was the most patient man I knew. And I was a very difficult child, I was told, and I remember some of it. I have calmed down considerably since." She chuckled. "He also lived a very long time, like your mother. I never had a mother. I never found out what happened to Margaret Noxon or her husband. I couldn't find any obituaries for them."

She hadn't looked back far enough in her search. "I'm so sorry—"

"You can tell me, *ma chère.*"

"I wish I had known them but they died when Brisdon was just a teenager. They were killed in a plane crash."

It took her a moment to take that in. "I see. How sad for my brother."

"They were travelling back from New Orleans, looking for you when the plane crashed on landing."

"Looking for me..." she repeated. The sun's rays high up through the trees sparkled over us as we walked. "How curious, don't you think? When my mother knew exactly where I was?"

"Yes, there are so many unanswered questions." She nodded her head as if she was resigned to it all and nothing could shake her any more.

"And these journals of his?" she asked.

"Brisdon wrote a series of diaries from the time he was very young up until his early twenties. He dedicated them to you, like a long and elaborate letter."

"Like a labyrinth of his life."

"Yes, his young life without you."

"And you have kept them?"

"I had to keep them. Now it's clear why..." Her laugh resonated with a particular beauty, full yet spare. "I only discovered the journals after Brisdon had disappeared. They contain stories—well—there are things he wanted you and no one else to know. The last journal in particular, the one about his time in Peru—"

I stopped walking and she stopped next to me. I didn't know what else to say. Brisdon's mysterious notebooks would be for her to discover, as they had been for me.

"They were like a travel log then?"

"Much more than that." We moved along again. I could detect the spicy scent of sweetgale when the wind rustled through the leaves, as if it were coming from Corinne and not the plants we passed. Then I stopped again. "Look there," I whispered. A tiny fawn was standing between the trees perhaps twenty feet away, grazing on some newly fallen leaves. "She's just a baby. Her mother must be close." The creature sensed us because she looked up and bounded away.

This was an enchantment; we were spellbound by our proximity, by our sheer fortune of having found each other. She took my arm in hers as we continued along the path. We were careful not to stumble over the surface roots of a copse of old trees, their trunks gnarled and grey and some of them so large it would take a snail its lifetime to encircle one. We passed meadowsweet and steeplebush and the upper branches of the trees were like the vault of a cathedral swaying in the wind above us.

"What happened to my brother?" she asked.

"I wish I could tell you. All we know is that his car went over a bridge in the middle of the night. We had only bought this property a few months earlier. It was all very baffling. I don't know why he came here that night."

"When people do strange things in Paris, it is often because of love."

Or from the fear of love, I thought. Her arm that was linked with mine felt secure amid all this uncertainty. "When you read Brisdon's journals, you will understand."

"I suppose my brother and I were meant to vanish from this earth for a time. But everything returns eventually, *n'est-ce pas?*" She squeezed my arm reassuringly. "Should we head back? You have been neglecting your family because of me. I will not stand for that."

"Do you have a family?"

"No children with Victor, no, and then it was too late. But after my father's death I met someone else. He is very good to me."

"I'm so glad. Who is he?"

"Jean-Luc Gaspard. He hates his name. He says it reminds him of a brand of French cigarette. He owns an antique shop on Rue du Faubourg Saint-Honoré. Do you know Paris, *ma chère?*"

"Yes, a little."

"Because of it, Jean-Luc and I have many beautiful things."

"And he doesn't mind that you have taken this journey on your own?"

"*Au contraire*, he encouraged it. I could only do this alone."

"Corinne, I want to invite you to stay on after my family leaves—"

"Yes, I would like that."

"Please stay with us for as long as you can." And with that she kissed me on the cheek.

"*Avec plaisir.*"

*   *   *

By the time Corinne and I returned from our walk, you could taste the impending rain in the wind skimming off the lake. Everyone except Atticus and Kai had come inside the restaurant. Mercy and I had cleaned up the dining room and changed the tablecloths. I asked Holly to stay on to help out and we worked together, side by side, and I told her I would miss her when we were gone and she just nodded. She rarely showed any emotion.

Then the rain began, the wind whipping the raindrops like rocks onto the old church roof. The door flew open and the dogs ran in followed by Atticus and Kai, drenched to the skin, even with their jackets held over their heads. The dogs shook themselves off. Max and I brought out bowls of salads for the family to help themselves, pasta salad and Caesar salad and coleslaw made for the afternoon picnic on the patio if the weather hadn't turned on us.

Understandably, much of the attention fell on Corinne. Had she only arrived at The Arms this morning? It all seemed familiar, somehow. It seemed right, as if I had known Corinne Lambert all my life. I didn't want Corinne to leave, it struck me, just like I didn't want to leave my life here at The Arms. I knew them both, I understood them both, and I loved them both.

"It's getting really, really dark out there," Isla exclaimed. We heard a rumble of thunder. It felt like midnight.

"Is it nighttime already?" Klara asked, confused, glancing around.

With that, the lights flickered and went out, followed by a ripping sound as if wood and metal were being wrenched apart and then a loud vibration where everything started to rattle: the floor, the walls, the furniture and the plates and glasses on the tables, the serving dishes and the salt and pepper shakers, all shaking as if in an earthquake. But it wasn't an earthquake. The dogs started to howl. For an instant, something blackened the stained-glass windows, as if a monster had risen up from the lake to engulf us.

In the moments that followed, all I could hear was the torrent of rain thundering against the roof. The emergency generator kicked in but the lights were dim and as my eyes adjusted to the new light, Klara exclaimed, "Is this the end of the world?"

"What the hell—" Morgan was the first to rush to the front door. Curan followed even as Harper pulled back his arm to stop him.

"Dad, don't—" The dogs, sensing excitement, bounced up and ran with them.

Max was beside me now, in the semi-darkness.

"Wait! Do we know it's safe?"

"Safe from what?" Morgan asked.

Churches are not built for us to look out. Within them we are meant to look inwards. The world moves on beyond their walls and spires and steeples, but inside a church, time stands still.

"I'll call for help!" Atticus cried out.

Morgan stopped him. "We have to know what's happening first." In his mind there was no use summoning the army if you needed the navy.

Max moved forward and I instinctively grabbed his arm as well.

"I'm just getting flashlights, don't worry."

Morgan opened the door and stepped into the rain. The dogs squirmed their way through the doorway. A few moments later he was back.

"A plane has crashed. A single-engine prop." Then he was back out the door with Curan.

Atticus was speaking with the emergency operator. Harper moved over to where Oliver was comforting Klara. Corinne asked if there was anything she could do. There was a tray of votive candles behind the bar where Kai was standing.

"Yes we can light some candles for more light."

Soon the room was lit up with tiny flames and then I heard a noise from the back of the dining room and Holly ran in, soaking wet, her chest heaving.

Kai called out, "Mom!"

"Kai! Thank God!"

"Were you out there?" he asked. "What did you see?" She looked around as if noticing the rest of us for the first time.

"Dad's plane. I think it was hit by lightning. *Lizzie* crashed."

Atticus was speaking loudly now into his phone. "It's a de Havilland prop that crashed. Maybe passengers..."

"Holly are you all right?" I asked.

"I was changing the sheets in one of the cabins when there was this big wind. I heard *Lizzie's* engine from above because I can always tell when it's *Lizzie*. But there was something wrong. The engine cut out..."

She was shaking. I helped her to a chair.

"Who was flying her today?" Kai asked. "Granddad?"

"I don't know. I don't know." She put her head in her hands.

"Kai, please get your mum a glass of water."

Holly pushed back the wet strands of hair from her face. "It looked like *Lizzie* was heading to land on the lake but she clipped the trees. She came down too fast and hit the schoolhouse with her floats. She almost crashed right into the church. Oh God, yes, I think dad was flying her."

She wanted to get up but I pressed my hand to her shoulder.

"We're taking care of everything. We've called for help."

Max brought over two flashlights and a lantern. Atticus took a flashlight and moved to the door.

"I'm coming with you," Kai called.

"While the boys are getting wet out there, what can we do in here?" Mercy asked.

"Let me help too," Corinne said.

"We should get some towels."

"I need a smoke," Oliver announced. He had no intention of going out into the pelting rain.

"In the kitchen then," I directed him.

"Smoking in a kitchen is bad luck," he responded and then laughed.

The door flew open and a gust of air teased at the candle flames. Curan came in to say the plane hadn't broken up too badly on landing. The pilot was all right.

"Is it my dad? Is it Willie?" Holly called out. But Curan wouldn't know Willie Bearheart.

"Are there other passengers?" Kai asked.

Suddenly, irrationally, I thought there could be someone else, that maybe Willie, who often flew tourists over the lakes, was bringing Brisdon back because his sister was here.

Then I scolded myself. Why in heaven's name would I think of that at a time like this?

"No, he's alone," Curan replied. "The plane seems to have skidded into the old well. It's all broken up too—"

Holly stood up. "I need to see."

"If it's your dad, he'll be fine," Mercy comforted her.

But she resisted. "I have to know." I could tell she was going to do what she needed to do.

"There's no fire," Curan pointed out, "but there's pieces of the plane lying all around so be careful."

I went to the door. The rain was still coming down in sheets. It felt like deep night even though it wasn't late; on a clear evening, the sun would be launching a spectacle of colour over the water. I stepped out as Holly took a flashlight from Max and ran ahead. As I stood on the top step, I shielded my eyes from the rain. Willie Bearheart's plane looked like a beached whale lying between the parking lot and a copse of trees.

Max had gone ahead. He held up the lantern, signalling to me.

"Look, Imogen!" He pointed. I could make out the schoolhouse, its windows dark, and above, a section of its roof had been sheared off by one of the plane's floats. We didn't say anything. We just stared. Then the shouts from Morgan and Curan and the barking of the dogs around the aircraft fuselage brought me back. I smelled burnt metal and diesel fumes mixed with wet earth.

"We need to get the dogs," Max said. Jasper and Sandro, covered in mud, were prancing around, getting underfoot.

"I'll take care of it," I told him.

That was when I noticed Holly standing back, apart from everyone else. Kai and Atticus were at the plane now and I would have thought she'd have raced forward to see about her father. Instead, she just stood there staring, as if in shock. Then she dropped the flashlight as if it had been too heavy for her hand. I took her arm. I said her name. She didn't seem to hear me. "Holly," I said again.

"Dear God, dear God—" she was murmuring. She was in shock.

"No, it's all right," I stressed. "Willie is fine. Your dad will be all right."

Then I lost hold of her arm as she sat down hard on the wet ground next to the flashlight. The rain struck her with a relentless rancour, like a punishment, while the distant sound of sirens drew near.

*   *   *

I once read that *disenchantment,* whether it's a minor disappointment or a major shock, is the signal that things are transitioning in our lives.

I finally coaxed Holly up from the ground and brought her back into the restaurant, giving her into Harper's care. They said a prayer together. Corinne didn't want to get in our way so I took her back to her cottage with candles and matches because the power from the generator didn't extend to the cabins. Then I went back to get the dogs. The paramedics were loading Willie Bearheart onto a stretcher the way they had done with Max that night at the Beechwood Christmas party. Kai went with his grandfather in the ambulance. Holly stayed with us until her brother Peter Bearheart, who was one of the local police officers at the scene, took her home. Until then she had remained sullen and fearful as if she had crashed the plane herself.

By nine in the evening the storm had been reduced to jagged bouts of rain. Workers in waterproof overalls with light-deflecting stripes on their coats taped off the area around the wreckage. They brought out their own emergency generator with floodlights. Then the Fire Marshall's truck pulled in.

The Fire Marshall had the weathered and serious look of someone who had faced a thousand fires. We greeted him as he came into The Church, shaking the rain from his coat.

"How's your evening coming along?" he asked with a deadpan expression.

"Are you serious?" Max asked.

"I can imagine things have been better. I should advise you that the investigation to determine the cause of the crash will take some days to complete. Then there's the clean-up. I hope you have good insurance."

"Do you know what happened?" I asked.

"Not yet. It could have been something mechanical. Let's get your electricity back and inspect the damage to your other buildings. Was there anyone in them?"

"No. We were all here together," Max replied.

"That was fortunate. I'll ask you not to go into any other buildings until we've determined that all is safe."

The utility trucks arrived. As they worked to restore the power, reporters with camera vans pulled up just outside the gate. Here, a plane crash, even just a small sea prop, was a big story.

When Max and I returned to The Church, Curan spoke up. "Imogen, honey, most of us think we had better head back home tonight."

I wasn't surprised. Actually, I was a bit relieved. We didn't know when the electricity would be restored. Tomorrow the grounds would be crawling with inspectors and salvage teams and the schoolhouse would still most likely be off limits.

"Mother shouldn't be in the dark more than she already is," Oliver remarked.

"Morgan and I will stay on." It was Mercy. "We can help out."

"I'll stay," Atticus spoke up. "I can get a ride back with them."

Finally, the rain eased up. Max and I went to say good-bye. Corinne joined us, grasping the hands of her new family. Curan and Harper were ready to get into the car. I gave Isla an extra-big hug for all her hard work over the summer.

When Oliver brought mother down to his jeep, Max bade his farewell and disappeared into his kitchen. He was never one for long goodbyes.

"So we have a new old sister-in-law," Oliver motioned to Corinne who was talking with Curan. "Is she staying on?"

"I hope so. I don't want her to leave. Not yet."

We embraced. "Next time try to liven things up a bit."

"There isn't going to be a next time."

"Talk to Max about that."

"What do you mean?"

"We had an interesting chat last night. Just talk to him."

As they drove off, Mercy took Corinne back to her cabin and I headed for The Church kitchen. I pushed through the doors to find the galley lit by a single oil lantern that Max had hung from a pot hook above the prep table. The light gave the kitchen a murky, underwater feel. Max had cleared away all the pots and pans and trays and dishes. A couple of gas burners were still lit on the stove, the bluish lights looking like two eyes alive in the dark. I didn't see Max right away.

"All you need is fire." His voice sounded far away but he was standing closer to me than I realized so he gave me a start. He was leaning against the wall, arms hanging limply at his side. When he looked at me in the strange light I could see the same desperate look I had witnessed during his heart attack. All the angst of that night came flooding back.

"What's wrong, Max?"

"Air," he said.

"What's that?"

"Fire needs air. We need air. And water. And time. Have you ever tried to hold any of them in your hands?" He lifted his hands from his sides, fanning his fingers out to show me. "They just slip away."

Perhaps it was the strange glow from the lantern that gave his words a touch of *Macbeth* madness.

"What are you talking about?" I led him to the small table in the kitchen and we sat. I took his hand. "What are you trying to tell me, Max?"

"I'm saying I'm lost, Gennie. I am nobody without my work. Without this, here, who would I become but another useless old man."

"My old man," I said.

He squeezed my hand. "This was your dream. Then we made it happen. Should we really be leaving?"

We intended to travel. And I wanted to be closer and more engaged with my family. But then, would we become a burden to them? Would we grow miserable being back in the city, a place that was unkind to anyone old or disabled? These thoughts had been plaguing me but I had pushed them down. I had pushed them as far down as I could for as long as I could.

"I don't want this to be our *Titanic*. A captain should never abandon ship."

"But we've sold it all," I reminded him.

We looked at each other and we were thinking the same thing. *Have we?* A piece of the roof on the schoolhouse had been sheared off by a plane that was now lying in pieces on our lawn. Would a buyer want to go through with the purchase now?

"It's not just cold feet," he said.

"I know. Let's talk about next steps tomorrow. Let's not worry about this anymore tonight. Who knows? Anything can happen."

And with that the lights came back on.

*   *   *

Everything is supposed to look brighter in the morning. But that next morning, after a fitful sleep, I awakened with a feeling of dread. The sound of heavy machinery rumbled outside. Max was nowhere to be seen but there was a full pot of strong coffee waiting for me in our little kitchen.

After a while, Max came in with Sandro. The fire crews had finished their inspection of the schoolhouse, he told me. The good news was that structurally, the building was safe to enter because only the exterior roof had been damaged. The bad news was that water had seeped inside from the rain last night, staining the ceiling and walls. They were putting a tarp over the roof to cover most of the damage until we got hold of our insurance agent.

"This will go on for days," Max groaned.

"Go cook something," I told him. "You'll feel better." There were still six of us who needed breakfast.

When Corinne came in to the dining room, Mercy took her arm. "Sit next to me. I still have so many questions."

I gathered up the burned-out candles and Max brought out bacon and eggs and toast with sweet jam and honey and hot Kona coffee.

"We're just missing Atticus," I said.

"Call his cellphone," Max suggested. It went to voicemail. I texted, *Coming to breakfast?* I waited. No reply.

"Just leave him," Morgan said. "Enjoy your breakfast, little sister."

Afterwards, everyone insisted on helping Max clean up, even Corinne. I slipped away and trudged through the wet grass. At the last cottage, I knocked loudly. There was no reply. I went around to the side window and peered in. The bed had been slept in but no one was there.

"Atticus," I called but the only answer I received was the trill of a warbler. He had to be somewhere on the property. I thought of the schoolhouse. It still had police-tape around it so I ducked under it feeling like a criminal.

He was there, sitting on a wicker chair by the fireplace. He hadn't turned the interior lights on so most of the room was in shadow. Jasper jumped up when I entered, all excited to see me. Atticus held him back. They had grown attached over the summer. I didn't know if I was inter-rupting something so I just said, "Atticus."

"I know you've been trying to reach me," he answered.

"We were worried about you."

I pulled up a chair next to him. In the muted light I could see the rain damage on the ceiling above us as the water had snaked its way along the edge and then down behind the piano. There were puddles on the floor. I could smell the dampness in the air.

"This is where I first met him," he said.

"Ah," was all I said. *Kai.*

"We both knew right away. There's that moment when you know, when you can just be yourself. Does everyone have that?"

"If we're lucky."

"I've been thinking about what you told us about Uncle Brisdon."

The seriousness of youth, I thought. Or was it that we just forget how to be young?

"What were you thinking?" I asked.

"Would you have supported him if you had known he was...you know...queer?"

"It wasn't that easy," I answered. "It was a different time."

"It's like we're stuck in the medieval ages."

"I don't know if we're stuck that far back, Atticus, but yes, to answer your question I wouldn't have turned Brisdon away."

"We all think differently, we act differently, we appear differently but we're all the same. Inside we're all completely and unavoidably the same. Why doesn't everyone see that?"

I wanted to say, *That's very wise of you,* but instead I said, "You just have to be brave, Atticus."

He thought for a moment. "Does being brave get easier as you get older?"

"No, it gets much harder."

"That's what I thought." I could feel a draught coming from the ceiling. "He's here, you know."

"Who? Kai?"

"No." He smiled shyly. "Kai is staying with his grandfather for now. I'm talking about Uncle Brisdon. I don't really remember him but I can feel him. Right here."

How remarkable, I thought. There was a noise from above us. Jasper barked and we looked up. Somehow a small bird had come through the damaged part of the ceiling. Realizing it was trapped it began fluttering around and around. Jasper jumped up barking and chasing it, trying to snap it up in his jaws.

"Grab hold of Jasper," I said to Atticus. We both had to duck a few times as the bird flapped over our heads.

"What is it?" Atticus asked.

"It looks like a house sparrow."

"That's funny, don't you think?" Atticus took hold of Jasper's collar.

"Poor thing." I ducked again. "I'll open the door."

We tried to shoo it out but it kept landing on the window sill, flapping and quivering against the glass. I attempted to corral it with a blanket while Atticus used chair cushions but this sparrow was stubborn. It would take off again and fly in circles past the open door and back to the window. Finally, after a few more turns around the room, it crashed into the window pane settling awkwardly on the sill. I reached out and caught it just as it tried to raise its wings. I could feel its little heart pounding against my palm. It looked at me.

"What were you thinking?" I said to it.

Atticus laughed. Jasper barked.

"Well done, Auntie. Is it okay?"

We moved to the doorway and Jasper ran out. "It was just dazed," I said and tossed the sparrow into the air so that it fluttered up into the sky and was gone. When Atticus and I came down the cobbled walkway towards The Church, Mercy was coming along the other way to meet us.

"They're looking for you, Imogen," she said.

"Who?"

"The police."

"Where's Max?"

"Morgan and Max took off in the truck a while ago."

Once again I heard sirens in the distance.

"Now what's happened?"

She shook her head. A familiar figure in a police uniform was waving at me from the parking lot. It was Peter Bearheart, Holly's brother. He had been leaning against his police cruiser until he saw me.

"Good morning, Mrs. Noxon."

"Peter, how's Willie?"

"Dad's going to be okay." It had stopped raining. He took off his police cap and turned it in his hands. "It seems *Lizzie* ran out of gas. It happens to planes a lot more than you think."

"Oh dear! Well, I'm very glad to hear about him, Peter. And your sister? She was quite upset—"

"Holly's very quiet right now. She's had a shock. But she'll push through it. Thank you for asking. But that's not why we're back."

"What's wrong, Peter?" Police cars were filling the parking lot. An ambulance was coming through the gate.

"Don't be alarmed, Mrs. Noxon. We've had to call in a special team."

"Has someone else been hurt?"

"Not exactly, ma'am. The recovery team found something in the well. When they were looking for pieces of *Lizzie* they saw something...well, something they didn't expect."

"What did they find?"

He just looked at me and somehow, beyond reason, I knew exactly what he was going to say.

*   *   *

Another black sedan pulled into the already crowded parking lot. There was something about an unmarked police car that was easy to recognize. Further ahead, workers were still sawing *Lizzie* up, steel blades screeching against metal skin with sparks and smoke hovering over them. For a moment I thought I would lose my mind. Constable Peter Bearheart brought me back to the dining room. Corinne was with Mercy and Atticus. Then Max and Morgan appeared from the kitchen, stopping dead in their tracks when they saw my expression. My voice trembled as I spoke.

"They found human remains at the bottom of the well." And we all thought, *they found Brisdon.*

"What is this, a Grimm's fairy tale?" Max growled.

"There's a detective here to speak with you," Peter Bearheart said. A severe woman in a severe suit was coming towards us.

"Mrs. Noxon?" she asked, not waiting for me to reply. "I'm Detective Milena Jablonski."

"Nice to meet you." I introduced Max. "Did you say *Jablonski?*"

"Yes ma'am."

"Are you related to—"

She cut in. "Yes, he's my father. The apple doesn't fall far from the tree, I know."

"He was the detective on the case of my missing husband years ago."

"Yes, that's why I'm here. Can we go somewhere to speak quietly?"

We took her to our apartment in the former rectory. I offered her tea but she declined.

"I need to be candid with you, Mrs. Noxon."

"That's fine."

"There appears to be the remains of two people at the bottom of your well."

"*Two* people?"

"We're estimating that they've been there at least ten, maybe twenty years." *Fifteen years,* I thought. Why isn't she saying fifteen years? She went on, "We can't see any clothing or identification but we'll know more when we bring them up."

"You think it's my husband then?"

"We can't say at this point."

Detective Jablonski placed her business card on the linen tablecloth. She advised us that she would be back after the identification of the bodies. I didn't like the way she said *the bodies.* There would be another series of questions to follow, I was certain.

When she was gone I drew Max aside. "You heard her. She suspects foul play. Maybe she even suspects *us.*"

"Did you kill them?" he asked.

"Oh Max, how could you even—"

He just laughed and put his arms around me. "Then you have nothing to worry about."

I was worried about Corinne. She seemed calm enough, taking things in stride, but I couldn't tell if she was feeling anxious, as I was. Back at the restaurant, Mercy came over to me.

"Would you rather be alone, Imogen?"

I thought, *I won't be alone, I've got Max and Corinne.*

"Yes, you should head home. You've been so helpful but you've got to get on with your own lives. We'll be fine."

When Morgan and Mercy had packed up everything and were ready to leave, the sun was already sinking behind the trees. I hugged them one by one, the last being Atticus.

"Be brave," I whispered into his ear.

I didn't need to convince Corinne to stay. She sat in our living room in Brisdon's old reading chair. We looked at the photo albums. When it grew dark she said, "I think I'll retire to my little cottage now." The impact of all these events must have been taking a toll on her as well. Later, for dinner, Max took her some duck confit cassoulet.

"Is she all right?" I asked when he returned.

"She said she's not hungry but when she smelled the wine reduction I could tell she would eat it." Max sat at his desk going through the insurance papers. The real estate folder lay next to him. "I'll call everyone first thing in the morning." he said. "I'm going to lie down."

He disappeared into the bedroom as I sat on the dining room window-seat looking out at the workers who had set up two spotlights and a tent over the broken well to shield it from the rain. After a while they raised something up from the scattered bricks. I turned to tell Max, forgetting he had gone. The forensic team disappeared from view. I couldn't wait by the window any longer, I had to see for myself. I threw on my raincoat and stepped into my boots and made my way over to the tent, once again ducking under police tape. The air had a sudden freshness to it like spring. I smelled rebirth instead of the decay of autumn. The misty rain on my face felt invigorating. The mosquitoes and moths were going mad in the spotlights. The forensic team must have gone to the recovery van to prepare for the bodies. Spread out on a white sheet under the tent was a jumble of bones the colour of cement. There were two skulls next to each other as if they had brought up a two-headed monster.

Something wasn't right. Where were their clothes? There was nothing on the sheet but bone and sinew and dirt. Then something caught my eye, glinting in the spotlight between the tangle of limbs. There were some small coins strewn amongst the bones and I realized they had brought up some of the dimes Brisdon had thrown into the wishing well as a boy. Then I saw something else, another larger coin, tarnished and attached to a chain. I bent closer and knew, suddenly, that it was Brisdon's medallion of Saint John the Evangelist. The certainty came rushing into my head with a roar. I stretched out my hand to touch it, to believe it was real, that all this was really happening. I reached into his chest where his heart had once been and clasped the medallion in my palm. Just then, I thought I heard a voice shout *Stop!* I jumped back and the medallion came away in my hand, jarring the skeletons apart and scattering their bones over the white sheet. I clutched the medallion and backed away right into Max who had come up behind me.

"Oh Max," I cried, "it's horrible!"

Max led me back to the house. I slumped down onto a chair with my raincoat and boots still on. I opened my hand for him to see.

"What is it, Gennie?"

"It's Brisdon's amulet. I recognized it. He wore it all the time. I didn't mean to pull it off like that."

He held me while I sat shivering in the chair. It was all over, all the waiting and the wondering if Brisdon would ever come back, even the unintended cruelty of Karen Noxon appearing like a renewal of lost hope. I cried. I was like Holly Bearheart who had collapsed at the sight of *Lizzie* smashed to the ground.

Max helped me to the bedroom. I undressed and he dried my tears with his chef's necktie. He lay beside me on the bed, holding me as my world spun in circles. Still clasping Brisdon's medallion in my hand, I closed my eyes and slept like the dead.

*   *   *

I was never approached about the two skeletons falling in on themselves. No one seemed to miss the medallion either, as if they hadn't inspected the bodies until they arrived at their lab or morgue or wherever they had taken them. I knew it was wrong not to say anything, that it could make me appear culpable for his death, but Max and I never mentioned it again. I put the medallion safely in Brisdon's Japanese puzzle box which I had kept and which only I knew how to open.

Over the next few days, without a kitchen to run, Max took over managing all the insurance and legal issues regarding the repair and reversal of sale of The Arms.

"Is this really what you want, Imogen?" he asked.

"I have no idea, Max."

"There appears to be some wiggle room for the buyers. They say the attraction of a property diminishes considerably once you find unburied bodies."

When the forensic team removed their tents and spot-lights, another crew sent by the insurance company arrived to repair the schoolhouse. Under the thunder of their hammers, Corinne helped us move the lounge furniture and piano away from the walls as if she were part of our team here, as if she belonged. The weather held; we were blessed by bright mornings and shimmering afternoons. Corinne and I sat in Muskoka chairs with our coffee, or with wine later in the afternoon, and watched the last of *Lizzie* being carted away.

The next morning, Corinne and I were up early. "Come join me at the lake," I suggested. "I have a spot where I enjoy the quiet." I wanted to share everything with her now. The more time I spent with her, the better I got to know the woman whose true identity had been stolen from us.

Steaming mugs in hand, we made our way past the remnants of the well, its broken bricks lying on the ground like smashed teeth. We paused there, neither of us speaking. The area was still cordoned off with police tape so we went around to the beach and along the water to the rocks. We settled on two flat stones.

"Look at that sky," I marvelled. The sun was rising.

"It's the colour of a healing bruise," she said.

A noise startled us. I thought it was one of the dogs.

"Who is there?" Corinne called out.

A figure came forward from the farthest point of the rocks.

"Oh Holly!" I exclaimed. "You startled us. What are you doing here?"

"I was waiting for you," she said.

There was something twisting in her face like a snake moving under her skin. I couldn't make out her eyes.

"Is something wrong, Holly?"

"I was there," she said.

"You were where?"

I think Corinne understood before I did, by the way she started forward, like a fish jumping from the lake.

"I was there the night your husband died," Holly continued.

"You were?" I wasn't grasping it. "You saw what happened?"

"We killed them," she admitted flatly. "We killed *your husband.*"

There was an impossible silence. I didn't know what I would have done if Corinne hadn't been with me. Corinne reached for my hand as if to reassure me.

Corinne spoke up. "Tell us."

"I'm sorry," she said looking straight at me. "You've been very good to me, Mrs. Noxon. And to Kai. You didn't deserve that."

Holly looked out over the lake as if contemplating disappearing within it. Then she sat a little below us as if at the feet of her judges, her executioners.

"What is it?" Corinne asked anxiously.

"I never told anyone what we did. You see, I couldn't lose Kai while he was so young. I had already abandoned him once. I couldn't do that to him again." She was looking right through us. "I wanted to drown myself. I wanted to take all I had done into the lake and drown it with me. I've tried to turn my life around but the whole time I was just spinning. When dad crashed *Lizzie* into the well, opening it up again, I knew it was all over, that they would find the men we left down there."

I couldn't speak. I looked to Corinne. I could tell her heart was racing like mine.

"You have to understand, I was a different person then. I was nineteen, the same age Kai is now. I abandoned him for the first three years of his life. I didn't care about him. My parents were raising him. Kai's father Kevin lived for trouble. But he's dead, thank God. He died of a drug overdose almost ten years ago. Back then no one knew I was First Nations or they wouldn't have accepted me. They were like white-supremacists but I still needed to be part of their group. I wanted to make as much trouble as I could. I needed to be heard."

"We're listening," Corinne said.

"We knew about this abandoned lodge. That sign as you come in from the road, the one saying *Shelter* was *my* shelter, like the shelter you've given me over the years and now..." She broke off and wiped her eyes with her sleeve. "The cabins were unlocked so Kevin and I crashed there when the weather warmed up. The place was all ours. Then you bought the place. Honestly Mrs. Noxon, I didn't know who you were. I had nothing against you or your husband. We would have been gone soon anyway when the cold weather came but your husband caught us one morning and kicked us out. And that made Kevin real mad. So he decided to get even. We brought along Terry, a big guy built like a gorilla and as dumb as an ox. We were just going to mess the place up, you know, that's all. Just to be mean."

"Oh Holly!"

"Go on," Corinne prompted.

"It had started to pour rain that night. I didn't even want to come along. But we were so fucking high. The boys grabbed a shovel and crowbar to break things up. Let's fuck up the church, Kevin said, but I didn't want them to do that because the church was sacred. It was really, really dark and Kevin and Terry were crashing about like idiots. Then I saw a tiny light in the schoolhouse window. I thought someone would burst out of there any moment with a shotgun but no one came out and I crept up to the window. I looked in and there they were, two men together on the floor, you know, *laying down with each other,* doing what God has forbidden. Then the light went out. I couldn't see anything more but I knew this was going to be bad. Kevin hated the gays. I think it was because of what happened to him in prison. I tried to stop him but he forced his way in. We used our phones for light. Kevin found them together on the floor and there was no stopping him. They never knew what hit them."

Corinne was holding my hand and I could feel her shaking. I wanted to cry out but something told me to hold back, to not say anything at all. Holly went on.

"I tried to stop it, I really did! They weren't moving anymore, they were dead. Then Kevin got scared. He didn't want to go back to jail. He was having a bad trip. So they picked up the men and dragged them out into the rain to throw them into the lake. But bodies are heavier than you think. That's when Terry saw the old well and yelled, let's throw them in the well! Kevin started singing, *throw them in the well, throw them in the well, hi-ho the derry-o we'll throw them in the well!* Then they shouted, *one-two-three-heave!* and the bodies toppled in. Terry went back inside and found their clothes and came out holding car keys. *We got wheels!* he yelled. Then Kevin told me to come back in the morning and clean everything up or else I'd be coming to jail with them. We got into the car and Kevin drove off. As we got to town we were going way too fast and suddenly the trunk popped up and startled Kevin who lost control on the bridge over the falls. We slid sideways and crashed through the guard rail and I thought we were all dead, I really did. We deserved it, I thought. That was my last thought. But big Terry was able to kick out the windshield and we got out before the car filled with water and they were both laughing as we swam to shore, it was just another rush for them but not for me, no. I just wanted to go home. I'd had enough."

I found my tongue now. "How terrible Holly. But you can't blame yourself."

"But I didn't stop them. And the next day I went back and I cleaned up all the blood. I found their clothes and stuffed everything into a garbage bag."

"How did the piano fall over?" I asked.

She looked startled. "I don't know anything about the piano, Mrs. Noxon."

"What about the other man?" Corinne asked. "The man with her husband?"

"We didn't know anything about them. I didn't know until I heard about your husband disappearing, Mrs. Noxon. But then something else happened. After I cleaned everything up, a construction truck drove in and parked right where we had dragged them the night before. I stayed out of sight. I prayed the rain had washed the blood away. Two men were unloading something heavy from the back of their truck. They carried it over to the well. I felt sick. All they had to do was look in. But they didn't, they were closing it up, capping it. I started to cry because I knew God was saving me. Plunging into the rapids that night cleansed me of my sins. I tried to make everything right. I went back to my little boy, to Kai. I took the housekeeping job here because of what I owed you. I watched your dogs lying by the well so many times, like in a vigil for those men down there all alone and forgotten. Like they could sense it, so I could never forget it."

She broke down, her head in her hands and all we could do was watch her sobbing. Corinne looked at me with an expression that asked, *What are we going to do now?* Then Holly composed herself.

"There's no coming back from this, I know. I've sacrificed my conscience to keep my son and now I have to lose him all over again. I understand that. God understands." She stood up. She was menacing now, hovering above us. "Whether I drown myself or turn myself in to the police I have lost my boy forever, either way."

"Not forever, Holly. He will always need his mother."

I was conflicted. I wanted to gather her into my arms like a broken child yet I was repulsed at the same time. Somewhere from the forest behind us came the *caw-caw* of a black crow.

Then Corinne stood up. Like a shot, she raised her arm and hit Holly straight across her face. It caught Holly off guard so that she stumbled, falling backwards onto the rocks. Holly scrambled up in shock. They just stood there facing each other. Corinne's neck had turned red.

"I don't know you," Holly said teetering, holding the side of her face.

"I am Karen Noxon," Corinne said, her words like ice, "and you murdered my brother."

I held out my hand to Holly. "You need to come with us now."

*   *   *

... I pulled out the moonstone ring I had bought in the Cusco market and told him it was the one in the legend, the real one this time and that it was enchanted and powerful. He held out his hand and said, put it on me Mr. Brisdon and I slipped it onto his ring finger. It fit snugly. He let out a laugh that was blithe and brimming with innocence. I laughed with him. Now we are married, he exclaimed...

"It is all in here," Corinne showed me.

It had been years since I looked at Brisdon's book of the dead and the strange emotions I had felt then came flooding back. We paged through it together. A paragraph here and a sentence there would amaze us and then confound us. We created a bond through these hours together even if it was based on a distressing story without an ending.

"The other man in the well—" Corinne started to say.

"Yes, it has to be *him*."

"How did they find each other?"

I remembered. "A long time ago a young man took me up to Brisdon's gallery to show me a painting. I think César was the painter."

Then she pointed to a line in the book; it was like the game *the danger of opening a book at random*. We read:

The Germans kissed. I wanted to kiss César right there, just to show them they didn't have a monopoly on love, or heaven, or moonstone rings. But the moment passed.

"He was so open and trusting then," I said. "Despite everything. After that there was no more heaven."

"*Ma chère*, you are the definition of heaven." She kissed me.

After that, we spent most of our time together. Max must have noticed the way I was cheered because of her, recovering from *the weekend from hell*, as he put it. Or my weekend of miracles, as I would later call it. The three of us stayed up late at night drinking the best wines. On mild nights we lit a bonfire in a pit along the beach. We were still waiting to hear if the sale of The Arms would be reversed, but right now, Max boasted, the fire pit belonged to us.

After the salvage crews were gone, the broken well stood out as a shattered testimonial.

"Only ghosts will live on in that well," Rosie said when she came back to see me. Corinne was still here. Somehow Rosie knew the prediction from her Tarot cards had come true. "You should get rid of it."

"*Une bonne idée*," Corinne agreed.

The next day, I arranged with the contractors who were finishing the schoolhouse roof to tear the well apart and cement it in, dimes and all, erasing it from the landscape forever.

Detective Jablonski returned the following Friday. This time she accepted an offer of tea as we sat in the dining room of The Church with Corinne. Max was away, meeting with our lawyers. I introduced Corinne as Madame Lambert, our good friend from Paris. We would have told her who Corinne really was if she had asked, but she didn't.

"The case is closed," the detective advised us. Brisdon had been identified by his dental records so I had no need to say anything about the medallion. The other body found along with my husband belonged to the artist known as CÁLA.

"His name was Luis Acosta," she advised us. "Did you know this man?"

Not Luis, I thought, César. "No, detective, I didn't know him." She scrutinized me for a moment, perhaps even detecting a soft ripple of reticence under my half-smile.

"How did you find out his identity?" Corinne asked quickly.

"We traced the serial numbers of a knee replacement." She pulled something from the briefcase she had brought with her. "There was only one item which we found with the remains of your husband and Mr. Acosta." I held my breath. She set a clear plastic bag on the table. It contained a silver moonstone ring.

"Oh." I breathed.

"Did this belong to your husband, Mrs. Noxon?"

"Yes," I said. I picked the bag up to take a closer look. "Yes, my husband bought this ring a long time ago."

"Then I'm glad to return it to you. If you could just sign these papers."

"Does the other man have relatives?" Corinne asked.

"None that we have found. We're still looking into it. He was an eccentric New York recluse. Everyone there assumed he had disappeared on purpose."

Before Detective Jablonski could ask any more questions, I pushed the signed papers towards her.

"And Holly—what will happen to her?"

I could smell chicory from the cup of tea the detective held in her hands. I would always associate that aroma with death now.

"Miss Bearheart will be sentenced in a few weeks."

"She and her son are like family to us."

She eyed us both knowing full well there was more that we weren't telling her.

"The judge may be lenient, if that's what you're asking. Duty counsel received your letter of recommendation. That was kind of you, under the circumstances."

Perhaps I had done it for Kai. I was concerned for him. He had no one now with his grandfather still in the hospital and Atticus away at university. Maybe we would reach out to him. Maybe, if Max was in agreement, he could stay with us if we ourselves were staying...

"Will they let this woman see her son?" Corinne asked.

"Yes, if he wants to see her."

"Good," I said. "That's important."

After all the paperwork was settled, Brisdon's remains could be released for cremation as I had requested. I couldn't bury Brisdon again, I wouldn't put him back into a dark and damp grave. His ashes would be delivered back to us in a simple box as I knew he would have wanted.

"You will stay until Brisdon's memorial?" I asked Corinne who I knew was ready to move on herself.

"Yes, of course."

"I was hoping to have it take place on the twenty-third."

"That's our birthday."

"Yes, I hope that's all right."

"Yes, it would be just right."

My family returned for the memorial, but just those of us who remembered Brisdon, except for mother. I remembered her saying once, *You are alive for as long as the last person remembers you.*

That day, Harper was the first to arrive with her father. She was to officiate at the small ceremony. She was still taking care of Curan and I was pleased to see that Curan looked so well. We all need someone to look after us, I thought. Even now, we had to look after Brisdon one last time.

When dusk arrived, the eight of us gathered on the pier leading out over the water. The cry of a loon echoed in the distance, the saddest cry of any bird I knew. Then there were no other sounds but the small waves lapping against the pier. A dragonfly skimmed silently over the surface and then paused, hovering there as if telling us it was time.

Harper had bowed her head and was intoning, "...*There's a time to cast away stones, and a time to gather stones together; a time to embrace, and a time to refrain from embracing; a time to get, and a time to lose; a time to weep, and a time to cast away...* Let these ashes be cast away as we release you, John Brisdon Noxon, into the water of ever-giving life..."

As I shook out his ashes I closed my eyes and remembered Brisdon as he had been. Then I imagined César and what they had meant to each other. I opened my eyes and my family was there. With heads bowed, they were all perfectly themselves: Morgan and Mercy looking solemn, Max hopeful, Harper enraptured, Oliver mischievous, Curan overwhelmed, and Corinne unshakable, my new sister.

And I thought, my God, how does anyone survive on this earth, or even eternity, without the people you love?

*   *   *

We come to beginnings only at the end.

"... Suddenly I didn't want Trinidad in my bed. I wanted to crawl under the warm covers and find César there, waiting for me.

I know it's wrong. I know it's reckless to want César. My longing is already getting mixed up with outrage and revenge stirring at the pit of my stomach.

There, there, my demon says to me, there's nothing to be done about a broken heart.

But the heart wants what the heart wants—and it wants blood."

Corinne closed the book and sipped from a glass of water. Her lips were pale, as if reading Brisdon's final entry aloud had drained them of all their blood.

"There seems to be so much he doesn't say."

"I couldn't have put it better myself." I agreed.

She was only taking that one journal with her, his *Peruvian* book of the dead. It would be enough for her to carry around so Max and I arranged to have the rest of the journals shipped to Paris. She had slipped a few photographs in-between its pages, one of her mother Margaret when she was young and still living in Scotland, and the one of her and Brisdon together before she was taken away. That one slipped out of the book now so I reached down to pick it up.

"*Merci, ma chère.*" I handed it to her. She looked at little Brisdon standing next to her in the picture. "I wish I could remember him. At least now I have a better idea of who my brother truly was."

"An enigma," I said.

"I meant because he married you."

I put out my hand to stop her from moving away from me just yet. "Corinne—"

"*Oui, ma chère?*"

"I have something I want to give you." I pulled Brisdon's medallion and chain from my pocket and handed it to her. "You should have this," I said and thought: *even if we will never know the true story behind it.* "Maybe, Corinne, in some way, it will bring you closer to him."

She clenched it in her hand and tapped her fist against her heart. "I am very touched. Thank you."

We made our way down the pathway to the waiting taxi. She shielded the low autumn sun from her eyes with Brisdon's book. The trees were starting to change colour, surrounding us with a golden world. She took a long last look at where the well had stood and where Brisdon had lain since before she knew she had a brother.

At the taxi, Max was shoving her oversized suitcase into the trunk.

"What are you going to do now?" she asked us. "What will happen to your Sheltering Arms?"

"Everything should be worked out by the end of the week," Max said. "Fingers crossed."

"You don't need to move across the world to be happy," she reminded us.

Emmet, the taxi driver, who had been waiting patiently, started the car engine.

"All set," Max proclaimed, dusting off his hands like they were covered in flour. He embraced Corinne and opened the door for her. "So you're heading home, then?"

"Oh!" she exclaimed. "I'm not returning to Paris just yet."

"Where are you going?" But the moment I said that, I knew her answer.

"To Peru, of course. To finish Brisdon's story."

As the taxi drove away under the arch, Corinne glanced back at us and waved and I saw that smile of Brisdon's that I knew so well.

Max was shaking his head.

"Unbelievable! You couldn't make this up!"

Now, as I linked my arm in his, we walked past the lawn that had been torn up by the plane and trucks and salvage equipment.

"We can fix all this," he reassured me, "if we stay." Then he tapped his chest to indicate the amulet. "Did you give her the gift?"

"Yes, just before she left."

"I think that was wise."

"To be honest, I didn't know if I had the courage to part with it." I knew Corinne would treasure it and I hoped her Paris antique expert, Jean-Luc, would recognize its value because Brisdon always said it was *important.*

I let go of Max so he could return to his restaurant to bake me something delicious. His Viennese pastries always cheered me up. When I reached the schoolhouse I made myself a cup of tea, but not chicory—and settled into a rattan chair by the window to gaze out at the lake that was sparkling in the late September sun, and where I hoped Brisdon had finally come to rest.

César

B risdon was a lunatic! *Dios mío*, he attacked me and then locked me in the boot of his car! And then he drove for hours while I was trapped in there banging and screaming and wetting myself out of fear for my life and then I almost drowned in the lake...

All right, maybe he saved me from drowning because I had never learned to swim, but that wasn't the point. It was pitch-dark. And pouring rain. We were both drenched to the bone. That's what unfulfilled love can do to you. It certainly drove Brisdon to madness, mad as a hatter. Didn't the Queen of Hearts sentence the Mad Hatter to death for murdering the time? It wouldn't only be time that was murdered that night.

I was certain Brisdon had never stopped thinking about me because he still wore the medallion. And here we were, lying on the ground in the dark, in the middle of nowhere, just like at Ataccala. We had never really dealt with what happened to us on that desert road. That night so long ago bound us together for life. For years Brisdon hated me because I left him on the road that morning and because he didn't believe that I loved him. Love and hate are the opposite sides of the same coin, *amigo*. But I couldn't let him dig up the dead to look for the living. That, too, was madness. So I stopped him. I tried to reason with him but he wouldn't listen. I wanted to shout out:

Are you a doctor? Are you a priest? What good will this do?

Por el amor de dios, of course I wanted to help those poor souls! But the *senderistas* were coming back, I was certain of it. *We have to leave!* I pleaded. I grabbed him by the waist and pulled him away as he fought against me, and in my victory I lost him.

Brisdon spent his entire adult life trying to forget that night. Brisdon didn't have a monopoly on guilt and nightmares. I was there too. I sketched and modelled and painted the horror of that night over and over, seeking atonement. I had a fever that would never break. But I would have rather been homeless on the streets of Lima with a clear conscience than CÁLA, the rich and revered artist—and be damned.

After Russell was gone from my life I turned back into the recluse that Jock had invented, but this time by my own choice. Then, finally, I had Brisdon back. Out of the blue. A ray of hope. And then, of course, Brisdon went a little *loco* but can I really blame him? Here we were again after all these years, wet and shivering and undressing and huddling under a blanket in the middle of a room that smelled like the catacombs of Lima. I knew this was what he had always wanted. Every kiss, every caress was like a brushstroke on an unfinished canvas. Then I heard a noise outside in the rain. There's someone there, I said. No, he replied, it's nothing. So I wrapped myself into him. It was like being in the back of the van that night, travelling down the road past Ataccala, huddled together before our world went all to hell.

Now, together again, we blew out the candles.

When the door crashed open and a flash of light blinded us, I knew that I was truly cursed because misfortune and misery had followed us here. From that point on it was all shouting and screaming in the dark. We were ripped apart and struck, over and over. *Someone is killing us*, I thought. There were three of them. I couldn't see but I could hear their voices. The leader was a woman but her voice belonged to a mere girl.

Motherfucking faggots! she raged.

And then the pain. They descended upon us like a pack of hungry jackals, shouting and striking us blow after blow. I felt my bones crunch. I couldn't see Brisdon but I could hear him. As I reached out a boot crushed my arm. We had no way to fight back. We were mere flesh and bone at the mercy of jaguars, so we curled up together to protect ourselves.

Use the shovel! she commanded. *Aww Holly...* I heard one of them protest. *Kick'em harder!* she yelled, *they deserve it!* She was goading them, firing them up. Now the strikes were from iron and steel and doing real damage and Brisdon was screaming and screaming. He was trying to crawl away so I crawled after him. The blows were becoming more methodical now. Sounds were growing distorted, being pulled into my ears, ending in the cacophony of a piano being pushed over on top of me...

When the pain woke me I heard more yelling but it wasn't Brisdon this time, it was our killers. I felt the ground moving under me. I could smell the earth as the rain washed my wounds. I tried to reach for Brisdon but my arms wouldn't bend. Then all went dark again.

I couldn't be dead because I was dreaming, unless the dead can dream.

I could hear a man singing a nursery rhyme, *The farmer in the dell, the farmer in the dell, hi-ho the derry-o, the farmer in the dell...*

Then we were back on that road to Ataccala, Brisdon and I, dusty, soiled and sweating, feeling the morning sun on our backs—the sun we had so feared. We were on our hands and knees digging in the dirt. There were muffled cries rising up from the earth beneath us.

I have one! Brisdon shouted and I joined him and we dug faster and we found a face and then a shoulder and then an arm and it was moving, it was an old woman and she was alive so we released her from the earth, pulled her right out and she started coughing up dirt and as soon as we laid her down on the ground Brisdon was back again digging into the upturned clay yelling, *I found another one!* So we dug again and pulled out a young man who didn't appear wounded at all and was smiling as we dragged him over to the old woman who was now lying on her side coughing out tiny stars and moons and planets and then we went back to the mound again and we pulled out the others from their graves until all of the massacred men and woman and children were raised up from the dark and were lying on the open ground writhing and crying, a miracle we thought, until we realized the *senderistas* had only used fear for bullets.

Then the open-backed trucks returned, trailing a cloud of dust behind them. They were filled with *senderistas* carrying real rifles now, with real bullets, bullets that would rip our skin and explode our bones and tear apart our intestines and spleens and hearts.

We were trapped. The men leapt from their trucks and aimed their rifles at us. I heard their leader shout:

... *One... two... three... fire!*

Then we were flying. That was when I realized, *Brisdon! I remember now! That day you saw me I was with my Argentinian uncles José Juan and Juan José on the boardwalk by the sea. They weren't tourists, or my lovers, they were just two endearing old queens lost in the nostalgia of their youth...*

Brisdon

uck fuck fuck!

They threw us down the old wishing well. I can't imagine a more inglorious way to die, naked and tangled together at the bottom of a dried-up waterhole. Even after all those vicious kicks and blows, we weren't dead! The fall didn't finish us off either, it just crushed more of our bones as we hit the bottom, toppling on top of each other.

That first night lying there, I felt around with my one good hand. I pulled César's body closer. In the end all we want is to be held. I felt his breath against my neck. I tried to speak but all that came out of my mouth was a gurgling noise from the blood in my throat.

When morning came, I heard shouting and I realized that the contractors were sealing up the well, just as I had instructed them, closing us in forever. I tried to shout back to them but I couldn't, as if a boot was still pressing into my throat. There was a loud *thud* and darkness swallowed us.

On the second night, the call of a lyre-tailed nightjar woke me from my dreams but I knew I was still dreaming. The bird's trill grew louder and then César was laughing beside me and the alpacas were grazing on the lush green plateau of Huayna Picchu. I could smell the wild fuchsia on the steppes, hear the rush of the Urubamba River below us, and taste the ancient dust of the ruins rising in the air.

Can you feel it, César? Something incredible is happening right here and now...

On the third night our tears flooded the well and we were buoyed up by the waves. My little demon appeared one last time to whisper, *The ocean is tears.* He was no longer frightening, he was just a sad and lonely guardian sent to watch over me from the time I was born, and now he was gone.

On the fourth night, César slipped away. I clutched him tight, blinded by a white rage until an angel appeared, chanting words from ancient Sanskrit parchments in order to release César from his earthly body. I relaxed my grip as the angel intoned:

O holy one, let the ethereal elements guide you towards the radiance of eternal life...

On the fifth night, a light shone upon my medallion of Saint John the Evangelist and the words written there were no longer from a dead language but a mathematical equation for the degrees of coincidence, illuminating how everything was linked by not seven, but *one* degree, and that we were never bound together by luck or misfortune at all, but by truth. Truth was the ethereal element that wrapped us in glory. Truth was the radiance, and the radiance was the enigma of the heart.

Of course nothing made sense—I was going stark raving mad lying there in the dark.

On the sixth night, I lifted out of my earthly body to watch the future rush ahead, days into weeks, weeks into months, months into years, our bodies honing to bone, ever so slowly in this other remote catacomb. Then I was brought back by Imogen's voice calling out my name. Once. Twice. And I thought:

Oh Imogen of my heart, this is not how I intended us to part.

But it wasn't only Imogen I heard; there was another voice, a voice I remembered as high-pitched and full of mischief. It was my sister Karen's voice and somehow, after all these years of waiting, I understood that she had come back for me.

Perhaps at the end of your life you get exactly what you wish for.

And now, on the seventh night, at the very end of this circle of time, I try to return to my mortal body. But César and I are no longer at the bottom of the well. The lid of our crypt has been wrenched open and we've been set free. I search for us in the schoolhouse but the wicker furniture has disappeared and the schoolchildren have returned, sitting at their wooden desks all in neat rows, as the young schoolmistress sings at the front of the classroom:

The wife takes a child, the wife takes a child, hi-ho the derry-o, the wife takes a child...

Next, I look inside the old church but the dining room has also been erased from time. The pews are back in place and all the seats are filled. The men hold their hats while the ladies wearing gloves fiddle with their pearls. Everyone is focused on the minister in his pulpit as he reads:

He cried with a loud voice, Lazarus, come forth. And he that was dead came forth...

The preacher's voice, travelling on the crest of Ariel's wings, leads me to where we lie. César and I are just rain-washed bones now, sprawled on a white sheet next to the shattered well. Someone has put up a tent to keep us safe.

Then, out of nowhere, a hand reaches down. *Stop!* I cry out, but it's too late. The medallion is torn from my neck—

Roger J. Florschutz was born in Toronto where he studied graphic arts and media writing. After separate careers in the food and beverage industry and the federal public service, he now lives in Ottawa with his husband, writing full-time. *The Peruvian Book of the Dead* is his first novel.

Printed in the USA
CPSIA information can be obtained
at www.ICGtesting.com
LVHW012311021223
765401LV00003B/160